Also by Frances Brody

Dying in the Wool
A Medal for Murder

Murder in the Afternoon

A
KATE SHACKLETON
MYSTERY

Frances Brody

MINOTAUR BOOKS

A THOMAS DUNNE BOOK

NEW YORK

This is a work of fiction. All of the characters, organizations, and events portrayed in this novel are either products of the author's imagination or are used fictitiously.

A THOMAS DUNNE BOOK FOR MINOTAUR BOOKS.
An imprint of St. Martin's Publishing Group.

www.thomasdunnebooks.com
www.minotaurbooks.com

The Library of Congress has cataloged the hardcover edition as follows:

Brody, Frances.
    Murder in the afternoon / Frances Brody.——1st U.S. ed.
        p. cm. (A Kate Shackleton mystery ; 3)
    ISBN 978-1-250-03702-2 (hardcover)
    ISBN 978-1-250-03703-9 (e-book)
1. Women private investigators—England—Fiction. 2. Murder—Investigation—Fiction.
I. Title.
    PR6113.C577M67 2014
    823'.92—dc23

                                                           2013039454

ISBN 978-1-250-06332-8 (trade paperback)

Minotaur books may be purchased for educational, business, or promotional use. For information on bulk purchases, please contact the Macmillan Corporate and Premium Sales Department at 1-800-221-7945, extension 5442, or write to specialmarkets@macmillan.com.

First published in Great Britain by Piatkus

First Minotaur Books Paperback Edition: February 2015

10 9 8 7 6 5 4 3

To my young assistant, Amy Sophie McNeil

SATURDAY
12 MAY, 1923
Great Applewick

Solomon Grundy,
Born on a Monday,
Christened on Tuesday,
Married on Wednesday,
Took ill on Thursday,
Grew worse on Friday,
Died on Saturday,
Buried on Sunday.
That was the end of Solomon Grundy.

Old rhyme

Prologue

Harriet held the cloth-covered basin in her thin hands, feeling the warmth. She and Austin trod the well-worn path from their long strip of back garden on Nether End.

Mam wasn't home. She'd hurried off to Town Street, to buy the Woodbines that Harriet accidentally on purpose forgot when she and Austin went to do the Saturday shop. Mam wanted a new house. She was sick to death of living in the back of beyond's backside.

The path led through a meadow of primroses, butter-cups and daisies. Far off, the church clock struck five.

Austin puffed at a dandelion clock. 'It doesn't work. This dandelion says three o'clock.'

Harriet, never short of an answer, sighed at his babyish ideas. 'Dandelion clocks have Saturday afternoons off. They belong to the dandelion clock union.'

He always believed her, believed her every word.

'Why is Dad still at work?'

'He has a special job to finish.'

'The sundial?'

'Yes.'

When they reached the stile Harriet handed him the basin, till she got to the top. He passed it back to her and she climbed down. Some of Conroys' sheep grazed here with their new lambs. One of the sheep would let you pat her, because she was hand reared, and called Mary; but Mary ignored them today, busy with her lamb. In her composition at school, Harriet had written, "Autumn is my favourite season". But perhaps it should be spring, or summer, or even winter.

When they were halfway across the field, a dark cloud covered the sun, turning the world to gloom. A thrush made a fuss in the hawthorn bush, complaining about the dust that turned leaves white.

From here, you could smell the quarry – stone and dust. There would be no one working, except Dad. At this time on a Saturday, no blasting would hurt your ears. No crushing machine would puff itself up, ready to swallow kids and grind their bones. Austin dragged his feet.

'Can you do this?' She clicked her tongue to make the sound of a clop-clopping horse.

He tried.

In silence, blown by the east wind, they slip-sloped to the quarry mouth. The quarry grew and grew, like an inside-out monster, bigger and bigger – hungry jaws ready to snap you up and turn you to stone. *Keep out!* the sign said.

The ground dipped and rose, puddles here, rocks there. On the far steep slope, a tree clung hopelessly to the side of the blasted rock. Next to it was a new mountain of fallen stone.

They walked the rough path passing the foreman's hut and big wagon that blocked the view when you were close enough. Beyond came emptiness, the dark shapes of huts and the far slopes.

The first drop of rain fell.

Shielded by the wagon, Harriet put her fingers to her lips and whistled, one long whistle, one short – their signal. If Dad heard her, they would not need to pass the empty sheds where goblins played hide and seek.

No whistle answered hers, only an echo.

'I don't like it.' Austin clutched her arm with his small, fierce hand. 'Whistle him again.'

She whistled.

4

On a weekday, or Saturday morning, there would be quarrymen with big voices, to yell to Ethan that his bairns were here.

No reply. When Dad worked, he shut out the world. He heard nothing and no one. So Mam said.

'Whistle louder,' Austin whined.

'Don't be scared. The goblins aren't here.'

'Where are they?'

'They go to Yeadon on Saturdays. Come on.'

The sloping, bumpy ground turned walking into a half run, eyes down, not looking at the crushing shed, the towering crane, the dressing and sawing sheds. A person's shadow grew longer in the quarry than anywhere else on earth. Pushing Austin to avoid a puddle, she stepped into one herself. Bomnation! Now her boots would be soaked through.

By Dad's mason's hut, the blue slate sundial shone grandly. Austin reached out and touched it. He traced the lines on the dial, placing his palms flat as if the slate would feed him a story through his skin.

Harriet put the plate of food on the sundial. 'Wait here.'

Afterwards, she could not say why she went into the hut. First she saw his boots, toes pointing to the corrugated roof.

Why would Dad be lying down?

Her head turned strange, as if it might split from her and float off like a balloon. She could not breathe out. Quarry dust dried her mouth. Something funny went on with her knees. Her skin prickled. She remembered the time when old Mr Bowman lay in the road outside the Fleece, and the greengrocer's horse and cart went round him.

Harriet dropped to her knees.

Dad's hard hand felt cold. His face looked away from her. His cheek was not so cold. His hair stuck up. She did what she sometimes did: combed her fingers through his hair, smoothing it. Some wetness from the hair came onto her hand. His scalp and hair smelled the same but different. She picked up his cap but it did not want to go back on his head, as if it had taken a dislike to him, no longer recognised him. She set Dad's cap down on the bench, but it slipped.

From a long way off, she heard Austin making little sounds of fright. Harriet shoved herself to her feet, pushing against the bench to help her stand.

She hurried to her brother and pulled him close.

'What's the matter?' he asked, in a weepy little voice.

She said, 'Just ... Come on ...'

'No!'

She placed her hands firmly at the top of his arms and turned him around, to point him homewards. He would not or could not budge.

'Shut your eyes, Austin. Shut your eyes tight and I'll lead you through dreamland.'

He did as he was bid, letting himself be spun round and round into dreamland. She guided him over bumps and hollows, telling him about the gingerbread house to his left, all trimmed with barley sugar. No, it wasn't raining. The fairy fountain spurted dandelion and burdock.

And she told herself that the dampness on her hand was raspberry sherbet, not blood.

But a country child knows a dead thing when she sees it.

MONDAY
Pipistrelle Lodge, Headingley

Time goes by turns and chances change by course,
From foul to fair, from better hap to worse.

Robert Southwell

One

The railway carriage lurched, flinging me forward. Bolts of lightning struck as the carriage toppled. Gasping, I grabbed for something to hold onto. The screech of brakes jerked me awake. I opened my eyes to find myself in bed, the journey from King's Cross to Leeds completed hours ago, and safely.

What woke me was the persistent, loud knocking at my front door. Since my room is at the back of the house, overlooking the wood, whoever had summoned me from slumber was hammering the knocker as if to tell me the house was on fire.

The clock on my bedside table said four o'clock. Sookie had made a pillow of my dressing gown and did not take kindly to having it pulled from under her; an unseemly intrusion for a cat in her delicate condition.

At the bottom of the stairs, I stubbed my toe on the portmanteau, dumped there last night by the taxi driver. I flicked on the light switch.

Turning the key in the lock and opening the door, I peered into the gloom, expecting some messenger of doom.

A woman, wearing cape and hood, stood in the shadow of the porch.

'Mrs Shackleton?' Her voice was slightly breathless, as though she were nervous or had been hurrying.

What sort of mad woman rushes out in the middle of the night and runs through the streets in the pouring rain?

'Yes. I'm Mrs Shackleton.'

'I must to talk to you.'

When I did not straightaway open the door wider, she added, 'My husband's gone missing.'

I felt groggy with tiredness. 'You best go to the police.' They would have detectives on night duty.

Her snort, part laugh, part groan, dismissed my suggestion before she spoke. 'The police? I've tried. They're neither use nor ornament.'

She seemed unaware of the time and offered no apology for disturbing me. A north wind howled down the street, driving horizontal bullets of rain.

Imagining that a person intent on foul play would not hammer the door knocker loudly enough to wake half of Headingley, I fumbled to undo the latch chain. As the light from the hall fell on her face, she looked very young, and pale as the moon.

Without waiting for an invitation, the woman stepped inside, dripping rain onto the mat.

I shut the door behind her. 'Let me take your cape.'

She unhooked and shook off a dark plaid cape, creating a pool of water on the polished wood floor.

'Thank you.' Her lips were pale but two unnaturally bright spots of pink lit her cheeks. Perhaps she suffered from consumption. The pulses in her throat throbbed. 'I left my umbrella on the train. I caught the milk train. I've run from Headingley station.'

I hung the cape on the newel post, again stubbing my toe on the suitcase.

'You'd better come through, Mrs . . .'

'Armstrong. Mary Jane Armstrong.'

The dining room doubles as my office but no fire had been lit in there for a week, since before I left for London. I led her through to the kitchen. 'This way. The fire will be out, but we'll be warmer in here.' She followed me. I handed her a towel. 'Dry yourself a little.' She moved like someone who had walked out of the sea and would shortly return to Neptune.

'I don't care about being wet.' But she rubbed at her hair which fell in damp wavy strands below her ears. Her hooded cape had provided little protection from the deluge.

She was in her mid or late thirties, about five foot four, plump and pretty with clear white skin and abundant hazelnut-brown hair, swept up and caught with tortoise-shell combs and pins. It looked as though it may have started out neat but now wavy tendrils escaped the combs. Strands of hair hung below her shoulders where the pins had fallen out. She wore a calf-length bottle-green skirt and white blouse, with a locket at her throat. Her shoes were so well polished that the rain slid off the leather.

I drew out a chair, leaving her to recover for a moment, while I went into the dining room.

Who was she, and what brought her here at this hour? Something about her seemed so very familiar. She reminded me of someone, and I couldn't think who.

I lifted the decanter from the sideboard, along with a brandy balloon. At the kitchen table, I poured brandy into the glass. 'Here. Drink this. You look as if you need it, and then you can tell me what brings you here.'

She cupped the glass in both hands and stared intently

into it, as if the amber liquor created a crystal ball and the future would become startlingly clear. Then she looked at me from eyes that were the same hazelnut brown as her hair. There was intensity in her gaze, as though what she did not find in the brandy balloon, she would see in my eyes.

Where did I know her from?

The impression fled as she screwed up her eyes tightly, sniffed at the brandy, and knocked it back in one quick gulp. She coughed and began to choke, saying between splutters, 'Eh, I thought it were ginger ale. What is it? Right burns my throat.'

'Brandy. It's brandy.'

'You should've said. I'll have another and take it more steady.'

I lifted the decanter and poured another finger of brandy. 'Sip it. Gently does it.' I had come back from London feeling a little tired, but now the tiredness fled. I said encouragingly, 'You'd better tell me what brings you here.'

She squeezed the glass so tightly it was in danger of cracking. 'Like I said, my husband's gone missing.' Mrs Armstrong spoke in a flat, tired voice. 'I don't know whether he's alive or dead. I thought of you because . . . well, I've heard that you find people.' She took another sip of brandy, and then lost interest and pushed the glass away.

'What's your husband's name?'

'Ethan. Ethan Armstrong.' She joined her hands and drew them close to her body, running the ball of her thumb across her fingertips, her only sign of agitation, and yet there was something so palpable in that agitation that it started butterflies fluttering in my stomach.

12

She tilted her head slightly to one side. 'I'd have known you anywhere.'

'Oh? We've met before?'

She gave a smile, and shook her head. 'Not met, not exactly.'

Perhaps she was a mad woman after all. My house-keeper has the flat adjoining the house. All I had to do was ring the bell. Emergency signal.

Calm down, I told myself. The woman's distressed. She doesn't know what she's saying. 'What do you mean?'

'You wouldn't remember.'

There is nothing more annoying than a person who will not spit out simple information. I have a good memory for faces, and there was something familiar about her, yet I could not place her. 'Was it during the war?'

'Something like that. Long ago, anyway.' She made a dismissive gesture, as if where and when our paths had crossed was of no importance.

'Have you come far?'

'From Great Applewick.'

I shook my head. 'Can't say I know the place.'

'No one does. There's not enough to it. It's near Guiseley.'

'Ah yes.' I pictured my journeys to Guiseley during the war, a small town, not much more than a mile wide, with a main street and a town hall that was given over as a hospital. 'The hospital, is that where we met?'

She looked at her hands. 'It could have been. Yes, that was it.'

People give themselves away in all sorts of small ways when lying. She changed the subject. 'Can I have a glass of water?'

I moved my chair, but she was already on her feet, at

the sink, her back to me, turning on the tap, running water into a cup.

What a cheek the woman had, talking her way in, hinting that she knew me, and now making herself at home. But perhaps her story was so terrible that she would have to work up to it slowly.

Holding the cup in both hands, she took a sip. 'I wish we had running water in our house. I'm to think myself lucky we have a well in the garden.'

Note to self: the first thing Mrs Armstrong mentioned was a well. A complaint about her living conditions, or an important clue? Perhaps she murdered her husband and dumped him in the well. How long would this take, I wondered, and what should I do with her at the end of it? 'So, Mrs Armstrong . . .'

'I don't like you to call me Mrs Armstrong. I'm Mary Jane.'

'Very well.' If she expected me to tell her to call me Kate, she could think again. 'Let me take some particulars, Mary Jane.'

At the top of the page, I wrote.
Mary Jane Armstrong – Monday, 14 May, 1923: 4.30 a.m.
Missing: Ethan Armstrong, husband.

'And your address?'

'Mason's Cottage on Nether End in Great Applewick.'

'Tell me when you last saw Ethan.'

'He went to work on Saturday, as usual. Ethan's a stone mason. Works at Ledger's quarry. Finishing time is one o'clock but he stayed on alone to get on with a special job. He's all for better working hours for quarrymen, and yet he's the one chooses to stay on when everyone else has knocked off.'

'So he went to work on Saturday morning at about . . .'

14

'They start at eight on Saturday, seven during the week. The children took him a bite to eat at five o'clock in the evening. I would have let him go hungry, till his belly brought him home.' She closed her eyes and for a moment her breathing came in short bursts. Her chest rose and fell. She took very deliberate deep breaths, and then paused, as though she would take a running jump at what she needed to say. I waited for her to continue.

'Harriet – she's my daughter – she says he was out cold, lying in his hut. He didn't stir when she touched him. She felt sure he was dead. Instead of coming straight home to me, she took it into her head to go to the farm, it being nearest, but having her little brother slowed her down. One of the men went back with her.' Her eyes widened and she jutted her chin, as though expecting contradiction of what she would say next. 'There was no sign of Ethan. The quarry was deserted. Arthur walked her to the road and sent her home. Then he went back to the farm for Austin, carried the little feller home on his shoulders.'

'What age are the children?' I wondered whether Austin would corroborate Harriet's story.

'Harriet's ten, Austin is six.'

'Did Austin see his father?'

She shook her head. 'Harriet said she kept him back, kept him out of it.' Mary Jane placed her hands on the table as though they no longer belonged to her. 'I hurried down to the quarry as soon as Harriet told me. Ethan was nowhere to be found. We haven't seen him since. I'm running mad with worry.'

'Could Harriet have been mistaken?'

'That's what I hope and pray. But I believe her. She's a truthful child and nobody's fool. Sergeant Sharp, he's our village bobby, he didn't believe her. Made that quite plain. Said a dead man doesn't stand up and walk. But give the sergeant his due, he pressed half a dozen quarrymen from the Fleece to search the quarry with lanterns, because by then it had come in dark. They were glad to do it, or some were. Ethan's a man people love or loathe.'

At least she spoke of him in the present tense. Perhaps he wasn't at the bottom of the well, unless dumped there by one of the people who loathed him.

'Do you have a photograph?'

She took an envelope from her skirt pocket. It contained a photograph which she slid across the table. Ethan Armstrong gazed at me: broad faced, clean shaven, and with a solemn expression. He was wearing uniform and an infantry cap badge.

'That was taken in 1917, so it's six years old but the best I've got.'

'What height and build is he?'

'He's five foot nine inches, with sandy coloured hair, well built, a strong fellow. He has to be in his line of work.'

'His age?'

'He's thirty-six, same as me.'

'Still clean shaven?'

'Yes.'

'How did you leave things with Sergeant Sharp, after the search of the quarry?'

I wondered whether he may have circulated a description to the local hospitals.

'He was fed up with me, especially when I told him we'd had a bit of a fall out that morning. He thinks Ethan has taken the hump and left me, and that Harriet is a little liar who seeks attention.' Her voice rose, as if she half expected me to take the side of the police sergeant and dismiss her fears. 'I haven't slept. I can't just leave it like this.'

I would have to tread a fine line. Either Ethan Armstrong had been murdered, or had abandoned his wife. 'Who are his friends? Is there anyone he would have confided in, or gone to visit?'

After ten minutes I had established who loved Ethan: his good friend Bob Conroy whose farm Harriet hurried to; Ethan's former apprentice, Raymond, now a mason in his own right; fellow trade unionists in the Quarrymen's Union, and radicals across the North of England who agitated for better pay and conditions for working men. That didn't exactly narrow the field.

Those who loathed him included the quarry foreman, who had defeated Ethan in his bid to call a strike last week.

'Mary Jane, you say you believe Harriet when she describes finding her father's body, even if the sergeant doesn't?'

Her sigh came from somewhere deep. 'I do, or I did. But now I begin to think she must have been mistaken. None of the quarrymen gave her credence. I began to think she must have seen some apparition.' Her voice lifted with hope. 'Bob thinks so too.'

'Bob Conroy the farmer?'

'Yes.'

Yet Bob Conroy had not been there to walk back with Harriet and search the quarry. I made a mental note that I must find out where he was on Saturday afternoon. This "good friend" might well be the Brutus who dealt the blow.

'Was there any further search yesterday? Did you contact anyone?'

She shook her head. 'Not a proper search, no. Bob said Ethan would be sure to turn up. He said that some comrades were meeting on Hawksworth Moor, a sort of labour rally.' The red spots returned to her cheeks as she coloured up with anger. 'I tell Ethan, we'd be better off if he put his energy into home and hearth. Bob took a stroll out to the moor, but he said he wasn't made welcome without Ethan, and no one knew where Ethan was.'

'Has Ethan disappeared before, without explanation?'

'Never.'

'How did Bob explain the fact that Harriet saw her father and thought him dead?'

'He said that she would have been scared in the quarry. Last year, someone fell to his death there. Perhaps she saw shadows, or imagined something. The children tell stories about the quarry. They think goblins live in little caves in the slopes. Bob said.'

My mind worked overtime. 'How long would it have taken Harriet to go to the farm, seek help, and get back to the quarry?'

She shook her head. 'I'm not sure. Arthur made her wait till he'd finished the evening milking.'

'An hour?'

'It could have been an hour, or a little less. It was half past six by the time I went to the quarry to see for myself, and here's the queerest thing . . .'

'Go on.'

She took a sip of water. Her hands began to shake. 'Ethan was making a sundial of blue slate, a very special job. Harriet and Austin both told me that when they arrived with the bite to eat for their dad, the sundial was standing there proud as you like, looking as finished as it might ever be. But by the time I arrived, after Harriet had told me her tale, it was going on dark. The sundial was smashed to smithereens, and there wasn't hair nor hide of Ethan.'

She put her head in her hands, and just for a moment I thought myself in one of the melodramas that mother and I sometimes go to see at the Drury Lane Theatre in Wakefield.

She looked up. 'What am I supposed to think? Harriet's not a little liar, but there was no sign of him.'

'Does Ethan drink?'

She gave a rueful smile. 'No one could work in a quarry with all that dust and not drink. But he wouldn't booze himself into a stupor at his work.'

'Might there be any other explanation for what Harriet saw?'

She rested her forearms on the table and leaned forward. 'I've been over and over that myself. Harriet's a daddy's girl. She'd heard us rowing. If Ethan said for her to tell me that he was laid out cold . . . But no, she wouldn't have kept it up.'

'What did you row about?'

She shook her head. 'Summat and nowt. I wanted him to do summat in the house, and chop a few logs, and not be working on Mrs Ledger's sundial for her birthday when he should be with us. And I feel so terrible now that we parted on bad terms but if he's taken that as an excuse to bugger off, I'll brain him.'

It vexed me that she seemed to be holding something back. And I am not so well known that my address is as familiar as 221B Baker Street.

'Mary Jane, if you want my help, you must be candid. You haven't even said how you found me.'

'Someone gave me your address.'

19

'Who?'

'Does it matter?'

It would matter very much if she would not tell me. After ten long seconds, she said, 'A relative of mine. She knew about you.' As if to forestall any questions about this helpful relative, she continued, 'It wasn't such a terrible row with Ethan. He'd taken no food with him on Saturday because I wouldn't put it up. Let his belly bring him home, that's what I thought. Of course Harriet had to defy me . . .'

We were beginning to go round in circles. It was time to stop talking and act. I stood up. 'You said the quarry opens for work at seven o'clock. It's just turned five. Let's go there now and you can show me where Harriet saw her father. I'd like to see it before men start work for the day.' I did not add that any evidence there may have been would likely have been trampled underfoot by searching quarrymen and the local bobby. 'Give me a few moments to get dressed.'

I left my visitor in the kitchen and tapped on the adjoining door that connects Mrs Sugden's quarters.

My housekeeper took a few moments to answer. She had drawn on the warm maroon check dressing gown that had belonged to her late husband, fingers fumbling for its silky, fraying cord. Her long grey hair was braided in a single plait. Without spectacles, the plain face looked naked and vulnerable.

I apologised for disturbing her and quickly explained about my visitor.

'And so I'm going to Great Applewick with Mrs Armstrong . . .'

'At this hour?'

'I want to get an early start, take a look at the quarry

where her husband was last seen, before men start work. I don't imagine they'll take kindly to a posh nosey parker tramping about.'

'I'm uneasy about this, Mrs Shackleton, on your own . . .'

I cut her off. 'You'll see the name and address on the kitchen table. Would you tell Mr Sykes where I've gone, and that I'll call on him when I have more definite information?'

Sykes, an ex-policeman, is my assistant and lives a short distance away.

I left Mrs Sugden with her uneasiness.

Mary Jane appeared at the kitchen door. 'I need the lavatory.'

'I'll show you. It's upstairs.'

My portmanteaux still stood in the hall. Mary Jane glanced at the suitcases. 'Are these to go up?'

'Yes but they're heavy,' I said lamely.

She picked up one in each hand. 'Not as heavy as kids and sacks of spuds.' She marched ahead of me up the stairs. 'Where shall I dump 'em?'

'In my bedroom – there. Thank you.'

She carried the cases into my room, and then came back onto the landing. I turned to her. In the dim light, with her high cheekbones and slanting eyes she had the look of a cautious cat.

I switched on the bathroom light.

She sighed. 'I wish we had a bathroom.'

When I did not answer, she said accusingly, 'I'm not unused to them you know. I wouldn't store coal in the bathtub.'

As I dressed, it occurred to me that anyone who could carry two full portmanteaux up the stairs would be able to

drag the body of an errant husband to some hiding place
in a quarry.

What did a person wear to go tramping round a quarry?
Corduroy breeches, cap and boots. It would be a men
only preserve. All the more important to get a move on
and arrive before the males of the species started work. At
least the rain had stopped. I dressed quickly, in a smartly
cut tweed costume. Country clothes, suitable for a shooting party. My stout shoes, bought last year in Harrogate,
would come in handy. A spare pair of Cuban heels and an
extra pair of stockings would not go amiss.

Mary Jane Armstrong waited for me in the hall. I
handed her Gerald's motoring coat. 'You'll need this.
There are goggles in the car.'

The coat reached her ankles. There it was again as I
looked at her, the niggle about where we had met before.

'Mary Jane, before we go, there's just one thing.'

'Yes?'

'Where do we know each other from?'

She tried to turn up the coat cuff.

'I can't say.'

'I'm not budging till you do.'

She looked at me, and then glanced away. 'It's a long
time since I saw you, Catherine. You were a few weeks
old. I was toddling about. A man came to take you away,
and I cried. I didn't want him to take you.'

She looked steadily at me, her feline eyes daring me to
contradict. 'My maiden name was Whitaker, same as
yours before you were given the name of the people who
adopted you. Catherine, I'm your sister.'

My heart thumped so hard I felt she would hear it.
Little wonder she had been reluctant to say how she
"knew" me. I was a few weeks old when I was adopted,

22

and I knew the name of my natural family, and that they lived in Wakefield. Beyond those simple facts lay a mystery that I had so far felt no inclination to unravel.

We stood a few feet apart in the hallway. Mary Jane Armstrong may or may not be genuine; she may or may not be a murderess.

I felt suddenly unsteady on my feet. I reached out and touched the wall, to anchor myself. Mary Jane looked at me with a mixture of concern, and something else. Fear? That I would turn her away?

'I'm sorry. I shouldn't have come.'

But she had come. And here we stood with our coats on, ready to go.

'How did you know where to find me?'

'Our sister, Barbara May. She always followed your progress.'

Progress. The word conjured up school history: kings and queens making epic journeys, lodging with favoured nobles; eating their subjects out of house, home and peace of mind.

And "Barbara May". Did everyone in the Whitaker family have two names? Was that the reason for my being turfed out of the clan? *We can't have a girl with just the one name. Get shut of her. That nice police officer and his wife will take her off our hands. Mr Dennis Hood and his charming and childless wife, Virginia, affectionately known to her friends as Ginny. She's a soft touch.*

Mary Jane was not even claiming to be the one who followed my progress. I had Barbara May to thank for that. Perhaps Barbara May would turn up next. Find my lost dog, love. Give me the loan of a shilling.

Mary Jane may be telling the truth, or she could be a glorious confidence trickster whose story I had swallowed without chewing. That would explain the lump in my craw.

'How did Barbara May find out where I live?'

'It was in the *Mercury*, when you married. Barbara May worked as a cleaner at the infirmary, where your husband used to work.'

I could not be sure, but thought she looked a little embarrassed. She did not explain whether Barbara May followed Gerald home, or poked about in the infirmary files for his address.

She added, 'Mam was very pleased when you married a doctor.'

Shut up, Mary Jane. Don't say any more.

In the thick silence, neither of us looked at each other as I hitched my satchel onto my shoulder, and reached out to open the door. The key did not want to budge, nor the knob to turn. Don't let her see how shaken I am. Don't let her see that I need two hands: the right hand to turn the handle, and the left hand to stop the right hand shaking.

'Right, Mary Jane. Let's go.'

I would think about this sister business later. For now, I must put it out of my mind and concentrate on the business in hand. She had come to me for help.

Two

As we walked up the road, my legs felt leaden and yet there was a strange lightness, as if I no longer belonged to myself and might float away.

We walked up the quiet street to the old stable my neighbours let me use as a garage for the Jowett. Silver cobwebs decorated the hedgerows.

There was lightness in Mary Jane's step as the motoring coat slapped her ankles, and an air of blitheness about her, as though she had shuffled off all her worries and everything would be all right, now that she had found me. Even through the fog of trying to make sense of her words, I recognised her mood. It was familiar to me from when I helped women after the war. The relief of having someone on one's side creates the illusion that all will be well. Now was not the moment to burst the bubble.

Sister. She was my sister. This little girl, Harriet, who had found her father's body, was my niece. And there was a nephew. What was his name? Austin. Little Austin, she had called him.

The horror of what those children had discovered hit me somewhere else, deep inside.

'Where are the children now?' I asked.

'I left them sleeping. I put a note on the table in case they wake before I get back.'

Early in the morning, everything makes more noise. The door of the old stable where I garage the Jowett creaked loudly as I opened it. Mary Jane gazed at the car. 'What a beautiful motor! The kids'll want a ride in this.'

She was acting as if we were about to have a day out, instead of beginning what might be a murder investigation.

'Shut the door when I drive out would you?'

She stepped well aside as though expecting to have her toes crushed by the car wheels.

When she had closed the doors, she clambered in.

I handed her the map. 'You'll have to tuck your hands up your sleeves to keep warm. I forgot to bring extra gloves.'

'I'll be fine.'

'Don't talk to me as I'm driving because the noise will fly your voice away. But you can put this map where I can get at it.'

She took the map. 'There's tramlines much of the way.'

There would not be too many opportunities for me to take a wrong turn on the twisting lanes that led from Headingley to Great Applewick, but it could not be entirely ruled out. The road towards Guiseley was not one I had driven in a long time.

As we left Headingley behind and drove into the country, pink streaks in the sky turned gold, and then faded to white. A half-hearted sun put in a wary appearance. Apart from the sound of the engine, the world was quiet and peaceful. Even horses and cows in the fields had not yet begun to stir.

Mary Jane turned up her collar and pushed her hands up the sleeves of the coat.

I glanced at her quickly. Here was someone who knew my birth mother, brothers, sisters, who had known my father, and formed part of their lives. All of them remained a mystery to me. As I carefully negotiated a bend in the road, a terrible loneliness came over me. Having refused to think about the family who gave me up, I had never needed to give them weight. Now she had pushed her way in, selfishly, without a by your leave.

A cart appeared suddenly from a lane on the left. The unblinkered horse tossed its head. A whip cracked. I slowed down and pressed the brake.

'I never forgot you,' she said suddenly, dipping her chin into her chest, then turning and looking at me. 'You were just a little baby. I said to Mam not to let the man take you. I thought he would drop you. He sort of crooked his right arm and balanced you on it. I remember saying that he would drop you. But no one listened. I cried when you'd gone.'

She had given me something to go on. I could test her claim. Ask Dad, did you go alone to fetch me? Did you carry me in the crook of your arm?

I drew into the kerb and brought the car to a halt. Not looking at her, staring at my hands on the wheel, I said, 'Why didn't you tell me when you stepped in the door? You should have told me straightaway.'

'I was going to tell you later.'

I turned to look at her. 'And what else are you going to tell me later?'

She looked back at me. 'You try it. You try saying something like that and see how you feel.'

She hadn't answered my question. If this was all some idiotic lie to get my help, she'd be sorry. But no one would invent such a story, would they? And there was something about her manner that made me feel at ease under my uneasiness, if that makes sense.

The way to Mary Jane's village took us out of Leeds, passing the village of Horsforth, and following the tramway. At a higher point in the road, we crossed the River Aire. It always surprises me how much life goes on around a corner, along a street you may not look at twice.

My new-found sister's directions were not of the highest quality. She called out things like, 'Go there,' meaning turn left, and 'You've missed it.'

Mary Jane was slow in telling me to turn for Great Applewick. I looked out for the next turning and entered Back Lane, a street of modest stone dwellings whose front doors opened directly onto the street. For a place whose name hinted at apple orchards, there was not a tree in sight. We turned again, passing Great Applewick Chemical works, a printing works and a sign pointing to "Golf Course".

Along Town Street, a mix of shops and houses, we passed school, church and Methodist chapel. Along Over Terrace, houses thinned out. Then came a rural lane, and two thatched sandstone cottages. Behind these dwellings spread narrow strips of fields and meadows into the open countryside. A little way on, Mary Jane pointed to a third house. 'That's us.'

I stopped the car opposite a two-storey sandstone dwelling, a couple of hundred years old. It was set a little way back from the road. The most cheerful thing about it was a blossoming apple tree to the left of the door.

The blinds were drawn down at its upper and lower windows. The stone roof looked much newer than the rest of the house. It was altogether more substantial than

Mary Jane had led me to believe. At first glance, almost the idyllic country cottage.

'It's lovely,' I said. 'But not thatched, like the other two cottages.'

She snorted her dislike of the cottage. 'I nagged Ethan into seeing to that. Have you ever tried living under a damp old roof where rats make their nests and birds think it's a free for all? And we've no running water like you. We've to fetch it from the well in the back garden.'

I was close up against a drystone wall and so we clambered out of my side, me first, curling my cold toes to bring them back to life.

'Ethan's not here,' she said flatly.

'How do you know?'

'He would have lit a fire. There'd be smoke from the chimney.'

We walked to the door stepping on pink blossoms blown from the tree.

She pulled a string through the letter box.

'Little monkey's taken the key off the string. She must have been scared someone would come.' Mary Jane knocked loudly, and waited. She knocked again. 'I'll have to thrown stones at the window.'

She bent down and began to scrabble about, picking pebbles from the verge. She took aim at the upstairs window and scored a hit that made barely a sound. The next pebble missed.

'If the children are still sleeping, what about you show me the quarry? Can we drive to it from here?'

She threw another pebble. 'I can't. I know I'm being a coward, but I can't go back there.'

'Then tell me where it is. I'll go.'

She looked relieved that I would be willing to go to the

29

quarry without her. 'There's two ways from here. Out of our garden at the back and follow the footpath, or back to the village and take the road by the side of the chapel. You can't miss the quarry.'

When someone tells you *You can't miss it*, that usually means *I* can't miss it because I know where it is, but you'll be lucky to find it.

Just then a noise came from the other side of the door. A bolt drew back. A key turned in the lock.

The small girl in the long white nightgown looked from her mother to me, and then beyond us, to the road and the motor, looking hopefully for someone else. Not seeing him, her shoulders drooped. She stepped back without looking at us again. Her long hair, tied with a ribbon, reached almost to her waist. A shiver ran through me. It was like looking in the mirror of the old wardrobe I had as a child. The girl's eyes were too big for her face, her hair parted severely above a pale high forehead. If I had doubted Mary Jane was my sister, those doubts fled when I looked at this little apparition of myself when young.

I followed Mary Jane across the threshold.

'Have you been all right?' she asked.

'Yes.' The girl's voice was sulky with sleep.

'This is Harriet. Harriet, say hello nicely to Mrs Shackleton who gave me a ride back from where I went to look for Dad. That was kind of her wasn't it?'

'Where did you look for him?' Harriet asked.

'Mrs Shackleton will look for him, in her motor car.'

So that's what I would do. The child had the sense to look a little sceptical at this idea. I wished Jim Sykes were here. He has children of his own and knows how to talk to them. Even my name sounded wrong in this house.

The girl did not look at me, but stood, watching, as her mother took off the motoring coat. I kept mine on.

'Why did you take the key off the string?' Mary Jane asked.

Harriet took the key from the lock and once more fastened it to the string. 'I didn't know who might be passing by and stick their big mitt through the letter box.'

She spoke calmly as if explaining to a child, and for the briefest of moments I thought she must be the mother and Mary Jane the daughter. Time played a trick so that Mary Jane became an old woman, and Harriet the calm and thoughtful adult. Beside her solemn daughter, Mary Jane seemed flibbertigibbet.

I glanced about the room. If one did not have to live here, one might describe it as picturesque, with its oil lamp on the dresser and candle holders on the mantelpiece. A well scrubbed deal table by the window held an enamel basin and jug. A pail and a bucket stood under the table. Another table stood against the wall, with chairs and buffets. A third, smaller table fronted by a spindly chair, held a Little Worker Lockstitch sewing machine. On either side of the range were fitted cupboards and drawers. On the far side of the room loomed a dresser. A blanket chest stood under the slope of the staircase. It was a crowded room. I pictured the family forever sidestepping, so as not to bump into the furniture.

Mary Jane raked at the ashes in the grate. 'We'll soon have a fire going. You go back to bed, Harriet. It's too early for school.'

The child sat on a buffet by the table, watching her mother.

Mary Jane picked up a newspaper and began to make a twist of it. Harriet leaped from the stool, snatched the newspaper back from her mother and smoothed it. 'Dad hasn't read that *Herald* yet.'

Mary Jane sighed. She reached for some shreds of bracken and placed a few chips of wood in the grate. 'You haven't fetched coal in.'

'I was going to do it.'

'Go on then!'

The sleepy-eyed child slipped from the buffet and picked up a scuttle from the hearth.

'Harriet! Put your shoes on.'

'Here, give that to me.' I took the coal scuttle from her. 'Where do you keep the coal?'

'Nay, Catherine. You mustn't do that.'

I ignored Mary Jane and followed as Harriet led me to a back door. It was bolted top and bottom. I shot back the bolts and the door swung open onto a long back garden with a couple of outhouses.

'That's coal 'ole.' Harriet pointed to the first shed.

Slipping on a pair of galoshes that were too big, she shuffled along beside me.

In the coal hole, I picked up the shovel. It grated on the floor as I slid it under the heap of coal, filled it, and tipped the coal into the scuttle. Coals tumbled from the top of the pile.

'You've to fill it to the top.'

I scraped the shovel along the floor once more.

'Do you know Dad, Mrs Shack . . .'

'Mrs Shackleton's a bit of a mouthful. You can call me Auntie Kate.' I hadn't meant to say it, but it came out.

She frowned, and I realised I had made a mistake. She watched me tip the next shovelful of coal into the scuttle. When she spoke, she did not call me Auntie Kate.

'Do you know Dad? Have you met him?'

She looked at me steadily, waiting for a reply. She would make a good interviewer. A felon staring into those wide eyes would be enticed into telling the truth.

'No, Harriet. I don't know your dad. But if you'll be kind enough and you don't need urgently to go back to bed, you could take me to the quarry and show me where he worked.'

It was hard, and perhaps even cruel, but I needed to talk to the child alone. After all, she claimed to have seen her father lying dead, and she did not look as if her eyesight failed her.

Harriet gulped. Her fists tightened. She no more wanted to go to the quarry than her mother did. But she was braver. 'I'll get dressed.'

Three

We walked in silence along the footpath. It was early enough for the wild flowers not to have opened for business. The quietness of the morning and the mildness of the scene lulled us into a gentle stroll, as though we had no particular destination. I hated to break the spell.

How do you start a conversation with a child when the question is, *Where did you see your father's body?*

'Your little brother came with you on Saturday.'

She kicked at a pebble. 'Austin, yes.'

'Do you know what time it was when you brought the supper for your dad?'

'The church clock was striking five. He'd been gone since morning.'

'Your mam said you put up the food yourself?'

'I am ten years old.' There was a hint of rebuke in her voice and perhaps a little doubt about my intelligence.

Grilling would lead me into troubled waters with this child.

The path turned muddy. I followed Harriet's footsteps as she skirted onto the damp grass. The river came into view, at the bottom of the steep bank. It flowed swiftly, giving off a soothing sound, and a terrible whiff of chemicals.

'I'm sorry to ask, Harriet. But would you tell me all about that day, as much as you can remember about Saturday.'

'What everything, from getting up?'

'Yes,' I said firmly.

Her gaze was incredulous. It said, *you've got a cheek*. Then she coloured up and said quietly, 'You don't tell people *all* your business.'

Mistake. I had asked too much and brought that deep-grained, early-learned Yorkshire caution into play. See all, hear all, say nowt. Eat all, sup all, pay nowt.

'Please, Harriet. It might help. Your mam has told me of course but everyone notices different things.'

She sighed, but did not answer.

I pressed on. 'Had your dad received any letters or messages? Did he say anything about visiting someone, or going off somewhere?'

I felt mean, introducing the possibility that Ethan may have gone visiting, but it did the trick.

'I don't know about any messages or letters. He was supposed to be going to Hawksworth Moor on Sunday, and he said he would take me and Austin.'

This was the trade union meeting Mary Jane had mentioned. Ethan must have intended to introduce his children to politics at an early age.

'Harriet, I want to find out as much as I can about what might have happened. Anything you can tell me might help, even if it seems a small thing. Tell me about Saturday.'

She had been dragging her feet. Now she made up her mind to help me. She held herself erect. Her steps became purposeful. I did not look at her. The energy in her voice made me kick myself for raising hopes that would not be met.

'Dad starts work later on a Saturday – eight o'clock instead of seven. We were still in bed when he left, me and Austin. He didn't call up that he was going, but when I went downstairs, he'd left me some tea in his pint pot. He allus does that. He likes it strong, with sugar, and he leaves some for me. I don't mind that it's cold. I like tea. I'm greedy for tea. Him and me both are. I'd heard him talking to Mam. He asked where was his snack. She said he mun come home at dinnertime. He said she knew fine well he was working the sundial. He'd finish it and come home when it was done and not before. She said what was the point of fighting for Saturday half day and then working it? And hadn't he promised to do the heavy work in the garden. He said he'd do it Sunday, and she said oh was he foregoing Hawksworth Moor and his socialist chums then, and he said he'd forgotten that. Then he left.

'I helped Mam all morning in the house and out in the garden. Which I have to do because she's making me a Whitsun dress and Austin Whitsun breeches and shirt, and she can't do everything. When it come to dinnertime, I said should I take summat to Dad and she said no, he was coming home. Me and Austin went along to the shops on Town Street, to the butcher and the bread shop. I got a cream bun with a hat on, and he got a jam tart.

'After we'd eaten us buns, Mam said where was her Woodbines, and I said I'd forgotten them. She said go get them and I said my legs ached and my arms ached from carrying shopping. And she said Oh all right then and went off herself. That was when I got the basin and put the boiled peas in it and cut a piece of cold bacon and covered it with a teacloth and said to Austin, come on, and shut up about it, and we'll be back before she comes home.'

Harriet impressed me. Her story came out in a matter of fact way. The row between Mary Jane and Ethan had been a petty squabble about what time Ethan would come home. Nothing that would make her slip to the quarry and murder her husband while her children were doing the shopping.

The path began to climb steeply. Scrubby bushes on the bank sloping down to the river turned a dusty white, which must mean the quarry was close by. And then I could smell it, a powdery dry smell that caught the back of my throat.

The track dropped and led us to a road that was little more than a bridleway. The quarry stretched before us stark and strange, a ravaged landscape. I reached for Harriet's hand, more to reassure myself than her.

'Harriet, is this what it was like on Saturday, or was there anyone here?'

'They'd all gone home. I whistled for Dad, but there was no answer. I didn't like to go walking through, just the two of us, but I'd come this far, so I did.'

'Can we do that now?'

She ran her tongue across her lips. With a stab of guilt, I remembered that the poor child had not had so much as a sip of tea, for which she was greedy, nor a slice of bread.

Harriet led the way along a rough path, saying nothing. We walked by a huge shed. Her breathing became louder.

'What's that?' I asked. The building to our right looked like a photograph I had seen of an enormous shack in a deserted gold rush town.

'It's the crushing shed.'

We passed a huge crane. A slope led up to a little hut

perched on top of rocks. When we had passed that, our way dipped down, and then became level.

She stopped by a makeshift three-sided shed, constructed of planks and corrugated iron, open at the front.

In front of it stood a long workbench. Beyond the workbench, on the ground, lay scattered pieces of blue slate.

'Was that the sundial your dad was working on, Harriet?'

'I think so. It wasn't broken when we came. It looked finished. At first I thought he must have gone home, by the road, and that was why we had missed him.'

'And where exactly did you see him?'

'Just there, lying just inside the hut.'

'Did Austin see him?'

'I don't think so. I made him stay there.' She pointed to the end of the table. 'He was scared. Some people say the goblins come out when the men leave the quarry.'

'Did your dad speak to you, or make any sound?'

'No.'

'Did you speak to him, or touch his hand?'

'Yes I did. He didn't answer. His hand was cold. But the stone is cold. So he would be cold.'

I went into the hut. She did not follow.

There was a rusty brazier and a blackened kettle. On the shelf to my left were tools and tin mugs.

Harriet followed my gaze. 'They're not Dad's tools. But that's Dad's mug and spoon. And them's Raymond's mallets and chisels.' She pointed to the bench that ran along the back. 'Mam and me made them cushions for Dad and Raymond.'

'Raymond was your Dad's apprentice?'

She looked pleased that I wasn't entirely ignorant. 'Dad's apprentice, until he came out of his time. Raymond's a mason in his own right now.'

'Was Raymond working with your dad on Saturday?'

'Only Dad worked on the sundial. Only Dad worked Saturday afternoon. Raymond is courting. He's to wed next Saturday. He and Polly will live with Raymond's mam and dad or Polly's mam and dad. Raymond's mam is nice but his dad is a nasty piece of work. Polly's mam and dad are nice but they have no room.'

Thanks to my persistence, the poor child was so busy trying to tell me everything that she did not know what to choose and what leave out.

She stared intently at the interior of the shed, as though still seeing someone there. She pointed to the place where she would not step. 'Here. He was lying here, with his head turned away from me. His cap had come off. Look – there it is!'

She pounced, forgetting her reluctance to step into the shed. From under the bench, she reached for an old tweed flat cap that once upon a time had boasted a check pattern.

She clutched the cap. 'I know Mam hopes I'm mistaken and I wish I was, because I don't want Dad to be dead. Sergeant Sharp believes I'm a little liar. I'm not.'

We left the hut. I picked up a large piece of slate with a smooth edge. Looking at the slate gave me something to do while thoughts raced through my brain. The way Harriet told her story, it had to be true.

A delicate straight line had been etched into the piece of slate. A wavy design decorated the edge.

'It wasn't smashed when we came.' She stood as still as the stone that surrounded us on the quarry slopes.

What anger and hatred lay behind the smashing of the

sundial, I wondered, and had that same anger and hatred been directed at Ethan? His craftsmanship was impeccable. I could see that from the fragment of blue slate with its smoothed edge. Why would he disappear? If we were to believe the worst, and imagine him to be dead when the children found him, what had happened to his body?

She followed me round the back of the hut. There were footprints there, and why should there not be? But one of the footsteps was no bigger than my own. Treading lightly, I measured the footstep against mine. I took out my camera. The light behind the hut was not very good, but I adjusted the setting and got as close as I could without distorting the footprint.

Now I regretted the child being here. Should I pretend I wanted a guided tour, just to give me an excuse to search? And what would I find? Any footprints, any clues, would be covered in dust, trampled by Saturday's search party, washed by last night's rain.

All the same, I took a look around. The place gave me goose bumps. This might be what the other side of the moon looks like. In the distance was a grey mountain of rubble, as if there had been a landslide.

What was I searching for? A scrap of cloth caught on a stone, a stain that might be blood, a clutch of hair? Most of our lives we do not look down, nor up either, but straight ahead. I stared at the ground. Sandy, stony, and giving away nothing.

Harriet stood ramrod straight, watching me. I should take her home. She had been through enough.

Her eyes met mine. 'I want you to look at summat.'

'What?'

She held out her hand. Led by her, I walked across the quarry, up and down the hilly ground, along a straight patch, by the crane, all the way to the other side where the hill sloped and a stubborn ash tree, white with dust, clung to the rock face.

The ground became soft. A jolt like an electric shock went through me as I saw what looked like a heel mark, and smoothness on the ground, as though it had been scraped flat. And again, another heel mark. It would not be enough to simply photograph these marks on the ground. I must measure the heel mark. It was too small to belong to a quarryman, unless there was a young boy here. Of course there could be some entirely rational explanation.

'Just a minute, Harriet. I want to take a photograph, to remind me of what the quarry looks like.'

I sat on a boulder to prepare the camera. This boulder would be my landmark. I would take a picture of my find, and the boulder, and of the straight line that led from here.

If I were right, and I wanted so much to be wrong, someone had dragged a body in this direction. That would explain why, by the time the man from the farm came back with Harriet, the body was gone.

Harriet watched as I took a photograph of this patch of ground, feeling uncertain even as I did so that this really did mark the spot where a body had been dragged. More likely it marked a spot where my sense of foreboding gathered in dry dust.

When I had taken the photograph, Harriet grasped my hand, tugging me to come with her. We continued our walk across the uneven ground.

At almost the furthest point, near the far slope, she stopped. The large, dark pool of still water formed an almost perfect menacing circle.

'What if he fell in there?' she asked. Her grip tightened on my hand.

Before I had time to answer, a piercing whistle shot through the quiet morning. We both jumped at the same time. I turned to see where the sound came from. A figure stood at the other side of the quarry. He lifted his hands to his mouth to form an angry trumpet.

The words weren't exactly clear, but his meaning was obvious enough. We stood our ground.

'It's Raymond's dad,' Harriet said quietly.

'The nasty piece of work?'

'Yes. He's foreman.'

'What's his name?'

'Josiah Turnbull.'

'He charges like a bull.' The man was bearing down on us so fast that I willed him to trip and fall flat on his face. 'Don't let's give him an audience, Harriet.'

I pointed my camera at the pool of still, dark water, and took a shot.

He was behind us, letting out some furious yell that turned into the words, 'What the blue blazes you playing at? We don't abide skirts here.'

I turned to face him. He wore cap, old corduroy trousers and ancient tweed jacket. The red muffler tied at his throat matched the colour of his bursting cheeks. His huge twin-peak nose had been broken at least once. An old scar started above his eyebrow and crossed his cheek in wayward fashion. He stank of stale beer and tobacco. With a shovel of a hand that was missing its little and ring fingers, he tried to grab my camera.

I was too quick for him. 'Please calm down, Mr Turnbull.'

'Don't you order me in my own quarry. I bark orders

here. Gerron home and give yer husband his breakfast.'
He turned to Harriet. 'You tellin' yer mad tales again?' As
he looked at Harriet, he saw the cap she clutched. He
moved his shovel hand, as if he would take the cap.
Harriet plunged the cap inside her coat.

While, he was momentarily silenced by the sight of
Ethan's cap, I said, 'I asked Harriet to show me the
quarry. I'm Mrs Shackleton, here to investigate on behalf
of Mrs Armstrong.'

He stared at me, and then at Harriet. The pause was
brief.

'Well you can 'vestigate somewhere else.' He stepped
even closer. Another inch and his bulk would topple me.
Turnbull and I eyed each other, which hurt my neck.
Harriet gulped, but did not budge.

'Were you among the men who searched the quarry on
Saturday night, Mr Turnbull?'

I sounded more confident than I felt. He was a man
unused to being challenged and just for a moment, he
faltered.

'What if I was?' He glared at Harriet. 'Yer dad's slung
his hook. He took the hump because he'll get no support
for a strike here. Satan had a silver tongue an' all and you
know what happened to him.'

'Last I heard, Mr Turnbull, Satan was alive and making
grand progress. Do you mind telling me when you last
saw Mr Armstrong?'

His toecap touched my shoes. 'Aye I do mind. And
you're trespassing.'

His bad breath formed fiery clouds that scorched my
scalp and travelled.

This was more than a nasty piece of work. This was a
violent bully. 'I dislike threatening behaviour, Mr

43

Turnbull. I hope when you consider you'll talk to me in a more courteous manner.' Some hopes. Hell would freeze over. The quarry would sprout blue roses. 'Come, Harriet.'

She threw back her head, gave him one more stare and we stepped round him, towards the quarry exit.

'Posh bitch!' he yelled.

The words hit me between the shoulder blades.

Harriet began to cry, but not until we were well away from Turnbull. 'He wouldn't be so rude and nasty if my dad was here.'

I searched for a hanky. 'I know. You stood up to him very well. I'm proud of you.' I didn't add that it would stand her in good stead for all the other big bullies she would meet throughout her life.

I felt shaken by the incident, not least because of having exposed Harriet to such an encounter.

We retraced our steps to the mouth of the quarry. 'Which way did you go on Saturday, Harriet?'

'We turned left here.' She pointed to the path we had just walked along. 'Only I went across the bridge to the farm.' She paused, as if waiting to be asked another question, then continued. 'I went to the farm because it was nearest and I thought Uncle Bob would come back with me and fetch Dad home. Do you want to go to the farm now?'

'No. You must go home and have your breakfast. But I would like you to show me the village. I'm going to call in to see the policeman.'

She nodded. 'It's this way then.'

We set off down the hill that led to Great Applewick. In future, I must make sure I go to the local police first. If it had turned difficult in the quarry with the nasty piece of work, I could have found myself on the wrong side of the local bobby, and I need all the support I can get.

Someone was walking uphill, a working man carrying a canvas bag.

'It's Raymond,' Harriet said as the young man surefooted his way towards us, swinging his arms like a soldier.

'Raymond your dad's apprentice?'

'He's a mason now, like Dad. But will never be as good.'

I would have liked to talk to him alone, in case he was as abusive as his father. Now that we drew close, Raymond slowed his pace, eyeing me cautiously. Thin and pale, like a long streak of whitewash, he wore baggy brown trousers and jerkin.

'You been in the quarry, Harriet?' he asked gently. 'You know it's dangerous.'

'It 'int dangerous to me,' Harriet said, still on the defensive after our encounter with Raymond's father.

'I asked Harriet to bring me. How do you do? I'm Mrs Shackleton, a friend of the family.'

We shook hands. The coldness of his touch matched his cautious aloofness. I held onto his hand, determined to melt him a little.

'You're Raymond Turnbull,' I told him, as if he needed to know. 'We just met up with your father.'

'Oh,' he said, and coloured with embarrassment as he glanced at Harriet, guessing our treatment at the hands of his father. 'I suppose he . . .'

'It's all right. I knew I wouldn't be welcome and intended to look round before you all started for the day.'

'Dad's always early.' Raymond turned to Harriet. 'I've just come for my tools.' Lightly, he touched her shoulder.

45

'I'm off up to the Hall to start another sundial to be ready in time for Mrs Ledger's birthday. It'll only be in sandstone mind, not that lovely blue slate.'

Harriet said nothing.

He was ready to walk away, but hesitated, and looked once more at Harriet, as if he wanted to say something kind, but could not find the words.

His fondness for Harriet would give me an advantage, and encourage him to talk.

She held out the cap. 'Dad's cap was under the bench.'

'We didn't see that Saturday night,' Raymond raised his eyebrows. 'Course it was getting dark.'

I disguised my question as a sympathetic comment. 'It must have taken you ages to search the whole quarry.'

He nodded. 'Sergeant Sharp dragged us out of the pub.' He looked at Harriet quickly. 'Not that we needed dragging. We wanted to help.'

'Did you . . .' Harriet began. She stopped.

'Did us what?'

'The pool . . .'

He reached out, but stopped short of touching her. 'No, don't think that, Harriet. That little lagoon, it's just run off groundwater. Once we get a spot of sunshine it'll be gone.'

Harriet stared. 'But I thought it was right deep. I thought all pools in the quarry was deep.'

He shook his head. 'This one 'int. We say that to keep kids out, because some of them lagoons are deep, in the old quarries where they've turned to lakes. Don't let on, Harriet. You're sensible, but there'll be daft kids coming in and getting themselves in bother, wanting to paddle.'

'Oh.' Harriet bit her lip.

'Raymond, what time did you last see Mr Armstrong on Saturday?'

'I worked till one o'clock and then went off for dinner, like everyone else. Ethan was still working on the sundial.'

'Did everyone leave the quarry at one o'clock?'

'Dad stayed a while. He always leaves last, being foreman. But he was in the pub by twenty past,' he added quickly, taking a sudden interest in the canvas bag he carried, not looking at us.

Raymond's precision disturbed me. It sounded uncannily like an alibi. Foreman Josiah Turnbull had been last to leave. Mary Jane had said that Ethan and Turnbull were at loggerheads over the vote for a strike, only days before, with Ethan urging action, but Turnbull coming out on top. I could easily imagine Turnbull goading Ethan. But I must stick to the facts. As casually as I could, I asked, 'How much longer do you think it would have taken Ethan to finish the sundial?'

Raymond frowned. He struck me as the kind of young man who would teaspoon out information without feeling the need to expand. To do any more would smack to him of stating the ruddy obvious.

Harriet came to the rescue. 'I wish Dad had finished it and come home.'

'So do I, Harriet. It would have been finished too, if your dad hadn't decided to add some little flourishes. He sent word up to Colonel Ledger to come and see it.'

'Colonel Ledger?' I asked.

'He owns the quarry. No one else would dare send for him to come, even though he's a man you can talk to. But that's your dad, Harriet. He stands on ceremony to no man. The sundial was for Mrs Ledger's birthday, see, and the colonel had drawn out the pattern. Ethan is used to working to finely drawn specifications. We don't just hew stone.'

He puffed with pride as he let me know his level of skill.

'I'm sure you don't. I've great respect for the mason's craft. Tell me, did the colonel come?'

'I don't know.' Raymond shrugged. His mouth turned down as he looked at Ethan's cap, as though it dawned on him for the first time that something bad may have happened to Ethan.

'Did you see Ethan again between one o'clock on Saturday and today?'

'No. I haven't seen him since.' He glanced at Harriet, as if more than anything he wanted to come up with some explanation. 'He might have tramped in search of another job.' He gulped, and looked away, as though what he regretted most in the world was being put on the spot. 'Anyhow, his tools is gone.'

Harriet raised her head and looked from Raymond to me. 'If Dad's taken his tools and gone somewhere, that'd mean I was mistaken about seeing him like that, in that way.'

We both looked at Raymond for confirmation of Harriet's hope. Her father may be safe, well, and chipping away with his mason's chisel somewhere.

'You could be right, Harriet,' Raymond said at last. 'Your dad could get a job anywhere. For two pins he would have gone to work on York Minster last year. He was offered it.'

I pushed Raymond a little further. 'Work like that would be very enticing for a skilled man. Why didn't he take the job?'

Raymond nodded at Harriet. 'Mary Jane didn't want to move, kids changing schools and all that.'

This puzzled me. After all, Mary Jane had been at pains

48

to tell me how much she disliked the cottage, with its well in the garden. They might have moved somewhere that had indoor plumbing.

The three of us stood in an awkward and silent circle. Harriet tossed her head. She looked at me reproachfully. She wanted me to find her dad, and here I was, asking useless questions. 'I'll let you catch me up.'

She began to walk slowly down the hill.

'What's going on?' Raymond asked. 'Where is Ethan?'

'That's what I hope to find out. You mentioned York, and work at the Minster. Do you really think he may have gone off in search of some other job, without saying anything?'

I had to explore the possibility, in spite of still holding to Harriet's belief that she saw a body.

Raymond coloured up. 'You mean because I wouldn't be sorry to see him go?'

'No I didn't mean that. But is it true?'

'Ethan lives in Mason's Cottage. That house always goes to a quarry worker. I'm getting wed on Saturday. If Ethan doesn't come back, we'll have somewhere of our own to live.'

And your nasty father wouldn't have to keep you and your wife under his roof.

'Thanks, Raymond.'

For a moment we stood, neither of us wanting to move off first in case there was more to be said.

Raymond sighed. 'I hope you find him.'

'So do I.'

I caught up with Harriet who was walking slowly. I wanted to know about her visit to the farm, but that would wait. She had been grilled enough and needed her breakfast and her sup of tea.

49

We walked in silence to the end of the High Street. If she wanted to tell me more, she would.

On the other side of the road, a greengrocer chalked produce and prices on his window. A van driver climbed from his cab, opened the back of his vehicle, took out a stack of newspapers and carried them into a shop.

'Do you have children?' Harriet asked.

'No. Only a cat.'

'Why don't you have children?'

'My husband didn't come back from the war.'

'That was a long time ago.'

'Yes it was.'

'What is your cat called?'

'Sookie. Do you have a cat?'

'No.' Without missing a beat, she added, 'Should I have gone to the village when I saw Dad? Should I have run for the doctor instead of going to the farm? Should I have gone straight home for Mam?'

'You did the right thing, going for the nearest adult.'

We crossed the High Street and turned into Easterly View, which had no view at all except the chemical works, but may once upon a time have had an easterly view. The sandstone houses stood in rows of six. Rounding the corner, we came to Town Street where church and chapel gazed sombrely at each other from opposite sides of the road, competing for the occupants of the pairs of well-built larger than average houses. One of these bore the West Riding Constabulary plaque.

'That's the police station, over there, near the church.'

'Thanks, Harriet. You go home now. You've done really well.'

She looked past me and then closed her eyes as if the sight were too much. 'It's Miss Trimble, the vicar's sister.

She'll ask me three hundred questions. I'm off home.'

Harriet turned, and ran.

From the corner of my eye, I caught a glimpse of a spare, grey woman bearing down on me from the direction of the church. Yes, I'll speak to you later, Miss Trimble. But first I must clear the decks with the local police. The knocker on the constabulary door hammered loudly enough to twitch every net curtain in the street.

Four

The door opened, and I stepped inside.

A jowly face with small eyes peering from nook and cranny sockets, gave the man the appearance of a bulldog.

'Good morning, officer,' I said as he closed the door behind me. I glanced at the stripes on his uniform. 'You must be Sergeant Sharp. I'm Mrs Kate Shackleton, a friend of the Armstrong family. Mrs Armstrong has asked for my help.' I handed him my card. His eyebrows arched high enough to let a train of hostile thought pass. 'I wonder whether you would be so kind as to spare me a few moments.'

He considered this request, taking in my appearance, reasonably well-to-do; my voice, educated; my demeanour, absurdly confident. He glanced pointedly at my card. A female investigator. His look said, It'll be talking monkeys next.

I could not rely on his knowing that my father is superintendent of the West Riding Constabulary, but I would be willing to flaunt family credentials. There is a trick to giving the silent impression that you have something up your sleeve. He gave way.

I followed him along the hallway, and into a front room that was designated as police headquarters.

He was a man recruited in the days when height and bulk was all, and any officer of the law worth his salt would tip the scales against a heavyweight champion.

His thinning hair lay neatly combed. There was enough flesh on his cheeks to make a second face.

As soon as we were in his office, he said in a cheerful voice, 'You'd better take a seat.'

He walked slowly round to the other side of his desk where he sat down in a padded swivel chair. Leaning forward, his forearms on the desk, fingers playing a tune on the blotter, he said, 'Do you have some information for me?'

'No. But after speaking to Mrs Armstrong and Harriet, I visited the quarry this morning. Harriet found her father's cap. Naturally Mrs Armstrong is very concerned and on her behalf, I wonder if you could tell me what line of enquiry is being pursued.'

'Mrs Armstrong lost the use of her legs has she?'

'She's exhausted and drained. I said I'd help as I've had some experience in tracking down missing persons.' I paused, giving time for my boast to make an impression. He did not look impressed. 'Would you tell me candidly, Sergeant Sharp, is this a missing person enquiry, or a murder investigation?'

'Murder?' His jowly jaw dropped. I caught a good look at the gold fillings in his bottom molars. 'Well, if it's murder, there's one person was spotted near the quarry in the afternoon and that's Mrs Armstrong herself, in her Scotch cape. Only she'd not be strong enough to carry a body and hide it somewhere.'

The image of Mary Jane hauling my suitcases up the stairs gave the lie to his belief, but I kept that to myself.

'And I can tell you,' he checked my name on the

53

business card, 'and I can tell you, Mrs Shackleton, that there's no sign of Ethan Armstrong in Great Applewick, alive or dead.'

'Mrs Armstrong hasn't seen her husband since Saturday morning. She wasn't near the quarry in the afternoon.'

'Aye, that's what she told me. Only someone else says different. And you'll understand that I can't say who it is, though it's a person whose truthfulness cannot be gainsaid.'

A person, he'd said. That meant woman, or he would have said man. If her word was worth so much to the officer, then she must be well connected. 'Miss Trimble, the vicar's sister?' I guessed.

He frowned.

I ignored the frown. 'Harriet found her father's cap under the bench in the mason's hut this morning. It was dark when you searched. Is it not possible that something else was missed? The men are already arriving at work, and it could be a murder scene. I believe Harriet. She saw her father dead.'

He sighed and shook his head slowly at the gulf between us. 'Now there we differ, Mrs Shackleton. Harriet may have seen her father having a lie down on work's time. They all drink. They all go up to the ale house, and he'd been there, I checked. Ethan Armstrong thinks himself a cut above, but he's as like as the next man to take a drop too much. This is the main point. His tools are gone. He and his missus had rowed – again. They're known for it. He's left. Now if he has gone for good, she stands to lose the house. It's a tied house. Obviously she's going to want to cling on.'

'But Harriet saw . . .'

'Did the little lad see anything? No, he did not.' The

sergeant blew out his breath and shook his head. 'You don't know what these young girls can be like, Mrs Shackleton. Young girls is noted for telling tall tales. It's a documented fact within the force. I don't think it started with the war, but the number of girls who reported secret liaisons with wartime spies and attempted abductions by white slavers is legion. Young Harriet Armstrong probably believes her own fancies. A little liar can cause a lot of trouble in a place like this. By taking her seriously, you're only encouraging her.'

'If it is Harriet's imaginings, where is Mr Armstrong?'

'How well do you know the Armstrongs?'

This was a difficult question, to which the answer would be not at all. 'It's a family connection,' I said truthfully. 'My father knew Mrs Armstrong's father, Mr Whitaker. He was a policeman in Wakefield,' I added, hoping this would elicit a little more interest.

'A policeman was he? Well then he wouldn't have thought much to his son-in-law, take it from me.'

'Why is that, officer?'

'Ethan Armstrong's a troublemaker. Tried to stir up the men to strike over summat that had nowt to do with them. Wanted them to support the miners at a pit owned by the colonel ten miles from here. The colonel is a fair man and a good employer. Armstrong doesn't know which side his bread's buttered. If and when I see him, I shall have one or two questions about wilful damage to a slate sundial.'

'Surely he wouldn't have destroyed his own work?'

'There's no telling what a man like that would do. His mind doesn't work like yours or mine.'

Sergeant Sharp was smarter than I had given him credit for. Rather than warn me off, he was trying to recruit me into the ranks of the reasonable: the good chaps who always share a sensible point of view.

'Won't you at least cordon off the mason's hut, in case this does turn out to be a murder enquiry?''

His small eyes narrowed. I had overplayed my hand.

'No, Mrs Shackleton, I will not.'

'You'll have no objections if I continue to make some enquiries?'

'All sorts of objections, but it's a free country, which it wouldn't be if men like Ethan Armstrong had their way.'

Five

I did not straightaway return to Mary Jane's cottage. It occurred to me that if Miss Trimble, the vicar's sister from whom Harriet fled, did indeed pop three hundred questions at a time, then perhaps my guess was correct and she was the sergeant's person whose truthfulness could not be gainsaid and who claimed to have seen Mary Jane by the quarry.

St Justin's church smelled powerfully of incense, Brasso and lavender polish. I walked down the side aisle. Abundant carnations decorated the altar and gave off an overpowering scent.

I did not sit long in the side pew in the gentle light from the stained-glass windows before Miss Trimble appeared. She recognised me as Harriet's companion, but hesitated to approach until I smiled and budged along.

'What a lovely church,' I remarked as she slipped into the pew beside me.

'Thank you. My brother and I do our utmost in the service of God and the parish. He could be answering the call in Brighton, but was guided to remain here, due to the church debt.' A certain tone of regret in her voice led me to think she would have packed for Brighton and let God take care of the debt.

'I'm Mrs Kate Shackleton, visiting with Mrs Armstrong today.'

She straightened a hymnal. 'Miss Aurora Trimble, sister of the vicar. I saw you earlier, with Harriet.'

'Yes. Her mother sought my help.' I thought it best to be direct, hoping that she would respond.

Miss Trimble sighed. 'I wish Mrs Armstrong would seek my help. As a young girl, when in service with the doctor, as Mary Jane Whitaker, she was a conscientious member of my Girls' Friendship Society.'

'That was a long time ago I expect.'

'1912,' she said firmly. 'On marriage, most girls join the Ladies' Friendship Society, though that is not a transition that applied in Mary Jane Armstrong's case. I had high hopes of her until ... Well, naturally, I cannot divulge. But I do now believe she may have been more sinned against than sinning. I have a missal that I should like to return to her. That was why I wanted to catch Harriet, and to enquire whether there is any news.'

'None I'm afraid.'

She sighed. 'Pity. But God works in mysterious ways. I know that Harriet wants to walk in the Whitsun procession under the church banner with some of her school friends and I would like to encourage that. If Mr Armstrong has left the village, then there would be no impediment.'

'Mr Armstrong would be an impediment?'

'Did you know the man?'

'No.'

'I am sorry to say that Ethan Armstrong is an atheist and a revolutionary. A man should keep his marriage vows –

made in this church — but it does not surprise me that he has gone.'

'You think he has just left without a word to anyone? Isn't that rather strange?'

'Strange men do strange things, Mrs Shackleton. He does not allow the children to attend Sunday school here or at the chapel. They go to the Quaker children's meeting and I believe he would stop that if he could. A most ungodly socialist.'

'But many socialists are Christians.'

'He is worse than a socialist.' She looked round. As though fearing the saints' images on the stained glass might overhear and be shocked, she lowered her voice. 'The man is a communist.'

'All the same I'd like to try and find him, or discover what happened to him.'

'Of course. And so would I. That is why I told the sergeant that I saw Mrs Armstrong by the quarry in the afternoon when I took my walk. I was trying to be helpful. I believe she went to plead with him not to abandon her, but that her pleas fell on stony ground.'

'You think he has left his wife and children?'

'It's just the kind of thing to be expected of a man like that, a communist. Of course, Ethan Armstrong is not dead.'

'How do you know?'

'God would not call him. God would not want him.'

Well, there we have it: the secret of eternal life. Become a communist and live forever, because there will be no place for you in heaven or hell.

'Are you sure it was Mrs Armstrong that you saw?'

'She wears a most distinctive tartan cape.'

'What time of day was this?'

'I take a constitutional after my afternoon nap. It would have been about four o'clock. I walk by the mill, across the river, along the side of the railway track and back across the other bridge. That's where I saw her.'

'Did she see you?'

'She had her back to me, walking towards the quarry.'

I began to see why Mary Jane had asked for my help. The sergeant did not believe Harriet. Miss Trimble told a tale of Mary Jane about to be abandoned by her husband. If this was a taste of village reaction, Mary Jane must feel very alone.

Miss Trimble brought a white calfskin-bound missal from her pocket.

A marker, a card printed with a prayer, fell from the book. I retrieved the marker, handed it to Miss Trimble, and watched as she flicked through the Sunday by Sunday entries, turning the pages more slowly until she reached Easter. She opened the book at the order of service for the Seventh Sunday after Easter: Whitsuntide. This was when Harriet expected to wear her new clothes, and, perhaps, to walk in procession. Miss Trimble inserted the marker. 'Please give Mrs Armstrong this when you see her. She'll understand.'

Six

It was eight-thirty when I arrived back at the cottage. I knocked and opened the door.

Harriet sat at the table. She paused, a spoonful of porridge halfway to her mouth. The fair-haired boy beside her glanced up at me, a puzzled look in his slate-blue eyes. The pale almost translucent skin gave him the appearance of a flower fairy who belonged in the leaves of a bluebell.

Harriet said, 'Mam's upstairs. You can have some breakfast if you want.'

'I'll wait, thanks.' I smiled at Austin. 'Hello.'

He mumbled something into his porridge.

Harriet said to him, 'This is Mrs ...' She changed her mind, or forgot my surname. 'You can call her Auntie Kate.'

Another mumble from Austin. Perhaps he was as reluctant to be familiar towards me as was his sister.

'To help us find out about Dad,' Harriet answered his mumble.

I caught his next words. 'Was the goblins there?'

She must have told him she'd been to the quarry.

'There 'int no goblins. That's just a story to keep kids out.'

61

He put down his spoon. 'I heard the goblin behind the hut, crunch. The goblin saw me.'

'Eat your porridge,' Harriet ordered.

I pulled up a stool beside the child. 'What was the goblin like?'

'Waiting.'

'He didn't see a goblin,' Harriet said wearily. 'If he'd seen a goblin, I'd have seen a goblin.'

The little fellow let out a wail. 'I heard a goblin crunch. It saw me.'

'Shut up.'

'You shut up.'

'No. I said it first. You shut up.'

What did a goblin sound like, I wondered? The footprints behind the hut had been on the large side for a goblin, but about right for a woman, or a small man.

Raymond Turnbull had small hands. Did he have small feet, too? He would stand to gain this house if Mary Jane received notice to quit. And Raymond Turnbull was courting. He would marry next Saturday. He did not seem to me to have it in him to kill. But his father did.

'I'll go up and have a word with your mam.'

The stone steps of the narrow staircase were used like shelves, with an item on the left side of every stair: shoes; boot cleaning stuff; button box; Oxo tin with recipes peeping out; an old biscuit tin bursting with documents.

On either side of the top step was a bedroom, the one on the left not much bigger than a cupboard.

'I'm in here,' Mary Jane called from the tiniest bedroom, where she was stripping a single bed. This was the children's room, and reeked of urine. Did poor little Austin always wet the bed, or was he distressed by his father's disappearance? Mary Jane rolled the sheet into a ball and dropped it in a pillowcase, saying, 'That's better. You can take the peg off your snitch.' She nodded me across to the other room as she unceremoniously slung the laundry down the stairs, expertly avoiding all the tins, boxes and shoes as she did so.

The opposite bedroom was larger, but not much. It contained a double bed and dressing table. Mary Jane sat down on the bed and patted the space beside her. Speaking quietly, she said, 'Harriet told me you saw Turnbull and Raymond, and that she found Ethan's cap.'

'Yes. And then I went to the police station. Not much joy with Sergeant Sharp, I'm afraid. He thinks Ethan has left you.'

'I knew he'd say that. Did you tell him about the cap?'

'Yes but it didn't make an impression on him. When the children have gone to school, I want us to go over everything, check whether Ethan may have taken some belongings, or left some clue that might give us a lead. I'll find out as much as I can today and that might force Sergeant Sharp to take the matter further. If he doesn't, I will.'

She nodded, reached for a bolster, began to take off its cover.

'After that, I'd like you to take me to the farm, and to see Colonel Ledger.'

She dropped the bolster. 'Why?'

'The farm because I want to talk to Bob Conroy and Arthur.'

'But why the colonel I mean?'

'Ethan sent him a note to come and see the sundial. If he came, he may have been the last person to see Ethan.'

She picked up the bolster and clutched it to her. 'He won't have. The colonel wouldn't come to the quarry.'

'All the same, we have to check. Is that Ethan's suit on the back of the door?'

'Yes. There's nowt in the pockets. I checked.'

'Do you mind if I do?'

She shrugged. 'Look at whatever you like.'

I stepped out of the way while she stripped two sheets off the bed. With an armful of linen, she moved to the door. Catching my eye, she said defensively, 'It's a good windy day for drying. The world doesn't stop turning.'

She tied the corners of the sheets to make a bundle and then flung the laundry down the stairs, walking down after it. I could hear her talking to the children.

I checked Ethan's pockets. Nothing in the trouser pockets. In the top pocket of the jacket were a couple of matches; nothing in the outside pockets; in the inside jacket pocket my fingers touched something Mary Jane had missed. It was a crumpled piece of newspaper, very tiny, an advertisement. It read:

```
A well provided and pleasant lady seeks well
  provided amiable gentleman with a view to
         joining lives and fortunes.
                Box No. 49
```

I smoothed out the creases. A check of the dressing table revealed nothing else of interest. I put the advertisement in my pocket and went downstairs.

Harriet had finished her porridge. Mary Jane took the dish, and looked at me. 'You'll have something to eat?'

It seemed rude to refuse.

I nodded.

'You can have an egg if you prefer. Georgina Conroy from the farm brought us half a dozen this morning, and a loaf of bread.'

'Porridge will be grand.'

A dollop of porridge fell into the fire and sizzled as she ladled a portion from the pan into Harriet's dish and passed it to me.

Harriet thoughtfully found me a clean spoon.

The next ten minutes involved children finding shoes and coats. Harriet claimed a headache and a belly ache and said she felt too poorly for school.

'Your headache will blow away as you walk along,' Mary Jane pronounced.

'What about my belly ache?'

'Do you want Syrup of Figs?'

Harriet did not. The children left for school. Not until she had waved them off did Mary Jane ask, 'What else did Sergeant Sharp say?'

'He doesn't believe Harriet's story. He says you rowed with Ethan, that you were seen by the quarry in the afternoon, and that Ethan has left you.'

'Who saw me?'

'Does it matter?'

'Yes! Harriet said Miss Trimble came bearing down on you before you went into the station. It was her wasn't it? Well, I wasn't anywhere near the quarry. Not until after six when Harriet finally came back after chasing off to the farm and looking for help.'

'You have a distinctive plaid cape.'

'Oh, so I'm the only person in Yorkshire wears a tartan cape?'

'Miss Trimble is sympathetic. She wants to help. She said to give you this.' I put the missal on the table.

Mary Jane stared at the prayer book, and then turned away. 'Let her keep it, swallow it page by page and choke on it for all I care.'

'Well, whatever happened in the past, she wants to make it up. She's concerned about you, and about the children. Though she doesn't have a good word for Ethan.'

'No, I don't suppose she does. It's Harriet she's after.' By the fireside was the set pot. Mary Jane lifted the lid and steam curled out. She lowered a sheet into the hot water, prodding it down as though trying to drown it. 'She wants Harriet for her precious Girls' Friendship Society. That's what she gives to her girls when they marry, a white leather missal. Only she took mine back after Harriet was born. Now she's changing her tune.'

I kept to myself the information that Harriet wanted to walk in the church Whitsun parade. But Mary Jane must know, especially since she was making a Whitsun dress for Harriet. I remembered that I used to like parades at her age, being part of something, that feeling of belonging.

Somehow I could not imagine Mary Jane wanting to march behind a banner. Now she stood at the sink, where she had propped the washboard, scrubbed at a bar of laundry soap, and at a stain on a sheet.

'What made you join the Girls' Friendship Society?'

A thin film of sweat shone on her brow. 'They were putting on a play. I fancied a bit of singing and dancing, but it was all very dull. Miss Trimble made it hard for you to get out, once she had her hooks in you.'

The sheet joined the other laundry in the set pot.

'Mary Jane, just come and sit down for a moment, and look at this.'

I showed her the cutting.

A well provided and pleasant lady seeks well
provided amiable gentleman with a view to
joining lives and fortunes.
Box No. 49

'This was at the bottom of Ethan's inside pocket. Does it mean anything to you?'

'It does not.' Mary Jane shook her head, and seemed genuinely surprised. She said almost cheerfully, 'Do you think he's run off to meet someone who's well provided and pleasant?'

'I don't know. What do you think?'

'If he has, she'll send him back by the first post. But I wouldn't set any great store by a newspaper cutting where Ethan's concerned. There's nowt that doesn't take his fancy.' She handed the cutting back to me. 'He cuts out the most peculiar items.' She said this as though speaking of an exotic animal brought from its far-flung country and missing its diet of wart-headed slugs. 'Look among his books if you don't believe me. Over here.'

By the side of the range, between the drawers and the cupboard was a space about nine inches high and eighteen inches deep. It was filled with books, shorter volumes upright, taller ones lying flat. There were volumes by Karl Marx, Friedrich Engels, William Morris, Bunyan, H G Wells and the English poets.

'Pick up any one of them books and some cutting will fall out,' Mary Jane said. 'And there's an orange box under the table, with more books. He's a one-man lending library.'

A child's scrapbook, lying on top of the books, was pasted with a dizzying range of snippets, and more loose cuttings, ready to be glued, covering topics such as birth control, over-population, Sitting Bull, under-population, Wild Bill Hickok, militarism, and South African gold mines.

'A man with many interests.' For the first time, I felt a real desire to meet this brother-in-law of mine, and a sense of foreboding, the feeling that I never would.

Mary Jane went to the far side of the room and raised the lid on a blanket chest. 'Look in here if you've a mind. This is all his trade union stuff and his politics.' She lifted out folders and envelopes. 'There's all sorts here – minutes of meetings, letters, resolutions, and who knows what. He's long stopped trying to interest me in it.'

I glanced at the material headed *Quarry Workers' Union*. An envelope, filled with loose papers, included cuttings from the *Daily Herald*, one of which was a letter written by Ethan concerning the poor health of quarry workers and their dangerous conditions of work.

'Did Ethan ever think of changing his line of work? Becoming something other than a mason?'

She smiled. 'A politician, you mean, or a full-time union man?'

'He seems to like paperwork.'

She laughed and the anxiety fled as her face lit up. 'That's just what I said to him. But he wasn't always so entirely caught up with motions and resolutions. He's never happier than when he's helping out on the Conroys' farm, on a Saturday afternoon or a Sunday, out in the fresh air. He used to want Austin to be a mason, but he seems to have changed his mind about that lately. He goes on something chronic about book learning. It hasn't struck him yet that the book learner will be Harriet.'

As I skimmed items from the chest, it struck me as likely that there would be a police file on Ethan Armstrong and his activities. Not that my father mentioned that aspect of the constabulary's work, but I was aware of it. Men considered radicals and potential revolutionaries had drawn a certain amount of official attention as early as 1911, and earlier still for all I knew.

I returned the manila folders and envelopes to the chest, and put the well provided woman cutting in my purse.

I glanced around the room. 'Has Ethan taken anything? Something that you may not have noticed at the time? A bag or clothes or papers? Does he have a bank book?'

'He went out in what he stood up in on Saturday morning.'

'We saw Raymond in the quarry. He said that Ethan's tools are gone. Doesn't that mean something?'

'It might mean someone's pinched them.'

'*Could* Ethan have gone off somewhere to find work?'

'Why would he do that on a Saturday, without breathing a word? It doesn't make sense. The only money, apart from my housekeeping, belongs to the union. It's in one of the tins on the stairs. He's the treasurer and collects the dues. And before you ask, I've already looked. There's not a penny missing.'

'What else is on the stairs, in the biscuit tin that won't close?'

'Policies, marriage and birth certificates. Look if you like.'

She expected me not to, but I fetched a couple of tins and began to look through. 'The police will do this, if they ever take Ethan's disappearance seriously, and so I might as well do it now.'

'Do as you like. I'm the one who asked you for help. But this one's of no interest to you.'

She picked up an Oxo tin of recipes and returned it to the stairs. I glanced through the papers in the biscuit tin. 'You have Ethan's life insured.'

'And he mine. But I wouldn't do him in for it. A poor man who's healthy is worth more alive than dead.'

She picked up a bucket from under the sink. 'I need water from the well.' She sighed. 'When your new parents took you from our house in White Swan Yard, I cried. Perhaps I cried because they didn't take me.'

The bucket clanked against the door as she went out. I returned the tin containing the policies to the stairs, and checked the Oxo tin. Under the recipes was a Yorkshire Penny Bank book, in Mary Jane's maiden name: M J Whitaker. She had three hundred pounds in the account, which had been opened in 1911 with one hundred and fifty pounds. That was an enormous amount for a girl who worked in service. What's more, she had never made a withdrawal. Her occasional deposits were never less than twenty pounds. Whatever Ethan had given her for house-keeping, or even if he had tipped up his wages, she would not have come up with such lump sums. 1911. Twelve years. I calculated that the date of the first deposit was a year before Mary Jane's marriage. From what little I had gleaned so far about our shared history, a legacy seemed highly unlikely. The poor, not the rich, give up their children for adoption. I returned the bank book to its hiding place, below the recipes, and replaced the tin on the stairs. Mary Jane may indeed be my long-lost sister, but she didn't know me at all.

Seven

Walking to Conroys' Farm would give me time to think. Mary Jane gave me directions but would not come herself, saying she would stop where she was, in case of news.

The sun shining across a glorious expanse of meadow and flowers on the other side of the dry-stone wall made it hard to imagine Ethan had met some foul end. This beautiful place struck me as a perfect spot for children to grow up. Mary Jane kept her cottage spotlessly clean. She grumbled, but I could imagine why she might be loath to leave. I wondered just how much she was hiding from me, and why. God knows I'm a fine one to talk. I don't go around advertising the fact that I'm having an affair with a man from Scotland Yard; that last year I came close to making a big mistake with a philandering psychiatrist; that I've made decisions that almost lost me my valuable assistant, and that I carry a secret that holds a man's life in the balance. Not to mention that five years on from receiving the *missing presumed dead* telegram, I still expect Gerald to walk through the door.

Next week, I have arranged to make yet one more visit to Catterick Hospital. I am not so stupid as to imagine I will find Gerald there. But there is always the faint possibility that he was overlooked in a small hospital, having lost his memory, or that he was found in France and brought home. So if Mary Jane has some secret bank account, that's her affair. Or is it? Does the fact that she's asked for help in discovering what happened to Ethan give me the right to pry into every corner of her life?

An old carthorse glanced at me before returning to the business of chomping grass and clover. A fingerpost pointed out the footpath to Little Applewick.

I followed a broad dirt track, leading to the river and the old stone bridge. Pausing to watch the fast-flowing water, I could feel myself back in a different age, when the bridge was first built, and the quarry an untouched hill. Something crashed into my legs, startling me out of my reverie.

It was a black and white dog, a sheepdog, a length of string tied to its neck. The dog wagged its tail, asking to have its head patted. I obliged. It waited with me, and we trotted across the bridge together.

At the railway line, the dog halted, and looked left and right, then up at me, as if to say, it's safe to cross. In the distance, a train hooted its way from Horsforth Station.

I had expected this hamlet to be deserted, except for the farm, but we passed an inn and brewery, and beyond that an abandoned cottage, its roof half collapsed. A brilliant laburnum tree flowered yards from the broken front door that hung by a single hinge.

After the deserted cottage, the lane narrowed. The east wind treated me to the stench of muck-spreading.

Beyond the parish boundary stone, a narrower track lay to the right. Dry-stone walls enclosed fields where sheep grazed, nibbling daintily at rough grass, lambs hobbling uncertainly beside them. In the next field, a cow lifted its amiable head, still munching hay as it stared at me.

The dog waited patiently until I opened the farm gate, and then bounded ahead, leaving me behind.

The two-storey farmhouse must have been a couple of hundred years old. It looked in good repair, with a solid slate roof. Smoke billowed from the chimney. Round about were several old barns and sheds. A couple of pigs spotted me before I spotted them. They snorted loudly, and a little derisively.

My feet squelched into foul-smelling mud. After that I was busy watching where I stepped. From the barn to my left came the bleating of a sheep and a low voice.

'Hello?' I peered in, my eyes taking a moment to become accustomed to the gloom. The friendly dog, now without its string, greeted me.

The man, whose wild grey hair sprouted from under his cap, knelt beside the silent ewe. He did not turn his head from the task of sticking his hand inside her as he said, 'You fetched the dog back?'

Guessing he was not addressing the ewe, I answered, 'He fetched himself.'

He nodded at the dog. 'Where was he?'

'On the bridge.'

'Not like him to disappear.' The dog looked from him to me, knowing himself to be the subject of conversation. 'Come on, old girl,' he cajoled the ewe. 'You're righted now.' He leaned back on his haunches, wiping his hands on an old cloth. A lamb's head appeared. We both watched as the lamb squeezed itself into the world. The small creature, its pale fleece striped with blood, struggled to find its feet.

'I'm looking for Arthur.'

73

'Then you've found him.'

'I'm Kate Shackleton, helping Mary Jane Armstrong look into the disappearance of her husband. Sorry, I don't know your last name.'

'Thah needn't bother wi' that.'

'Arthur, I believe Harriet came to you in her trouble on Saturday.'

'Aye, and a right bad turn it gave me when she came with her tale.'

His eyes were on the lamb as it found its feet.

'I believe she came for Bob Conroy. Was he not here?'

'She brayed on t'farmhouse door all right and come to me when she got no joy.' He stood up and stretched. 'I were milking.' He gestured at the ewe. 'This 'int my job. I'm herdsman but it's that kind of set up here, all turn our hands as necessary.'

'It was kind of you to go with her.'

'Course, Ethan weren't there.' Arthur took out his pipe as he watched the ewe lick the lamb's head. 'I'm glad young Harriet didn't find Bob Conroy.'

'Why's that?'

'Don't thah know? Bob's own younger brother Simon met his end in that quarry last lambing time.'

'What happened?'

Arthur struck a match on a stone. 'He got word that a lamb strayed into the quarry. It were a Sunday, so no quarrymen about. Simon went on his own, to try and fetch the creature back. Poor man took a terrible tumble. Some are saying it was his ghost that Harriet saw, on Saturday.'

The whiff of pipe tobacco mingled with the smell of hay and muck. I supposed there was no reason for Mary Jane to have mentioned this earlier death. But it made me think

74

differently about the quarry. Small wonder the children were afraid.

'Did you see anything at all unusual in the quarry when you went with Harriet?'

He sucked on his pipe. 'Usual or not I wouldn't know. I've only ever passed it by, not gone circulating there.'

'By the time Mrs Armstrong got to the quarry, the sundial was broken.'

'Nowt to do wi' me. Never touched it.'

'Were you out and about at all on Saturday afternoon, after one o'clock? I'm wondering whether you saw anyone by the quarry.'

'I saw nowt but cows, ewes and lambs. I'm eatin', sleepin' and dreamin' cows, ewes and lambs. And it's worse than usual without Ethan strolling up here after he's had his tea to give us a hand.'

'Ethan helps on the farm a lot does he?'

'He does, when he's not out and about changing the world. And afore you ask, he's said nowt to me about slinging his hook and I've no notion where he might have gone. I only hope Harriet was mistaken.'

'Did he come here last week to help?'

'He did come, but not to help. He took it hard when Bob told him he's sold out to the colonel. Ethan was disgusted that Bob'd given up the farm after all these years.'

Something else that Mary Jane had not thought to mention. I acted as if I knew.

'When did Ethan find out that Bob had sold the farm?'

Mistake. He clammed up and turned his attention to the dregs of tea in a tin mug, letting on not to have heard me. But I guessed the sale to be recent. Arthur had not yet taken it in. Some new owner may not want the services of an old man.

'I'm not being nosey, Arthur. It's just that I want to help Mary Jane find Ethan, if he's still alive.'

'I know that, missus.' He tossed the tea leaves from his mug across the dirty hay.

'Then let me ask one more question. You said Ethan was here last week, but not to help. Was he here for some other reason?'

Arthur shrugged. 'He went in the house with yon. Don't ask me what that was about. Nowt to do with me.'

'Thank you. I hope things work out for you. Perhaps you'll stay on when the farm changes hands.'

His mouth turned down at the corners as he gave something like a laugh. 'The colonel won't keep it as a farm. We all know what he'll do.'

'What's that?'

If he had heard, he did not answer.

He walked to the cowshed as I approached the house. Last week was a bad time for Ethan Armstrong. His friend sold out to the colonel, no doubt in Ethan's view a bloated capitalist; he lost a strike vote, and he fell out with Mary Jane. Ostensibly about summat and nowt, as she said. But did she keep a secret from him – such as her bank deposit? If so, perhaps the row was more serious than she claimed.

I knocked on the farmhouse door. It took a minute or so before the door opened. A woman with a friendly smile greeted me warmly. I introduced myself, saying my piece about investigating Ethan's disappearance.

She stood back for me to step inside. 'I was expecting you.'

I stepped onto the doormat, trying to wipe my shoes and then deciding that it would be best to take them off altogether.

'Nay lass, leave thah shoes on. We don't stand on

76

ceremony here. We're used to a bit of muck. Come and sit down. I'm Georgina Conroy.'

She was attractive, but not in a conventional way. The attractiveness came more from her liveliness and her energy, her ready smile. With capable hands jutting from dark sleeves, she reached for a bottle that had a teat attached. 'Come and sit by the fire and be warm. You can talk to me while I keep yon creature this side of paradise.'

The lamb curled in a box by the fire. Bobbing down, she put the teat to the lamb's mouth. 'I can listen and faff at the same time, and I'll make us a pot of tea in a minute. Eh, it's a bad business, Ethan going missing. I went down there with eggs this morning, hoping Mary Jane would have news.'

Her attention went to the lamb and for a moment we sat in silence.

Sitting in the comfortable room with its blazing fire, I relaxed for the first time that day. I forgot for a moment that I was supposed to be working. Though the farmyard had a run-down look, this house could not have been a greater contrast. It smelled of freshly baked bread. The black lead fireplace and hearth shone from serious polishing. Gleaming brass pots and warmers hung from hooks on the wall. A blackened kettle sang on the hob.

The flagged floor had been treated with something red, perhaps a bright lead paint, and was strewn with peg rugs of different ages, sizes and colours. The furniture comprised a heavy old oak dresser displaying gleaming crockery, a solid table covered in a practical oil cloth, sturdy dining chairs, and a couple of rockers by the hearth. A smaller scrubbed table stood by the large flat sink.

'Sorry about this. I'll give you a cup of tea in a shake.'

77

'Not to worry about that. You have your hands full.'

'Not so full that I don't mind my manners. But you're right. Work on a farm is never done. That's why neither me nor Bob was here Saturday when Harriet come by.'

'If it's such hard work, perhaps you won't be sorry to move on.'

She sighed and looked so full of regret that I felt tactless to have mentioned it.

'I'll be right sorry to leave this farm, but it's been hand to mouth for years, and worse since the tragedy of last year.'

'That quarry seems an unlucky place.'

'Aye. Bob were that upset that he wasn't here for the lass, and just as upset that . . .' She paused.

'What?'

'Oh nothing. I shouldn't say. Me and my big mouth.'

Who could be more welcome to a detective than a person with a big mouth? 'Mrs Conroy, I'm trying to find out what happened on Saturday. If you can help in any way, I'd be most grateful.'

'Well, Ethan took it badly when Bob told him he was selling up. This farm has been Ethan's bolt hole when he and Mary Jane didn't see eye to eye. They fell out about it, and Bob felt right bad. So Bob was dead upset not to have been here for Harriet, as if he'd let Ethan down twice.'

'Where was Bob that afternoon?'

'In the far field, clearing a ditch. With the size of this place, it's all hands to the deck most of the time and we're coming to the end of the lambing so it's twenty-four hours some days. I'd gone to check the ewes while Arthur was milking.' She patted the lamb and stood up. 'I'll make that tea now. Arthur will be ready for a cup.'

Through the window, I saw a girl sweeping the yard. She looked as if she ought to be at school.

'Is that your daughter?'

'Oh no. I have no children. She's just a kid that does for me.'

'She's very young.'

'She's gone thirteen. I keep her out of charity really. I'm sure there's older lassies in the village would do better, but I can't turn her out.' Mrs Conroy tapped on the window. 'She can have a cup of tea and take some to the men.'

The girl turned quickly. She looked a sullen little thing. A moment later she dropped the broom and came through the door, wiping her feet. She ignored the two of us but went to the lamb, stroked its head and spoke a word or two.

Mrs Conroy called to her. 'Take out this tray to Arthur, and if you see Mr Conroy let him know we've a visitor.'

The girl went out, leaving the two of us at the table. Georgina Conroy returned to the topic of the missing Ethan.

'I made Mary Jane and the bairns stop here for their dinner on Sunday.' She shook her head sadly. 'Not that she had much appetite.'

'That was good of you.'

'That's what neighbours are for.'

'It must have been a hard choice for your husband to sell up.'

'He'd come to a fork in the road.' She turned her head, so that I would not see the tears in her eyes. From her apron pocket she drew a hanky and blew her nose. 'He's a fine fellow, Ethan Armstrong. A man of principle, even if wrong-headed at times. Bob tried to persuade him to stand for member of parliament, did you know that?'

'No.'

'Ethan came to talk to me last week. It was as though him and Bob had both come to the end of something. Mary Jane and Ethan, they were like oil and fire.'

'What did he say?'

She shook her head. 'It wouldn't be fair to repeat it. But he told me he just had to get out of the house. Mary Jane never let up with her dissatisfactions. But then, all these meetings he goes to. If I were Mary Jane, I'd be suspicious.'

Her words gave me an opening. I brought out the news-paper cutting. 'Does this mean anything to you?' I passed her the cutting, hating to do it because it was an intrusion into Ethan and Mary Jane's privacy. If Mrs Conroy talked freely to me, perhaps she would tell all to others. Yet she seemed a decent woman, fond of Ethan, Mary Jane and the children.

A well provided and pleasant lady seeks well provided amiable gentleman with a view to joining lives and fortunes.
Box No. 49

She looked at the cutting. 'Where did this come from?'

'Ethan's suit pocket.'

'Did you show it to Bob?'

'I haven't met your husband yet.'

'Well, if anyone would know, Bob would, but he's said nowt to me. I know Ethan has been unhappy, but I shouldn't think he would answer an advertisement in the press. Besides, it'd be bigamy wouldn't it? He's a law-abiding chap, for a revolutionary.'

'Mrs Conroy, if there's anything at all – even if it seems

insignificant – that you can tell me, that might help solve this puzzle, please do.'

She sighed. 'I just can't fathom it. I wonder now if his head hasn't been turned by some firebrand socialist female who preaches free love. But it's no more than a feeling.'

I persisted. 'I'm talking to everyone who may be able to help. It could be that some little thing you tell me will fit with something else, and make sense.'

She thought for a moment, and seemed reluctant to speak. I waited.

Mrs Conroy blew her nose. 'Don't mistake me. I wouldn't say this to anyone in the village. I'm telling you candidly and between these four walls because you've taken on to help Mary Jane. And I hope you can, and I hope I'm wrong. I feel for her because she was an incomer, like me, and people round here will take a quarter of a century before they'll say to your face that you never will fit in. But they talk about her in the village in a way they don't talk about me because I don't give them anything to go on.'

'What do they say?'

'Oh it's nonsense. Gossip and tittle tattle. It doesn't amount to enough currants to throw at a bun from t'other end of kitchen.'

'It won't go any further. I want to help if I can.'

'I don't know what they say about her. When they see me, the whispering stops. I just hear her name, that's all.'

'Linked to any other name?' I prompted.

'Aye. Linked to the names of who she used to work for.'

'The doctor?' I remembered Miss Trimble telling me that Mary Jane was in service there.

81

'No. Not the doctor. After she left off working for the doctor and his wife, she went to the big house for several years, with the the Ledgers. Ethan reckoned that's where her grand ideas came from. The cottage wasn't good enough for her, once the novelty wore off. But I don't blame the lass, and I don't blame Ethan.' Her voice softened when she mentioned Ethan's name. 'Ethan was very kind to me.' Mrs Conroy hesitated. 'There is just one thing.'

'Oh?'

'I feel terrible betraying a confidence ...' She pushed her hands into the pockets of her pinafore. 'Ethan came to talk to me one night last week, when Bob was in the Fleece. Him and Bob weren't speaking by then. Ethan asked my advice.'

'What about?'

'About himself and Mary Jane. They'd had a big row, he wouldn't say what about. He said it wouldn't be so bad if she would at least be more sympathetic to The Cause, as he calls it.'

'Then he must think you are sympathetic to ... the cause.'

'Me? I haven't a political bone in my body, but I make a point of never contradicting, and that lets men think you agree, which is always the best policy.'

'Thank you for telling me.'

'Please don't let on to Mary Jane. He shouldn't have come. I'd be mortified if she knew. Their troubles were between the two of them.'

She stood at the door to see me out. As I left the farmyard, the girl was sweeping the yard, and teasing the dog as it darted for the sweeping brush, wagging its tail, wanting to play.

'Clever boy. Who found his own way back from them bad children, bad, bad, bad, bad.'

'Where did the dog go?' I asked. 'Did someone take it?'

The girl pretended not to hear me.

It seemed she was happy to talk to an animal, but not to a human being. I followed her lead and spoke to the dog, patting his head. 'You brought me here didn't you? What's your name?'

When the dog didn't answer, the girl spoke for him.

'Billy.'

'And what children whisked you away, Billy?'

'Harriet and Austin took you,' the girl told the dog. 'But you come back.'

Eight

Bright sheets and pillowcases billowed in the breeze in the Armstrongs' back garden. Clearly Mary Jane did not let a possible tragedy interfere with domestic activities. She stood by the door, beating a rag rug, stopping as I came within earshot. 'Would you believe what those kids of mine have done?'

'They're at school aren't they?'

'Huh! Set off to school nice as ninepence and never arrived. I had a child bringing me a note from the teacher about their absence. Where do you think they went?'

I hate it when people pose questions when what they mean to do is tell you something, but I played the game. 'I don't know where they went, Mary Jane.'

I followed her into the house where she lay the beaten rug down carefully. 'Up to the farm they went, sneaky as you like, grabbed the farm dog, tied it on a piece of string and let it sniff Ethan's cap. They've been haunting fields and ditches. It makes me look such a fool with the teachers.'

That explained the wandering sheepdog. It must have grown tired of being pressed into service and escaped. 'Poor kids.'

'Aye, poor kids indeed.' She stared at my muddy shoes as I sat myself down in the one good chair. 'But at least they're trying.'

In other words, I wasn't trying. 'Look, Mary Jane, you haven't been straightforward with me. You led me to believe that you'd be out of this house, with its well and its hard work, and out of this village where you claim no one likes you, that you'd be out like greased lightning given half a chance. And then I find out that Ethan could have found work in York. And you didn't tell me he was being encouraged to stand for parliament.'

She gave a dismissive gesture. 'Oh that.'

'You say Miss Trimble doesn't like you, but you don't say why. Sergeant Sharp doesn't like you, but you don't say why. You told me you came to Great Applewick to work for the doctor . . .'

'I did at first.'

'. . . and now I discover that you worked for Colonel Ledger . . .'

'For Mrs Ledger . . .'

'Mrs Ledger then. So will you go to the Hall and ask a simple question? Did Colonel Ledger go to the quarry on Saturday?'

The house was spotless, but Mary Jane pounced at a smudge on the fender, rubbing at it with a rag. 'I don't have to ask because working there I know all too well that the Colonel wouldn't have gone to the quarry. As for Sergeant Sharp not liking me, well it's no mystery. If you want to know, I once laughed at him.'

'Why?'

'Because I didn't know any better and I couldn't help it.'

'What was funny?'

'Whenever there's a village do, he stands up and gives a recitation. If Ethan had warned me that it wasn't a comic turn I wouldn't have showed myself up. I couldn't stop laughing. When I realised he was in earnest, I tried to pretend it was a cough from a tickle in my throat.'

'He won't remember, or hold that against you.'

'Oh he will. He was spouting Horatius.' She threw out her chest, took a deep breath and began to recite, '"Lars Porsena of Closium, by the Nine Gods he swore, that the great house of Tarquin should suffer wrong no more." It was all his dramatic actions got me going. "East and West and South and North," flinging out his arms hither and thither.'

In spite of my annoyance with her, she made me laugh. I could picture the solemn moment and Mary Jane getting the giggles.

'What about Miss Trimble? Did you laugh at her too?'

Mary Jane heaved a sigh. 'Do you do this to everyone you investigate for? Demand a life story? I mean, say I'd robbed a bank, what would that have to do with Ethan going missing and whether you could find him?' She picked up a teacloth from the oven door and hung it on a hook. The missal sent by Miss Trimble still lay on the table. She picked it up. 'I might as well tell you or someone else will. When the girls in her friendship group marry, Miss Trimble gives them a missal bound in white calfskin. She keeps an eye on the calendar and if the date of the first confinement is less than nine months after the wedding, she takes the missal back.'

'Oh, I see.'

'That tells you what kind of a place Great Applewick is.

I should have gone when Ethan had the chance.'

'Why didn't you?'

'I don't know why. I can't remember.' Mary Jane made fists of her hands and growled her frustration.

'There must be a reason you wouldn't leave. It was only as far as York, not the other side of the world.'

'The children,' she said quietly. 'I was thinking of the children, if you must know.' It was not a good answer, but would have to do. For now. She changed tack, becoming exasperated – with me. 'And I told you Sergeant Sharp would be no help. He thinks I smashed the sundial and drove Ethan away. In his book, Ethan's a revolutionary and I'm no better than I ought to be.'

We were getting nowhere. Time to move. 'Come on, Mary Jane. You're going to show me the way to the Hall. We need to ask Colonel Ledger whether he went to the quarry, or if Ethan went to see him.'

'Can't you go on your own?'

'I need you to show me the way.' I guessed that the Ledgers may be more willing to answer questions if I turned up with Mary Jane, their former employee, now a damsel in distress.

White clouds scudded across a blue sky. A man with a cart rattled past us across the cobbles. A woman came from the bakery, basket over her arm.

A carter and his mate manhandled a beer barrel to the trap door outside the Fleece. The pub's worn sign creaked in the breeze, its paint peeling. The sign showed an exceedingly woolly sheep hovering miraculously in mid air, back curved, eyes shut.

The patient brewery carthorse pawed the ground, nostrils flaring a small cloud into the morning air.

When we reached the war memorial, I paused. Mary Jane stood beside me.

For the last couple of hours, I had put out of my mind the thought that Mary Jane was my sister. Now I wondered what the recent years had meant for this family of mine that I knew nothing of.

'Mary Jane, did any of our family perish in the Great War?'

'Yes. Our brother Bert, cousin Geoffrey and Uncle Tommy – our dad's brother.'

'Uncle Tommy wasn't too old to enlist?'

'He was. He went almost right through, thinking he could keep an eye on their Geoffrey and our Bert.'

Mary Jane watched me reading the names on the War Memorial. 'Your husband's name will be on one of these, Catherine.'

'Yes.'

My only disagreement with Gerald's family had been about their wanting to put his name on their local war memorial, among the list of the dead. Why should he be there? I'd asked. Missing does not have to mean dead. In the end, they had his name inscribed without my permission.

I gave myself a little shake. 'Come on. Let's get to the Hall.'

Mary Jane seemed better, once on the move, taking me to the top of Town Street, pointing out the chemical works and the mill.

I tried to imagine what it must have been like for her to come here as a girl and go into service, far from her family. 'Where is the doctor's house, where you came to work?'

'Back there, not far from the vicarage.'

We turned into a lane where Mary Jane came to a halt. 'You'll find your way from here, along Back Lane, past the reservoir, and up the track.'

'Mary Jane, we're doing this together.'

She made a derisive noise. 'It's pointless. The colonel wouldn't go chasing to the quarry at Ethan's beck and call. Not a man in his position. You needn't bring him into this.'

'You asked me to investigate. Let me say who we need to and needn't talk to.'

She hesitated, and then fell into step with me. We walked in silence along a narrow lane, between rows of lime trees. The sunlight formed shadowing patterns on Mary Jane as she walked so that the light and shade on her changed with every step she took.

You're my sister, and I don't know what to make of you. I feel suspicion and mistrust, as though you have drawn me into a web.

The substantial house appeared suddenly, behind a low dry-stone wall. Because of its distance from the mill chimney and the smoke, the sandstone was not blackened but held the warmth of its original colour. With its immaculately kept drive and extensive gardens, the dwelling gave off an unmistakeable whiff of abiding privilege.

'Tell me about the Ledgers, Mary Jane. Colonel Ledger commissioned Ethan to make the sundial. And he owns the quarry ...'

'And quarries all over the place, and mines. His own family were in glassmaking. It's Mrs Ledger's side that were the big landowners. They have an interest in the mills as well.'

'What kind of man is he?'

'He's approachable. People like him.'

On either side of the iron gateway crouched a carved lion. I stroked the mane of the one nearest to me. 'Has the walk given you courage? Shall we beard the Ledger lion in his den?' She did not answer. 'You have a simple enough question to ask of Colonel Ledger. He's your husband's employer after all.'

'I can't. I can't humiliate myself by asking.' A bitterness entered her voice. 'Ethan wouldn't have gone off without a word to someone. Only it wasn't me, that's all. Someone will know, but not the colonel.'

'What's Mrs Ledger like?'

'She's . . . exquisite. You'll never have met anyone like her.'

'How did you come to work for them, when you started out by working for the doctor and his wife?'

'Mrs Ledger took a fancy to me when I came up here to fetch medicines. She asked the doctor could she have me. Well, I was only fifteen and cock-a-hoop to be chosen. I worked here until I married.' She seemed on the verge of tears, as if being here brought back some memory she would rather forget. 'When I left, Mrs Ledger thought I would marry Bob Conroy and live at the farm. Her family and his have a long connection. But I married Ethan, and I know she was disappointed. And then last week, Ethan tried to make the quarrymen go on strike because of something happening in another mine. And I felt sorry for those people in the mine having their wages cut, and Ethan took donations. Why wasn't that enough? Ethan was brass faced. He'd lost the battle, he said, but he'd win the war. I feel bad about everything. Mrs Ledger will look at me and she won't say anything, but she'll think I married the wrong man. And I didn't, Kate. I love Ethan.'

There were tears in her eyes, and now I felt mean at having pushed her so hard. 'You go back to the cottage. I'll see you there when I'm done.'

I gave the lion one last pat, and walked through the gateway, leaving Mary Jane staring after me.

Nine

The central part of Applewick Hall could have been a sixteenth-century manor house. Wings on either side had been added later, built to accommodate a large family, or to impress. The lowness of the surrounding walls did not shut off the occupying family from their neighbours. That suggested good relations prevailed, and perhaps a sense of noblesse oblige on behalf of the colonel and his lady, and their predecessors.

One gardener busied himself in a bed of flowers. Another pushed a wheelbarrow past the side of the house. Somewhere out of sight, Raymond Turnbull would be chipping away at the new sundial. There would be groom, chauffeur, butler, housekeeper, and a mop of harassed maids.

It did not surprise me that after working here Mary Jane felt dissatisfied with her cottage. As I looked at the grandeur of this house, I understood a little of the passion for improvement and equality that drove Ethan Armstrong. What a grand opinion he held of himself to send word to the colonel – landowner, squire and baron of all he surveyed – to come and inspect a slate sundial.

I knocked on the heavy door, still toying with how to

approach this family. You can talk to him, Raymond had said.

The maid who answered the door was so surprised to have a lady visitor present her calling card and ask to see the colonel that she gave me the wrong answer.

'Mrs Ledger is indisposed.'

'I'm here to see Colonel Ledger, if you would be so good as to give him my card.'

She nodded dumbly, and thought for a moment before deciding to open the door wide enough for me to step inside, into a high hallway with an ornate ceiling halfway to heaven, massive rooms to either side, the hall continuing into infinity, and a staircase leading to the stars.

Before the crick in my neck became serious enough to require medical attention, the maid returned and led me into a drawing room.

'The colonel will be with you shortly.'

This gave me a little time to gawp. A family portrait hung on the wall opposite the draped window. I assumed I was looking at Colonel and Mrs Ledger and their two sons aged nine or ten, along with a pair of well-fed hounds. Mrs Ledger, if the likeness were true, would not have been out of place in a Gainsborough portrait: an aristocratic beauty, with lively eyes and an amused mouth. Seated on a garden chair, she wore a blue summer dress, all folds and pleats, the sleeves ending just below her elbows in a flourish of lace. The colonel's gun was propped against the tree, as if to show he had just returned from shooting. One boy stood on a rope swing, the other boy leaned against his father. I recognised the artist's name as someone who exhibited at the Royal Academy a few years ago.

'Do you like it?' The voice startled me.

I turned to see the man himself, tall, spare, with black hair only a little streaked with grey.

'It's splendid, a photographic quality almost. When was it painted?'

'About three years ago, when the boys were home from school.'

He indicated the pair of brocade sofas on either side of an ornate fireplace. 'Won't you sit down?' He glanced at my card, 'Mrs Shackleton.'

I chose the seat with my back to the window. We faced each other across the broad expanse of oak flooring, divided by a Persian rug.

'Thank you for seeing me, Colonel.'

He looked at me steadily. 'I'm curious. I receive few lady callers.' A trace of a smile appeared on what was really quite a handsome face.

'I'm here on behalf of Mrs Armstrong. Mr Ethan Armstrong has been missing since Saturday . . .'

The change in his manner was barely perceptible, a slight narrowing of the eyes, a movement, not quite a twitch, between nostril and lip. He waited.

'Colonel, do you have any idea where Mr Armstrong may have gone, or why?'

'Can't help, I'm afraid. First I heard of his failure to put in an appearance was on Sunday morning outside church. Young Raymond Turnbull turned up, twisting his cap and telling me in his round the houses way that I could wave the blue slate sundial goodbye. But perhaps you can tell me something, Mrs Shackleton.' He leaned back in his master-of-all-I-survey manner. 'You say you are here on behalf of Mrs Armstrong.'

'Yes.'

'How is it that Mrs Armstrong has involved you? And

what makes you think I would be privy to the movements of one of my stonemasons? Mary Jane should go to the police, if she's so concerned.'

'She did go to the police. Sergeant Sharp seems to think that because Ethan Armstrong's tools are gone, he has left the area to find work.'

'That's possible. Stonemasons believe they can set their own rules and their own hours, especially a man like Armstrong. Did his wife tell you that he's an agitator of the first order?'

'Yet you keep him on.'

'He's good at his job, but if he wants to find another, that's up to him.'

'Mrs Armstrong thinks that's unlikely and . . .'

He put his head to one side, like a hawk about to pounce on a sparrow. 'What is your connection with Mrs Armstrong?'

I was supposed to be the one asking questions. 'Our families have a long-standing connection. I said I would help if I could.' That sounded almost plausible and had the merit of several grains of truth. My superintendent father took such an interest in the Whitaker family that he adopted me from it. 'Sometimes it's easier for an outsider,' I added, with the air of someone frequently called to mend bridges between husbands and wives.

'Easier for an outsider to . . .?'

'To ask awkward questions. Colonel, did you go to the quarry on Saturday? I know that Mr Armstrong asked if you would inspect the sundial.'

For the first time in our conversation, he hesitated, for just a little too long. He smiled. 'Armstrong rightly held himself and his craft in high esteem. He did send word that I might wish to inspect the work in progress because he had been forced to make a slight variation in my design for the sundial.'

'Did you go there, Colonel?'

He allowed himself the smallest of chuckles. 'I did not. I have, or had, every confidence in Armstrong's workmanship. The sundial was to have been brought up here on Monday morning, early, and placed in the rose garden, ready to be unveiled on my wife's birthday. My wife will have a considerably inferior birthday sundial, though aptly of our own sandstone.' He rang a bell. 'Let me show you something. It may help explain what could have happened.'

A butler appeared so quickly that he must have been listening at the door.

'Fetch me the blueprint for the sundial, and Armstrong's note.'

The butler nodded, and was gone.

'Did you know Armstrong, Mrs Shackleton?'

'No. My parents' connection was with Mrs Armstrong's family.'

'He's the kind of man who thinks horny-handed sons of the soil are the undiscovered geniuses of the world and that they should be – what was that line of Shelley's? – legislators of the world also. It galled him that I gave him a blueprint for the sundial that was accurate to a thousandth of an inch. It disturbed his view of me as an unthinking exploiter of the land and its rightful inheritors.'

The butler returned carrying a thick card folder fastened with tape. He placed it on a low table and carried the table to the oriental rug. There he undid the tape, opened the folder, and spread the blueprint.

'Look.' The colonel nodded at the table. 'Here it is; the

base a Doric column pedestal, the face of the dial simplicity itself. Armstrong wasn't to know that I didn't do the calculations personally. Some Persian chap worked out the sums centuries ago. All I had to do was find the correct pages in the appropriate books and re-draw the plan to scale. This set Mr Stonemason a challenge. He has to show how clever he is – and he is clever. He is working in blue slate, a material he has no experience of. He suspects I have chosen this so that he will fail and look a fool. He's wrong of course, but that is what he thinks.' The colonel pointed to the plan with the stem of his pipe. 'Armstrong taps with his chisel, patiently, carefully, till he has all his straight edges and a smooth surface. Doing it all himself, not trusting the initial part of the work to a labourer or to his former apprentice. Precise movements, going gently so that the slate won't notice it's being transformed; won't fight back and get the better of him. He has to coax it into shape. Because, like stone, slate has a life of its own. It can have some fissure you can't see with the naked eye. It might crack while you're carrying it to where you want it to be. Perhaps water seeped in thousands of years ago and left air pockets, so a man could chisel as carefully as he likes and he'll hit one of these pockets. All his work will go for nothing as the stone fractures and shatters to pieces, and then . . .'

The colonel took a sheet of paper from an envelope and handed it to me.

The note was written in the meticulous copperplate hand that had become familiar to me as I sifted through the papers in Ethan Armstrong's chest.

Sir,

There is a small flaw in the slate which will mar its appearance. I can disguise it entirely by carving a flower, and would carve three additional flowers so as to make this pattern a harmonious whole. Will you call to give your approval to this alteration of the plan?
Ethan Armstrong

The note was entirely matter-of-fact without a polite salutation or a respectful close. I returned it to the table.

'So you see,' the colonel said, 'I was meant to know that for the sake of symmetry he would improve on my plan. I, who go to the mines and quarries once a year if that, and rely on reports from my managers, am being asked to attend and inspect this perfect work that I should have insisted be carved on my property, and not in the quarry. No, Mrs Shackleton, I did not go to the quarry. I sent word for him to get on with the job and have it here first thing Monday morning. What happened after that? Well, your guess is as good as mine. Either he festered on my reply and brought his hammer down on the whole operation, or he wasn't as clever as he thought and his concealment of flaw by flower did not work. The slate defeated him.'

'Who brought the note from Mr Armstrong, and who took the message back?'

'I don't know who brought it.'

He rang the bell. Once again, the butler appeared in an instant.

'We've done with this.'

'Very good, sir.' The butler returned the blueprint and Ethan's note to the folder, and tied the tape carefully.

'And Rigby, who brought that note from Armstrong?'

'One of the quarry labourers, sir. I couldn't say more than that.'

The butler waited, as if he expected to show me out.

It was clear that my interview was at an end.

'There is one other thing, if I may.' I looked towards the butler, and back at the colonel.

'Leave us, Rigby.'

'Sir.' The butler disappeared as quietly as he had come.

'Harriet Armstrong went to the quarry on Saturday evening to take her father some food, and hoped to bring him home. She gives an account of seeing him lying in his hut. Dead. When a farm worker and then Mrs Armstrong went to see, he was not there. The sundial was smashed. Mr Armstrong has not been seen since. I thought it best to make a few preliminary enquiries before this becomes a murder investigation.'

His mouth opened in astonishment. 'You suspect murder?'

'Harriet strikes me as a sensible child. I'm inclined to believe her, though others don't.'

'Why wasn't I told?' He rang a bell.

The butler reappeared.

'Ask Sergeant Sharp to call and see me. And send a message to the quarry foreman to get himself here in double-quick time.'

'Yes, colonel.' The butler nodded his way out.

I stood to leave. 'Thank you for your time, Colonel.'

He jumped to his feet. 'Wait! I'm going to fetch my wife. She'll want to know about Harriet finding her father. She's fond of Mary Jane. Do please sit down. Would you care for anything? A glass of sherry?'

'No, thank you.'

He turned at the door. 'I've seen you before some-where, Mrs Shackleton.'

'I was thinking that, too,' I said. 'But I can't think where.'

I did not trust him but had no choice other than to wait. Ethan Armstrong must have been a thorn in the colonel's side – a thorn to be rid of. The colonel needed time to think, having learned that Harriet saw her father's body before there was time for the killer – Ledger's minion? – to remove it. Ledger had gone for his wife not out of consideration for Mary Jane, but to keep me waiting. While he did what? Talked to the sergeant, and made sure the investigation was closed down before it began.

After six or seven minutes that seemed like hours, Mrs Ledger floated into the room wearing a navy and sky-blue morning dress with wide sleeves and a square neck. The sapphire at her throat matched the colour of her eyes. The severe style of her golden hair gave her the appearance of a carved Dresden doll. She smiled a pearly smile that nevertheless betrayed concern.

In my country costume, I suddenly felt like a poor governess. Mary Jane was right, she was exquisite. But she was wrong when she said I would never have met anyone like her. I had met many women like Mrs Ledger, delicate, feminine, and with a steely determination to never exert themselves in any direction. Perhaps that was harsh, but it was how she struck me. In the face of such superficial perfection, I could understand why Mary Jane had been so reluctant to set foot inside the gates of Applewick Hall.

Mrs Ledger sat beside me on the sofa. 'I am so very sorry to hear about Mr Armstrong, and distressed for Mary Jane. I wish she had come to me. Her husband is a political firebrand but a supremely good workman, the colonel tells me.'

'I believe he narrowly missed engendering a strike in your quarry.'

She looked at me shrewdly. 'Yes, that's true. But my husband tells me we must move with the times, and try to understand people like Ethan Armstrong.'

Or eliminate them.

'How is Mary Jane?'

'She's bearing up.'

'And the children?'

Her interest seemed genuine. Briefly, I told her about Harriet finding the body on Saturday, and this morning taking the farm dog out to search. She listened carefully, then said, 'And the boy? Six years old is is too young to understand about death. Let's hope that Harriet was mistaken.'

After a few more moments, I made my excuses, and left.

As I stepped from the house, I did a quick calculation. It occurred to me that the money in Mary Jane's bank book was deposited while she worked for the Ledgers. Perhaps Mary Jane herself had a radical streak and had seen some opportunity for profit here. In spite of Mrs Ledger's wealth and a certain sympathy, I would not suspect her of generosity. In my experience, the wealthy hold on to what they have.

The gardener still meddled in the flower bed. I spoke to the back of his head. 'Excuse me.'

He looked up from his work and gave me a suspicious glare.

'Where is the rose garden?'

He straightened up and pointed. 'Over yon.'

'Thank you.'

As I walked across the lawn in the direction of the rose garden, I felt disappointed that this visit had not taken my investigation much further forward. All I had was a suspicion that Ethan's attempt to call a strike had tipped the colonel over the edge. Of course he could have sacked Ethan without a reference, turned him out of the tied house, made life exceptionally difficult. It made no logical sense that he would murder, or arrange for murder. But under that charming mask was a hard-nosed businessman, with sons ready to inherit, and who wanted to hold on to what was his.

In the rose garden, one or two of the bushes showed promising buds. It was too early for roses. I heard the sound of someone at work, a rhythmic tapping that chimed with birdsong from the concealing hedge. I approached cautiously, not wishing to startle Raymond and cause his hand to slip and ruin a second sundial.

I need not have worried. He ignored my presence and continued with his work. Nearby was a wrought-iron seat. I made for that, as though watching men at work was my chosen vocation in life.

He'll stop in a minute, I thought. He'll stop because he's nervous and my watching him might make him uneasy.

He stopped.

'Don't let me put you off.'

'Did you want something? Only this is supposed to be a surprise, and if Mrs Ledger saw you come in this direction . . .'

'Raymond, will you do something for me? It will mean going back to the quarry when you finish work here.'

'Is it to do with Ethan going missing?'

'Yes.'

He came across to the bench. 'Tell me what you want me to do.'

'Ethan was carving four flowers on the sundial, to cover a flaw in the slate. It was his final touch. Will you look through the fragments? If there are four flowers, then he had finished the work. I don't know whether it will help to find that out, but it might.'

'You think he's dead don't you?'

'Yes I do.'

'Me too.'

'Raymond, who would want to kill Ethan?'

I held my breath during Raymond's pause, half expecting that he would accuse his own father of killing Ethan. Although I tried to look impassive, he read my glance.

When he finally spoke, his shyness prevented him meeting my eye. 'I'm in the Quarry Workers' Union. We voted for a strike. Word got back to my father, he's the foreman – you met him earlier – exactly how everyone voted. Ethan knew there was a traitor in our midst. He said to me no matter where he went, there was always a boss's nark or a government spy. He said people must be afraid of him to watch him so closely, and that gave him heart. If someone has harmed Ethan, it wasn't my Dad. Dad's a bully. He tackles people who can't fight back. Only this is what I want to tell you. Ethan said he'd found out who it was went telling tales.'

'Did he tell you who?'

'He wouldn't. He just said he would make sure it never happened again. If you heard Ethan speak, you would understand how his mind works. He says that battle lines are being drawn. He talks about the promises that were made when he went to war. Better housing, homes fit for heroes, decent schooling. He thought he was fighting for a better world. And what have we got, that's what he asks. Well, the answer's nowt. The working man got nowt. I'm getting wed on Saturday, and it's a choice of stopping with her mam and dad, who haven't space to scratch, or my mam and dad. And my dad knows I'm in the union. He doesn't let me forget it. You saw what he's like.'

I had indeed seen what Mr Turnbull was like, bully, big bruiser, with no love for Ethan or his politics.

Ten

As I walked back from the Hall, skirting the reservoir, passing the allotments, I tried to make sense of what I had learned so far. Both Ethan and Mary Jane had longings to be elsewhere, in a different kind of life, but something held her here; him, too, if my guess was right. Wanting to move on in life reminds me of a person who spoils for a fight but thinks better of it because there is no one nearby to hold his coat while he rolls up his sleeves. Perhaps Mary Jane blamed Ethan for caring more about his fellow workers than his own family, and Ethan blamed her for being stuck in her ways, and there they stayed — until Saturday.

As I neared the village, I remembered that Miss Trimble had been so sure that she had seen Mary Jane by the quarry in the middle of the afternoon. Yet Mary Jane denied that. Perhaps it would be worth another visit to Miss Trimble. Her returning the prayer book, and everything she had said, made me believe she was now sympathetic to Mary Jane.

I found my way to the vicarage, prepared myself for a great deal of irrelevant gossip, and tapped on the vicarage door. No reply. Perhaps she was in the church, rearranging the carnations.

The church was deserted. I tried the vestry door. It was not locked. Out of curiosity, I opened the parish register.

Harriet would be eleven in September. We were now in May. That made the date of her birth September, 1912. I flicked back the pages. Sure enough, there she was. Typically of the family, she possessed two names: Harriet Winifred. I turned back the pages through the summer months of 1912, and back into the spring. No entry of a marriage between Ethan Armstrong and Mary Jane Whitaker. January – nothing; December, 1911 – nothing; November, and there was a note of the marriage, and the signatures of Ethan Armstrong and Mary Jane Whitaker, witnessed by Bob Conroy and Barbara May Dawson. So Bob Conroy, who Mary Jane had rejected, cared enough for both of them to be best man; and the oracle sister Barbara May, maid of honour.

A respectable ten months elapsed between the marriage and Harriet's birth. Unless Miss Trimble's arithmetic was seriously at fault, she must have had some other reason for demanding the return of the missal than that Harriet was conceived out of wedlock.

Why would Mary Jane have misled me in that regard? Just as I had begun to trust my sister, that trust ebbed away. What made her lie? A lie against herself.

I closed the door of the vestry behind me. An old woman hobbled through the church doors and took a place in a rear pew.

I left the church for the vicarage, to try again.

When no one answered my knock, I peered through the kitchen window. It was a neat, modern room, with a gas cooker on which stood a bright copper kettle. A blazing fire burned in the grate; no sparing of coals here. Following the path round the side of the house, I looked

106

through the next window into what must be the parson's study, its walls thickly lined with books, a manuscript on the table.

It was through the parlour window that I saw Miss Trimble. She lay motionless on the hearth, her head dangerously close to the corner of the fender.

The front door was locked. I hastened to the back door. It opened. Hurrying through the kitchen into the hall, I called, 'Anyone home?'

No one answered.

I opened the parlour door. *Be alive.*

She must have been about to ring the bell pull and had fallen. My first mad thought was that perhaps she saw a mouse and fainted, but the rug was skew-whiff, as though she had tripped.

'Miss Trimble?'

My anxiety and lack of sleep must be playing tricks. She breathed. I felt sure she breathed. Her terror-stricken eyes flickered. Her lips moved. I came close to listen, 'Bitter,' she said.

'It will be all right.'

I fetched a rug from the sofa and covered her, adjusting her into the recovery position. No bones appeared to be broken. She was so very cold.

I took her hand, felt for a pulse in her wrist. Under her nails was wool from the carpet. She must have clutched at it in her desperation. 'Can you feel anything?' Her eyes flickered with fear. 'Does it hurt anywhere?' I asked.

She stared hard, the fear stronger now. I realised that she could not move her head, to nod, or to say no. With a harsh grating sound, she made a slow, difficult exhalation, as though this shudder would be her last. With superhuman effort, she held my gaze, and made the smallest of inhalations, her eyes alive with alarm at the shrill, creaking sound that came from her very being. She gasped a single word, 'Dandy,' her weak voice barely audible, yet urgent with desperation.

The poor woman was out of her mind, halluncinating. 'I'm going to call the doctor. It will be all right. Don't worry.'

The fear in her eyes held me still. Kneeling beside her, I held her hand, supported her head. She became calm, and very still. Her look held something greater than fear – loss, love, terror, and then she was gone. I closed her eyes.

Slowly, I retraced my steps to the hall, and picked up the telephone receiver. 'Please connect me to the doctor, straightaway. This is an emergency.'

'Who is calling?' the operator asked, more from nosiness than efficiency.

'My name is Mrs Shackleton, calling from the vicarage. Connect me now please.'

The woman lying on the hearth rug would preside over no more Girls' Friendship meetings.

For such a portly man, the doctor trod lightly. He was no longer young but gamely creaked to his knees to examine Miss Trimble. Seeing that it would be harder for him to get up than down, I placed a raffia-backed chair nearby. He used this to lever himself to standing, and then asked me about finding her, nodding his head sadly as I gave him details.

'Madam, I am obliged to you. The poor lady was asthmatic and had a heart condition.'

'You believe that to be the cause of death?'

He frowned, his manner changing as he heard the challenge in my voice.

*

I left the vicarage feeling faint, and as if every bone in my body had melted. Had Miss Trimble died because she knew something, and was that something her reported sighting of Mary Jane by the quarry? But she had already made a statement about that. The doctor clearly did not want any complications. Heart failure, always a satisfactory cause of death. But the wildness in her eyes when she first looked at me, the sense that she was trying to tell me something, overwhelmed me. Perhaps my nerves played tricks, or my instinct for foul play betrayed me into believing Miss Trimble had been murdered.

It was a short stumble to the churchyard. Some enterprising soul had created a circular wooden bench around an old oak tree. The shivers began as I sat down. With trembling hands, I fumbled for the brandy flask in my satchel.

I had been on the go since four-thirty this morning. My visit to the quarry, to the police house and Applewick Hall had brought me no nearer an answer regarding the fate of Ethan Armstrong, alive or dead. I needed to think, before seeing Mary Jane again. The effort of trying to make sense of Ethan's disappearance made my head ache. What little information I had gathered was in danger of being obliterated from my mind by this sudden death that the doctor seemed determined to regard as natural.

If I knew more about the people concerned – my own flesh and blood, for instance – then I would be better placed to understand what was going on. Harriet had told me of her fear that her father lay at the bottom of the pool in the quarry. Was that because it was easier to confide in a stranger, or was there a darker reason? Perhaps in some part of Harriet's being lurked a mistrust of her own mother, as well as fear for her father. That would explain why the children crept from the house on Saturday with the snack for their father while Mary Jane was out; why they lassoed the farm dog into service. It would explain why Miss Trimble saw a figure in a plaid cape near the quarry in the afternoon.

Austin claimed to have heard a goblin hiding behind the hut. A real aunt would know whether Austin's imagination teemed with scary bogeymen, or whether he caught the sound of someone who did not want to be seen or heard – a killer, lurking behind the masons' shed.

Surely that could not have been Mary Jane? She would not have let her own children find their father's body. That would be unnatural.

How long I sat there, I did not know. There was some vague thought at the back of my mind that the vicar would wish to speak to the person who found his sister's body. I heard the noise of the children, coming out of school. One or two made a shortcut through the churchyard, paying me no heed.

And then someone spoke. Clearly, I heard the name. Ethan Armstrong.

Where had the voice come from? Had I conjured the name?

I walked the path between the graves, looking not at the old stones, but at the new. Ethan Armstrong, stone mason, must have carved some of these names. Perhaps Raymond, Ethan's apprentice, would carve his master's name, if ever Ethan's body was found.

And then I saw him, bending over a grave, rocking back and forth, muttering to himself. Had I found Ethan Armstrong? My own voice sounded strange as I spoke to him.

The man turned to look at me. It was not the man whose

photograph Mary Jane had shown me. He did not look embarrassed, but seemed unaware of his rocking and his muttering. He stared at me for a moment, as though trying to work out what country was this, what person accosted him.

Then he stepped back, staring at me, suddenly realising the strange impression he created. A gaunt, wiry man with long arms, he dipped his head to one side and raised his hands in a gesture of harmlessness, or surrender. With some effort, he smiled, showing even teeth near enough to white. The broad forehead and heavy brow gave him a sad look. He had the fresh-faced ruddy skin of a country man, his eyes the colour of stone.

'My wife, Georgina, she said to look out for you. You must be Mrs Shackleton.'

'Yes. Mr Conroy?'

'Bob. Excuse the muttering. I was talking to my brother.' He nodded at the grave. 'He was killed in the quarry last year.'

'I heard you speak Ethan's name. You were telling your brother about him?'

'Yes,' Bob Conroy said softly. 'My brother Simon was the true farmer, a shepherd. He lost his life in the quarry, rescuing a lost lamb. This business with Ethan brought it all back.' He stepped a little to one side, allowing me to join him.

I read the inscription, and the date of Simon's death, just a year, a month and a day ago.

Bob watched me, and then said, 'Ethan carved a text on the back of the stone as well. Read that.'

He waited. I stepped from the path and read the inscription on the reverse of the headstone.

111

He who does not enter the sheepfold by the door but climbs in by another way, that man is a thief and a robber; he who enters by the door is the shepherd of the sheep.

These lines from the Gospel of St John struck a wrong note. They were not the lines I would have chosen for a shepherd who died trying to save a lamb.

I bowed my head to the gravestone, with the feeling that I was being introduced to the dead man when it would be more usual to make the acquaintance of the living. 'Ethan carved this?'

'Yes.'

'You're Ethan's good friend I believe?'

He jutted his chin forward in an almost aggressive way. 'Yes. Friend and comrade. We were at school together. We fought together. Harriet has to have been wrong. He'll turn up.'

The forced optimism in his voice did not light his eyes or change his serious expression.

Perhaps it was the breeze through the leaves of the willow tree, or realising how outnumbered we are by the dead. A sense of foreboding sent a shiver through me.

'I've written letters,' Bob said, 'to our comrades, to ask whether Ethan has been in touch with them. I've posted half a dozen letters today. I can't understand that he would leave without a word.'

'When you say you've written to comrades, do you mean wartime comrades?'

'I mean his friends in the trade union and labour movement. And yes, some of them served in our regiment.'

I remembered the amount of paperwork in Ethan's chest, the painstaking minutes of meetings in Ethan's writing and in another hand, perhaps Bob Conroy's. Letter writing would give Bob something to do, and he would know all the people Ethan may have been in touch with.

'I'm glad you're doing that, Mr Conroy. So you and Ethan are fellow revolutionaries?'

He laughed gently. 'Ethan's a visionary, but he has no illusions. Those who fear we're on the eve of a revolution overestimate us. There are too many powerful people who'll fight tooth and nail to keep things as they are.'

'Then Ethan must have enemies?'

'We're not important enough for that, though Ethan would think differently.'

I looked again at the inscription on the reverse of the shepherd's gravestone. 'You said Ethan carved this?'

'Yes.'

'It's . . .'

'Go on.' His head jutted, like a tortoise peeping from its shell. 'Tell me what *you* think he meant by it.'

When I did not answer straightaway, he sighed, as if reluctant to continue, as if the man in the grave may have ears that flapped. 'Shall we sit down somewhere Mrs Shackleton?'

We walked the path, beyond the older graves and the willow tree until we came to the seat I had vacated not so long before.

'Will this do?'

Conroy sat with his back to the tree, like some latter-day Green Man who might find his way into the trunk and never be seen again.

'So tell me, Mr Conroy, why did Ethan carve those cryptic lines from scripture?'

'Our farm is adjacent to Ledgers' land. We have the freehold. Last spring, a child brought word to say that one of the lambs had lost its way and was by the quarry. It was a Sunday you see so there was no man at work to pick it up and bring it home. I don't know exactly how it happened. But Simon went alone to save the lamb. Next thing I heard, he lay dead in the quarry bottom.' He sighed. 'I carried him home myself.'

His large hands cradled his kneecaps, as though he were a boy who had fallen and grazed himself and was trying to make it better. He rocked slightly.

I thought he had forgotten that he intended to explain the inscription, but after a long time, he said, 'Those words that Ethan carved, "He who does not enter the sheepfold by the door but climbs in by another way, that man is a thief and a robber", he meant Colonel Ledger.'

'Colonel Ledger? Why?'

'The colonel wanted to buy our farm. Ethan thought that Ledger was behind Simon's death. Oh he didn't say that to me. He didn't have to. We each knew what the other was thinking right enough. Ethan believed that Ledger wanted Simon out of the way. Without him, he thought I'd sell. He made an offer while Simon was alive, and he made another, the week after Simon was buried.'

'Why would Colonel Ledger want your farm?'

'Because the existing quarry is near exhausted. The colonel sent his engineer across one day to our far meadow. Simon caught him taking samples. There's a rich seam – a millstone grit that's high quality. We're near the railway line. He has the labour force here. As long as Simon was in this world, there'd be no question of selling up. With Simon gone, Ledger counted that I would give up the land. I almost did. Hadn't the heart for going on. But Ethan encouraged me. He said to hold fast. What if I had a son, he said, and then I would be sorry to have lost the farm.'

'But your brother's death was an accident. He'd gone to find a lamb that had strayed.'

'Yes. And that's what I think. But Ethan has a mind to see beyond to other motives, and sometimes he's right. We never found out what child brought the message.'

'Did he think the colonel pushed Simon to his death?'

'Not the colonel himself, but he could have made his wishes known. It wasn't Ledger made us the offer directly, it was his man.'

'But you didn't sell then.'

'Ethan persuaded me not to. He helped me whenever he could. But it was no use. We had a bad winter, sick animals, the price of feed has been more than I could stand. A week ago yesterday, I told Ethan that I'd accepted the colonel's offer'

We sat in silence. At a nearby grave an old woman set down a mat and knelt. She began, in an increasingly loud and complaining voice, to tell the occupant of the grave about the door coming off the kitchen cupboard.

After his outpouring of emotion and suspicion regarding his brother's death, Conroy placed his palms on the bench and seemed to be gathering his composure.

I risked a question. 'Mr Conroy, perhaps you can help with something that puzzles me.'

'What is it?'

I handed him the cutting.

A well provided and pleasant lady seeks well provided amiable gentleman with a view to joining lives and fortunes.
Box No. 49

'Does this mean anything to you?'

He scanned it, and then blushed. 'I hope Mary Jane

doesn't think Ethan would chase after another woman.'

'She didn't know what to think.'

Conroy shook his head. 'He wouldn't do that.' He stood. 'I have to get back to work.'

We walked together through the churchyard. As we reached the lych gate, I tried once more. 'Do you know why Mary Jane wouldn't leave Great Applewick last year, when Ethan could have got work on the Minster?'

He hesitated. 'Don't think ill of Mary Jane. You see, there's more to it.'

For a moment, he looked as if he regretted his words. 'She . . . you see . . . well, they have two bairns buried in the chapel graveyard. Perhaps that's what keeps Mary Jane tied to this place.'

'I didn't know,' I said simply.

'I don't think she likes to talk about it. Shall I show you?'

We crossed the street to the rival place of worship and walked beyond the chapel to where the neat gravestones stood row on row. It was a small headstone. Two children, born after Harriet, had died within a month of each other, at ages three and two; one named after his father, and one named after me.

'They caught the whooping cough,' he said simply. 'Mary Jane was beside herself with grief.'

He left me standing there. Sometimes it seems the world is just one great big sphere of loss, spinning fast, trying to topple us all over the edge.

Slowly, I walked back towards the cottage. It struck me that there was a great deal Mary Jane did not like to talk about.

Eleven

As I turned the bend, a few yards from the cottage, the children dawdled towards me along the lane. 'Are you off somewhere?'

Austin said, in a sulky voice, 'I don't want to go again.'

Harriet sighed. 'We have to apologise for taking Billy and making him search for Dad.'

'Billy?'

'The sheepdog.'

'Did you cover much ground?'

Harriet shook her head. 'Billy didn't want to do it. He ran off.'

'Didn't go to the moor,' Austin chipped in.

'The moor?'

'That's where we would have gone to search,' Harriet said quietly. 'That's where we go sometimes.'

Austin looked hopeful. He shifted his weight from one foot to the other, and back again. I waited to hear what he would have to say.

'We can go in your motorcar.'

'Another time. I have to talk to your mam.'

'Where do motorcars go?' he asked.

'Motorcars can go anywhere.'

Harriet tugged at his sleeve. 'Come on!'

'It was clever of you, Harriet, to think of giving Billy your dad's cap to sniff, and to search.'

She didn't answer. They set off walking, slowly, as though whatever energy they had for the day was used up this morning, trying to turn a sheepdog into a bloodhound.

I knocked and opened the cottage door. The room sparkled, neat, tidy and spotlessly clean. While I had dropped everything to rush to Mary Jane's aid, she played the good housewife.

As if she read my thoughts, she said, 'If Ethan comes back, I want him to see everything's as it should be. I don't want him to think he can upset me. I won't go to pieces because he takes it into his head to disappear.' She waved at the chair by the fire. 'Better sit down and tell me how you got on.'

I flopped into the chair.

'You mucked up your shoes again.' She sat on a buffet and unlaced my shoes. 'You can't go round looking like you've tramped across Hawksworth Moor. I'll polish them for you.'

I felt too done in to argue, and did not know where to start. I should begin by telling her about Miss Trimble, but had not taken it in myself yet.

'Did you go out this afternoon?' I asked.

'No. Why?'

'I just wondered.'

'I've known you for eleven hours and you don't just wonder. What's happened?'

She spread a newspaper on the table, placed my shoes on it, and then brought the boot blacking box from its place on the stairs.

'I'll get to it,' I said, thinking of Miss Trimble. 'But I've

118

learned that Ethan had quite a week last week. Saturday before last taking a collection to some miners who were on strike.'

She brushed the mud from my shoes. 'Yes I know.'

'On Sunday, Bob told him that he'd sold the farm to Colonel Ledger.'

She paused, brush in midair. 'He never? I didn't know that. What was Ethan thinking of that he never told me?' She dabbed the brush into the polish and began to apply it.

'Were you speaking? I know you weren't getting on.'

'Who's been saying that? We were getting on fine, in our fashion.'

'Saturday he took the donations, Sunday found out about the farm, and Monday lost the strike vote.'

'And I'm glad he did. How are people supposed to live if they've no wage coming in?' Her shoe polish applying gained a furious speed.

'He found out who'd been betraying him – telling the foreman the way the vote had gone.'

'Well, what's so secret about it? There's always some big mouth. I don't see what any of this has to do with him being found . . . like Harriet said, or disappearing.'

'It all paints a picture, Mary Jane, a picture of a man going through a crisis. Did he talk about any of this?'

'No.' She began applying polish to my second shoe, with a rhythmic movement, staring at the leather. 'You think I'm hiding something.'

'Either that or I'm missing something. There's a difference.'

'Well, go on. What do you want to quiz me about?'

'Was something wrong between you? Only it's bound to come out if there was. Ethan had talked to Mrs Conroy, found a sympathetic ear.'

'Never!' she picked up a polishing brush and began to furiously polish the toes of my shoes, spitting for good measure. 'He didn't like her. I was always the one who liked Georgina.'

She finished polishing the shoes and returned them to me, bobbing down, putting the shoes on the rug. I looked at the top of her head – chestnut hair, with not a single strand of grey. She sat down on the chair opposite me.

'Mary Jane, if Harriet's worst fear becomes reality and the police become involved, they will start from the assumption of foul play. There'll be a list of persons of interest. Starting from the bottom, Raymond will have questions to answer, as Ethan's former apprentice . . .'

'Oh you can rule that out.'

'Let me finish. As Ethan's former apprentice, he says himself he will take over the job, and this house.'

'And where do we go?'

'It's a tied house.'

The reality dawned on her. 'But . . .'

'Josiah Turnbull, foreman, Raymond's father, he was a sworn enemy to Ethan and he got the better of him in the strike vote. They could have come to blows. He was the last to leave the quarry on Saturday. And then there is Colonel Ledger . . .'

'Are you mad? The colonel . . .'

'Ethan was a thorn in his side. The colonel admired Ethan's skill, gave him a job to do that might well require some personal contact, with the colonel himself, or one of his minions.'

'You should be writing detective stories. All this is fantastic.'

'Wait. That was the list working from the bottom. You

might find yourself at the top, Mary Jane, and that's why I wish you would tell me a straight story.'

'Everything I've told you is true.'

'No. It's not. You and Ethan had fallen out. The kids took him food secretly because . . .'

'I wanted him to come home, that's why I didn't pack him food.'

'You lied about why Miss Trimble took back the missal. I checked the parish register. Harriet was born way beyond nine months. A whole four weeks more.'

She smiled. 'All right. But she does do that to people. I've seen it happen. If you must know I stopped going to that church and went to the chapel. I don't like Miss Trimble, and I don't like the vicar. He's a snob, dead posh, and full of himself. He has a parish with people drawing water from the well and not affording candles, and he's had a bathroom put in and a kitchen, all done up and charges it to the parish. Ethan was right about him. And we do get on, Ethan and me. We have our differences, but we're two of a kind him and me, mad at the world, that's what he said, and it's true.' She folded her arms tightly around her and shut her lips as though she might never speak another word.

I was beginning to feel a tiredness creeping up from my toes. The task of putting on my shoes suddenly seemed enormous. 'Mary Jane, the reason I asked you where you were this afternoon is because something very serious happened at the vicarage, concerning Miss Trimble.'

'Good. She's a cow.'

'You wouldn't speak ill, if you knew.'

'What? Are you saying she's dead?'

'Yes, and I found her. She died in my arms. It was terrible. The doctor says heart failure, but I'm not so sure.'

She closed her eyes. 'I'm sorry she's dead. She was nice to me when I first came, then turned spiteful.'

I put on my shoes. As I did up the laces, I thought, if we'd been brought up together, I would know her so well, be able to read her outbursts and her silences. 'I've found out a lot today, Mary Jane. At some point it might begin to make sense. I won't come back tomorrow. I'm going to see my father in Wakefield. Someone ought to make Sergeant Sharp take Ethan's disappearance more seriously.'

'And what am I supposed to do in the meantime? I feel useless.'

'What about your mother, and Barbara May? Shouldn't they know what you're going through?'

She sighed. 'As long as they don't know, it doesn't feel real. But I might have to tell them.'

I stood up to go. 'I'm not giving up. Don't think that. If you need me, ask Sergeant Sharp to telephone me, or you can send a telegram.'

She followed me to the door.

I walked to my car, climbed in.

'Wait!' She was behind me. 'Kate, wait! Budge up. I have to talk to you.'

I moved along on the seat. She climbed in. In the distance, a train sounded its hooter.

Not looking at me, staring ahead, she said, 'You're right about saying I wouldn't go when Ethan was offered work at the Minster. I did want to leave this place, and then when it came down to it, well I just couldn't. I can't explain.'

'Try.'

She was silent.

Remembering what Bob Conroy had said, I asked, 'Is it something to do with the two children?'

Her voice was barely audible. 'Something like that.'

'Tell me.'

'I can't.'

'Bob told me that you lost two children, and that they're buried in the chapel graveyard.'

She paused before answering. 'Yes. That broke my heart.' She looked at her hands. They were chapped and red from her day's washing. 'There's something else. I expect you took a gander at my bank book. You don't miss much.'

'Yes, I saw it.'

'I showed it to Ethan last week. He'd never known about it, but he was so upset last week about everything that was happening, the poor miners, locked out and starving. It's not a strike at the colonel's pit, it's a lock-out. I told him, if he wanted to do what Bob said and stand for parliament, I would put us a deposit on a house, I would help him. He got it out of me, where the money came from.'

Mary Jane came to a full stop. The shadow of the hedgerow lengthened.

'Where did the money come from, Mary Jane?'

'It was a kind of dowry, from Mrs Ledger, when she thought I would marry Bob Conroy. When I told Ethan, he was blue with fury. Said he wouldn't touch the money. Swore at me, called me names.'

'Did he think there was more behind Mrs Ledger's gift than kindness?'

'Yes. And he was right. I wouldn't tell him. But that only made him imagine the worst. He says people like her don't give money for nothing.'

I was glad we were sitting side by side in the car because I felt that had she been opposite me, and we could look at each other, she would not speak.

123

'I was just fifteen when I went to the Ledgers and I was pretty little thing, and very shy. Mrs Ledger made a big fuss of me. I knew nothing about being a lady's maid. She showed me what to do. She dressed me up in nice clothes. It was like playing, having a jolly time. And I didn't feel like a maid at all. The colonel took our photographs. Artistic, the colonel called them. I would have liked to send one home but they wouldn't have understood. They wouldn't have seen the artistic quality. They would have said they were saucy.'

I wondered how saucy, but thought it best to let her keep talking. 'Mary Jane, I'm in a photographic club. I've probably seen the sort of picture you're talking about.'

'So when she gave me the money, I put it in a bank book and I never told Ethan. Well, you don't, do you? What fool of a woman getting wed would let her husband know what she keeps in reserve? Only last week, when he was that down in the dumps, and was thinking what else we would do, I said to him that we could put a deposit on a place, and he could go into business on his own account, or stand for parliament, or whatever he wanted. And he'd already started work on the sundial. I think he wanted to do it so perfectly, to show he could, and then smash it, because of who it was for. And I think that he's gone, and won't come back. Or else something worse has happened.'

We sat in silence for a long time.

'Is that why you wouldn't go to the Hall, to ask the colonel whether he'd been to the quarry to see the sundial? Are you still attached to the Ledgers, after what they did? You were not much more than a child.'

'No. I'm not attached to them. I think Miss Trimble must have caught a glance or something in the air between us, between the colonel and me. I don't know. She took against me, and I could imagine why. I know I should have left here long ago, but sometimes you're bound to a place, no matter what.'

'Because of your children in the churchyard?'

She sighed. 'That's it. It's stupid isn't it? I can't leave the children. They're still mine. What would they think if they knew, and if they knew I could just walk away?'

'But you have Harriet and Austin to think of.'

'I know.'

'Mary Jane, you've come to me for help. And I'm doing what I can. But I'm not proper family, like your mother, or your sister Barbara May. With Ethan gone, you'll need them. Tell them. If Ethan has abandoned you, or met with some accident, you'll need your real family.'

She opened her mouth and shut it again. Whether she would have agreed, or contradicted, I didn't know.

Mary Jane climbed out of the car. 'I'll think on it. I might go see my mother tomorrow.' She turned back. 'And Kate, don't tell anyone about the Ledgers and me, and about the money in my bank book. I won't ever touch it now. It will be for Harriet, and Austin.'

As I started the motor, she called again. 'Wait!' A moment later, she appeared with armfuls of folders and newspapers. 'Take this stuff of Ethan's. I can't bear to read it. But it must give some inkling as to what was going on in his life that I didn't know about. I want you to read it.'

Twelve

It was hard to concentrate on the road when the image of Miss Trimble's body seemed real enough to be in the car with me. Look at the road, I told myself. Keep an eye on the tramlines.

It was not that I missed the turn for Kirkstall but that I mistook an earlier road for it and ended up on steep hills, scenic but unfamiliar, taking me to a high point beyond woods where the journey stretched on into a bitter chill before I had to stop and consult the map with shivering fingers, and come home via Butcher Hill and a roundabout route through West Park.

As I drew into Headingley, I remembered that this was my housekeeper's night for exchanging books with our neighbour across the road, the professor's sister.

Instead of going straight home, I drove to Woodhouse, to talk to Mr Sykes. Jim Sykes is my right-hand man, an ex-policeman who likes nothing better than to corner and capture a guilty party. This morning he would have been to Marshall & Snelgrove's department store, where an ocelot coat went missing some weeks ago. Sykes had suggested a training course for sales staff. The first of these events he had undertaken this morning.

Talking to Sykes about the events of this long day might help me make some sense of it all.

When I reached Woodhouse and knocked on the Sykeses' door, Mrs Sykes answered. She is a round, friendly woman who beamed a greeting and asked me in.

'There's tea in the pot, and you'll have a scone with me. They're fresh baked today.'

'That sounds lovely.'

She put a plate of scones on the table, and a butter dish, plate and knife. 'They'll be swallowed up in minutes when that lot come back. Jim and the kids are on the moor, playing cricket, though they'll be at it in darkness if they don't come back soon.'

As I buttered my scone, I glanced about the house. This was only my second time of being indoors here. It was a neat terrace house, with this one room downstairs, two up and a cellar. The leaded range shone, from the application of black lead and elbow grease. A low fire burned in the grate. The rag rug was a riot of colour with no discernible pattern. I guessed that they had all joined in the making of it on winter nights.

The Sykes family have lived in Woodhouse for six years, three years less than I have lived in Headingley.

Mrs Sykes watched me bite into the scone. 'It's a new recipe, with a bit of cheese. My own invention.'

'Delicious.'

'Then you'll take one for Mrs Sugden.'

'Yes I will, thank you.' Mrs Sugden would not be pleased if Mrs Sykes's scones turned out better than her own.

'Jim's that pleased with himself today over the Marshall & Snelgrove business. I can tell you now what I can't say in front of him. He's a changed man, since working with you, Mrs Shackleton. It suits him to have that bit of independence, and the chance to drive the motor car now and then.'

Why thoughts of remuneration should have popped into my head at that moment I don't know. It occurred to me that I do not pay Sykes enough money. But this isn't a proper job. We never know what might come next, or if anything will come next.

As if she guessed my thoughts, Mrs Sykes said, 'He appreciated that bonus you gave him after the business you took care of for the jeweller.'

That had been the least I could do. The case was one over which we did not see eye to eye, and never would. 'I'm glad.' I polished off the scone and refused another.

'And there's summat else, though don't let on I told you. If we hadn't had that holiday in Robin Hood's Bay, our Thomas wouldn't have made himself useful to the joiner there and developed his taste for carpentry. Then he wouldn't have got his apprenticeship.'

'He's got an apprenticeship! That's wonderful. I didn't know about that.'

She put a finger to her lips. 'Jim'll want to tell you himself.'

'Then I won't breathe a word. I have one or two things I need to talk over with him.' I carried my plate and cup to the sink.

'Oh leave that.'

'I'm going to walk along in the hope of meeting them. Mr Sykes and I will take a turn on the moor and talk about something else that's come up.'

Her eyes sparkled. 'More jobs?'

'Sort of,' I said. 'A family connection.'

'Ah.' She nodded. Everyone knew that where family comes in, money does not.

*

Woodhouse Moor is one of the precious green spaces close to the city centre. As I walked onto the moor, I spotted Jim Sykes and his children. Thomas, at fourteen the elder of the two boys, sauntered along carrying the cricket bat. Half running, half walking, the younger girl and boy threw the ball back and forth, laughing if one of them dropped it. Sykes came a little way behind them, and raised a hand in greeting.

I thought back to last year, when Dad first suggested that Sykes come and work for me. We had arranged to meet on the moor. He was seated in the centre of the bench that stood to the right of the path. Both of us were wary – me at the thought of interviewing a prospective employee on a park bench, he because wary is part of his character. He had worn a trilby that day and as he whipped it off, I looked for a pin hole at the back of the hat – for his extra eye, the one in the back of his head.

It was growing dark enough for the children to keep missing the ball. Sykes stretched, caught it, and threw it back. As we grew close enough to see each other better, I noticed how cheerfully he strode along, looking much happier than when we first met. Back then he was unemployed, and very much out of favour with the constabulary. One of his superiors had arrested the wrong man for a crime, and when Sykes attempted to right a wrong, it was made clear he had no future. After being forced into a corner, he saw no choice but to resign from the force.

Thomas spotted me and waved. He broke into a sprint. Last year he was all elbows and knees. He was still a little gangly but had lost the awkwardness.

'Hello, Mrs Shackleton. Do you notice summat different about me?'

'Thomas! You're wearing long trousers.'

'Guess why.'

'I can't think.'

'Guess.'

'I can only think you must have a job.'

'I started my apprenticeship today.' He was practically bouncing with delight.

'If you do as well there as you did making the nameplate for my house, they'll be glad to have you.'

He had made the nameplate of English oak, and named the house *Pipistrelle Lodge*, after the bats that inhabit the adjoining wood.

The younger two Sykes children stood back, giving Thomas his moment.

Then we all fell into step walking to the edge of the darkening moor.

'Tell your mother I'll see her later,' Sykes said and the three of them hurried off in high spirits. No doubt we old ones had slowed the youngsters down.

'Great news about Thomas,' I said.

Sykes gave one of his rare smiles. 'I expect Rosie told you. She can't keep quiet about it. Worse than the lad himself.'

The street lights flickered into life. By the time we walked once around the moor, Sykes had told me as much as I needed to know about how well he prepared the staff of Marshall & Snelgrove to spot likely shoplifters.

My story took a little longer, beginning with Mary Jane's arrival at my house in the early hours of this morning.

He listened gravely. 'I had no idea you were adopted.'

'It's not something I've thought about for years. Though now I have no choice but to think about it. I'm going to Wakefield tomorrow to speak to my father. He and Mother have to know that I've been contacted by this sister of mine. Dad will tell me I'm too close to be helping Mary Jane of course, no objectivity, and he'll be right. It doesn't help that I have to squeeze her like a tube of toothpaste to get information.'

'What does she hold back?'

'There's something I don't like about the local bigwigs, Colonel and Mrs Ledger, Great Applewick's nearest thing to lord and lady of the manor. It turns out that Mary Jane worked as Mrs Ledger's maid. The relationship was not entirely conventional, if you take my meaning.'

Sykes, admirably, did not raise an eyebrow, or if he did, the gloom prevented my noticing. 'It happens.'

'Mary Jane has a rather large insurance policy on Ethan's life, and a bank book he knew nothing of until days before he was either murdered or disappeared. Two hundred came from Mrs Ledger, deposited before Mary Jane married Ethan. I don't know about the other hundred. It was paid over in smaller amounts.'

'That's a lot of money for a lady's maid, or a stonemason's wife. Did she drop any hints as to how she'd . . .'

'Earned it?'

'Yes.'

'Saucy photographs. It sounds harmless but anyone looking with an objective eye would put Mary Jane on the list of suspects for Ethan's murder, if he found out and threatened to leave her.'

'Along with the Ledgers, though I expect the colonel would be unlikely to dirty his hands. Anything else I should know, Mrs Shackleton?'

We were overtaken on the path by a huge dog, bounding free as its owner let it off the leash.

131

'Ethan was offered work elsewhere last year, but she wouldn't go.'

'Because of the Ledgers? Is she still . . . in touch?'

'I don't believe so. It was a long time ago. She's thirty-six now, with a daughter of her own. She'll probably look back on that episode and see it quite differently. There's something else. She lost two children after Harriet. They're buried in the chapel graveyard. Bob Conroy, he's the farmer and Ethan's old friend, believes that makes it hard for her to leave, but I'm not sure I agree with him.'

'Could be,' Sykes said. 'Some people make visiting graves an important part of their lives. Now, can you tell me a bit more about this Miss Trimble? Finding her must have been a terrible shock.'

A group of dog owners had gathered with their animals and were chatting a few yards away. With some effort, I forced myself to voice my barely supportable suspicions about Miss Trimble's death. 'I'm sure she was poisoned, though the doctor looked at me as though I were mad. Is there or isn't there a connection? I just don't know.'

'If the police come in on the case, it's not something we'll need to pursue,' Sykes said grimly.

'I can't let it go, Mr Sykes. She's my sister. Those children . . . the little girl reminds me so much of myself at her age. She's brave, and desperate to know whether she can trust the evidence of her own eyes. I can't desert them. Do you understand that?'

'I do. But does that mean you must go on investigating personally? I'm sure when you see the superintendent tomorrow, he'll . . .'

'Dad will order me to steer clear. But let me tell you a little more.'

I described Josiah Turnbull, quarry foreman, and his

132

son Raymond, and my meeting with Colonel and Mrs Ledger.

Sykes listened carefully, asking for details, descriptions.

I had parked my car by the edge of the moor. As we drew close, Sykes asked, 'So what exactly would you like me to do?'

'It wouldn't hurt if you paid a visit to Great Applewick, just to take a little snoop about. If someone has murdered my brother-in-law, I want to know.'

'Even if it is your sister?'

I did not answer that directly. 'There's an advantage in that no one there will know who you are, and that includes Mary Jane. You might be able to pick up some useful information, though I don't know how you'll go about it. It's the kind of place where a stranger sticks out like the barber's pole.'

'I'll put my thinking cap on.'

'And this is going to sound very sneaky.'

'Go on.'

'Before I left, I urged Mary Jane to tell her mother, or her proper sister, the one she's close to and was brought up with, that her husband has disappeared. They're her real kin and will be far more help to her than I in the family stakes, whatever the outcome. If Ethan has abandoned her, or met with some accident or . . .'

'Been murdered.'

'. . . then she'll need her family. She said she might do it, visit her mother tomorrow I mean.'

'But you don't think she will?'

'The children will be at school. She trusts Harriet to take care of Austin so she might well go off visiting. If so, I'd be interested to know what tram or train she catches.'

Sykes does not miss the slightest hint or intonation.

'You don't trust her, and you wonder whether she may go see someone else altogether?'

'I don't believe Mary Jane killed Ethan. But she doesn't help herself. She can be frank to the point of foolishness, or she tells a stupid lie, or holds back. She's trying to be private in a situation where that just won't do.'

Sykes darted a quick look at me and I felt slightly uncomfortable, as though he were saying, *Well then, who's just described herself?*

Thirteen

The house was empty. I switched on the light in the hall. Along with the day's post, Mrs Sugden had placed a note on the hall table.

Supper on plate on pan
I made the telephone calls —
  1. *No hospitals in vicinity report accident victim answering Ethan Armstrong's description*
  2. *Your dad — tomorrow lunch, 12 noon — will meet you at Websters*

One of the letters was from Marcus, another from the Yorkshire Mutual Insurance Company. But before I read the post, I would look for Sookie. She must have had her kittens by now.

I called her name.

Of course she never answers. I knelt on the floor and looked under the dresser. Not there. Nor was she curled on the sofa in the drawing room, or on a dining room chair. I went upstairs. Mrs Sugden always closes every upstairs door. No Sookie fastened in the spare bedroom or the bathroom. Not in the airing cupboard. What a relief. Mrs Sugden would be most annoyed if Sookie had her litter on the linen. She was not under my bed, nor on the rattan chair by the washstand. It is pointless to look out of the window for a cat in the gathering dark, but all the same I did it. I took a cardigan from the drawer.

Where could she be?

There would probably be some old Chinese proverb that warned against looking for a black cat in a dark wood, and if there wasn't, there should be.

All the same, I would try one quick whiz around the garden and wood. I picked up the torch and let myself out the back door. Sookie has a den in the snowberry bush. I peered through the gap, her doorway. The torch's beam caught a startled dormouse.

Slowly, I circled Batswing Wood, looking among felled logs where soft bark might provide a bed. A pipistrelle bat grazed my hair.

'Sookie!'

If she gave birth here, some fox might kill her kittens and her too, in her weakened state.

I gave up and went back into the house. Mrs Sugden had left me a pie and pea supper.

As I ate the pie and peas, I read Marcus's letter.

Dearest Kate

I raced to Kings Cross station hoping to see you off. Your train was just leaving the station. So sorry to have missed you and not said a proper goodbye. Our time together lit my life.

Till next time. Soon, I hope.

All my love

Marcus

Ten out of ten for brevity, Marcus.

I had come back from London only yesterday, and it seemed a lifetime ago. During our time together, I had a feeling that Marcus would ask me to marry him, and I could not think of a kind way to say no.

I enjoyed his company. I had slept in his bed. But that did not mean I wanted to be the wife of a police inspector, living in Hampstead, waiting for my man to come home. All the same, his letter cheered me. The warm glow made me feel guilty and dissatisfied that I would never again be someone who would fall hopelessly, helplessly in love.

The Yorkshire Mutual Insurance Company letter lifted my spirits. The managing director asked me to telephone to arrange an interview with himself and Head of Claims. If this was to do with tracking down fraudsters, it would suit my cohort Sykes down to the toecaps of his shiny boots.

I retreated to my darkroom. A black cat in a dark wood.

We had converted a pantry into a darkroom shortly after moving into the house. It had the advantage of being light-proof and the disadvantage of incurable stuffiness.

I had used a six-exposure spooled film to take photographs in the quarry. Carefully, I unwound the film into the tank. I poured in the developer, and waited. My green "safe" light was more agreeable to work by than the red.

Minutes ticked by. I poured off the developer, and added fixer solution. My green thought in a green shade became the wish that life could be fixed as easily as the image on a photograph.

I had done something sneaky. As well as my photographs in the quarry, I had taken two on the farm. One ostensibly of the lamb but including Mrs Conroy, and another of Arthur with his hand in the ewe. I always have an eye to submitting my photographs for competitions.

My prints of the broken sundial, the vista of the quarry, the worktable, turned out reasonably well.

My surreptitious portraits of farmer's wife and labourer would not win any prizes.

Now it was time to attend to the photographic plate I had used to capture the image of what appeared to me the imprint on the ground of a man's heel, and what could have been the mark of a body being dragged. I had taken this photograph by the edge of the quarry pool where the ground was damp and the impression clear.

When I took it, I had thought the pool deep enough to hide a body. That was before Raymond enlightened me. A person in boots could step into that deceptive pool without wetting his or her ankles.

All the same, I wanted the picture.

I have a little book that I like to read – *The Gentle Art of Photography*. The anonymous writer says that every photograph ought to be an exact reproduction, in monochrome, of the scene at which the camera was pointed.

The scene at which I had pointed my camera, using my trusty Actinometer to judge the exact exposure required, might or might not turn out to look like the marking of a heel and the drag of a body. Who would drag a body to a pool only a few inches deep?

When I allowed myself a peep, the picture had begun to emerge, showing the faintest contour in the ground, and the shape of a boulder.

It is a fine line between developing and over-developing, just as between telling the truth and a little bit more, or less, than the truth. What would this image say, except that I was on the wrong track, had allowed my imagination, and Harriet's childish fears, to run away with me?

I poured the developer back into the measure glass, set the dish on end and tilted the plate out of it, gripping the edges with my fingertips. The detail looked foggy but the dark rock was clearly visible and made me believe the negative was sufficiently developed.

Each time I take a sheet of self-toning printing out paper from its wrapper, there is a sense of wonder, and delight. Photographic material is treated so carefully by the manufacturers, so reverently packaged that it is a joy to handle. If only life took such good care of humanity! I placed the glossy side against my negative, fixed the back of the frame in position, and carried it through the kitchen, to place in the light.

By then I was ready for my bed. The bedroom door stood slightly ajar. I pushed it open, and only then heard the faintest of meows.

Sookie blinked when I switched on the light. She lay in the bottom drawer of my dresser, which I had left open when taking out a cardigan. I knelt down to take a closer look. She stared at me reproachfully. *Don't just gawp, fetch me some food.* Blind kittens squirmed, piling themselves on top of each other as they groped for her nipples. A black one, two black and white, two tabby, and then a strange looking little hybrid, ginger and tabby and white. Six kittens.

I sighed and went downstairs for milk and victuals.

A lamb bleated in my bedroom drawer. A child tugged my hand. Mrs Sugden, who was not Mrs Sugden said, 'Six children'. Sookie and her kittens came into focus in the developing tray. I could not find my way out of the dark wood and it was not Batswing Wood. The path led some-where else, to a shallow lagoon, where a body lay.

When I woke my own voice had spoken in the dream, crying, 'It's not deep!'

The person who dragged the body to the lagoon was like me. He, or she, thought the water would be deep and that a man with stones in his pockets would sink without a trace. Ethan's body had been dragged to the lagoon, and then moved. But where?

TUESDAY

You can allus tell a Yorkshireman — but you can't tell him much.

Traditional

One

Jim Sykes woke on Tuesday morning knowing for sure that something about this Mary Jane and the missing husband chimed wrong. He intended to pick out the false note.

Sykes stood at the kitchen sink, bobbing down to see himself in the mottled mirror propped against the window. He slicked his hair. Looking through the mirror, he saw his son, Thomas, seated at the table, spooning porridge into his gob.

'I'm borrowing your bike, Thomas.'

The lad's jaw dropped. Not a pretty sight, with a mouthful of porridge. 'Aw, Dad!'

'Shut your mouth, there's a tram coming up Woodhouse Lane.'

'How'm I gonna get to work?'

'Run.'

'Aw, Dad!'

Sykes put his hand in his pocket and fished out a tanner. 'You're best off on the tram till you find where you can safely park your bike.'

'I know where to safely park it.' Thomas picked up the coin, weighing up the inconvenience against the bribe.

'What'll I say to people? They know I come on a bike.'

'Well, today you've come by tram.'

After he had pedalled half a mile up Otley Road, Sykes wished he'd let Thomas have his way and take the bike. It was too long since he'd been in the saddle and it took a greater amount of puff than he'd ever remembered.

Poor Thomas. Once you were old and out in the world a long time, you forgot what it was like to be the lad among a posse of men, not knowing what to say about this or that, not having the words for the simplest of things. Thomas had set himself up as the apprentice who came on the bike. Now here he was, a day into the job, being the lad who caught the tram. It was enough to confuse a young fellow.

Sykes felt the sweat rolling down his back. Why didn't he think of it before? He turned into North Lane. He'd catch the train, himself and his bike on the train from Headingley Station. At the thought of it, he pedalled with new vigour, holding on with one hand, loosening his tie. The breeze tickled his cheeks and cooled his throat.

The station master held the watering can steady above the potted floral display. 'Nay lad, you'll not get to Great Applewick from here. You need to go into Leeds and change trains.'

Sykes sighed. He took out a large hanky and mopped his brow. Some travelling salesman he would turn out to be. On the rear of his bike he had strapped a brown attaché case, full of neatly folded ladies' stockings and men's socks. Sykes's cover, as he carried out his investigations into the disappearance of Ethan Armstrong, was to be a traveller in hosiery. Last night, he had visited his market trader friend who owed him a favour or two from the old days. If Sykes needed to do any observing, he would take out his bicycle repair kit and mend a puncture. Slowly.

By the time he'd got lost – wouldn't let on to Mrs Shackleton about that – and then found his way along Great Applewick High Street, it was nearly noon.

Holding a mental picture of the place as described by Mrs Shackleton, he followed the High Street, turned right along a row of terraced houses, and left onto a track.

Now he wished he'd stayed in the town, found a hostelry and refreshed himself. Just as he considered turning around and retracing his wheel marks, he noticed that the grass by the side of the track turned a greyish white. He must be close to the quarry. No point in attempting to "observe" there. In his brown suit on his boy's bike, he would be a figure of fun within a minute of arrival. He would bear right, which should take him on to Nether End.

He slowed down as he drew near to what he took to be Mary Jane's cottage.

If he were still on the force, there would have been some well thought out cover for him, though he could not think what. No nearby hedge stood in need of trimming. The dry-stone wall deserved a little attention, but if he busied himself with that he would make a pig's ear of the venture, not to mention being wrongly dressed. No. The only thing for it was to keep a good distance between himself and the cottage, and observe.

The dilapidated stone wall gave him the advantage of being able to clamber over it, haul his bike after him and crouch unobserved. If spotted, he could claim to be mending his puncture off the road, so as not to be knocked down by non-existent traffic.

After almost an hour watching the cottage, Sykes's

right leg with its pins and needles had him near screaming point. For all he knew, Mary Jane was out to market. Only the knowledge that women did their housework in the mornings kept him as close to his spot as lichen clung to the wall.

The cottage door opened. He peered over the wall cautiously. Kate had said that Mary Jane may go somewhere, and to watch her.

A girl came out first, followed by a boy. They turned to wave, and then hurried along the lane, as if they would be late back to school. They had been home for their dinner. Mary Jane stood in the doorway and waved until they reached the bend in the lane. From behind, Sykes could not get much of a look at her, only her piled-up hair, the grey dress and the ties from her white apron.

Sykes's stomach rumbled. His head throbbed. His calves ached like billy-o. The woman wasn't going anywhere. He was wasting his time. He rubbed his hands to try and bring some feeling back into the fingers. Do a few squats. Remember that physical training instructor from his early days in the force. Back straight, knees bend, up down, up down. If anyone walked by this wall they'd think he'd escaped from a loony bin. He looked at his watch. Only half past one. Go somewhere, woman, if you're going. Sykes risked standing, pushing himself to his feet like an old man. Leg swing, leg swing, holding the wall. That felt better. Arm swing, left right, left right. Don't push your luck. Down behind the wall. Crouch and observe. Who owned this field? Would some irate farmer turn up, bull in tow? It's your own fault if you're gored, man.

At ten minutes to two o'clock, the door opened.

Mary Jane stepped out. She locked the door, and

pushed the key through the letterbox. She wore a grey, calf-length coat and brimmed hat, black stockings and black ankle boots. She did not carry a bag. Sykes watched her, noted her height, about five feet four, the jut of her slender shoulders, the way she walked, head erect, very straight. She held herself like Mrs Shackleton, something contained and untouchable about her. The difference was that where Mrs Shackleton walked quickly, like a person with an appointment to keep, her sister Mrs Armstrong moved slowly, as though she had a long way to go before nightfall and must pace herself.

This way of walking would make it difficult for Sykes to follow her on the bike, especially downhill. But he dared not risk leaving the bike by the side of the wall. Losing it would be too high a price.

He lifted the bike across the wall and placed it down gently. Still stiff from the long watch, he climbed over the wall, knocking a stone loose. Too bad.

Sykes mounted his bike. He thought he looked every inch the commercial traveller, though he wished that instead of hosiery the brown attaché case contained a morsel of bread and cheese.

Riding was agony now, torture. He tried peddling while raising himself from the saddle. *You can have your bike back, Thomas. Never again.*

Mary Jane looked neither right nor left as she walked past the mill. Sykes listened to the clanging music of the looms, admired the cathedral arches of the mill windows, and thanked God that he didn't work in such a place.

She turned up a narrow lane, crossed a bridge. Someone coming the other way across the bridge acknowledged her but they did not stop to speak. If this were Rosie, she would be stopping on every corner to pass the time of day and would be a devil to follow. Mary Jane was easy. No one caught her in conversation.

Ah, so that's where you're going. She entered the railway station. Sykes leaped onto the bike, forgot his aches and pains and pedalled as fast his legs would allow. He wanted to be in the queue behind her, and listen when she asked for a ticket.

She had already gone through the barrier when he arrived. He spotted her, on platform one.

'Is number one the platform for the Leeds train?' Sykes asked at the ticket desk. He guessed she may be going there to connect with another train.

'Aye. Train in three minutes.'

Sykes bought a ticket. He wheeled his bike through. Now there would be the complication of putting his bike in the luggage van and having to lose sight of her. Couldn't be helped. He admired Mary Jane's timing.

The train steamed in. An elderly man opened a carriage door for her. She nodded an acknowledgement and stepped elegantly into the train, with a smooth unhurried movement.

The muscles in Sykes's arms ached as he manoeuvred the bike into the luggage van.

It was a relief to stand upright.

The guard blew his whistle. The train slowly left the station. Its sound and movement lulled Sykes into a reverie. But when it stopped, he peered out – just in case.

She wasn't going to Leeds. This was Horsforth. She was getting off. Confound the woman. Sykes leaped into action, bumping into the conductor as he grabbed his bicycle, apologising, saying this was an emergency, thrusting the ticket under the conductor's nose, pushing his way out of the carriage and onto the platform.

He need not have worried. Mary Jane strolled leisurely from the station. Sykes followed, wheeling his bike through the barrier, feeling foolish. He could have taken the train to Horsforth this morning. It would have shortened his ride considerably. The train did not go from Great Applewick to Headingley, but it did go to and from Horsforth.

Mary Jane left the station, like an actress making an entrance. She strode in a stately fashion, as though a brass band marched behind her.

By the kerb outside the station, Sykes paused, as if resting a moment, and checked his pockets.

Mary Jane stood still and looked about her. From further down the road, a man climbed out of a Wolseley. He wore a good, dark suit. A cashmere coat was draped over his shoulders. He walked with an easy, confident stride. She went to meet him. All he did was touch her hand but there was something in the touch, in the way they fell into step and turned together. They would not notice him even if their backs were not turned to him, so absorbed were they in each other. The man helped her into the car, in a slow and deliberate manner.

The motor pulled away from the kerb.

Sykes forgot his saddle soreness and began to pedal, and pedal, and pedal. He freewheeled downhill, keeping the motor in sight, until it drew up outside an inn. He would kick himself if this turned out to be some wild goose chase and the woman was not Mary Jane Armstrong. What if he had watched the wrong cottage? No. Dismiss that thought. It was her all right.

The man stepped out of the car. He opened the door and offered his hand to the woman. Head erect, as if she stepped from fancy motors every day of the week, she glided onto the pavement. Together, they entered the inn, going not in the front door, but round the side.

Sykes cycled closer, wheeled his bike to the back of the inn and padlocked it to a railing. No assignment was worth the loss of Thomas's bicycle. He unfastened his traveller's attaché case from the carrier. Then he remembered to remove his bicycle clips.

The polished oak door swung open into a vestibule with inner doors on either side, half glass panelled. To his left, picked out in dark green leaded lights, were the words TAP ROOM, and to the right, SNUG. He decided on the snug with the guess that from there he would have a view across the bar into the LOUNGE.

A waiter in long white apron stood behind the counter, polishing a glass with great concentration. He wore his hair in the style of Rudolph Valentino, darkened with pomade and slicked back. His small moustache was equally well pomaded. He turned to face Sykes, with a cheery, 'What can I get you, gov?'

'Do you have food on?'

'We do. Pie and peas.'

'Then I'll have plate of pie and peas and a pint of your house bitter.'

'Good choice, sir.'

The waiter disappeared. Sykes guessed he had gone to the kitchen to place the pie and peas order. While he was gone, Sykes looked across the bar into the lounge. No sign of the car driver and the lady.

Sykes found his way through the lounge, out to the back where a pair of lavatories sported newly painted doors that neither reached the lintel of the doorway nor the ground. Sykes went inside. Neatly cut squares of newspaper hung on a nail. He availed himself of the facilities, then returned to the snug. His pint sat on the table, along with a knife and fork.

Through the window, he saw the motor, gleaming in the afternoon sun. There would be some other dining room, a function room upstairs, perhaps a private room. This couple did not wish to be seen together in public.

Sykes took a long drink of the foaming pint, and then wiped the back of his hand across his mouth.

'Here you are, sir.' The waiter balanced the plate on the palm of his hand. The sharply folded starched white teacloth over the waiter's arm came perilously close to Sykes's left eye.

What will they rush me for this, Sykes asked himself. You were always charged well for clean aprons and snowy white cloths.

'Thank you.' Steam and a succulent odour of gravy rose from the pie. 'Looks good.'

Well, hang it. Whatever the cost, he deserved this after his morning's exertions, for effort if not for results.

The waiter nodded at the attaché case. 'Traveller are you?'

'After a fashion. Hosiery and such like.'

'Ladies' stockings?' The Rudolph Valentino waxwork waiter looked suitably impressed.

'Some,' said Sykes. 'I'll open the case for you after I've had my dinner, if you like.'

The waiter shook his head sadly. 'Out of my reach I shouldn't wonder.'

'You never know,' Sykes said cheerily, cutting into the pie.

'Enjoy it.'

'I intend to.'

Moments later, the waiter was back, bringing a second pint. 'On the house.'

'Cheers!' said Sykes, glumly wondering if this was meant to cost him a pair of stockings. If so, he should have his stockings-worth. He nodded through the window. 'That's a fine motor.'

'It is.'

'Belongs to the landlord?'

'No. He hasn't given up the horses yet. That's the colonel's.'

'Colonel Ledger?' Sykes stabbed a guess.

'Aye. You know him?'

'Know of him that's all. I suppose everyone round here does. Do you think he'll be interested in a pair of stockings?'

The waiter smiled. 'He could well be, but it'll be more than my life's worth to bring it up. Mind you, he's an approachable chap. You can talk to him, not like his late father.'

He retreated behind the bar, polished a glass, and then disappeared.

Sykes ate slowly, savouring the pie. Not in every job would there be the good excuse to sit in an inn beyond your means and enjoy a leisurely dinner. He laid down the knife and fork, but left some beer at the bottom of his glass. How long could he sit here without looking like a man who had nothing to do? There was not even the excuse of keeping out of the rain. It was a fine day out there.

Well, he would risk it. He took out his notebook. Travellers had to keep a note of their stock after all, and plan visits. Here would be as good a place as any to loiter over his paperwork.

The waiter appeared again behind the bar. 'Anything else, sir?'

'No. But I'll pay for what I've had.' Sykes pushed the pencil behind his ear.

He walked across to the bar, carrying his plate with him.

'Thanks,' the waiter said.

Sykes paid and went back to his seat. As an afterthought, he opened the attaché case and took out a pair of stockings. 'My compliments.'

'That's very swell of you,' the waiter said. 'I wasn't angling for . . .'

'I know you weren't. But the food was good, the ale superb, and you gave me a free pint. What more could a man want?'

Except, in future, a little more information. Always good to have someone to come back to.

'Excuse me, sir.' The waiter went to answer a bell.

Sykes picked up his case. It would look odd to stay here much longer. Besides, the place would be shutting soon.

In the yard, he put on his bicycle clips and unlocked the bike slowly. He re-fastened the attaché case to the carrier, and snailed his bike along the yard.

The man and woman came through the side door and walked to the motor. They were not touching. There was about a foot of space between them. Sykes wished he could read that space, and work out what it meant.

Courteously, the man extended his hand to help her into the car. She seemed to demur and would have walked away, but he insisted. She climbed in, a little awkwardly, Sykes thought.

He expected the car to turn and climb the hill in the direction it had come, but it went down, and so he followed.

153

The man drove with one hand on the wheel, and the other on the woman's shoulder.

By the time Sykes reached the bottom of the hill, the car was drawing away. The woman stood on the other side of the road, at the tram stop that would take her back to Great Applewick.

Two

'A late lunch,' Dad had agreed.

It was already the middle of the afternoon; a very late lunch indeed. And I was not sure there would be enough fuel in the tank for me to reach Wakefield.

The Jowett and I powered along familiar routes through the smoky city, past warehouses, mills and engineering works. Grime darkened my motoring goggles. Wiping them with gloved fingers did not help much. And then the world opened into countryside, fields, pit shafts, and ramshackle cottages.

At Newton Hill, I stopped for fuel. As I climbed from the car, a stocky red-haired attendant appeared from a hut. He wore dark blue overalls and brought the reassuringly powerful smell of engine oil in his wake. 'Come far have you?'

'Just from Leeds. Would you top up the spare can, too, please?'

I was glad to stretch my legs and shake off the dust. My day had started with a vividly disturbing dream in the early hours. A ghostly Miss Trimble stood beside the bench in the churchyard, wearing a moleskin-coloured dress, her head half turned towards me. On either end of the bench sat two spectres coated in white quarry dust, all three fighting for attention, all speaking at once. What did the dead say?

Miss Trimble murmured, 'The Ladies' Friendship Group will go to bits without me . . .'

The dead shepherd said, 'My dog Billy, he listens for my footsteps.'

Ethan's words vanished before I caught them.

'Off into Wakefield, miss?' the attendant called to me.

'Yes. Being taken to lunch by my father.'

'All right for some!' He whistled as he filled the tank.

The sun shone, and made the world a more cheerful place, for those not pestered by ghosts from the past.

All these years, I had chosen not to think about being adopted, pushed it to the back of my mind. Now, thanks to Mary Jane, the information exploded, and kept on exploding.

Every family is complicated in a different way. I can entirely hold onto the whole lineage of my adoptive mother's family. The first baron earned ennoblement as a thank you for his niftiness with a pen on behalf of Elizabeth I. Mother drew it all out for me on a sheet of foolscap when I was five. She let me crayon the squares that denoted generations. She provided me with an atlas so that I could pinpoint her ancestors' land-grabs.

The attendant finished filling the tank. He began to wash flies and dirt from the windscreen. 'Don't know how you saw through this, miss.'

'You're doing a grand job,' I said. But my thoughts were elsewhere.

Dad's family is military. He was the first to find his way into the police force. One entire shelf of the family china cabinet holds polished medals, won in campaigns dating back to the late seventeen hundreds.

My husband Gerald's family also has certain features that allow me to get the hang of them. They crossed the border from England to Scotland and back again. When I think of the Shackleton family, my image is of a kilt-wearing exodus from Edinburgh of clever women and medical men.

Where do I fit into any of this remarkable history?

Nowhere. If we go by blood, I have as much notion of family history as the sparrow pecking at something by the petrol pump.

When I was about seven, Mother told me that I was adopted, and tried to explain what it meant. After the explanation, she took a quarto sheet and said did I want to have it drawn? I said no, and scribbled on the sheet.

By turning up unannounced, Mary Jane had forced me to look at a bloody great fault line running through my own history. My blood ties were to Mrs Whitaker, Barbara May, and the lost brother, cousin and uncle who died in the Great War.

'All done,' the attendant said.

I settled my bill and gave him a tip for his cheerfulness. He was a man who loved his work.

As I drove away, I could not shake off the image that Mary Jane had planted in my mind: an infant being carried from a Wakefield house in the crook of my father's arm.

I parked in the Bull Ring, just as if I had come on the tram, swapped my motoring bonnet for a navy Sans Souci wide-brimmed hat, tucked my big coat in the back of the motor, and then walked to Cross Square, already ten minutes late, and Dad is so very punctual.

We had arranged to meet in Websters. That was the place Mother and I used to haunt before I was married, when we were on one of our shopping expeditions. It seemed strange to be meeting Dad there, among the smartly dressed shoppers.

Dad waved to me, stood up, and drew out my chair. Heads turned discreetly in our direction. Dad, having shed his gabardine raincoat, looked striking in his West Riding Constabulary uniform. At six feet tall, he is not a man to pass unnoticed.

He smiled.

'Sorry I'm late, Dad. I stopped for fuel.'

'It's all right. Our new Chief Constable is out and about today so there's no one will be looking at a watch.' He pointed to the menu. 'I've ordered for us. Hope that's all right. I knew you wouldn't be much longer.'

'What am I having?'

He looked a little sheepish. 'I asked for the mince for us both. I've got a bit of a toothache and I don't want to do much chewing. But if you'd rather . . .'

'The mince will be grand.'

He leaned forward, his eyes twinkling with anticipation. 'Now what's all the mystery? You don't usually ask Mrs Sugden to telephone me at work and arrange lunch.'

I unfolded my serviette.

'Did she get it wrong?' Dad raised an eyebrow. 'Was I meant to ask your mother along as well?'

'No. I wanted to talk to you. Well, both of you really, but I thought if I talked to you first . . .'

The more I muttered and prevaricated the worse it would be. I know Dad so well and I could see straight away that he thought I had news about me and Marcus Charles. I guessed that Aunt Berta had been talking to Mother about how much time I spent with Marcus during my week in London.

158

I could hear my aunt's voice, loud and clear across the telephone lines. 'Ginny, my dear, Kate was off with that policeman chappy of hers no end of times, and did I see him? No. Did I hear anything? No. But something's going on, believe me.'

Dad says that if the constabulary were half as good in making use of the telephone as Mother and Aunt Berta, communications in the force would be greatly improved.

What he said next confirmed my opinion. 'Your Aunt Berta tells us she was sorry not to meet Inspector Charles when you were in London. He sounds a good fellow.'

'Yes he is.'

'You know, you mustn't feel obliged to carry on with your detective agency for the sake of Jim Sykes. I know it was my suggestion that you take him on in the first place, but he'd find another job. And so would Mrs Sugden.' He looked at me and at once realised his blunder. 'Am I jumping in with two left feet?'

'Yes you are. Dad, I don't know what Aunt Berta said, but you know what she's like for matchmaking. I've no plans to give up my work, or leave my little house.'

'Sorry, only . . .'

'The reason I wanted to see you, Dad . . . I don't know where to begin. It's nothing to do with Marcus, or my visit to London.'

'What then?'

No other way than to just begin, just say it. 'Someone arrived on my doorstep in the early hours yesterday. There's a mystery surrounding her husband's disappearance. She's got it into her head that I'm the person to find him.'

Dad nodded. 'I can see why she would think that. You have had some success in that department.'

'Her name is Mary Jane Armstrong. Her maiden name was Whitaker.'

For a moment, he looked puzzled, and then the penny dropped. 'Whitaker?'

'Yes.'

'From Wakefield?'

I nodded. 'She says she was brought up in one of the Yards off Westgate.'

'White Swan Yard?'

'That's the one.'

'Well then, she's picked the right name and right yard. Do you believe she's genuine?'

'I think she's my sister, yes. We don't look all that much alike, but there's something there, some connection. She has two children and, oddly enough, the girl reminds me of myself when I was her age. About ten.'

He picked up a knife with his right hand, passed it to his left hand and back again before returning it to the table.

'I suppose there was always a chance this could happen. How did she find you?'

I gave a brief account of how one of my other sisters had kept track of me.

Dad leaned forward. He spoke quietly. 'You don't have to do it you know, if you don't want to. You can pass the case to the police.'

'I already have, or tried to, and so did Mary Jane. The local sergeant mounted a search on Saturday night but drew a blank.'

'Where does she live?'

'Great Applewick.'

'Do you want to tell me about the case?'

'Well yes, I think I should because it's not as straight-forward as it seems. There was another death yesterday, a

160

Miss Trimble, and I can't help but connect them. There ought to be a post mortem to ascertain cause of death, but I believe the doctor will sign the death certificate without one.'

He began to look interested, immediately grasping what was unspoken. We could pick up the case and run with it through our meal and beyond. But for once what was uppermost in my mind was more personal, closer to home. 'Before we get on to that, I'm hoping you'll tell me something.'

The waitress brought our mince, potatoes and peas, nicely covered with suspiciously dark gravy.

'What do you want to know?' Dad asked, when the waitress had gone.

'I'm not sure. Mother once or twice broached the subject of my adoption. I suppose she thought she had to. But I didn't want to know at the time. Now there's no choice.'

'Wouldn't you be better talking to your mother about it?'

'Not yet. Only when I've sorted out my thoughts. You see, Mary Jane said *you* came to fetch me. She claims she tried to stop you.'

'I don't remember that. There were other children about.'

'So she's right. You carried me from the house.'

'Your mother was outside. I'd borrowed a motor. Ginny wouldn't come in. I'm not sure what she was afraid of. Perhaps she thought there might be tears, or a scene. Your mother upsets easily.'

'That's why I want to have everything clear in my mind. If you can answer my questions, then all I will have to do is tell Mother that I've finally made a connection with my original family. I don't want it to be some great drama.'

God knows there had been enough of those. Mother has not got over the loss of Gerald any more than I have.

Dad concentrated mightily on chewing mince, and crushing a piece of potato with his fork. He was trying to eat using only the left side of his mouth.

'You need to see the dentist, Dad.'

'I know. Only you know my opinion of those fellows.'

'Make an appointment all the same.'

'I will.' He swallowed. 'Heard about a new tooth wallah opened up somewhere off Kirkgate. Thought I'd give him a try.'

'Do. Shall I come with you?'

'That'd look fine wouldn't it?' He forked half a dozen peas. 'What else do you want to know?'

'Why that family? Why did the Whitakers give me up?'

Dad laid down his knife and fork. If we had not been in a public place, I swear he would have stood up and strode about the room – a combination of toothache and uneasiness. He frowned.

'Your mother and I . . .' He paused. This was how it would be now. Even the word mother would ring with a different sound. 'We'd been married for three years. She was impatient for children. We'd never discussed adoption, but one day I arrived home early. She wasn't there. When I asked where she'd been, it was to the Bede Home . . .'

'The orphanage?'

'Yes. They had these annual pound days, when people gave a pound of flour, a pound of sugar, and so on, and she'd taken part in that. Turned up with I don't know how many pounds of this and that she'd collected from her friends. That was when I knew. We chaps don't always see into a person's heart. Well, it stayed with me, the thought of her going to the Bede Home, and what she said about all the boys there. They were all boys. I kept half expecting her to suggest adopting one. But she didn't. There came one of those cold, foggy days in October – I went home feeling very downhearted. One of my best men had died suddenly, a heart attack. He was just forty-five years old, with eleven children.'

'Eleven?'

'Kate, it was the last century. There was little or no knowledge of . . .'

I knew what he meant without his having to continue. If it had not been for Marie Stopes and her ilk, I would not have dared what I had with Marcus last week. But it did set me thinking. If my natural mother had been so damned fertile, why had I not managed to produce a child before Gerald was snatched away?

'You were just a few months old. Mrs Whitaker was forty-four, and worn out. She had daughters old enough to take care of you, but they had to go out to work. I had not thought when I went home and told Ginny the story that she would decide to visit Mrs Whitaker. But that's what she did. And that evening, she told me that she wanted us to adopt you.'

'As simple as that?'

He hesitated, and in that moment I knew that it had not been at all simple. My mother would have weighed up all sorts of probabilities. Knowing her as I did, I guessed that she had inspected the other children to make sure they were physically sound and had their wits about them.

Dad said slowly, 'The moment she saw you, she wanted to take you home. We talked about it, and . . . I'm sure your family didn't want to part with you, but under the circumstances . . .'

I nodded. I would not help him with this. It was up to him to tell me what I wanted to know, and I would not divert him by questions.

'Go on,' I said, having picked up this little policeman's phrase from Marcus Charles.

'Your mother never kept it from you that you were adopted, as you know. But you were not curious as a child. Once the twins had arrived, you seemed more determined than ever to be of our family, and no other.'

That was true. I remembered well enough my baby brothers brought from the nursing home, and feeling protective towards them, and wanting them to hurry up and grow so that I could play with them, and boss them about.

Dad continued. 'Your mother had several pretty speeches planned, in case you asked her questions, but you never did.'

Why would she have needed pretty speeches, I wondered, except to cover something sordid? 'Did money change hands?' I asked.

He shook his head. 'No. I made sure that the family benefited from the police benevolent fund, and a collection was taken. Work was found for the older children. When two boys wanted to go to Canada, I wrote them a letter of introduction to the mounted police.' He smiled. 'They'd spent weeks learning bareback riding at a farm in Outwood. I believe they've done well for themselves.'

'Do the family still live in White Swan Yard?'

He knew exactly who I was asking about, not "the family", but my mother.

'Mrs Whitaker lives in the second house on the right. I call on her from time to time. She asks about you.'

A sudden heaviness filled me so that I felt glued to the

chair. If a fire bell rang, I would have to be carried out.

The waitress appeared and asked brightly whether we wanted pudding. We did not, but ordered a pot of tea.

When she had gone, he said, 'I expect you'll want to meet Mrs Whitaker?'

'I suppose I should. She must be getting on.'

'Well into her seventies. I'm glad you've asked me about her. So often in life we leave something too late.'

Fortunately, he did not press me as to when I would go. Something told me it would be better to see my mother, and tell her, before I went to visit this other mother, in White Swan Yard.

We sat in silence for a while until the tea came. I stirred the pot, and then poured.

'I shall have to let it cool,' Dad said, rubbing at his jaw.

The toothache did not stop him spooning in plenty of sugar.

'Tell me,' he said, 'this missing husband of Mary Jane's. Did you make much headway?'

'No. And it's a very strange case. His children, his daughter at least, saw him lying motionless in the quarry. And now he's nowhere to be found.'

'Motionless?'

'Dead. I believe he was murdered and that someone was still there, lurking nearby, and disposed of the body.'

'The local sergeant, you said he had the quarry searched.'

'Yes. I could be wrong. Harriet could be wrong, she's the little girl, but somehow I don't think so. The sergeant chooses to disbelieve Harriet – a fanciful tale. He thinks because Ethan's tools are gone he's left, after an argument with his wife. And then the death of the vicar's sister, Miss Trimble. I'm sure there was something she could have told me. I know this sounds far-fetched.'

Dad stirred his tea. 'The missing man, what's his name?'

'Ethan Armstrong.'

Dad's spoon came to a halt. He stared at me.

'Ethan Armstrong, of Great Applewick?'

'Yes.'

'And he works as . . .?'

'A stonemason.'

'Ah.'

'What is it?'

He began to stir again, forgetting that the sugar must be long dissolved.

'Katie, I'd like you to come back to the station with me. I want you to tell me everything you know.'

'But . . .'

'It'll be best if I don't say more. But of course if I have details then . . . there'll be a much greater chance of finding him.'

He was not looking me in the eye as he took a sip of tea. He winced as he did so, but that could have been because of his troublesome tooth.

Dad took my arm as we crossed the Bull Ring, as though he half expected me to walk under an electric tram. He chatted away as we strolled down Wood Street.

His words floated away.

Mrs Whitaker lived in the second house on the right, in White Swan Yard.

Dad held onto my arm, though we were safely out of the way of tramcars. 'Your mother hopes you'll come over to stay for a couple of days. She dragged me to the Empire last week to see *Blood and Sand*. And there's something on at the Grand that she talked about. *Orphans of the*

Storm, that was it. I'll happily get you tickets if you want to see it.'

Second house on the right, in White Swan Yard.

We were on Back Bond Street, and in a moment would walk across the threshold of the red brick West Riding Constabulary building.

Second house on the right, in White Swan Yard.

I stopped. Never had I felt less like giving a statement, which was what he was asking me to do. Poor Dad. He had done his best to make this seem like a routine matter that would take a moment. But I knew him too well. Why had he changed so quickly when he heard Ethan Armstrong's name?

I had wanted to wash my hands of the case, and leave it to someone else – Sergeant Sharp, Jim Sykes – but now I realised this was my case. Mary Jane had asked me.

White Swan Yard, the second house on the right.

Something did not feel right about accompanying my father to the station.

'Why, Dad? Why are you suddenly interested? Before you heard Ethan's name you were quite happy to leave it with the local sergeant.'

Dad had assumed his professional manner. He was no longer my father, but the superintendent, speaking calmly, as if he were addressing a public meeting instead of his daughter. 'The man's missing. It's our jurisdiction. I shall check whether a report has come through.'

'Anything I tell you will be second hand from Mary Jane and Harriet and . . .'

'Exactly.' Dad held the door for me. 'You've already covered the ground. That could save us a great deal of time.'

'Dad! You're asking me to . . .'

But we were already inside the building and walking through the lobby, the tap-tap of my low heels echoing across the tiled floor. We passed a plain-clothes man on the stairs. Dad nodded to a young fellow who carried a heavy file of papers; he spoke to the chap in a low voice.

In his office, Dad drew back the chair for me, and sat down behind his desk.

I heard the strain, my reluctance, as I said, 'Mary Jane gave her own account in the local police station. I really have nothing to add.'

'Katie, what's got into you? You want to find the man don't you?'

'Yes of course. Only there's something you're not telling me. That's not fair.'

Dad sighed. 'Ethan Armstrong is a person of interest, because of his political activities, let's put it that way. Have you looked round their house?'

'Yes.'

'What did you find?'

I shook my head. 'If he's on your list because of political activities, I'm sure you know the sorts of things I found. Nothing was hidden. He's involved in a trade union. That's not illegal is it? Dad, you know what it's like for men who came back from the war expecting a new world, homes for heroes and all that. It doesn't surprise me that they should try and do something about it.'

'But there are ways and means, Katie. Some of these groups stir up trouble, call for a general strike, call for workers to take over the means of production. They think they're in Russia and it's 1917. They went to war as factory operatives and farm workers, and came back knowing how to kill. There are men who look the same

168

on the outside, but what goes on in their minds cannot easily be read.'

I smiled. 'Dad, he writes letters. There was some stuff about a merger between unions – mine workers and quarry workers – and support for men on strike, or locked out, at a pit where wages have been cut. He collects all sorts of bits and pieces of knowledge by way of newspaper cuttings, and has his own library of books that he lends out. Nothing sinister. Nothing sinister at all. He took a collection for families of striking miners, but there's no money missing or anything like that.'

There was a tap on the door. Dad called out, 'Come in!'

The young man we had passed on the stairs padded silently across the room. He handed Dad a note that said, 'No report on Ethan Armstrong.'

Dad glared at him. 'In future, fold notes if you mean them to be confidential. Not that there is any need. This is my daughter, Mrs Shackleton.'

The young man coloured up, 'Sorry, sir. Madam.'

'Get onto Otley, Simpson. See if they're sitting on a missing person's report on Ethan Armstrong, and a sudden death . . .' He looked at me.

'Trimble, Miss Aurora Trimble of the Vicarage.'

'Yes, sir.' The young man stepped smartly to the door.

Dad interwove his fingers and studied the palms of his hands. His tone was conciliatory. 'I'm sure you're right about Armstrong. It's not me who draws up these Home Office lists, and there's a great deal of local discretion. It's quite likely that Sergeant Sharp is making his own enquiries. He won't have told you that, but he'll be on the case. I'm not asking you to make a formal statement or anything like that . . .'

Aren't you, I thought. That's what it sounded like when you heard Ethan Armstrong's name. Only my reluctance has made you change tack.

'Just tell me about it, Katie. Likely as not by the end of the day it'll be sorted out one way or another. And it's possible a report is on its way through. So what did Mary Jane have to say?'

'If the report will be here by the end of the day ...'

Dad was not to be deflected so easily. 'I'd rather hear it from you.'

There was no escaping the grilling.

'At about five o'clock on Saturday, Harriet took her father some food to the quarry. He was working alone, putting finishing touches to a sundial for Colonel Ledger. Harriet describes seeing her father, and felt sure he was dead. She went for help, to the nearest neighbours – Conroys' farm.'

'Sensible girl.'

'I went to the quarry with her, first thing yesterday morning, and took some photographs.'

'Do you have the photographs with you?'

'They show nothing conclusive.' I took the prints from the satchel and laid them on his desk. 'This is taken behind the hut. You'll see footprints. Nothing unusual in that, but one of them is on the small side. It could be a woman's footprint, or the footprint of a small chap, or a lad. Austin, the little boy, thought there was a goblin behind the hut. There are all sorts of scary stories about the quarry, designed to keep children out. But he could have heard something. Then there's this.'

He studied the photograph of the shallow lake, the foot-print, the drag marks on the damp ground. 'Yes, I can see how this looks. The lake ...'

'That's what I thought. It looks deep, but it's run-off groundwater and rain, quite shallow, not deep enough to hide a body.'

'Are you sure?'

'One of the other masons told me.'

'All the same, we might check.'

'It did occur to me that . . .'

'Go on, Katie. However silly it may sound.'

'Someone who doesn't know the quarry might have thought as I did, and dragged the body to the lagoon. Once he realised his mistake, he would have to find another way of disposing of it.'

'May I keep these?' Dad's fingers itched around the photographs.

I shrugged. 'If you're investigating and I'm not, then they're no use to me. But why so cloak and dagger with me? He's a respectable working man, with an interest in improving conditions. What's so revolutionary about that?'

'Katie.' Dad spoke in his you-know-far-less-than-you-think voice. 'Ethan Armstrong is part of an extensive network. Don't underestimate the motivation of people who want to radically change our society. We have to be careful. These men have access to explosives. And there are still lots of wartime weapons about, brought home by soldiers. All over the country we have to keep an eye on tight-knit groups of politically motivated men, and not just the Irish.'

'I didn't trip over any anarchist bombs or pistols. The Armstrongs live on a dreary lane called Nether End. It's a damp cottage with the benefit of a good roof and a garden at the back where they grow a few vegetables. Ethan Armstrong may have access to explosives but it strikes me he's a man who makes more use of pen and ink.'

171

Dad nodded. 'You're a good judge of character, Katie, but you haven't met him in person remember. From everything you say, this may have nothing whatsoever to do with politics. It could be purely a domestic matter, or some workplace disagreement. There might turn out to be a very simple explanation. Now leave it to us, Katie. Don't go back there.'

It had not been my intention to go back there, yet it surprised me that Dad should issue what amounted to an order. 'You're right that it's difficult for me to be objective. That's why Sykes is in Great Applewick today, taking a look round.'

'Then get him out, please.'

'Dad, what is it you're not telling me?'

Because what I'm not telling you is that Mrs Sugden is also itching to board a tram to Great Applewick to do a little snooping of her own. Helping Sykes with store detection went to her head.

Dad drummed his fingers on the desk. 'You are far too close to this than anyone ought to be. Mary Jane should have shown more thought, more discretion.'

'Discretion isn't the uppermost thought when a woman's husband has gone missing.'

He nodded, and said gently, 'That's the other reason for you to draw back. Leave this to me. And take a tip regarding Harriet's story. You can't always rely on what children say, especially girls of that age. They like to romance. Once they have the limelight they want to keep it, and stick to a tale, no matter how fanciful.'

Three

I had walked the short distance from Back Bond Street to Cross Square enough times that I could point myself in the right direction, like a blinkered horse. But on the corner of Wood Street, an old soldier played such a haunting tune on his flute that he stopped me in my tracks. I dropped a coin in his cap. So many brave men, out in the world trying to scrape something that passed for a living. I wished I had it in me to either not look, or to take up some noble cause.

I thought of Mary Jane's words about who in our family was lost in the war. A brother, a cousin, an uncle. Don't be curious about that family, I told myself. Don't wonder what they are like, whether someone has perfect pitch, a madness for horses, a passion for photography or for Rudolph Valentino, is well read, would have flourished in some sphere of life if given the opportunities I have been given.

What was it Dad had said? Mrs Whitaker had lost heart when her husband died, lost heart for keeping me.

But had all of them lost heart? With ten other children, at least some must have been working, and others big enough to feed and change a baby. They could have kept me.

But I was glad they had not.

Lost heart. Well, I knew how that felt. I had lost heart myself. Lost heart for helping Mary Jane. My reason for sending Sykes into the fray was because I could not face it. Mary Jane should not have come to me. Her father had been in the force. There would have been someone still, someone her mother knew – even my own Dad – to whom she could have turned. She knew from her sister Barbara May that I had lost Gerald. By turning up on the doorstep, she had robbed me of choice. Well, I had that choice back, and I had made it. Let the West Riding Constabulary investigate the death or disappearance of Ethan Armstrong.

The Whitakers were not a family I wanted to be part of. From everything Dad had told me, and that I'd heard from Mary Jane, they struck me as an odd job lot. Bareback riders who set out for the other side of the world; a Nosey Parker cleaner, Barbara May, who had found out where I lived; a lady's maid, Mary Jane, paid by her boss to pose for saucy photographs, and left forever dissatisfied. They were people who went in every direction and none, travelling in circles, meeting themselves coming back. They were a family driven by necessity, with never a moment of leisure to ponder on what might be wonderful in life, or having the capacity to strike out in some useful profession.

But curiosity made me want to see where I came from, not the family, just the yard.

White Swan Yard, second door on the right.

Back through Cross Square, past Bread Street and across Westgate, and there it was: White Swan Yard. I stepped through the opening and into the courtyard. Only a look, that's all. A look at the place.

A slightly sour smell of drains and cabbage mingled with the hoppy, beery aroma from the White Swan. A line of washing hung across the top end of the yard, a greyish sheet, a petticoat and a pair of drawers. Halfway up the yard, a woman in a long black dress and white pinafore scrubbed a windowsill. An enamel bucket on the ground beside her was surrounded by splashes of water. A contented dog lay on the flags, lazily scratching its ear.

No strangers ever came into this yard, I guessed. They would have no reason to do so.

I glanced at the second house on the right. A white curtain covered the lower window pane, and a partly unrolled paper blind shaded the upper part. Step and windowsill were scoured clean. Blue curtains hung at the upstairs window. The door was painted brown.

The door of the first house opened. Small children tumbled out.

Was she there, in the second house, the woman who had given birth to me and had given me up? If I stood here long enough, would some unknown brother come home for his tea, or did she live alone? Perhaps she worked for her living, or looked after grandchildren. I had no idea. There would be one easy way to find out. All I had to do was knock on the door.

But I didn't want to know. This was enough. Just to look. My hand made a fist, but not so that my knuckles would rap on the panel of that door. I left the yard and walked up and down the street, crossed and re-crossed the road, and then came back into White Swan Yard, to the second house on the right.

Eleven kids Mr and Mrs Whitaker produced, and for all I know several misses in between. Who did Mrs Whitaker give away? Me. Logic and sense told me that it was

175

nothing to do with the look of me, the touch of me, the smell of me, and yet how could she do it? Like an unwanted kitten, I was snatched and despatched.

My fist clenched, ready to land a knuckle punch on the door. But I did not need any more complications in my life. Mary Jane had butted in and got in the way of other plans.

Tomorrow I would visit the insurance offices, take on an assignment, I hoped. I would write a letter to my lover, arrange to meet him again soon. On visiting day, I would go to Catterick Hospital to . . . I did not let myself fully acknowledge that I would look for Gerald among men who had lost memories, suffered such injuries that they would forever desire to turn away from the world. Some smaller hospitals in various parts of the country had finally closed their doors, men moved to Catterick. It was an outside chance, but all the same . . .

The brown door of the second house on the right in White Swan Yard took on a life of its own. Every other feature in the courtyard faded to nothingness. There was just me, and that door.

If there were voices indoors, would I hear by inching nearer? Perhaps Mary Jane had taken my advice and even now was telling her mother all her troubles, including reporting the uselessness of that sister who was given up. They'd done the right thing, getting shut of her.

No sound.

What if she dies tonight, this woman who gave birth to me? Would it matter that I never saw her? I could choose not to knock. All I had to do was leave the yard, turn right, walk back to my motor, and drive home.

Dad was right. Let the police help Mary Jane. If ever a matter was a police matter, this was it. I'd said so from the beginning. When the dust settled, then I might come back here, and knock on the door.

Besides, I should tell my real mother first, the woman who brought me up, the one who nursed me better when I was poorly. The one who always moans that no one but me will go to the pictures with her. It's not true of course, but she says it to bring me back.

The sleepy dog on the pavement became bored with staring at me and shut its eyes.

I knocked on the door.

And the window was so close; I could look through it, across the gap between the curtain and the blind. There she was, sitting in a chair by the hearth. Some leisure then, she enjoys a sit down, peace and quiet.

She pushed herself up from the chair, a gaunt, grey-haired woman in a long dark skirt, a navy tabard over a long-sleeved jumper. I glanced away so that she would not see me looking. And then the door opened.

We stared at each other for a moment. Her skin under her high cheek bones was as lined as the tram terminus, criss-crossed with fine wrinkles. Her eyes narrowed, as if she thought she ought to recognise me.

'Mrs Whitaker?'

'Who's asking?'

'Kate Shackleton. You may know me if I say Catherine Hood.'

Her hand went to her heart. What an idiot I am. She could drop dead from shock and it would be my fault.

At the second house on the right in White Swan Yard, a woman dropped dead from shock today when confronted with her long lost daughter. A person close to the family said . . .

Sorry, Mary Jane. I didn't manage to find your missing husband, but gave your mother a nice enough heart attack. Perhaps when Ethan's body turns up you could arrange a double funeral.

But she did not drop dead. Instead, she opened the door wider.

'You better come in.'

As she spoke, she glanced at the mantelpiece as though there might be a clock, to mark the precise moment of the infant Catherine's return. There wasn't.

She did not blink or look in the least surprised but said in a conversational way, as though picking up a topic she had just dropped, 'I thought for a minute I was looking at my aunt Phoebe. You take after her.'

'I was just passing,' I said. 'I won't keep you.'

No more than you kept me.

I glanced around the house. There were few comforts. Apart from the chair she sat in, only a couple of buffets and a table.

She saw me looking. 'You were well off out of it, lass.'

I hadn't meant it to come out in the way it did. 'You had eleven children? Here?'

'Ten, without you. Will you sit down?'

I saw that she meant me to take the chair, but I pulled a buffet from the side of the table and sat on that.

She returned to her chair. 'You were just passing?'

Thirty-two years it had taken me to "just pass".

'I met Dad for a bite to eat in Websters.'

'Very nice.'

'I asked him about you. I thought it was about time we at least said hello. I hope that's all right.'

'It'll be all the same if it's not. You've said it now.' She looked at me from top to toe, my hat, coat, stockings and shoes. 'Did he tell you how it came about that you were taken to live with them?'

'Yes.' She did not use the word adopted. 'You were widowed.'

She sighed. 'Aye, that was it. And I'm sorry you was widowed by the war. Our Barbara May told me.'

'Barbara May seems to know quite a lot about me.'

She nodded with pride at Barbara May's extensive knowledge. 'There's always one knits the family together, remembers birthdays, marriages, deaths, the bairns' names. In our family it's Barbara May. She runs rings round us all. She found out where you live. She said she'd take me up there to see, and we could look through the window if you weren't in. I said no. But now you're here. Is it down to Barbara May that you've come?'

'No. It's because of Mary Jane.'

'Mary Jane?' She drew back her head, pulling her chin into her neck, as if a little more space was needed to take in this piece of unlikely information.

'She came to see me.'

'Did she now? Then she must be in bother. She never goes to see no one unless she needs summat. What's up?'

I wished now I had kept Mary Jane out of it. I wished now I had left this visit to another day. 'You don't see much of her and the children then?'

'No. Mind, Ethan calls in. He's a good lad. If he's at one of his meetings roundabout, he makes a point of coming in, and never empty handed. Allus a couple of eggs, or a corner of ham, or a pound of flour. Once he brought me a chicken.' She chuckled at this extravagance. 'By, it took some plucking.'

I smiled, and stood to go. 'I'll call and see you again another time, if that's all right.'

'If you like. If you've a mind to.'

'Well, goodbye.'

What should I do? Shake her hand, kiss her cheek, or touch her hair? I did nothing. As I stood by the door, she put her hand on my arm.

'What's up with Mary Jane that she came mithering you?'

There was no point in lying. She would find out soon enough.

'Ethan's gone. She hasn't seen him since Saturday.'

She reached round me and unhooked a coat from the back of the door. 'I better go to her.'

'No really, I'm sure . . .'

'I'm the one she should have come to. Will you take me there? I know you've got a motor car. It's blue.'

Barbara May must have told her.

'Pass that shopping basket, eh?'

I picked up a shopping basket from the side of the table.

'We can call and get one or two items, since she won't be expecting us – me at any rate.'

I could say no. I should say no. What the hell was I doing here?

We were outside. She was locking the door and letting the key on its string fall back through the letter box.

The dog looked up. It hauled its old body from the pavement and stood wagging its tail.

As we left the yard, the dog trotted behind us.

'That dog's following us.'

'Oh aye. Benjie's my dog. He won't be left behind.'

At the greengrocer's, and the butcher's, Mrs Whitaker asked for the shopping to be put on the slate, but I paid. Why did I have the feeling I would go on paying, and not entirely in cash?

*

180

She sat ramrod straight for the entire journey, motoring blanket round her shoulders, the large dog in her lap, only its head peering out from the blanket. Sometimes it looked with a worried gaze as we passed through quiet lanes, occasionally barking at nothing. When we were in the noise and smoke of the city, it relaxed and shut its eyes.

This is the best thing I could do, I told myself. Now Mary Jane will have someone who really is family to be with her, and the police to investigate Ethan's disappearance. I can bow out.

It was turning dark when we reached Great Applewick. I followed the familiar road to Mary Jane's cottage. The curtains in the downstairs room were drawn back, the blind up. A candle burned brightly on the window sill, as if to beckon Ethan home.

Mrs Whitaker opened the blanket and out jumped Benjie. The dog ran to the door of the cottage as though he knew all along this was our destination.

I helped Mrs Whitaker from the car and we walked together to the door of the cottage. She opened it and walked straight in. The children were in their pyjamas. Mary Jane sat at the table, drinking tea and smoking a cigarette.

She looked up in surprise. 'Hello, Mam. Didn't expect you.'

'When were you going to tell me?' Mrs Whitaker asked, unbuttoning her coat.

'Grandma!' Harriet ran to Mrs Whitaker who grabbed her and kissed her.

The dog had been relieving himself against the apple tree. He came rushing in. The room grew smaller.

I hovered in the doorway.

Mary Jane looked at me accusingly. 'You said you wouldn't come today.'

'I can't do any more, Mary Jane. The West Riding Constabulary are looking into Ethan's disappearance. It's out of my hands. When I've something to tell you, or there's something I can do, I shall be here.'

Harriet was all ears. Mary Jane stood up and came outside with me, shutting the door behind her, saying, 'Little pigs have big ears.' When we were out of earshot, she said, 'Nothing? Nothing?'

'I haven't abandoned the case.'

'The case? So I'm a case?'

'You know what I mean.'

'Mam'll love this. Turning up here, bossing us all around. That stinking dog of hers. Have you smelled its breath?'

'The children like the dog. It'll divert them.'

'Oh it'll do that. They'll have it on a string taking it round the village.' She drew on her cigarette, the tab so small it must have burned her nicotine-stained fingers. 'Thanks for nothing.'

I opened the door and called goodnight to Mrs Whitaker and the children. Mary Jane went inside, shutting me out.

Just as I climbed in the motor, Harriet ran across, barefoot, holding something. 'Raymond brought this for you. It's pieces of slate from the sundial.'

She handed me a cloth knotted at its four corners, with something hard inside. These would be the flowers that Ethan had carved to disguise the flaw in the slate. If there were four, he had completed it. If three or less, he had been interrupted before the work was finished.

One more piece for the jigsaw, or perhaps not. I put the package on the seat beside me.

'Thanks, Harriet.'

'I'm glad you brought Grandma.'

'So am I. Goodnight then.'

'Goodnight.'

She was still standing in the road when I started the motor. 'Go inside. You'll catch cold.'

'Do you believe me? Do you believe what I said about seeing Dad, because Sergeant Sharp thinks I'm a little liar.'

'Yes, Harriet. I believe you.'

'Has someone killed Dad? And Miss Trimble?'

'I don't know.'

'And do you think . . .'

'What?'

'If I'd taken Dad's dinner to him sooner, would everything have been all right? Is it my fault, Auntie Kate?'

It was the first time she had taken up my invitation to call me auntie.

'None of this is your fault, Harriet. You ask your grandma. She'll tell you the same.'

Four

It was after eight o'clock when I arrived home to a house in darkness. I switched on the light in the hall. The second post lay on the hall table. I walked through to the kitchen, where a mean little fire gave off a sulky glow.

When I tapped on the door to her part of the house, Mrs Sugden did not answer. Back in the kitchen, I built up the fire, turned on the gas ring and filled a kettle.

On the kitchen table were two notes. Note one read,

6 o'clock. Sookie fed and stroked. Looked in three times at two hourly intervals. Kittens satisfactory. Eliz. Merton.

Elizabeth Merton lives across the street. The professor's sister, she acts as his housekeeper.

Note two lay sealed in a manila envelope, with my name on the front, in Mrs Sugden's neat round hand. I took out the small ruled sheet of writing paper.

You are right. It is all hands to the deck in such a case. Taking tram to terminus. Meeting at Spiritualist Church in Great Applewick this evening.

I'd said no such thing about all hands to the deck. Mrs Sugden had got bored with her knitting, run out of library books, and fancied a little nosey sleuthing.

The doorbell rang. I hurried to answer, expecting a weary Mrs Sugden, exhausted by fleeting spirits and the return tram journey, lacking the energy to delve into her bag for the key.

'Hello. You look how I feel.'

It was Sykes. He took a parcel from the saddlebag of a bicycle which he then wheeled into the hall. 'I brought us a fish and chip supper.'

Never had I been so glad to see him. 'Come through to the kitchen. Did you know Mrs Sugden has gone off sleuthing?'

'Aye. She called round to tell Rosie. She said that she knew of a spiritualist church out there, and if she paid a visit, it might yield dividends.'

'What kind of dividends?'

'She reckons that the people who visit the spiritualist church to commune with the departed know everything there is to know about the not yet departed.'

I mashed tea.

Sykes opened the newspaper parcel. In an instant, the kitchen smelled like a fried-fish shop.

I put the teapot and cups on the table and turned to open the cutlery drawer.

'Forget knives and forks. Don't make washing up.' Sykes divided the fish and chips. 'Do you have pickled onions?'

I opened the cupboard door. 'Pickled onions on the top shelf. You'll have to reach them.'

I found a pickle fork, giving it a thorough rinse under the tap; Mrs Sugden goes overboard on the silver polish.

As we tucked into our supper, I broke the news to Sykes that Dad had warned me off investigating on behalf of Mary Jane. 'I'm just glad he didn't have men there today, falling over you and me and Mrs Sugden.'

'You went across?'

'I took Mrs Whitaker to Mary Jane's.'

'Mrs Whitaker?' Sykes speared an onion.

'Mary Jane's mother.' And mine, of course.

'Ah.' The onion fell back into the jar. Sykes had difficulty recapturing it. He wore his *What am I supposed to say next* look.

I sighed, and explained. 'I screwed my courage into my knuckles and rapped on Mrs Whitaker's door.'

White Swan Yard, Wakefield, second house on the right.

'Was this the first time you've seen your ... Mrs Whitaker?'

'Yes, and to hand it to her, she was off to Mary Jane like a shot. A friend in need and all that. It's likely Mary Jane and the children will get more from her visit than from anything I can do.'

What I avoided saying was how I felt about Mrs Whitaker. Sykes would not expect some heartfelt outpouring and I still felt too uncertain of my feelings to know what to think, much less what to say.

'Was Mary Jane pleased to see her mother?'

'Not enchanted, no.'

Sykes offered me a pickled onion, which I accepted. He forked out two more for himself.

I could tell by the concentration with which he munched his extra scraps of crunchy fried batter that he had more to tell. He made a tightly screwed up firelighter of his portion of greasy newspaper. 'I saw Mary Jane today, first in her doorway, waving the kids off to school after their dinner. And then she came out in a smart grey coat and a hat with a flower on and took the train to Horsforth Station.'

'Horsforth? I wonder if that's where the oracle sister Barbara May has fetched up? She's the one that keeps tabs on the whole family.'

'Not unless Barbara May wears a mohair suit, sports a cashmere coat, drives a Wolseley and goes by the alias of Colonel Ledger. They disappeared into a private room at the Station Hotel.'

A chip stuck in my throat. 'I suppose it had to be her, if you followed her from the house?'

He went to the sink, turned on the tap and washed his hands, keeping his back to me. 'You have a similar way of walking. Don't take this wrong.'

'Go on. I won't throw pickled onions at you.'

'How to describe it? Gliding, upright, as if you've got a cooking pot on your head.'

'Thanks.' So what I imagined was my fine deportment, encouraged by Aunt Berta, also belonged to Mary Jane. I would have to ask her sometime whether she was ever made to walk with a dictionary on her head. 'How do you know the man she met was Colonel Ledger?'

'The waiter's a friendly chap, especially if he's given a pair of stockings.'

Little wonder Mary Jane had been cagey with me. Perhaps she had been having an affair with the colonel all these years. The Station Hotel. Colonel Ledger must be

187

worth a fortune, and Mary Jane made do with the Station Hotel.

'Did the waiter say whether these are regular get-togethers for the pair of them?'

'I didn't push it. But I'm sure I could find out.'

I wiped the kitchen table, giving myself time to think. 'Put another cob on the fire would you?' I wanted to show him Ethan Armstrong's papers, and the pieces of the sundial, but I needed time to take in his information about Mary Jane. 'I'm going to check on Sookie and her kittens.'

I needed to be out of the room, to think. My mind raced in a dozen different directions as I pictured Mary Jane and Ledger.

I walked upstairs slowly, carrying scraps of fish for Sookie. She and the kittens were sleeping. On the floor by the drawer was an old newspaper, with an empty dish, and an almost empty saucer. I took them into the bathroom, rinsed them under the tap. When I went back into my bedroom, Sookie was awake and looking at me.

It is always useful to have something new and very definite to worry about. What if she, or one of the kittens, clambered over the back of the drawer into the void? Someone, the obliging Elizabeth Merton say, might come into the room and, unthinkingly, shut the drawer, squashing bodies.

There was nothing I could do about that at the moment, except pull the drawer all the way out. Good idea. Sookie didn't think so. She scowled. Her roof was gone. Some cats just don't allow themselves to be grateful.

'Are you all right?' Sykes called up the stairs as the drawer thumped the floor.

'Yes.' I didn't need him to fuss.

Sykes stood at the bottom of the stairs. 'Rosie does that, gets it into her head to rearrange the furniture all of a sudden. Keeps us on our toes.'

Sykes had made a fresh pot of tea.

In the centre of the kitchen table, I placed the cloth that Harriet had handed to me. Unfolded, it revealed four shards of blue slate, each carved with a delicate flower.

'What's this?' Sykes asked. 'Are you collecting bits of slate now?'

'When Ethan was making the sundial, he came across a flaw in the slate. He carved a flower to cover that flaw, and then intended to do three more. I asked Raymond, the other mason, to search in the broken pieces of slate, to see whether Ethan had finished the work.'

Sykes picked up each flower in turn. 'It looks as if he did finish it.'

'Yes. So he is unlikely to have destroyed his own work in frustration. The colonel suggested there could have been a fault in the slate, some hidden crack that foiled Ethan's best efforts, and that the sundial split at the very last moment. But from looking at these pieces, I'd say he finished it and would have been satisfied.'

Sykes pondered. He was leaving it to me to comment on Mary Jane and the colonel, but he said, 'After today, should we regard what the colonel says as gospel?'

'Probably not.' I rewrapped the pieces of slate in the cloth.

'Of course, this meeting between them this afternoon might have been quite innocent.'

Sykes never thinks anything anyone ever does is innocent. He was trying to make me react. I said, 'If it was innocent, why didn't Mary Jane see him openly?'

Sykes shook his head. 'I don't know. Perhaps she didn't

want to run the risk of going to the house and seeing the colonel's wife.'

I went into the dining room and brought back the papers from Ethan Armstrong's trunk that Mary Jane had pressed me to take.

'Dad won't be too pleased that I have these. His line of enquiry is that Ethan was up to no good, politically. Special Branch have him on a list.'

Sykes let out a whistle. 'Shouldn't you turn these papers in to them? If it's political, it's specialist stuff, Mrs Shackleton.'

'We're specialist people, Mr Sykes. We have to be able to understand all sorts of matters to make our way through this undergrowth.'

'But we're off the case, aren't we?'

'I suppose so. But that doesn't stop us being curious, does it?'

'No,' he said thoughtfully. 'And if the constabulary and special branch are looking through one particular lens, it wouldn't hurt us to glance down the wrong end of the telescope.'

'At the colonel, and my sister?'

He nodded, then added, 'If only to eliminate them.'

'Or not.'

'Or not.'

We divided Ethan Armstrong's papers between us and read carefully.

After an hour, Sykes said, 'They don't want much, these trade unionists. Only to build a new Jerusalem in England's green and pleasant land.'

'I don't think it's quite as unselfish as that. They want a forty-four hour week, better pay and conditions. There's nothing here that would help women and children.'

'Paying a man well helps his family.'

'Not necessarily, Mr Sykes.'

I looked at the names of the union members, and wondered which one might have been a traitor to his comrades. The familiar name was Raymond Turnbull, Ethan's old apprentice, and son of the quarry foreman. I told Sykes of Raymond's comments – that Ethan said they had an informer in their midst. 'Whoever it was reported back which men were willing to go on strike.'

'There's always one,' Sykes said. 'Some people get a thrill out of passing on information. Makes them feel important.' He was picking up the newspapers, glancing at the dates. 'This is odd. Our man Armstrong has all these *Daily Heralds*, and then there's last week's *Wakefield Express*, and look, it has that same ad on the front page, the one you told me about.'

He passed the newspaper to me.

```
A well provided and pleasant lady seeks well
  provided amiable gentleman with a view to
            joining lives and fortunes.
                 Box No. 61
```

The telephone rang. I jumped. 'That might be Mrs Sugden. If she wants a lift back from some godforsaken place, I hope you'll feel up to going because I don't.'

'As long as it's not on that damn bike,' Sykes said. 'I swore I'd never climb on it again, but it was that or cold fish and chips.'

I picked up the receiver.

'Katie?'

'Oh, hello, Dad.'

'How are you?'

'I'm all right thank you.'

'You didn't come to see your mother.'

'No. I shall though. Tomorrow.'

There was a short silence. He was thinking, Good, that means she's listened to me and is leaving the Ethan Armstrong case alone. Or is she? To be sure I had taken his point, he said, 'I just want to tell you, everything is in hand. You needn't worry yourself any more about that matter we spoke of.'

'Good. And, Dad, there's something I should tell you. I called on Mrs Whitaker today, and gave her a ride out to see Mary Jane. I thought that might be best.'

During the six-second silence that followed, I could hear him thinking. Slowly, he said, 'Good idea. It will save you having to be there, won't it?' So that was his message. Loud and clear. I waited, counting to five in my head to see what would come next. He said, 'It's likely there'll be someone up from London.'

'Ah. Do we know who?'

'I have to go. There's someone at the door.'

'Goodnight, Dad.'

'Goodnight, Katie.'

Sykes had heard enough of the conversation to know who I was talking to.

'We're warned off?'

'Doubly warned off. But I'm sure he now owes me explanations. I'd like to know if I'm right that Miss Trimble was poisoned.'

'It's puzzling,' Sykes said. 'The disappearance or murder of Ethan was clumsy, bungled, with his daughter seeing his body, and the body disappearing. Miss Trimble's death was very neat. If you hadn't spotted her through the window and gone in there before her brother came home, her death would almost certainly be put down as natural causes.'

Sykes looked at his hands carefully. They were black with print from the newspapers. 'I don't suppose . . .'

'What?'

'Well, I know we're ordered off the case, but I have all this hosiery and a little case to carry it in. It's sale or return, but it seems a pity to return it when I've not much else to do tomorrow.'

'And you might make a few sales in Great Applewick?'

'Door to door.'

'I don't see why not. Let's go together to this insurance appointment tomorrow morning, and then we'll go our separate ways, and see what the day brings.'

At that moment, the front door opened. A great sigh travelled down the hall, followed by Mrs Sugden's weary footsteps. Something told me she had drawn a blank at the spiritualist meeting, but at least she was home, and safe.

She stood in the kitchen doorway, unpinning her hat. 'It wasn't an entirely wasted visit. I met the housekeeper from Applewick Hall. She and I got on very well.' Sykes raised his particularly mobile left eyebrow at me.

Mrs Sugden came sniffing, peeling off her gloves. 'You've had fish and chips?'

'Yes. Sorry we didn't save you any.'

She snorted. 'I wouldn't thank you for them.'

'Did the housekeeper say much else about the Ledgers?'

'She says the colonel and Mrs Ledger are utterly devoted to each other.'

'Take the weight off your feet.' I drew back the third kitchen chair.

Mrs Sugden unbuttoned her coat and sat down. 'All the staff watched the unveiling of the sundial today. It was Mrs Ledger's birthday, and their wedding anniversary.'

Sykes fetched another cup and poured tea.

Mrs Sugden glanced critically at the tea. 'It wasn't a good night for the spirits.' She smiled. 'Not very useful was it? But the members of the Spiritualist Church welcomed me most warmly. Said join in again any time.' She looked all round, checking the kitchen to ensure we had not made a terrible mess or dropped chips on the clean floor.

Mrs Sugden does not usually omit chapter and verse.

'What else?' I prompted.

'Summat and nowt.' She waved her hand dismissively.

'Something about Mary Jane?'

She sighed. 'The servants at the Hall don't like her.'

'Any particular reason?'

Mrs Sugden almost blushed; something I did not think possible. 'They say she set her cap at the colonel, and that Mrs Ledger had to get shut of her – give her a dowry and marry her off. She was meant to marry a chap from the farm, Bob someone . . .'

'Bob Conroy?'

'That's the one. But Ethan Armstrong swept her off her feet.'

Sykes shot me a questioning look.

'Bob Conroy is Ethan's best friend. I saw him in the churchyard yesterday. He was very upset about Ethan going missing.'

Sykes's fingers drummed silently on the table. 'Was he upset because he was responsible for Ethan's death?'

WEDNESDAY

So a' bade me lay more clothes on his feet: I put my hand into the bed and felt them, and they were as cold as any stone; then I felt to his knees, and so upward, and upward, and all was as cold as any stone.

Shakespeare, *Henry V* II, ii

One

On Wednesday morning, I unfolded my sheet of foolscap notes. Sykes and I had written one each the previous evening. Mine read:

APPROXIMATE TIMINGS
Ethan last seen alive: 1.10pm Saturday by Josiah Turnbull, quarry foreman
5.15pm – Ethan's body found by Harriet
5.50pm – Arthur from farm: no sign of Ethan – sundial intact
6.30pm – MJ to quarry – sundial smashed
7.30pm – search of quarry by Sergeant Sharp, Josiah & Raymond Turnbull and two other quarrymen

QUERIES
What is going on between Col. Ledger and Mary Jane?
Significance of the "well provided woman" advertisement?
Mary Jane – opportunity to 'visit' Ethan at work during afternoon when children shopping. Claims not to have done so.
Miss Trimble reported seeing person (Mary Jane?) in plaid cape at 4 pm.
Who broke the sundial – is this a diversion?
Ethan A. – associates and friends?

Enemies?
Coincidence of shepherd's death in quarry last year?
Link between Ethan's death and Miss Trimble's death?

POSSIBILITIES
Foul play — Ethan attacked; assailant hid when children
approached; assailant hid body when children gone.
If body hidden, cannot be far away, unless moved at night — by
whom?
If Ethan attacked, how? Where are his tools?

My map and matchstick men figures, with arrows from
one to another, were of no great help. In large letters
came the question — WHO BENEFITS FROM ETHAN
ARMSTRONG'S DEATH?

There was a simple answer to the first question. Mary
Jane had Ethan's life insured, but as she had reminded me,
a fit working man was worth more alive than dead. Of
course if he had found out something about Mary Jane that
put their marriage in jeopardy, this would change.

If Mary Jane and Colonel Ledger were having an affair,
and Ethan had found out, then it may be convenient for
the colonel to have Ethan out of the way.

We were off the case. But there must be something that
would shed a little light, if only to satisfy my own curiosity. Once more I picked up the advertisement, that had
reappeared in the Wakefield Express. A well provided
woman seeking a similar mate.

The man who kept a closer eye on newspapers than
anyone else I had ever met was Mr Eric Duffield, local
newspaper librarian at the Herald on Albion Street.
Fortunately, I had sent him a bottle of whiskey at
Christmas, as thanks for his help in the Braithwaite case.

I went into the hall and lifted the telephone receiver. Moments later, Mr Duffield assured me that he would be able to see me at 10.30.

Sookie appeared on the stairs. She padded into the hall at a stately pace. The slightest movement of her head told me that something was required. I followed her into the kitchen. Now I would have to open the door, let her out, and wait for her to come back.

She marched out of the back door, tail straight as a flag-pole. While she was out, I located the trug Mrs Sugden had set aside, put in an old blanket and took it upstairs. Gingerly, I lifted my once immaculate white jumper and its complement of kittens into the trug, counted that all were present and correct, and manoeuvred and pushed the drawer back into place, shutting it firmly. If Sookie didn't like it, she could lump it.

By the time I went downstairs, Sookie was back at the door. She deigned to eat her food in the kitchen, as an indication that she was back to normal.

After our meeting with the director of the Yorkshire Mutual Insurance Company, Sykes and I congratulated ourselves on scooping another assignment. We were to be retained in connection with investigations into insurance fraud.

We parted on Park Row, Sykes to the railway station, carrying his attaché case of hosiery, me to make the short walk to meet Mr Duffield in the offices of the *Herald*.

I did not have to wait long before my courtly friend greeted me and we made our way in the rattling lift to the top floor of the newspaper offices.

'Personal advertisements are perpetually intriguing,' Mr Duffield agreed when I told him about the cutting that had aroused my curiosity, reciting the wording that I now knew by heart.

'A well provided lady, eh?' The lift clattered to a stop. He clanked open the door for me. 'Either the lady in question is casting her net wide or there is a recommended wording – perhaps advised by some matrimonial agency.' He tapped the side of his nose indicating private information to be imparted in his own good time.

Mr Duffield looked just the same as I had seen him last – calm, unhurried, well turned out in his boiled shirt, his fingers black with newsprint. We reached the newspaper library, with its high windows, ancient wooden tables and a multitude of cupboards and filing cabinets. Pale morning light shone through the windows. The air reeked of ink, hair oil and tobacco. Mr Duffield was lord of all he surveyed: piles of newspapers, file drawers of cuttings, an index system that would flummox Special Branch.

'Please.' He drew out a chair beside his desk and bowed me into it before taking a seat himself.

'Would you reply to this?' I asked. 'If you were looking for a wife I mean.'

'That depends,' Mr Duffield said cautiously.

'On what?'

'Was I in much of a hurry, for instance? Perhaps a wife might be required urgently, say if I were a sick man, in need of nursing, or thought I might soon become sick.'

'Then wouldn't you advertise for a nurse?'

'Nurses can be expensive. A well provided man has stayed prosperous because he has not let go of his money, and the same with the lady in question, one presumes. Money finds money.'

I tested out the suggestion that this personal advertisement may be a code.

'Now there's a thought.' Mr Duffield wrapped his lips around his teeth. 'What a thought indeed. That might explain this answering advertisement, or should I call it a twin advertisement?' He rifled through the papers on his desk until he found a *Harrogate Advertiser*. 'Peruse this if you please, my dear Mrs Shackleton; the selfsame paragraph.'

Sure enough, the wording in the *Harrogate Advertiser* was identical.

```
A well provided and pleasant lady seeks well
provided amiable gentleman with a view to
            joining lives and fortunes.
                 Box No. 53
```

It was this week's paper. 'The cutting from Ethan Armstrong's pocket, and the advertisements in the *Harrogate Advertiser* and the *Wakefield Express* are word for word. Only the box number is different.'

He nodded sagely. 'Yes. It strikes me as odd that this person advertises in different parts of the county. She casts her net wide.'

I felt a tingle that I really was onto something, but what? It was possible that Ethan Armstrong had cut out this advertisement because it amused him, but somehow there seemed to be more to it than that. It could have been placed by a husband-hunting woman; or by some Russian spy communicating with his treacherous dupes. 'Would you be able to discover details of the person who placed this advertisement?'

Mr Duffield picked up on my buzz of excitement. 'Most cloak and daggerish. How very appealing.' He smiled his sepulchral smile. 'I cannot help as far as the Harrogate paper, but have a young friend on the staff of the *Wakefield Express*, my landlady's daughter. She was given the job on my recommendation. She may be able to put us on the right track. Bear with me.'

He picked up the telephone. While he waited to be connected, he put his hand over the mouthpiece.

'I suspect the advertiser is a bigamous creature and marries men across Yorkshire, travelling between them.' He bared tombstone teeth in a broad smile. 'Perhaps if we find her out, we shall crash our way into all the weddings and when the parson says . . .'

'Does anyone know of any impediment . . .'

The connection was made. Not wishing to hang on his every word and dampen his conversation, I quelled my excitement by turning the pages of the *Wakefield Express* and reading about Princess Helena Victoria's forthcoming visit to open the YMCA Bazaar at the Town Hall. Perhaps this mysterious advertisement may conceal some plan to assassinate a royal personage.

After several moments, Mr Duffield replaced the receiver with a sigh. 'No luck I'm afraid. The advertiser mailed the copy, including postal order payment and the request that replies be sent to a Leeds post office box number.'

'Isn't that a little unusual? Wouldn't your newspaper usually require a postal address?'

'Not when something is paid in advance. And of course, in a matter like this, there is some delicacy involved on the part of the advertiser. My young friend remarked that it was very brave of the lady to make her requirements known.' He rocked back and forth in his chair, hooking thumbs under the lapels of his coat.

I gazed at him steadily, listening to the devious tick-tock of my own thoughts. After all, the worst he could say was no.

'Mr Duffield, might I ask one more favour?'

'What is that, Mrs Shackleton?'

'Help me compose a reply to this well provided lady. I think there will be only one way to discover who she is, and that is to invite her to meet a well provided gentleman.'

Mr Duffield summoned his clerk to man the desk, while he and I retreated to an old oak table in the corner of the room where dust danced in the single shaft of foggy light from the high window.

After several false starts, we produced a fair copy of a letter to be addressed to a fair lady.

My dear lady

I am a childless widower of more than middle years, in not unsound health, and with, I believe, some good years ahead of me. In temper I am equable, in person clean living and sober.

Since the death of my wife, I shut up our country dwelling and now keep a floor in a respectable house where my landlady provides meals. Do not think this a sign of impoverishment, only that I choose not to deal with the vagaries of housekeepers.

Import and export occupied my youth. I now enjoy an income of one thousand guineas a year, which allows capital to remain untouched. My family own a flat in Mayfair, London, and occasionally I visit the capital.

I should relish the prospect of a friendship, or more, with a respectable lady whose means need not match my own (and if they did would be untouched by me). I have no strong objection to children as long as they be of quiet temperament.

Will you do me the honour of meeting me? I shall book a

table for lunch at the Griffin, Boar Lane, Leeds for noon this coming Sunday. Excuse presumptuousness and please feel at liberty to alter this arrangement if it does not suit.

After some discussion regarding the complimentary close and signature, Mr Duffield said that the lady would want to meet Mr Right, and a rock of a man. He plumped for P L Wright, Peter Wright. We could not decide what the L stood for but agreed it gave the moniker a flow, suggesting light, love and filthy lucre. He signed,

Yours sincerely
P L Wright

Mr Duffield frowned. 'What about an inside address? I prefer not to give my own.'

'Since the lady advertises in the Wakefield paper, a Wakefield address would be best. I have just the one.'

Mr Duffield agreed to write the letter in his best gentleman's hand. For my part, I would speak to Mother and ask her to keep a close eye on the post, to ensure no letter was returned to sender, addressee unknown.

We completed the task and agreed that it would not be long before discovering whether our advertiser was a flesh and blood creature or a secret code.

'We have a delivery going to Wakefield this morning. I shall ensure that my letter is despatched from the newspaper box office to the lady's post office box by this afternoon.'

When I arrived home and let myself in, the telephone was ringing. Mrs Sugden answered.

'One moment please.' She put her hand over the mouthpiece and whispered loudly. 'It is a chief inspector from New Scotland Yard.'

'Chief inspector?'

'That is how the operator announced him.'

'Thank you.' I took the receiver from her. 'Hello. Mrs Shackleton speaking.'

'Kate.'

'Marcus?'

'Yes.'

'Only Mrs Sugden thought the operator said chief inspector.'

'Ah. I was going to tell you about that.'

'You've been promoted?'

'Yes.'

'Congratulations. Wasn't that rather sudden?'

'It was in the air,' he said modestly.

First I knew that promotions dropped from the air. He was better at keeping things to himself than I had realised.

So Marcus has been promoted. More money. The

205

requirement for a wife? Those thoughts raced through my mind before anything to do with investigations occurred to me.

'I'm in your neck of the woods again, sooner than expected.'

Even the construction of his sentence left me unclear. Was he here now, or to be expected? I did not ask that.

'Business or pleasure?'

He hesitated. Why did the man telephone to me if he planned to say nothing?

'There's a terrible crackle on the line, Kate.'

I tried again. 'May I ask what area you are visiting?'

He said, cautiously, 'It's a little to the north and west of you.'

'Marcus, is this a geography test?'

He laughed. 'I hope we may meet up, and I didn't want to spring it on you at a moment's notice.'

Another brief exchange led me to gather that he would be basing himself at Otley police station, the headquarters for Great Applewick. I replaced the telephone in the cradle. Unless something dire had happened in Otley, events in Great Applewick merited the personal attention of the man Scotland Yard most frequently sends in our direction. I would have to wait and see whether his investigation focused on Ethan Armstrong's disappearance; or Miss Trimble's untimely demise.

But where did I fit in?

One thing was for sure and certain. I dared not now leave it till Sunday before telling my mother about meeting Mary Jane, and Mrs Whitaker. Marcus would have made courtesy contact with the headquarters of the West Riding Constabulary – Dad. And Dad would say to Mother, 'I believe Kate's friend is in the vicinity.'

I went upstairs and changed into an afternoon dress with matching coat.

'Are you going out again?' Mrs Sugden asked as I tripped downstairs and lifted my motoring coat from the hook. She can be very perceptive.

'Yes. I'm off to Wakefield, to visit my mother.'

Mrs Sugden looked surprised but was tactful enough not to remark on the fact that it wasn't Sunday, and we had a case.

'The thing is, Mrs Sugden, my father wants me not to take Mary Jane's enquiries about her husband any further. And nothing will convince him more that I'm following his wishes than going to see my mother on a weekday.'

'And are we off the case?' Mrs Sugden asked.

'Well, of course. We wouldn't fly in the face of a hint from the superintendent of the West Riding Constabulary would we? But if you plan further visits to a spiritualist church, well it's up to you what you do in your spare time. And don't be surprised if on the way you see Mr Sykes, selling stockings from his attaché case.'

My mother has the art of making a house comfortable and has passed that trick to me. She likes colourful throws over the furniture, uncluttered rooms, and rugs that look as though they may have flown in on their own initiative from Persia. Even before my parents moved to Sandal, when we lived in a West Riding Constabulary house as I was growing up, it was unlike any other police house in Wakefield. Of course, not every police officer's wife has her own income to fall back on.

She was in her favourite corner of the dining room, curled in a chair by the window, reading. There was a fire in the grate and the room oozed cosiness. I took off my motoring coat.

Mother glanced up at me with such a look of pleasure, full of smiles. She marked her place in the book, set it down and rose from her chair. 'I'm sure you'd be better coming through on the tram than driving all this way. You'll catch a terrible chill one of these days.'

'Too many stops on the tram. It drives me mad.'

She moved to the sofa, patting the place beside her. 'Come and sit down and tell me how you are.'

I draped my coat across the back of the sofa. 'Couldn't be better.'

'And how was Berta?'

'Aunt Berta's on top form. She sent you that scarf you wanted from Derry & Toms.'

'How lovely!'

Admiring the scarf would put off the moment when I would broach the subject of Mary Jane and Mrs Whitaker, not to mention using my parents' address as a mysterious lonely hearts letter drop.

Mother took her button scissors from the sewing box. She cut the string of the Derry & Toms parcel and shook out the colourful silk scarf. 'Perfect. That will go very nicely with something I'm having made up for the summer. I'll show it to you later. Now tell me all about your visit to London. And what's this about that nice Inspector Charles coming in this direction again?'

'He's a chief inspector now. He's been called in to investigate some events in the Otley area. And that's partly what I've come to talk to you about.'

As we sat side by side on the sofa, she listened while I told her the story of Mary Jane's arrival at the house, in the early hours of Monday, the events of the past three days, Ethan's disappearance and Miss Trimble's death.

'Good heavens! And all I've done is reread a couple of chapters of this book that I can't make head nor tail of.'

We were both acting as if there was no great weight to my having met Mary Jane, but it was no use pretending. 'Mother, it was really the Mary Jane visit I wanted to tell you about. Because it led me to Mrs Whitaker in White Swan Yard.'

'Ah.' Mother sat back on the cushions as though she had lost the energy to hold herself upright. She did not look at me.

Finally she said, 'I knew there was something. When Dennis said he'd given you lunch yesterday, and you'd gone back to the station, he said you'd be coming soon and telling me all about everything. I hope he's better at concealing what he knows from criminals. I can always tell when he's holding something back. Silly me. I thought it might be something between you and Marcus Charles. He seemed so charming when we met him in Harrogate last year. But it wasn't that at all. It was your . . . your mother.'

I put my hand on her arm. 'You're my mother. No one else. How old was I when Dad brought me from the Whitakers'?'

'Eight weeks I think. You would keep a kitten with its mother longer, but I wanted to be sure, and she . . .'

'Was glad to be rid of me.'

'No! Not at all. You mustn't entertain such a thought. But if a thing is to be done, it's best it's done quickly.'

For a moment, neither of us spoke. 'Mother, Mrs Whitaker and I had very little to say to each other. I took her across to be with Mary Jane. I'm not part of that family.'

She smiled. 'It's all right. It had to happen. Well, I suppose it didn't have to happen that you should meet her but as one grows older there are all sorts of regrets, not for what you've done but for what was left undone. And who knows, you and she may get to know and like each other.'

'Anything's possible I suppose.' I paused. 'Dad said he fetched me out of the Whitakers' house, and you stayed in the motor.'

She looked at her hands. 'Even at the last moment, I feared she might change her mind.' She turned to me, gave her warmest smile, and took my hand. 'But I thank God every day that she didn't and that you came home with us.'

Later, as she poured the tea and we dived into potted beef sandwiches, Mother asked about my visit to London last week.

She waved her hand dismissively as I began to tell her about my shopping trips and the dinner party Aunt Berta had given. 'Berta's told me all about shopping trips and menus. You went on a tour of Scotland Yard on your last day. Tell me about that, and how things were left with Marcus Charles. If he's coming up here and likely to visit, then I need to know how matters stand, or don't stand.'

I took my time over the sandwich.

'It was absolutely grand, and totally disastrous, if you must know.'

'That sounds interesting, which bit was which?'

'We got on really well. He managed a day off, which we spent together.' I did not mention that we also spent the night together, and that was fine too.

Mother is very good at hearing an unspoken but.

'But?'

210

'Mother, he is so old-fashioned!'

She shot me a surprised glance, which made me think Aunt Berta had tittle-tattled about my nights on the tiles. 'He didn't strike me as old-fashioned when we met him in Harrogate.'

'You saw him for five minutes. When he toured me round Scotland Yard, he told me all about how they recruited policewomen in 1918, and then had to let them go, because of financial cuts. He said that when they first started, the women walked in twos . . .'

'Well, yes, they would . . .'

'With two stalwart and time-tested policemen walking six to ten yards behind them. He was sorry that had been stopped. He was sorry that women were finally given powers of arrest. He thought it a mistake that there was now a woman in CID.'

'Is there really?'

'Yes. One. Among three thousand men. I met her. She's very plucky and has a lot of commonsense. But I don't know how she puts up with it. Marcus and I got on really well except when it came to any matter of conse-quence whatever, and then we disagreed.'

'But opposites attract, look at me and your father.'

'Not this opposite. It's too late for me to change my spots. And now he's up here to look into something that I've learned a little about, and talked to Dad about, I'm sure that . . . oh never mind.'

'Have a scone.'

I took a scone. Scones can be a bit claggy. I don't really like them, but it had never before occurred to me to refuse, any more than one would stay seated in church when everyone else stands or kneels.

'I don't like scones.'

Mother poured more tea. 'Calm down, dear. Nothing is so important that you should become upset about it. I'm reading a book by Helena Blavatsky. I can hardly follow it but it does give some extraordinary perspectives. There are so many other philosophies. Would you like to hear what I make of it so far?'

'Not just now.'

'So the crux of it is this,' she said. 'You want to stay on this case and your father and Marcus have squeezed you out.'

She surprised me with how quickly she picked up on what I had not said.

'Yes.'

'Well, in my humble opinion – and of course I know nothing – I think it would be very foolish of the murder squad and the West Riding Constabulary and . . .'

'Special Branch . . .'

'. . . and Special Branch to exclude you. And after all, this Mary Jane is your sister, Kate. Visiting relatives isn't yet against the law, is it?'

'No it's not.'

My mother's revolutionary stance towards the British establishment did not entirely surprise me. I believe I get my directness from her, and my deviousness from Dad.

'Thank you, Mother. That's just what I wanted to hear. And Mother, if a letter is delivered here for a P L Wright, Esquire, would you please open it, and let me know straightaway?'

Before I had time to explain, the telephone rang.

'Oh leave it, Kate. It'll be Martha Graham. The woman is bridge mad. I told her I'm not playing today.'

'I best answer. If she hears me, she'll know that you're otherwise engaged.' I picked up the telephone. 'Hood residence.'

'Hello, Kate.' It was Marcus. 'I'm in Great Applewick. We've found something. I wonder whether you'd like to come out here?'

Would I like to come? Try and keep me away. 'Possibly,' I said. Better not seem too keen.

'Do you need me to send a car?'

If they had found something, that something could only be a body. Ethan Armstrong's body.

Three

On arriving in Great Applewick, I could not have answered a single question about the journey from Wakefield; landmarks, traffic policemen, other motors, bikes, or my own state of mind. Only driving along Nether Edge, passing first one cottage and then another, negotiating the bend in the road, did I blink into awareness like a subject roused from a trance. The sense of dread settled somewhere around my jaw and sent waves of anxiety through my body, tautening every nerve.

As soon as Mary Jane's cottage came into view, I noticed the constable posted at the door. I parked in what was by now my usual place, by the dry-stone wall opposite Mary Jane's cottage. The constable watched me climb from the motor. He waited until I stood beside him.

'You can't go in there, madam.'

'I need to speak to Mrs Armstrong.'

He shook his head. 'No one is to pass the threshold.'

I looked beyond him through the window. A woman I did not recognise was seated at the table, her back to me.

'Chief Inspector Charles asked me to call, constable.'

'You can't go in,' he repeated.

'Where is Chief Inspector Charles?'

'At the quarry. You won't be able to go in there neither.'

'Who is that in the cottage? And where is Mrs Armstrong?'

'That's Mrs Sharp sitting with the lady.' He peered in the window, as if to make certain of his facts. 'She's the local police sergeant's wife.'

Mary Jane was not with her.

'Where are you going?' shouted the constable as I disappeared round the back of the cottage.

'To the lavatory.'

'You can't . . .'

I heard no more as I rushed to the privy and slammed the door shut behind me. It was spotlessly whitewashed and the seat scrubbed clean. Neat string-threaded squares of the *Daily Herald* hung on a nail. I wondered whether Marcus Charles would have that fact reported to him by Sergeant or Mrs Sharp. The Armstrongs wipe their bottoms on a radical newspaper.

When I came out, Mary Jane was at the window.

'What's going on?' I mouthed.

She raised the window and leaned out. 'Oh it's all right. They want me to stay indoors so as not to be upset that they're searching.' She pulled a face and lowered her voice. 'Mrs Sharp has kindly come to sit with me. I can't very well turn her away can I? That inspector was very nice. I came to lie down. I have such a headache, Kate. I can't be making polite conversation.'

You poor idiot. You're virtually under arrest, and probably will be by the time day is out. 'Where are Harriet and Austin?'

'Staying at school until the upset at the quarry is over.'

'What about their grandma?'

215

Mary Jane pulled an exasperated face. 'You should hear her snore! We had words and she's gone home. I've promised the kids can visit her on Sunday.'

'You lie down and rest then,' I said. 'I'll see what's going on.'

She disappeared from the window. I ladled water from the well bucket, took a drink, and washed my hands.

The constable must have heard our voices. He appeared, face clouded with suspicion.

Slowly, I walked back to my motor.

At the entrance to the quarry, a length of red tape stretched between two portable posts. I popped around to the other side as a uniformed man hurried across to stop me. I got my piece in first. 'Would you please tell Chief Inspector Charles that Mrs Shackleton is here.'

He would have liked to order me back to the other side of the tape but satisfied himself with an officious, 'Wait here please, madam.'

An eerie silence lay over the quarry. The mason's hut was cordoned off – a little late in my view. I strained my eyes to try and make out whether the remnants of the sundial still lay in a heap but could not see because of the contour of the ground.

Beyond the foreman's hut, the constable approached two men who had their backs to me. I recognized Marcus's easy stance and his broad shoulders. He turned and acknowledged me, raising his hand in greeting. When he moved towards me, I noticed that the other man held a bloodhound on a leash.

Marcus drew close, his eyes searching out mine, trying to speak without words. Was it sympathy he conveyed?

He held out his hand and took mine, holding it with a

terrible gentleness. 'Kate. Thank you for coming. I should have sent a car for you. Are you all right?'

'Marcus, what's going on?'

As if it wasn't obvious, as if I didn't know.

'I'll explain.' He took my arm, to lead me towards the foreman's hut.

'You'll be warmer inside. I'll have someone take you to the station for a cup of tea.'

'No, Marcus. I want to see. I want to see what you're doing.'

He hesitated. 'We're just getting started. It took longer than expected because I had to wait for Mr McSnout to be brought. His minder had taken him for a walk on the moors and it was a while before we could get them here.'

'Mr Mac who?'

'McSnout's the number one bloodhound, and McManus his handler.'

I followed his glance. The man Marcus had stood with a moment ago was showing something to the hound. It was Ethan's cap, the one Harriet had found under the bench in the mason's hut, and that she had tried to encourage the sheepdog to sniff and pick up the trail. Harriet had the right idea when she harnessed Billy into service, but the wrong dog, covering the wrong terrain.

The bloodhound wagged its tail. Head close to the ground, the dog moved at a speedy pace towards the mason's hut, the handler following, holding the hound on a long leash.

Two figures emerged from the foreman's hut to watch.

Marcus glanced at them. 'We've sent the quarry workers home, all but the foreman and his son.'

'Josiah Turnbull and Raymond.'

'You've met them?' He did not sound surprised.

'On Monday.' Now was not the moment to speak of the bad blood between Turnbull and Ethan Armstrong, or to say that Raymond would take over Ethan's house and his job. Perhaps Marcus had already found this out. 'They're not exactly disinterested,' was all I said.

We were watching the dog. It reached the mason's hut.

'Yes,' Marcus said, misinterpreting my comment about the Turnbulls' interest. 'The older chap's deeply cut up by the situation. He and Ethan were sparring partners in politics, but respected each other. We may need his help if Mr McSnout finds something of interest.'

Someone, he meant, not something. Ethan Armstrong's body, he meant.

Turnbull appeared far more subdued than when I had seen him last. He pretended not to notice me, and gazed across the quarry. Raymond stood beside his father. He gave one of those understated Yorkshire greetings – more than a flicker of the eyes if you are close enough to catch it, but less than a full nod. I acknowledged.

The dog did not, as I had expected, move to the lagoon but led its handler further into the quarry, round a bend, out of view.

No one spoke, not Marcus or me, or the Turnbulls, or the constable on sentry duty, or Sergeant Sharp who had appeared from somewhere and stood a few respectful yards from Marcus.

The air hung still. A light fleecy cloud sped by, as if it wanted to be well away from this melancholy scene. The silence crackled.

After what seemed an age, the dog handler reappeared. He raised his arms above his head and moved them three times, forming an x. Marcus reached for my hand, gave the smallest squeeze. He waved to the police photographer who emerged from the open door of the foreman's hut. Mr Turnbull cleared his throat and spat in an arc. The photographer took one last long drag on a cigarette, discarded the tab end and ground it with his heel.

My chest heaved. Not enough air reached my lungs. I stood very still, my mouth open for breath like a just-caught fish.

Marcus signalled to the Turnbulls, and to the photographer. Mr Turnbull strode past me, Raymond coming after with a wheelbarrow. In the wheelbarrow were picks and shovels.

Raymond turned to me. 'It might not be him.' He tilted the barrow. Pick and shovel slammed against each other. 'We'll lift the rocks gentle like, the tools are just in case.'

After speaking to the dog handler, Marcus walked back to me.

'What is it?'

'There's a fall of rocks up at the far end. I've said not to begin moving anything until I'm there. We'll have a photograph first.'

'I want to see.'

'No, Kate. This isn't for your eyes.'

'If Mary Jane hadn't come to me, no one would be looking for Ethan Armstrong.' Without meaning to, I turned and glanced at Sergeant Sharp, who hovered sheepishly, waiting for instructions. 'Marcus, why did you send for me if I'm not to be part of this?'

'Because, Kate, I have reason to believe Mary Jane has some awkward questions to answer, and I want you to be with her when I put them to her. You know her better than I do. You'll know whether she is being truthful. And I want you to know that I'm treating her fairly and justly.'

He was looking not at me but at the dust on his shoes.

You want me to know you are treating her fairly and justly because if I think you do not I shall hold it against you forever. Well yes, you are right about that.

'If I'm here for Mary Jane's sake, then let me be witness to what McSnout has found. Ethan Armstrong was my brother-in-law. Mary Jane will want the truth. And please don't feel you need to protect me. I was in France during the war, you know that. There can be nothing in this quarry worse than the sights I saw there. The horror lies in imagining, and waiting.'

He nodded. 'Very well.'

He called to the sergeant. 'Sharp, would you see that we have a stretcher ready, and bring the doctor along as soon as he arrives?'

The sergeant saluted and went towards the quarry entrance.

I fell into step with Marcus as he walked the dusty track that led past the crushing shed and on to the far end of the quarry where the dog handler and McSnout stood. The hound's ears trailed the ground as it sniffed at the rocks.

Marcus exchanged a few words with the handler, and I caught Mr McManus's words, 'Mac's never been wrong yet.'

'Did you search here on Saturday evening?' Marcus addressed Mr Turnbull.

Turnbull wore a red handkerchief tied at his throat. He touched his fingers to it, as if the knot was too tight and might hang him. 'Aye, sir. We walked the whole quarry with lanterns after what Ethan's little lass had said. There was no sign of Ethan.'

'And this rock fall, was it just the same on Saturday as it is now?'

'No. A few more rocks have fallen, sir, but not so very many.'

'Have you taken a photograph?' Marcus asked the photographer.

'I have, sir.' He was a keen-looking young fellow with a fair moustache. He handled his Thornton Pickard reflex camera protectively.

Marcus turned back to the Turnbulls. 'Go to it then, chaps. Steady like.'

Father and son bent to the task of shifting rocks. They rolled a boulder, pushing it aside.

Dog and handler turned away from the scene, a look of regret in the bloodhound's big brown eyes.

'Excuse me, Mr McManus.'

He paused.

'Would McSnout have followed the man's scent around the quarry or come straight to the spot? Only I thought perhaps Mr Armstrong, the missing man, had possibly been dragged towards the lagoon on the other side.'

'Could have been.' McManus held the leash loosely. The dog sniffed the ground. 'McSnout wouldn't follow the scent all around the quarry, he'd go to where it was strongest. He knows who he's looking for.'

'Thank you.'

We watchers, Marcus, the photographer and I, stood clear as the Turnbulls, father and son, carefully shifted up rocks and stones.

Raymond let out something like a strangled yelp and jumped back as if scalded.

Marcus moved closer to look.

It was a hand, palm uppermost, as if in supplication.

Marcus signalled to the photographer who moved in

221

with his tripod. We stood as still as children playing statues while the photographer clicked.

Marcus turned to me, a question in his eyes.

'I'll stay, Marcus,'

'If you're sure.'

After his involuntary cry, Raymond worked with a will, not able to lift the rocks and stones quickly enough for his own liking. Mr Turnbull slowed to a snail's pace, as though delay might put off the horror of this discovery.

A sleeve, dusty and torn, click of camera; a ripped trouser leg, the palest of legs smeared with dirt and blood, click of camera; a boot that had come off; another hand; hair stiff with dust, and a face bruised and bloodied, dusted with white; click, click, click. This unreal figure, now revealed, did not look crushed and broken but dirty and dishevelled, almost as if he had only fallen, bruised his face, and then slept deeply.

Once again the photographer replaced the plate and took another image. So this was Ethan Armstrong, writer of letters, champion of the working man, father, husband, carver of slate and stone.

Raymond Turnbull did not shift his gaze from Ethan. He bent to touch his hand, as if he might bring him back to life. Josiah Turnbull moved towards his son, to speak to him, or touch him, then changed his mind, stood still, and looked away. Poor Raymond. He appeared in a state of shock. It was not fair. An older man should have had this task. On Saturday he would be married. No young bridegroom should carry such horror to his bed.

Sergeant Sharp and the constable who had stood sentry tramped towards us carrying a stretcher. They laid it on the ground, making way for the doctor who bent to look at the body. He straightened himself, spoke briefly to

Marcus and then squatted beside Ethan, touching his hand and face as if in a farewell.

When the doctor stood, Raymond pushed in front of the constable. 'I'll lift him. Let me and my dad lift him.'

With great tenderness, Ethan's old enemy, Josiah Turnbull, and Ethan's once upon a time apprentice, Raymond Turnbull, lifted the body onto the stretcher.

Now it was the doctor who led the way.

The wheelbarrow was abandoned.

Marcus and I walked behind in procession.

'Let me break the news to Mary Jane, Marcus.'

'Very well.'

We stood at the mouth of the quarry, watching as the stretcher bearing Ethan's body was carried carefully towards the waiting vehicle.

I touched Marcus's sleeve. 'She'll want to see him. Will you take him to her?'

Marcus did not look at me. 'I've instructed the driver to take him to the hospital. Mrs Armstrong will need to do a formal identification there. I'll be applying to the coroner to order a post mortem.'

Ethan Armstrong's arm suddenly slipped from under the cover and dangled to the side of the stretcher, pointing one last time to the earth. I shuddered.

Marcus squeezed my arm. 'Are you all right?'

'Yes. Just . . . I wonder whether it was an accident, that there was a landslide . . .' It would be better to believe that, but then I would have to think that what Harriet saw was an apparition. 'It couldn't have been, could it?'

'That's what we'll find out.'

'Why did you put a man on Mary Jane's door?'

'I didn't want her taking it in her head to come up here that's all,' he said evenly.

'And the sergeant's wife to sit with her?'

'To keep her company.'

'Marcus, the children will be coming home from school shortly, if they see a policeman on the door . . .'

'The children will stay at school until they're collected. I talked to the girl earlier and explained that we were looking into her father's disappearance. She's a good little witness. Didn't waver from her story one jot.'

We had reached the top of the quarry. He moved away from me and spoke to the driver who supervised the loading of the stretcher and the closing of the vehicle doors.

A moment later, Marcus was by my side. 'I see you have your car just there. Do you want me to drive you? We can go see Mrs Armstrong together.'

'I'll be all right.'

'Then I'll follow. We'll go in together and you can break the news. I'll be able to answer any questions she has.'

He suspected her involvement. Everything about his manner, his voice, remained neutral, but the suspicion trickled under his words and made me feel on edge.

The short journey to the cottage went too quickly. I wanted an age to pass before having to break such devastating news.

And the children, soon they would need to know the awful truth. Would we have to see their little faces melt into perplexed misery?

I stopped the car. Marcus's driver brought his vehicle to a halt behind me. Marcus leaped out first and spoke to the constable on the door. The constable nodded and moved round the side of the cottage. When Marcus knocked, it was Mrs Sharp, the sergeant's wife, who opened the door. That infuriated me. A scream crawled under my skin.

Marcus spoke in a low voice. Mrs Sharp disappeared into the cottage, came back carrying her coat. She and Marcus stood under the apple tree, exchanging a few words, and then she left.

Mary Jane stood up from where she had been sitting at the table. There were two cups. She and Mrs Sharp must have been having a chat. Perhaps Marcus had instructed her in what he hoped to get out of Mary Jane – any little slips, criticisms of Ethan, complaints about her marriage.

Marcus came in behind me, close on my heels.

Mary Jane stared at me, waiting for me to speak, one hand placed flat on the table to support herself.

'You'd better sit down, Mary Jane.' She did not move. 'Sit down, please.' I took her arm and led her to the chair by the fire. She melted into it, shaking her head, knowing what we would say.

'Ethan's body was found in the quarry. I'm so sorry.'

She closed her eyes. 'But the men looked. They searched on Saturday.'

Marcus stood back and let me explain.

'He was . . . at the far end of the quarry. Mr Turnbull and Raymond helped recover him. He was . . .'

Marcus gave me a warning prod in the small of my back. Don't say too much.

'Oh my God,' she lifted her white pinafore and covered her face. 'Poor Ethan. What happened? Why would he be at the far end of the quarry?'

Marcus said, 'We shall investigate that, Mrs Armstrong.'

'Where is he?'

'We've taken him to the nearest hospital. Otley.'

'Why? Why haven't you brought him home?'

'I'm sorry not to be able to do that. The coroner will

need to be informed, but I would ask you to come with me and make a formal identification.'

It occurred to me there was no need to hurry her in this way. Formal identification could wait. I glanced at him quickly. He was not looking at me. *You want to ask Mary Jane questions, while she is still upset, while you think she may give herself away.*

He said, 'Your husband's body will be returned to you for burial when formalities are completed.'

I pulled up a chair beside Mary Jane and took her hand, peeled the apron back, to see her face.

She seemed not to take in the information. 'So . . . do you mean he's not to be brought home to me, not to be laid out?'

'That's right,' Marcus said. 'Not straightaway. But as I say, I can take you now . . .'

She wailed, that is the only way to describe it, a heart-felt wail of pain, and then, 'Ethan, my poor boy. Is he very disfigured?'

Although I had watched his body lifted free, I suddenly could not remember whether his limbs hung useless from broken bones, whether the mark on his face was a bruise, or dirt.

She turned to me.

I said, 'He looked to me as though he were sleeping.'

She shook her head as she rocked back and forth. 'I'll go to him. I have to see him.'

'Shall I come with you?'

Marcus went to the door. He spoke to the constable.

She was pale, and looked at me from red-rimmed eyes. 'How am I going to tell Harriet and Austin? She was right. Harriet was right, and I knew it. I said so.'

'You don't have to think about that straightaway. They're in school, until we collect them.'

'And what must they be thinking?'

Marcus said, 'Mrs Sharp arranged for them to stay in the head teacher's office by the fire. Their teacher is giving them tea. Don't worry about the children, Mrs Armstrong. The children will be all right. But I wonder if you would be kind enough to help clear up something that puzzles me?'

He did not look at me. The axe was about to fall.

Mary Jane looked white and shaken. She stared at Marcus, reading behind the mask of his grim look. She did not answer.

'I'm sorry to ask you questions at a time like this, Mrs Armstrong, but I'm sure you understand we must find out everything we can.'

'Does it have to be now?' I asked. 'Can't this wait?'

'Best not,' Marcus said.

The door opened. Sergeant Sharp stepped inside. This was like some weird dance where all the participants knew their routine in advance, and only Mary Jane and I were out of step.

Sharp held out his truncheon. On it hung a canvas bag, covered in coal dust.

Marcus looked at Mary Jane. 'Do you recognise this bag, Mrs Armstrong?'

Her eyes widened. 'It looks like Ethan's tool bag.'

'Did you put it in the shed, under the coal?'

'No!'

'Bring it across here please, sergeant.'

Sergeant Sharp was about to deposit the dusty bag on the table. I whipped a newspaper from behind the coal scuttle and set it down.

Slowly, the sergeant lowered the bag.

'Open it,' Marcus ordered.

The sergeant opened the bag gingerly, trying in vain not to blacken his fingers.

'Withdraw the tools with care.'

Sergeant Sharp first lifted out a chisel, and then a mallet, setting each one carefully on the newspaper.

'Please inspect the tools,' the inspector said to Mary Jane.

She stared. In a whisper she said, 'Yes. They are Ethan's tools. There's a carving on the handle of the mallet, a star and his initials.'

'How do you think they came to be in your coal shed?'

'I don't know.'

'Look carefully at the mallet, Mrs Armstrong.'

She did so.

'What do you see?'

'A mallet. Ethan's mallet.' She looked at me, as if I could prompt her in what her reply ought to be.

'And the head of the mallet?' the inspector asked. 'There is something on the head of the mallet.'

'I can't see anything.'

'I think our scientific people will find traces of blood and hair there.'

She shook her head. 'I don't know what to say.'

I put my arm around her. 'You don't have to say anything.' I glared at Marcus. 'Is this really necessary?'

'I'm afraid it is.'

'I've no idea what his tools are doing there. I don't know.'

'Very well. Thank you, Mrs Armstrong.' Marcus nodded at Sergeant Sharp. The sergeant returned the tools to the coal-blackened bag, and the whole lot into a large evidence bag. Then he went out.

Mary Jane held onto the arms of the chair, her

knuckles were white. She looked at me. 'They think I killed him. Catherine, tell them I didn't.'

'Nobody in their right mind thinks that.' I glared at Marcus, who said nothing. I put my hand on Mary Jane's. 'I brought in coal on Monday. I would have seen that bag. It wasn't there.'

Marcus said, 'Shall we go, Mrs Armstrong? I'll take you to identify your husband. Mrs Shackleton may wish to accompany you.'

'Yes!' I said quickly.

Mary Jane said, 'Go and fetch the children, Kate. Take them to the farm. They've stayed there before sometimes.'

'But you won't be gone long. I'll mind them here. You'll want to see them, and they you.'

'Not just yet. I can't tell them. I can't . . . Tell them . . . Say . . . I don't know. But I don't want them here. I don't want them to see me like this.'

Her breath came in short bursts. Sergeant Sharp reappeared. 'Come along, Mrs Armstrong. I'll sit with you.' He picked up her cape from the back of the door. 'This yours is it?'

It was the plaid cape Miss Trimble claimed to have seen Mary Jane wearing by the quarry at four o'clock on Saturday afternoon.

'Yes,' she said.

I moved towards her. 'I'd better come with you.'

'No. The children, see to Harriet and Austin.'

She was gone. Marcus stood by the door. 'Kate, I'm sorry. You do understand I have a job to do.'

'I told you. I filled a bucket of coal out there, it all came tumbling down. There was nothing. Why would she hide incriminating tools in her own back yard? It doesn't make

229

sense. And I thought you were simply taking her to do an identification. If you're going to interrogate her . . .'

'I'm not. But obviously there are questions. A woman answering her description was seen by the quarry that afternoon, when Mrs Armstrong claimed to be here alone . . .'

'Miss Trimble said she saw a woman in a plaid cape. Do you think mills produce just enough material for one cape? There must be dozens of cloaks and capes similar to Mary Jane's.'

'She and her husband had quarrelled. She has a large insurance policy on his life.'

'He's a mason, a man in a dangerous trade, why wouldn't he be insured? There's a policy on her life too. And that bag of tools wasn't there! Someone has put it there.'

Marcus frowned. 'You must understand. We're the professionals. We know how to carry out a thorough search, and we know how difficult that can be for people who are not fully trained.' He gave a gracious and patronising nod of the head. 'But we will look at every possibility. Once we have the post mortem report, I shall have a better idea how to proceed. Now if you'll excuse me.'

His hand was on the door knob.

'What about Miss Trimble's death? Isn't that suspicious, and Mary Jane was nowhere near the vicarage. I can vouch for that. I was. Why don't you arrest me?'

'Miss Trimble's death isn't unexplained. She had asthma and a weak heart. She died of respiratory failure.'

Sergeant Sharp was at the door. 'Mrs Armstrong is comfortably seated, sir.'

I felt utterly helpless. 'Will you be bringing her back?'

Marcus bristled. I half expected him to tell me he did not operate a taxi cab service.

Sergeant Sharp looked human for once and said, 'I shall escort Mrs Armstrong home if that's required, sir.'

'Thank you.' Marcus sounded weary, probably regretting my involvement, or perhaps my existence.

Tactfully, the sergeant disappeared.

'Bye, Kate.'

'Bye, Marcus.'

He came close to me, leaned forward and kissed my cheek. 'Sorry. This must be very hard for you.'

'You're talking as if she's guilty.'

'I hope she's not, for her sake, and for yours.'

I didn't answer but followed him outside.

Mary Jane was looking at me through the car window. Perhaps the full weight of her plight dawned on her. Her lips formed the words, 'Help me.'

I nodded and raised my hand.

She said something else I couldn't catch.

The car drew away. I went back inside.

Now I had to face the children. Mary Jane should be telling them. Their grandmother would have been good at this. She knew Ethan, liked him.

It had to be done. If I did not tell them, they would find out. There would be some classmate, even now, earwigging as grown-ups talked about Ethan's body being dug out from under rocks.

The children would need their nightwear. Toothbrushes stood in a cracked cup on the window bottom. I found a bone-handled bag on the back of the door and began to gather stuff together.

Four

Rather than take the Jowett, I walked the lane slowly and turned into the village, snailing my way towards the school. There is something about an empty school that makes me imagine generations of children, reluctant, keen, smart, dim; playgrounds that might be heaven or hell. The yard sloped upwards. I entered the door marked Boys.

Only my footsteps on the wood floor broke the palpable silence. On a cupboard in the hall stood a big bell. I resisted the urge to pick it up and toll the death of Ethan Armstrong.

Passing empty classrooms and turning into another corridor, smelling of chalk and feet, I had no idea where to look. Upstairs. Trying the door of a broom cupboard. A sudden panic seized me – that I would never find my way out.

And then, at the end of a long corridor, a door stood slightly ajar. I headed for that door.

Someone heard my footsteps. The door opened and a gaunt woman, hair done in salt and pepper ear pleats, strode to meet me. She was entirely dressed in ghostlike grey.

We introduced ourselves. Miss Patterson, Harriet's form teacher. She frowned at the prospect of handing the children into the care of someone she did not know, and I liked her for that.

I heard Harriet's voice before seeing her. She was reading aloud.

In the snug study, Harriet and Austin sat on small chairs by the fire. Harriet stopped reading. They both looked at me, and at Miss Patterson.

Miss Patterson said, 'Your Aunt Kate has some sad news for you.'

For God's sake, how did you do this? Sykes would know. He has children. My mother would know.

'It's Dad,' Harriet said. 'What about him?'

'Your dad is dead.'

Everything about Harriet slackened, her head dipped, her arms seemed to lengthen. I reached out, lifting her from the chair and held her to me. She began to cry.

When I tried to hold Austin, he wriggled and pushed me away. 'What's the matter?' He fixed himself to the little chair, like a snowman in hard frost.

'I was right,' Harriet said. 'We won't see Dad again, Austin. He's died and gone to heaven.'

Austin looked at her, and at me, as though we were mad. 'How can he? He has to come back and go to work. He didn't polish my boots for school. Where is he?'

'In heaven.'

'I don't want him to be in heaven.'

Miss Patterson said, 'Let us pray for him, children.'

She knelt and we all copied her, not knowing what else to do. She recited the Twenty-third Psalm, and it occurred to me that if you are a school teacher you had better have something on the tip of your tongue for every

233

occasion. When she finished, Harriet and I said, Amen. Austin repeated the Amen, then looked about expectantly as though believing we had chanted a spell and some sea change would occur in the room.

He wet his lips quickly with a pointy little tongue and listened for footsteps in the hall.

The three of us left the school, walking down the sloping yard.

As we reached the lane, Harriet asked, 'When will Mam be back?'

'Probably not tonight.'

'Soon?'

'I hope so.'

'I want to stop at home,' Austin said. 'I don't want to go to the farm.'

'I'm taking you in the motor car.'

That quietened him until we reached the cottage. I helped him into the motor.

Harriet said, 'I've forgotten something.' She ran to the cottage door, and then beckoned me.

She unlocked the door and we went inside. 'At play-time, I saw policemen in the High Street outside school. I saw a man with a bloodhound. Did that dog find Dad?'

'Yes.'

'Where was he?'

'In the quarry.'

'He's been there all this while, on his own?'

'He's not alone any more.'

'Is Mam with him?'

'Yes.' It was a white lie, with a syllable of truth. 'They've taken him to Otley, to the hospital and your mam . . .'

'The hospital?' Her eyes flashed with hope. The hospital was where people were made better.

'To a special part of the hospital where they take people who have died. And your mam has gone there.'

Harriet turned away from me. She picked up a teacloth and took the lid off a bin, lifting out half a loaf.

'It's hard to take in, Harriet. I'm so sorry. Such terrible news.'

She placed the bread on the cloth, tied all four corners. 'Austin doesn't understand. He's too young.'

'Do you understand?'

'I think so. It means I'm half an orphan.'

'Yes.'

She nodded gravely. 'When will Mam come back?'

A new determination grew in me. 'As soon as I can fetch her back, which will be very soon, believe me, Harriet.'

Austin had moved into the driver's seat and was playing with the steering wheel. That's all I needed, a runaway car and a squashed six-year-old. He looked cheerful. 'This motor can go anywhere,' he said. 'You told me.'

'Yes.'

'Take us to heaven. I want to see my dad.'

I started the motor. 'We'll go to the farm now.'

'No! Heaven. Go to heaven.'

'Motors can't go to heaven.'

'But you said . . .'

Harriet looked at him, and then beyond him across the fallow field as though gazing somewhere far off in time and space. 'We won't see Dad again, Austin. Dead means like the two little ones in the grave who'll never grow old. Dad will go to be with them. It's their turn to have him.'

Five

Sykes stood at the gates of Great Applewick Mill as women and girls poured out; an opportunity not to be missed by any hosiery salesman worth his garters. A pair of stockings over his arm, notebook at the ready, he grinned in what he hoped was an endearing, cheeky manner at the first young woman to come through the gates. 'Taking orders – delivered on payday.' Mouselike, she scurried off. He tried a wink at a red-haired beauty.

She returned his wink. 'Can't afford it, love, unless a pretty face makes you feel generous.' She lingered long enough to be persuaded.

That did the trick. Not only did he take orders for thirty-seven pairs of stockings, but invitations to a dance in the village hall, the picture palace in Yeadon and a wedding on Saturday. If these women came up trumps with cash on Friday, selling stockings would earn him more than Mrs Shackleton paid for a fortnight's work. Small consolation for finding himself no further forward in his investigations.

He had watched police arrive in force in the village, the West Riding men providing backup for Mrs Shackleton's friend from Scotland Yard. Bobbies went door to door in the village, asking questions. Sykes followed with his attaché case, only to discover how little the inhabitants of Great Applewick had to say. All the police questions concerned Ethan Armstrong. If there had been a post mortem on Miss Trimble, no one was telling.

Sykes headed for the farm, wanting to talk to Bob Conroy, Ethan's friend from boyhood. But the closer Sykes came to his destination, the less he believed he might interest Bob Conroy in hosiery.

Not far off, smoke from the farmhouse chimney mingled with soft white clouds. Closer, and he caught the whiff of manure, pigs and earth.

A police sergeant wearing the West Riding Constabulary uniform walked towards him from the direction of the farm. Sykes wished he was not carrying his attaché case. His years in the force made him realise how his assumed itinerant salesman character might arouse suspicion.

'Nah then, lad,' the sergeant said in a bluff, affable voice. Meaning, who are you, where are you going, what's your business here?

At being called lad, Sykes's grip on the case handle tightened. 'Afternoon, officer. Am I on the right road for the farm?'

'Aye. Though whatever you're after this won't be a good time.'

'I'm selling. I find the wives in the outlying farms appreciate a look at a bit of haberdashery and hosiery.'

The sergeant gave him a penetrating look. 'Yon won't be a good stopping off point today.'

'Oh? Why's that?'

'I've just delivered some news that'll not put the lady of the house in the mood for purchasing.'

Sykes was being warned off, but if the Conroys had received bad news about Ethan Armstrong, now was exactly the time to call. He would either be sent packing, or learn something about the friendship between the two men. If Ethan had confided in anyone, it would be his friend Bob Conroy.

Sykes played the interested outsider. 'I heard there was a bit of activity round the quarry, and that quarrymen had been sent home.'

'Where did you hear that?'

'I took some orders by the mill gates,' Sykes said. 'I'll be back to make my deliveries Friday,' he added quickly, so that the sergeant would feel confident of knowing where to find this travelling salesman if the need arose.

The sergeant adjusted his helmet. You recognise me, Sykes thought. You don't know me personally, but you recognise another bobby when you see one and you think you must be mistaken and so you are uneasy.

'You'll get no joy at Conroy's farm today,' the sergeant said.

'Then I might just make an appointment to call again next time I'm round.'

'As you like. It's a free country.'

'Thank you. Good afternoon, officer.'

Sykes strode on, glancing back to see the sergeant climbing a stile, into a field where four cows grazed. From this, Sykes guessed that the sergeant had not found Conroy at home and was setting off to look for him.

Sykes pushed open the farm gate. In the field to his left, a little girl piled couch grass onto a fire, warming her hands as she did so. Sykes said hello. 'That's a grand blaze.'

The girl gave something close to a smile. She was dark as a gypsy, her movements smooth as a wriggling eel's.

'What you burning?'

'Couch grass.'

He looked at her dirty hands, pencil-thin arms and legs. 'Did you pull it all up yourself?'

She shook her head. 'Just some.'

In the field beyond was another fire. A black cauldron hung over the flames with two crouched figures beside it, one of the men holding an animal. From this distance, the scene struck him as some ancient ritual of sacrifice. I'm a townie, Sykes thought to himself. Coming here spoils my view of the country entirely.

'What are they up to?' he asked the girl.

'Over thur?' She looked at him as if he must be stupid.

'Yes.'

'Cutting tails.'

'What tails?'

'Lambs' tails.'

This was a girl who did not run to more than two words at a time. Sykes wished he hadn't asked. 'Is one of them Mr Conroy?'

'No.'

A dog began to bark.

The girl threw more couch grass on the fire, turning her back on him.

'I have a girl your age. She likes chocolate. She won't mind if you have this chocolate bar and I'll get her another one.'

She turned. He held out the chocolate.

'Fur me?'

'Aye.'

'Thanks, mister.'

'What's your name?'

She thought for a long moment. 'Millie.'

239

'Whose girl are you?'

She did not answer straightaway, as though the question was too difficult, and then the words came to her. 'Hurs.'

'Did you know Mr Armstrong?' he asked the girl, immediately wanting to bite his tongue for putting Ethan Armstrong in the past tense.

She nodded.

'Come to the farm a lot did he?'

Her canny glance told him she would not give much away, even if she could. She held the chocolate in her hand, close to her chest, as though it would be snatched away. 'What does tha want wi' me, mister?'

'Nowt.'

She broke off a piece of chocolate, popped it in her mouth, and slipped the rest of the bar in her pocket. She stooped for more couch grass. The burning grass crackled. Millie wiped a hand across her smeared face.

Sykes said, 'There is summat.'

'What?'

A flash of inspiration led him to say, 'How did Mr Armstrong and Mrs Conroy get on when he came to see her?'

Mrs Shackleton had said that Armstrong supposedly talked to Mrs Conroy about his troubles. What if it wasn't that at all? Armstrong and the farmer's wife were lovers. Conroy had found out. A fight. A deadly blow. That would explain why Conroy was not here when Harriet came running. Conroy was already in the quarry, blood on his hands.

He waited for Millie's answer, willing her, please give me more than two words.

'Don't know.' She fingered the chocolate bar in her pocket, not looking at him. But he had the feeling of being close to something.

240

The eye in the back of Sykes's head blinked. He turned and saw the farmhouse door open. 'Bye, Millie. Don't eat the chocolate all at once, lassie.'

The woman at the door watched as Sykes approached.

When he drew close, he saw that she had a round, open face and mesmerising blue eyes. Her look was curious as she waited for him to speak.

'Good afternoon, madam. I wonder if I might interest you in some very fine hosiery at a reasonable price? No obligation for taking a look.'

She looked beyond him as though he may be some ne'er do well who had an accomplice lurking round the corner, waiting to pounce.

'I'm Jim Sykes, and this week I'm in the area with some superior items manufactured from viscose which if you touch between finger and thumb I guarantee you will imagine to be silk.'

She hesitated.

'A lady like yourself would, I'm sure, appreciate the quality.'

She opened the door wide enough for him to step inside. 'I'll spare you five minutes. Only because it's a change to have a salesman who isn't flogging cattle feed.'

Sykes glanced around the kitchen. 'You keep a lovely place, and a grand fire, Mrs ...' Just in time, Sykes stopped himself from saying her name.

'Mrs Conroy.'

'A lovely place,' he repeated.

'I try. It's a losing battle with men trooping in for their meals.' She moved from the kitchen towards a door at the far side of the room. 'Come through, or whatever you have to display will end up smeared with dripping and smelling of smoked bacon.'

He followed her into a Sunday best room, with over-stuffed horsehair sofa and chairs, oak sideboard suitable for a giant's parlour and enough ornaments to keep an auctioneer busy for a week.

'Do you manage this place all on your own?' Sykes waited until she sat down on the sofa, motioning him to put down his case and be seated.

'I've a girl to help, and a woman comes in from the village twice a week.'

'Well, I take my hat off to you, Mrs Conroy.' He set the case between them, and flicked open the lid. Drawing out a pair of stockings, he held them up to catch the light. 'The silkworm himself wouldn't tell the difference between this and the real thing.'

She took the hose from him with long, slender fingers – a pianist's hands, but roughened by work. 'That's a right nice stocking. What would you rush me for 'em?'

'How much would you say they're worth to a lady like yourself with an ankle worth showing to the world?'

They haggled amiably for several minutes. 'You drive a hard bargain,' Sykes said, 'but since I've come this far and you're buying three pairs, you shall have them.'

'Well, be quick about it before my husband gets back or he'll be on at me for wasting brass.'

Sykes took out two more pairs of stockings and a sheet of tissue paper.

'Not so fast. I must make sure that the other two pairs aren't inferior.'

'I can see no man will get the better of you, Mrs Conroy.'

She laughed, a warm genuine laugh.

'Will your man be back soon? Perhaps I can interest him in a pair of socks?'

'He has socks enough to last a lifetime. His mother used to knit them for him as a punishment.' She spotted children's socks. Sykes lifted out a pair of boy's and girl's socks. 'What about something for the children?'

'I was thinking of that.'

'How many bairns do you have?'

'None of my own, sadly, but I've two little ones coming to stay who've had a dire loss. Stockings won't make up for that but if I take a pair for each of them, they'll know they're welcome when they come.'

'Might I ask what dire loss the two little ones have suffered?'

'Their father,' she sighed. 'He was found dead in the quarry earlier. The police sergeant, probably you passed him in the lane, he came to tell me.'

'I'm sorry. You should have said. I would have come another time.'

She went to the dresser, opened the top drawer and took out a purse. 'Nay, I wasn't close to the man. But he was a childhood friend of my husband. My mister will take it hard.'

As they stood by the sofa, she counted the money into his hand. I wonder, he thought as her fingers grazed his palm, was there something between you and Ethan Armstrong? When you say you were not close, do you protest too much? The thought lingered as she walked him to the door and wished him good day.

As he drew level with the girl in the field, Sykes balanced his case on top of the dry-stone wall. 'Millie!' he called.

She looked up from her fire.

'Here. A pair of stockings for you.'

Her eyes widened. 'Why?'

'To keep you warm, why else?'

The girl took the stockings from him and slid them into her apron pocket.

It was then that Sykes heard the unmistakeable sound of Mrs Shackleton's Jowett approaching.

He said goodbye to the girl and walked to the gate.

Mrs Shackleton stayed in the motor. She spoke to the children who climbed from the car. Like two little rag dolls with the stuffing knocked out of them, they stepped slowly and cautiously through the gate, keeping to the edge of the path, trying to avoid the mud.

Sykes caught a glimpse of Mrs Shackleton's face in an unguarded moment as she watched the children. He looked away because the sadness was too naked.

He walked to the car and said cheerily, 'I never miss an opportunity to show my wares. And that's what I shall do now, as you tell me what comes next.'

He opened the attaché case and set it on the seat beside her.

'I don't know what comes next, Mr Sykes. I've just had to break it to those two children that their father is dead.'

He could have choked on his cheeriness. 'Where's their mother?'

'Taken to formally identify her husband's body. But I know she'll be questioned.'

'By your chief inspector?'

'Yes. Ethan's tools were hidden under the coal in her outhouse. As if she'd be so stupid.'

People had been hanged on less evidence, Sykes knew, but he kept the thought to himself. 'I passed the local sergeant earlier. He's on his way to some far-flung field to seek out Bob Conroy and tell him the bad news.'

'That's kind of him,' Mrs Shackleton said, making a show of picking up a stocking. 'Unless...'

'Unless what?'

'He could be acting on instructions. If I'm not mistaken, Chief Inspector Marcus Charles thinks Mary Jane killed Ethan. He may suspect that she had help from Bob Conroy. Mrs Ledger said both Bob Conroy and Ethan were smitten by Mary Jane, and Ethan won her.'

Sykes held out another stocking, lisle this time, in what he thought of as "unnatural flesh" colour. They had a slightly orange tinge that he had never seen in a human being. Absently, she took it from him. Sykes thought the best thing to say now was nothing, but he said, 'What about a possible connection between Ethan Armstrong and Mrs Conroy? She's got something about her.'

Mrs Shackleton looked at him quickly. Two pink spots appeared on her cheeks. It reminded him that he must tread carefully. This investigation was too close to home for her to feel objective about it.

She let the flesh-coloured stocking fall back into the case.

Six

Sykes marched away down the lane, carrying his attaché case. I hurried to the farmhouse, feeling guilty about letting the children go in alone. But at least Georgina Conroy now knew about Ethan, and so it would not be up to Harriet to try and put the bad news into words.

I tapped on the door and went inside. 'Sorry. I sent the children ahead. I was waylaid by a man selling stockings.'

'Did you buy?'

'No. Did you?'

'I felt sorry for the poor chap. And he has the gumption to get himself out and about and try and earn a living. Not like some poor souls who have the stuffing knocked out of 'em and never see how to put it back.'

Mrs Conroy already had the children sitting by the fire, trying on new socks.

'It looks as if you two are settling in all right,' I said, immediately regretting my choice of words which made it sound as if they would be here for the duration. Both Harriet and Austin ignored me. Harriet seemed to struggle to get the heel of the sock in the right place. Austin's foot was still inside the stocking leg.

With her back to the children, Mrs Conroy cast me a

tragic glance. 'Eh what a to do. But the bairns can stay here as long as need be. Put Mary Jane at ease over that.'

I helped Austin try on his new socks. He let me do it, though would not look, and would not answer when I asked did he like them.

Declining the offer to stay for tea, I was just about to leave when the door burst open and a cold blast of air filled the room. Bob Conroy stood in the doorway, looking at the farmhouse kitchen as though he had never seen it or the occupants before. He stumbled a few steps into the room. Ignoring his wife's warning glance, his face contorted with emotion. He swooped towards the hearth and the two children.

Georgina Conroy shut the door behind him and uttered a warning, 'Bob!'

But he was on the hearth rug, between the children, silently putting his arms around the pair of them, drawing them to him. 'You can stay as long as you want, and your mam, too, when she comes home.'

'Of course they can, my dear,' Georgina said evenly.

She walked to the door, where I stood waiting to take my leave. Mrs Conroy sighed at her husband's demonstrativeness. 'The poor bairns don't need outpourings of sentiment. They need a bit of calm and care.'

Feeling I had left the children in safe hands, I said goodbye. Next stop, Applewick Hall.

The powerful conviction that the Ledgers had some connection with Ethan's death was not my only prompt for driving to Applewick Hall. Marcus had been quick enough to tell me about Mary Jane's insurance policy on Ethan's life, yet he did not mention her bank book. I felt sure he would have asked me about that had he come across it. I wanted to know why Mary Jane met Colonel Ledger on Tuesday.

I parked my motor in front of Applewick Hall, hoping my noisy arrival and obtrusive placing of the motor would alert the occupants. At the front door, I gave the knocker a whopping thump, and waited. A word from someone "important" carries a great deal of weight. Tipped as future lord lieutenant of the county, Ledger was "important". I had no compunction about pulling any string that might ease Mary Jane's way. The butler remembered me from my previous visit. 'I'm here to see Mrs Ledger, on a matter of urgency.' Best be conventional, and start with her.

'Madam is not receiving visitors at present.' He hesitated. 'Would you care to leave your card?'

'No. I shall wait and see either Mrs Ledger or the colonel. They will not thank you for turning me away.'

Without another word, he opened the door and led me into the drawing room, where I had waited on my previous visit. The family portrait dominated the room. Colonel and Mrs Ledger in all their glory gazed down at me with something like disdain. The two little boys, bright-eyed and confident, brought a touch of joy to the scene. The elder had curved brows that gave him a surprised, slightly supercilious look, like my cat when she thought herself ignored.

I did not have long to wait. Mrs Ledger glided into the room. She approached me cautiously. 'Mrs Shackleton?'

'Mrs Ledger.'

'Won't you sit down?' There was something curiously brittle about her that I had not noticed before. A tremor of irritation came from her as I took up her invitation and sat on the sofa that faced the portrait, looking at the woman and the painted image of her. 'You are here on a matter of urgency, I understand?'

'Yes. You'll have heard that Ethan Armstrong's body was found in the quarry.'

She nodded gravely. 'We were told of course. Sergeant Sharp telephoned to my husband. A tragedy.'

'Mrs Armstrong has been taken to make formal identification of the body, and for questioning by the police. I thought you would want to know, because of how long she worked for you.'

She looked at me steadily, trying to work out what else lay behind my words.

'Oh?' She looked surprised. 'When you say taken for questioning, do you give me to understand that some suspicion hangs over Mrs Armstrong?'

'I believe so, though I'm sure it's entirely unfounded.'

'It's absurd if she's suspected. But I'm not sure what I can do. Did she ask that you come here?'

'No. I took it upon myself. Because she worked for you, when she was very young, and because her husband was your employee.'

Mrs Ledger gave me a sharp look, as if to assess what Mary Jane may have said.

'She was my maid, yes. But that was a long time ago. Is there something she needs, for herself or the children? Naturally if there's anything we can do to help . . .'

At that moment the door opened. Colonel Ledger feigned surprise. 'I'm sorry, my dear. I didn't know you had company.' For a moment he seemed to look through me, as if our meeting on Monday was a decade ago and he had trouble placing me. Flattering.

Finally he said, 'Mrs Shackleton.'

'Colonel.'

He strode across the room and sat down beside his wife. A united front. 'I've heard about Armstrong being found. Bad business. Wish now that I'd thought to send my own hounds to the quarry earlier.'

Mrs Ledger stretched her fingers towards her husband's hand, without touching. 'I expect it is better that the police deal with these matters, Colonel.'

She called him colonel? I tried not to smile.

And now she did touch his arm. 'Apparently Mrs Armstrong has been taken to identify the body, and for questioning.'

He blinked several times. 'Why? I mean, this is no time to question her.'

I decided not to tell him about Ethan's tool bag hidden in the Armstrongs' coalhouse. As briefly as I could, I hinted at Marcus's suspicions.

The colonel sprang to his feet. 'But that's absurd! I shall speak to the man. Mary Jane's sent you here?'

'No. I offered to go with her to Otley, to the hospital, but she asked me to collect the children from school. They're with the Conroys.'

'My dear,' Mrs Ledger said quietly, 'I think we should let the police deal with this in their own way.'

He sighed, strode across the room, and returned to his seat. 'You're right, darling. You're right, of course. But I shall contact my solicitor all the same.'

His agitation showed in the movement of his jaw, the flexing of his fingers.

Mrs Ledger patted his arm. The two of them, side by side on the sofa, would have made a perfect second portrait. Older, but with none of their confidence, none of their certainties dented. Supply a solicitor. Talk sense to the constabulary.

Calmer now, he spoke again. 'You did the right thing coming here, Mrs Shackleton. I shall look out for Mary Jane's . . . for Mrs Armstrong's interests.'

But would he? The part of me that had been brought up expecting men to take charge, men to put things right, wanted to let go, wanted to let him look out for Mary Jane. But the little voice in my head said, Don't trust him.

'Colonel Ledger, may I ask what you and Mary Jane discussed when you met on Tuesday?'

His mouth dropped open. Mrs Ledger turned her head towards him. Her small tongue darted across her lower lip. She knew.

'Tuesday?' He shook his head. For two pins he would have me escorted out.

If I were to get information from him, he needed to know that I could be trouble. 'When you met at Horsforth railway station and drove to the Station Hotel.' He opened his mouth to deny, or accuse me of being mistaken, but before his words tumbled into the air, I said, 'Only I wonder if she gave her bank passbook into your safekeeping?'

He looked surprised. 'Why would she give me a bank book?'

'Because the money is in her maiden name. It's what you gave her when she was in your wife's employ, and what you've given her since.' The last part was a guess, but it hit home.

Colonel and Mrs Ledger froze, but only for a fraction of a second. He gulped. She cleared her throat, as if to speak, but he was ahead of her. 'Did Mrs Armstrong explain the money?'

'She told me that when she was fifteen you photographed her in artistic poses.'

He gave a small smile. 'Quite innocent.'

Mrs Ledger echoed her husband. 'Entirely innocent.'

There was a long silence. They were not going to say more, and why should they? I rose to go. 'Then if you don't have the bank book . . .'

As I stood, so did the colonel, unsure whether to see me out.

'Wait!' Mrs Ledger gave a light, tinkling laugh. Her husband smiled at her, waiting to see what lead she would give him. She said, 'Please sit down, Mrs Shackleton. It's all very simple. Mary Jane was a pretty little thing and she certainly knew it. My husband is a keen amateur photographer and he took some portraits of her in a Grecian robe, terribly proper, which she, in her naivety, believed to be immensely daring. I'm sure if we can turn them up you may see for yourself. I gave her money when she was twenty-three, and about to be married. There was no connection with the photographs. At one of our harvest suppers, it was clear to anyone with eyes to see that Bob Conroy fell for Mary Jane. He spoke to the colonel one day and sought her hand, as though we were her parents. I found that touching, and if you must know, I looked on my gift to her as a sort of dowry. There have been connections between my family and the Conroys' for generations. As it transpired, Ethan Armstrong stole her heart, and that was not a match made in heaven. But if some police inspector believes Mary Jane would have killed her husband, and he's whisked her off to the Otley police station for a confession, then he should be packed off to some backwater of Empire.'

The colonel said, 'My dear you must be more temperate in your comments. It may be that the chief inspector simply wants to give Mrs Armstrong the opportunity to think more clearly, away from her home and children.'

'And your tryst on Tuesday?' I persisted.

He sighed. 'Not a tryst. She asked me to advise her. She lives in a tied house and feared eviction. I assured her that no such occurrence would take place.' He turned to his wife. 'That was all, my dear.'

'Of course.' She squeezed his hand.

'Now if you'll excuse me, I shall call my solicitor and have him get onto the police. It's outrageous that Mrs Armstrong should be separated from her children. I would have identified Armstrong.'

He sprang from the sofa. At the door, he turned back. 'Are the police aware that Mrs Armstrong has her own deposit account?'

He would wash his hands of her in a moment if he had to, to save his own reputation.

'No.'

'Good.' He closed the door gently as he left.

Mrs Ledger's smile condescended. 'Mary Jane was with me for years. I grew fond of her. I hope this can be sorted out quickly. But the children will be well looked after at the farm, with Mr and Mrs Conroy.'

Something in her voice seemed to be drawing a line under the past.

'Of course, it's your farm now.'

Her nostrils flared almost imperceptibly. 'You won't expect me to comment on that, and I'm surprised that Conroy would speak of the sale so prematurely.'

It saddened me that what Ethan most argued against had come to pass. An age-old farm would be torn open and quarried, without Ethan standing in the way of progress.

Yet there was something else going on. I sensed it but could not give a shape to what niggled at me.

After a few more moments, the colonel returned. 'My

253

solicitor will be onto the police straightaway. He will look after Mary Jane's interests.'

Mrs Ledger stood up and joined her husband. 'Thank you for bringing this to our attention, Mrs Shackleton.'

I'd made a mistake. These people could not be trusted. Mary Jane would be in their power. The solicitor would look after her interests only if those interests coincided with the Ledgers'.

I drove slowly back through the village, ready to make my way home. Yet I was drawn to Mary Jane's cottage. If she had not given her bank book to Colonel Ledger for safe-keeping, then where was it? And who had placed Ethan's tools where they might be found and used against Mary Jane?

The merest whiff of smoke still rose from the chimney, a forlorn signal meandering uselessly towards the clouds.

I drew the key through the letter box and unlocked the door. Straightaway I knew the house was not deserted. Someone was here. I felt a presence, like a drawn breath. A footstep sounded on the stair.

'Mrs Shackleton.'

'Mr Sykes! What are you doing here?'

'Same as you, I expect. Wondering who planted the tools in the coalhouse, wondering whether there was anything the police missed.'

'And is there?'

'No. Not that I can see.'

'I don't know where Mary Jane has put her bank book. I thought she may have given it to the colonel, but if she has, he's saying nothing.'

'You went to see them?'

'They're worried, but making light of it. Mrs Ledger

claims the saucy photographs were simply artistic, Grecian toga stuff. They probably have the photographic prints and negatives to prove it, and anything else will mysteriously disappear.'

'Still, it does put them on her side.'

'It puts them on their own side, Mr Sykes. They'd sacrifice Mary Jane in a moment.'

'Your chief inspector has nothing concrete against Mary Jane, except the hidden tools. Anyone could have put them there.'

Sykes was already putting together a case for the defence. He rubbed his chin. 'There'll be a great deal of speculation in the local hostelry tonight.'

Mr Sykes places great store by pub gossip because it gives him an advantage over me who wouldn't be able to indulge in the same kind of information gathering.

'If you must. But be careful. We don't know how many plain-clothes men might have the same idea.'

He met me halfway.

'I haven't forgotten I'm due at the insurance offices at nine o'clock in the morning. Just a couple of pints and an hour's earwigging, and then I'll find my way home.'

I scribbled a note for Mary Jane and set it in the middle of the table so that she would spot it as soon as Sergeant Sharp brought her home; if he brought her home.

'You'd better leave first, Mr Sykes. I shall pay my condolences to the vicar.'

There was a connection between the death of Ethan Armstrong and that of Miss Trimble, and I intended to uncover that link.

Seven

A craggy man with a well-fed belly greeted me in a soft cultured voice. I guessed the vicar to be an Oxford man, and remembered his sister saying that he would rather have served God in Brighton than in the wilds of Yorkshire. He gave the impression of a man who had been over-condoled and there was the possibility I would be rebuffed. Perhaps this was not the moment for him to confront the woman who had shared his sister's last moments.

With my practised skill, I introduced myself with full credentials including my status and profession, Dad's job and Mother's title. That did the trick.

Wearily, he picked up a book from the hall table. 'Come into the study, Mrs Shackleton. So, I have you to thank for finding my sister.'

I said a few appropriate words. He opened the book. 'Condolences,' he said, turning it towards me. 'People have been very good. She didn't realise how loved she was.'

I glanced at the pages, full of signatures, prayers, and flowery sentiments.

I was meant to take the pen. 'I'm sorry to say I did not

know Miss Trimble, having only met her that morning. If you'll give me a moment . . .'

Even with a moment, I could think of nothing to write.

'Poor Aurora was in high spirits that day,' he said glumly. 'The lord gave her joy in her final days on earth.'

'Was she joyful for a particular reason?'

He pushed his sermon in progress away. 'She'd spent a happy week in Clitheroe with our cousin who is married to the verger there. And of course, she loved the church windows, you see, leaded lights, heavenly stained glass.'

'In Clitheroe?'

'No. Here. Poor Aurora.'

For a long moment, as I wrote something anodyne in the condolence book, I tried to think of how to phrase the question: is there anyone who would have wanted your sister dead? Instead, I said, 'You have a lovely church.' And then I remembered that one of the windows was plain glass. 'Were you to have a new window?'

'Yes. That was why she was so happy. Farmer Conroy spoke to my sister about it on Sunday. He would pay for a new one, in memory of his parents and his brother.'

Bob Conroy. So he intended to donate some of the proceeds of his farm sale. He was in the churchyard after I left the vicarage, by his brother's grave, talking to the dead, distressed. I kept my face as expressionless as a poker player as I wondered had Bob Conroy helped Aurora Trimble into the afterlife so that she could not give evidence against Mary Jane?

Mr Trimble was speaking, asking me a question.

'Sorry. What did you ask me?'

'Did Aurora say anything before she died?'

Oh dear. Gerald used to play a game with a doctor friend. One would name a person living or dead. The other had to quote or invent Famous Last Words. I was tempted to invent something marvellous now. But I had been hopeless at the game.

'She said only two words, Mr Trimble. "Bitter" was the first.'

'Bitter, or *bitte*?'

'Pardon?'

'She spoke German you know. Just like her to be so polite, even on the point of death.'

'Why would she speak to me in German?'

'We had a cousin to stay from Baden-Baden. Perhaps she . . . No, she would not have mistaken you for our cousin. Did my sister say anything else?'

This was even worse. Now he would think I was deaf, or making it up. 'She said, "dandy".'

'Dandy?' He shook his head in puzzlement.

I waited, to hear what other languages she may have spoken, to other cousins, in which the word "dandy" meant thank you and goodbye.

When I drove back to the cottage, a light shone in the window. Mary Jane was home. I tapped on the door, which was locked.

'Who is it?'

'It's me.'

She unlocked the door and opened it, waiting for me to step inside. She looked wrung out and exhausted.

'I wanted to make sure you're all right. Was it terrible?'

'Yes.' She returned to her chair by the fire and stared into the flames. 'So final. It's not him any more, Kate. Ethan's gone. People say oh he's just a shell. I never knew what that meant. I wish I hadn't seen him like that.'

'Have you eaten?'

'I'm not hungry. And look at that lot.' She waved her arm at the table. There was a pot of stew, a cake, a pie. 'People left stuff on the doorstep. For the kids probably. They don't like me.'

'That can't be true. There'll be a lot of sympathy for you in the village.'

Reluctantly, I confided my visit to the Ledgers and the colonel's telephone call to his solicitor. 'Now is there anything I can do?'

There was not.

I ignored the rebuff and picked up the bed warmer from the hearth. It was a silver shoe, waiting to be filled with boiling water. I took it to the table, lifted the kettle and began to pour. 'I'll put this in your bed. You look done in.'

She made no objection. While upstairs, I checked under the mattress for the disappeared bank book. Not there.

We sat on either side of the fire. She gazed at the flames. 'What did you say to the children?'

'I told them as simply as I could. Austin, well, he didn't understand.'

'No. I don't suppose he would. You probably think I'm a coward not wanting to tell them myself.'

'Of course not.'

She poked the fire, stirring up the flames. 'Only when our dad died, Mam told us all straight away, all the details. He was brought home into that downstairs room and we all had to sit there, him lying on a board on the table. We all had to kiss him. It was horrible. Then go to the funeral, and I was too little, and my legs ached but no one noticed. I just had to try and keep up. I always said that if ever my children . . . I wanted to protect them. And you can't. I see that now. There's no way to do it. Mam did what she thought best.'

'Do you want me to stay with you?'

'No. The inspector, chief inspector, whatever he is, said nothing will happen now until after the post mortem and after more information has been gathered, whatever he means by that. I'll just have to get through. I'll be best on my own. Mrs Conroy will take care of the kids. I want a little time to be here, just a bit longer. Ethan loved this place, and I couldn't wait to be out. Well, sometimes I couldn't wait to be out and other times . . . I loved it too, at first. People will be calling on me tomorrow. I'll have to put up with it. I'll be best on my own.'

'All right. You know where I am if you need me. Ask Sergeant Sharp to telephone me.'

She nodded.

There was a knock on the door.

'I can't bear it, Kate. Say I've gone to bed. Say you're just leaving. Anything.'

She let her shawl drop to the floor as she hurried to the bottom of the stairs.

'Hello again.' It was Bob Conroy.

'Mary Jane's gone to . . .'

But she was there beside me, running to him, saying, 'Bob, oh Bob.' He stepped inside and took her in his arms.

I left.

By the tram stop on the main road, I stopped and picked up Sykes.

'Is something wrong?' he asked.

'I don't know.'

The one person who had claimed to see Mary Jane in the vicinity of the quarry at a crucial time was Miss

Trimble. Miss Trimble was dead. The person who hovered near the vicarage at her time of death was Bob Conroy. But the doctor had certified death from heart failure. And doctors are never wrong. I should put thoughts of poison out of my mind.

THURSDAY

Sage snail, within thine own self curl'd,
Instruct me softly to make haste,
Whilst these my feet go slowly fast.

Richard Lovelace

One

Thursday was my favourite day as a child. It was the day the grocery box came from Lipton's store, with a bar of Fry's Five Boys chocolate. Thursday was the day when I came home from school with nothing to do, no ballet class (Monday and Wednesday); no visit from my home tutor (Tuesday) who smoked a pipe, wore a smelly tweed jacket, picked his nose and did all the sums himself as I pretended to follow while watching the dry skin fall from his chin onto the page as he rubbed bogeymen into his beard.

This Thursday I lay in bed, my first long lie in since returning from London last Sunday. Mrs Sugden fussed over me and brought up breakfast. 'Stop where you are, Mrs Shackleton, you look done in.'

I felt done in, but from the frustration of making no progress, and the growing certainty that the investigation into Ethan Armstrong's death was slipping from my grasp.

When I am stuck, it can help to tell myself the story of what has happened so far, which I did, hoping then to project into where I should look next. A powerful image held me back. Each time I ran through the story, the embrace between Mary Jane and Bob Conroy brought me to a halt.

Conroy had concluded his deal with Ledger. It would be simply a matter of time, selling up of farm stock and equipment, and then Conroy would move on. But where would he go, and with whom – his own wife, or Mary Jane, her children, and her bank book?

Unable to go forward, I went back, to the vicarage drawing room and Miss Trimble's last words. Bitter. Well yes, a bitter pill to be dying. Dandy. A person? During my brief time in Great Applewick, I saw not a single person who could be accused of snappy dressing.

Mrs Sugden came into the bedroom to pick up my breakfast tray. 'Do you want anything else?'

'Yes but I'll get it.'

'You rest. Everyone who carries a lot of cares in their head should have one day a month in their nightdress.'

'In that case, I'll have the dictionary please. Miss Trimble's last word was dandy, and I can't imagine what she meant to say.'

'Then don't,' Mrs Sugden said. 'She was probably rambling. Rest your brain or you'll be rambling yourself.'

I glanced at the clock. Nine-thirty. I would lie till ten-thirty, with my eyes shut, and see whether any amazing insights occurred.

Mrs Sugden returned, dictionary in hand. She stood by the trug of kittens and read, 'Dandy. Noun. A fop; coxcomb; something very neat and trim; a subsidiary attachment to a machine; a chamber in a pudding furnace; a Ganges boatman; a cloth hammock slung on a bamboo staff used in India like a palanquin; a sloop-rigged vessel with a jigger mast; a small sail carried at the stern of a small boat; a jigger: Dandy, adjective, pertaining to or characteristic of a dandy or fop. Dandy-brush, a whale-bone brush; Dandy-note, a Custom's permit for the removal of goods from a bonded warehouse.' She shut the book. 'Now are you any wiser, Mrs Shackleton?'

'No.' I wasn't going to ask her to read the definition of palanquin.

She sighed. 'It's unlikely, but if she felt herself to be ailing . . .'

'Yes?'

'Well, there's *dandy fever* isn't there?'

'You're right. But is she likely to have caught *dandy fever* in Great Applewick, or during her visit to Clitheroe, and self-diagnosed her condition as she lay dying? I don't think so.'

The puzzle remained. I decided against staying in bed any longer. After my bath, I walked about the wood, hoping for inspiration. I was still there, admiring blue-bells, when Marcus called my name.

He strode towards me, arms open, 'My wood nymph! Now I see you in your own habitat.'

'Welcome to Batswing Wood.'

'It's lovely here.'

We perched on the log that forms a bench. He looked around. 'You even have a natural stage.'

'Yes. The local children put on their plays here. All a little precocious, lots of academic and medical parents come to dote in the summer before they flee on their long holidays.' He had not come to discuss the merits of Batswing Wood and my learned neighbours. 'Will you have lunch, Marcus? I'm sure it'll stretch.'

'Perhaps a quick bite.' He made a playful dart for my ear.

'You have a driver with you?'

'Yes.'

'Ask him in. Mrs Sugden will look after him.' I reached for his hand. 'Let's go inside.'

He pulled me back. 'I'm sorry. I shouldn't be joking about. I'm putting off what I have to tell you.'

'Go on.'

'The post mortem on Ethan Armstrong, it took place early this morning.'

'Don't tell me here, Marcus.' I stood up. It was ridiculous and irrational, but I didn't want the words spoken in my little wood. Not that the bluebells would hear, but the words might bounce from tree to tree forever. Whenever I came out here to think, or watch the squirrels, I would hear what he had to say. 'Let's walk up the road. It won't take long and you can tell me there, away from my wood.'

He did not argue. I called in at the kitchen door and asked Mrs Sugden would she put together something light, and ask the driver to come inside.

We walked to the top of the road, past my neighbour's big house where the gardener paused in his hedge trimming. The path led us into another wood, not my wood.

'Tell me now.'

'Ethan Armstrong was killed with a blunt instrument, his own hammer, by a blow to his skull.'

'So it was someone tall.'

It was Bob Conroy, Josiah Turnbull, one of Ledger's men, anyone, but not Mary Jane.

'Not necessarily. There are bruises around the kneecap, a cracked patella. The most likely explanation is that the assailant hit him there first so that he buckled at the knees, and then brought the hammer down on his head. He suffered a depressed skull fracture and bleeding to the brain.'

'Do you have any leads?'

'It's early days, Kate. We know now how he died, and approximately when. I have to find out why, and who.'

'When do you plan to tell Mary Jane?'

'Let her take in the death first, and then the manner of it.'

'She didn't do it you know.'

I should tell him about Bob Conroy, but if I did, that would implicate Mary Jane.

He did not respond to my claim for Mary Jane's innocence. 'You have some papers that belonged to Mr Armstrong, trade union material and so on.'

'Yes.'

'I'll take them with me please.'

'Very well.'

We walked back to the house. 'I so much wanted to see you again, Kate, but not like this.'

'I know.'

He gave a rueful laugh. 'I'm invited to lunch on Sunday with you and your parents. Your father telephoned this morning, under instructions from your mother I expect.'

'That sounds right. Well, I know Dad will be glad to meet you, and Mother has spoken of you several times since your fleeting encounter in Harrogate.'

'Where will we be by Sunday?' he asked, and answered his own question. 'I just don't know. You'll understand if I have to cry off at the last minute?'

'Mother and I are used to that with Dad.'

He paused at my gate. 'There's something else, Kate.' I waited. 'When I bring Mrs Armstrong back into the station, I might call on your services, to be there with her.'

'Well, of course.'

'To be there with her, to observe.'

269

'Marcus, what are you getting at?'

'I want you to know that everything will be fair, and done properly. Did you know I've had the Ledgers' solicitor chap bending my ear?'

'I'm afraid that's my fault. I thought they might want to help Mary Jane because she used to work for them. Now I wonder if they'd repay a closer look from you.'

'Kate, you're not suggesting that Ledger killed Ethan Armstrong?'

'They recently bought Bob Conroy's farm. The person who'd stood in the way of that for years was Ethan Armstrong. Ledger has problems at one of his coal mines. Ethan tried to call a strike.'

'And Ledger defeated Armstrong at every turn. He wouldn't need to resort to foul play. The colonel could have chewed up Armstrong and spat him out whenever he chose. Come on, Kate. Let's have that bite of lunch.'

I could have said more. I was tempted to tell him about the bank book, Ledger's photographs of Mary Jane, the "dowry" from Mrs Ledger. But that would reflect badly on Mary Jane's character and the outlook for her was bleak enough already. For now, I would keep that information to myself.

I took Marcus to the dining room where Ethan Armstrong's papers were piled at one end of the table. On top was the personal advertisement of a well provided woman looking for a well provided man. As casually as I could, I said, 'I'm enquiring into this.'

'You've written a letter?'

'Composed a letter, yes.' No need to bring Mr Duffield into it.

He smiled indulgently. In that moment, I could have walloped him, and I am not given to violence as a rule.

FRIDAY

To inform — or, in official speech, "to approve" — seems as much in the nature of an Englishman as it is to kick a ball or to drink a glass of beer.

Wilfred Macartney, *Walls Have Mouths*

One

At ten o'clock on Friday morning, I parked the Jowett on Courtyard Street, just a few yards from Otley police station. I walked into the station, carrying a bag of sandwiches for Mary Jane, and a flask. This could not have been what she had in mind when she turned up on my doorstep asking for help.

The duty sergeant was expecting me. He bounced from behind his counter and escorted me upstairs.

Minutes later, Marcus stood to greet me, in his borrowed office. The room was painted institutional green, with worn linoleum and a powerful smell of stale ash from the metal waste bin. Every story and account I had ever heard about imprisonment came into my head at once. I felt utterly inadequate. Marcus put on a cheerful look and asked about my journey, as he might ask a stranger. The exchange felt formal, anxious even. From his point of view I could see why Mary Jane might look guilty. *Don't acknowledge that even to yourself, Kate. Act as if she is innocent and she will be.*

'Thank you for coming, Kate. I know this must be difficult.'

'What's happening, Marcus?'

273

'A solicitor, Mr Nelson, has been appointed by the Ledgers to act for Mrs Armstrong. He'll be here at eleven and I shall interview her in his presence.'

'Under caution, you mean?'

He ignored my question. 'There's something you could do for me, and for her too. I don't want to have to recruit yet another policeman's wife.'

'Where is Mary Jane? How long has she been here?'

He hesitated. 'We brought her at eight. She's in an interview room. No one is giving her the third degree, Kate. Believe me, she will be treated with utmost courtesy and fairness. I've had Colonel Ledger on the phone this morning.' He pulled a wry face. 'Between you and the colonel, she can be sure her interests are well protected.'

'If she's been here since eight, that means you're leaving her to stew, in the hope that she'll be so softened up.'

'Now really, Kate, you know me better than that.'

'Do I? Well go on, what is it you want me to do?'

Whether his slight blush came from embarrassment or annoyance I could not tell. 'I'd like you to be with her and watch her reaction when two other individuals are brought in for questioning.'

'You want me to inform on her?'

'You asked to see her, and I'm finding a way for that to happen. If you agree, I'll take you to a room that over-looks the main entrance. From the window, you'll see who comes and goes.'

'Marcus, don't play games with me. You think she killed her husband and had an accomplice who dragged the body across the quarry because she wasn't strong enough. Someone who wanted rid of Ethan.'

He did not meet my glance. 'Let's just see what happens, eh?'

'And if I don't agree?'

'I shall bring in the duty sergeant's wife.'

'And I won't get to see Mary Jane.'

'I'm sorry, Kate. I'm trying to do my best, and be fair. I really and truly hope to eliminate her from enquiries.'

'She'll come through with flying colours because she's innocent.'

'I should like you to watch her reactions. Listen to what she says when she sees them.'

'Who are these people?'

'There will be two, brought in succession.'

I looked at him steadily. He suspected Mary Jane. He doubted that she would have had the strength to drag Ethan's body across the quarry unaided. From her performance swinging my suitcases up the stairs on Monday morning, I could have put him right on that.

'If those are your terms for my seeing Mary Jane, I shall do it.'

He came round the desk and stood beside me, bobbed down, and took my hand. 'Kate, I would trust you to the ends of the earth.' Then you are a fool, I thought. But of course, he was lying.

'She's on the first floor. I'll take you to her. You can leave your bag here.'

'I brought sandwiches for her, and a flask.'

'I'll see she gets them later.'

'I can at least take in cigarettes?'

He nodded.

So this was what it was like to be on the wrong side of the law. I slipped cigarettes, matches and, surreptitiously, notebook and pencil into my pocket.

She was sitting on a bench by the window in a small room

that looked to have been partitioned off from a larger one. More institutional green – olive walls, khaki door and window frames. A small oak table, stained with teacup marks and the burnt-out cigarettes that had been placed on its edge dominated the centre of the room, along with three bentwood chairs. On the table stood a tin ashtray, a glass of water and a jug.

I took out a packet of cigarettes and a box of matches. Mary Jane lit up and inhaled. 'Can I keep these?'

'Yes.'

'They think I did it.'

'The truth will come out. I'm sure of it.'

She gave a rueful little grin. 'I'm not sure, not sure at all. The truth has a way of hiding under stones.' She turned to the window and looked down into the street. 'They had me in a room without a window earlier. It was horrible.'

'Chief Inspector Charles is a fair man. He'll keep an open mind, believe me.'

And if I am not mistaken, he will even now be listening through this thin partition wall.

'You would say that. They came for me before eight o'clock this morning. I've no idea what's happening, apart from this solicitor who's supposed to be coming. I can't believe this. It's like being in some horrible dream. They think I did it, just because of some dratted insurance policy that wasn't even my idea. Ethan came home with that suggestion. I wouldn't entertain it. Get them to ask the insurance man. He'll tell them whose idea it was.'

I didn't know how to answer. If I said the solicitor would make sure everything like that came out, it would sound as if I thought she would be charged. In the silence where there should have been my reassurance, she said, 'I don't understand how the tools ended up in the coal shed. Kate, ask Harriet about it. She picked up Ethan's cap. Did she pick up his tools as well? She might think she'll be in trouble.'

'Do you want me to go and see the children?'

'Yes. I said they could see their grandma on Sunday and now I don't know whether they'll let me out of here before then.'

'Do you want me to take them?'

'Would you?'

'Yes. They'll be glad of that. I know Austin didn't want to go to the farm.'

'Poor Austin.' She sighed. 'What a mess. Sometimes don't you just wonder how differently your life might have turned out? And then you find it's too late.'

Shut up, Mary Jane. Walls have ears. But I couldn't say that, so I interrupted her. 'Mrs Conroy gave the children each a pair of socks.'

But she was no longer listening. Her attention was on something going on below.

I looked out of the window.

Turnbull, the quarry foreman, swaggered between two uniformed policemen. He threw out his chest, jutted his chin defiantly.

Mary Jane stared. 'They're bringing in Turnbull! He never liked Ethan. Maybe they don't think it's me. They want Turnbull to get the wrong end of the stick, so that he'll give himself away. He has a temper on him. You should see that poor wife of his, and I'll tell you what, she doesn't try to hide it any more. She walks around not caring who sees her black eyes. If he killed Ethan . . . I tell you what, Kate, I said to his wife once, I said to her, he has to sleep. If he were mine, I'd take a knife to him. If he were mine, he'd wake up dead.'

Shut up, Mary Jane. Don't say things like that in here.

She took another drag on her cigarette. 'I want to go home. If I'd known I was going to be pulled in here again, I'd have kept the children by me. Only I thought it would be better for them not to see me crying. When are they gonna let me go? This damn toff of a legal eagle we're waiting for is probably off playing golf. Who is he anyway?'

If Marcus were not listening, I would have admitted to her that I had been to see the Ledgers, and that Colonel Ledger had contacted his solicitor.

The ash on her cigarette lengthened. I went to the table and picked up the battered ashtray. Too late, the ash fell from her cigarette as she once again stared through the window. 'Hey! Look at this. They're fetching in Raymond Turnbull as well. Well, they can't suspect Raymond. Do you think he'll give evidence against his dad?'

'Mary Jane, they're probably just gathering information.' But I allowed myself to hope. Only one constable escorted Raymond.

Mary Jane stubbed out her cigarette. 'Raymond's getting married tomorrow. Me and Ethan were supposed to be at the wedding. He worships Ethan. If he knows anything, he'll tell it. He will.' Her voice fell to almost a whisper. 'He'll get our house. It always goes to a mason.'

There came a muffled sound from the other side of the partition. Marcus had said he wanted Mary Jane's reactions to two men who would be brought in. Well, now he had her reaction. No doubt in just a moment more I should be called away. I strained my ears for another noise from beyond the partition, or the corridor, but all was silence.

Mary Jane couldn't be still. She sat down. She stood up. She walked across the room. She went back to the window.

'Oh look!' Mary Jane's joy transformed her face. 'He's come to tell them that it wasn't me. I knew he'd stand by me.'

I looked down. The man approaching the door below strode purposefully, unescorted. It was Bob Conroy.

How long would this go on? Would we have to watch the entire male population of Great Applewick cross the threshold of Otley police station?

She banged on the window, trying to attract Bob's attention.

The look of pleasure made her face young. At the sight of him, care fled, her cheeks flushed. He had not heard her, but she smiled. 'You know who'll stand by you in dark times.'

It was the line of her high cheekbone, the curve of her eyebrow, the shape of her mouth.

And I knew. It hit me like a punch in the gut.

I took out my notebook and quickly scribbled, *You need the lavatory now!*

She looked at the page, and was about to rephrase my words back as a question, when I shook my head. Her mouth fell open as she looked at the thin partition wall, and at the door. The penny dropped.

'I need the lavatory, Kate. I can't wait.'

'I'll get someone.' I tried the door. It was locked. I rattled the knob, and urged her with my eyes to play her part.

'It's . . . you know . . . Kate, do something or I shall be so embarrassed.'

279

I knocked loudly on the door. When the constable unlocked it, I said, in the same voice I would use to report an unexploded bomb, 'Where is the nearest ladies' convenience?' I could see from his face that he did not know. No one had asked him such a question before.

'I can find out,' he said thoughtfully.

'This is an urgent female matter,' I whispered so as not to embarrass the female in question. 'I shall vouch for Mrs Armstrong's return.'

With that I grabbed Mary Jane's hand and raced along the corridor and down the stairs.

'Where are we going? Are we running away?'

'We're not running away. We're looking for a lavatory.'

We hurried along the corridor, down a flight of stairs.

It was a gent's lavatory and it stunk but had the advantage of being unoccupied. I kept my back to the door.

'What is it?' Mary Jane asked. 'Is it to do with Bob Conroy?'

'No.' *Though I know you probably feel you made the wrong choice and wish you'd married him.* 'Mary Jane, it wasn't that. It was the expression on your face when you saw him. You suddenly looked younger, and I thought where have I seen that face before?'

There was little light in the room, yet the striking similarity would not go away.

'What are you talking about?'

'You told me that it was because of the two children you wouldn't leave Great Applewick. That puzzled me, because you didn't mean Harriet and Austin. You let me think you meant the two little ones in the chapel graveyard. But that wasn't true. It was the other two children who kept you here. The boys, the Ledger boys.'

She took a shuddering breath. 'How ... what made you ...?'

'The portrait that hangs in the Ledgers' drawing room. The likeness is there. So obvious. That's why the Ledgers wanted you out of the way, in case someone guessed, perhaps even the boys themselves. Children always think they don't really belong to the family they are born into. Those Ledger boys, they're yours aren't they?'

'I swore to never . . .. You're guessing.'

'Mary Jane, your life may be at stake. I'm on your side, perhaps the only one who truly is on your side.'

'Bob . . .'

Footsteps approached along the corridor. I put a finger to my lips. The footsteps continued. When the footsteps had passed, I said, 'Tell me I'm right.'

'I . . . I . . . Oh Kate, I can't.'

'Trust me. I'm your sister, the one you didn't want to lose. Well, you've got me back. Now tell me.'

'Mrs Ledger couldn't have children. She ... We went on holiday together, the three of us. The mistress was called away because her mother was sick. It was just the colonel and me, and somehow ... He fell in love with me Kate, he truly did. Mrs Ledger was very understanding, said she would keep the child and no one need know.'

'And that happened twice?'

I tried to keep the disbelief from my voice that Mary Jane could have been so naïve. The colonel wanted an heir and a spare and not succeeding with his wealthy land-owning wife, the two of them had contrived to deal with the situation in a more subtle and effective way. They must have been disappointed when Mary Jane did not take the money and leave the area. Mrs Ledger's tale regarding wanting Mary Jane to marry Bob Conroy and stay on the farm was a lie. Ethan the stonemason was the man most likely to move on. Ethan the troublesome stonemason was always the favoured choice of someone to take a trouble-some maid off their hands. But perhaps Ethan the stonemason had found out.

'Did Ethan know about the Ledger children?' I asked.

'No. Nobody knew, except the doctor and nurse, and they were well paid to keep quiet. The nurse has a house in Ilkley, rent free for life.'

'You're sure?'

'Yes.'

'Do you think Miss Trimble might have guessed?'

Because if she did, I thought, it may have cost her life.

Voices called to each other, that the women had vanished. Marcus ordered someone to go outside and search.

I whispered again, 'Could Miss Trimble have guessed? Think!'

'There was a day, a Sunday, when the Ledgers came with the boys to church and the little one began to cry. I jumped up from my seat and I was about to go to him. I didn't mean to, it just happened. Ethan wasn't with me. I was in the aisle, hurrying towards their pew and Miss Trimble gave me such a look, just as Bob came and took my arm and led me outside, and I pretended I'd felt faint.'

I nodded.

'You better use one of those smelly lavatories, Mary Jane. It'll probably be a while before you can go again. I'll hold this door.'

Moments later, we stepped into the corridor. The constable who had tailed us covered his embarrassment with bombast. 'You shouldn't have run so far ahead of me. I went walking on. I didn't imagine you would have entered a gentlemen's convenience. There's a search going on.'

'Sorry. It was an emergency. We couldn't see the ladies' convenience.'

We trailed in silence behind him. When we returned to the interview room, the constable opened the door for Mary Jane, but barred my way.

She gave me a brave smile and raised her hand.

Marcus's familiar footsteps came up the stairs. I had never seen him out of breath before. 'You gave me a fright.'

'Sorry.'

Back in his vomit-coloured office I reported on what he knew very well, having listened from the other side of the wall.

'She was not surprised to see Mr Turnbull, the quarry foreman. He's a violent man who dislikes Ethan. She thinks you may suspect him. Raymond Turnbull, she says her cottage would go to him – it's a tied house and he marries on Saturday and needs a roof – but that he wouldn't have harmed Ethan.'

'Thank you, Kate.'

'And Bob Conroy . . .'

'We weren't expecting him.'

'Mary Jane thinks he still has a soft spot for her. He wanted to marry her before Ethan pushed him out.'

'I don't think he need concern us. He has an alibi for Saturday afternoon.'

'That's very convenient.'

'A watertight alibi with two impeccable individuals.'

'Was one of these impeccable individuals Colonel Ledger?'

'You won't expect me to confirm or deny that.'

'Conroy has sold the farm to the colonel.'

'That wouldn't have a bearing on the case.'

'There's something going on, Marcus, and it makes me think that this solicitor, the Ledgers' solicitor, isn't going to look out for Mary Jane's interests.'

'Why do you think that?'

I did not tell him. If there was dirt to be uncovered then I would have to do some shovelling. 'Marcus, I did as you asked. I observed Mary Jane, I told you her reactions. Let me ask you something in return.' I came as close to him as if we were about to make love, looking into his eyes, almost touching his body with mine. 'You needn't say yes or no, but if I am right, just let me know in some other way, a nod . . .'

'Or a wink,' he said half jokingly, scratching his neck under the stiff collar, not knowing what I was about to ask.

'Or a wink. Someone reported on Ethan's political activities, meetings he attended, people he met. Someone said how the vote went when a strike was called. The guess would be that information came from a member of the quarrymen's union, but I think it came from Bob Conroy. Bob and Ethan went to the same political meetings. Ethan spent his spare time helping on the farm. He confided in Bob. And Bob betrayed him. Am I right?'

Marcus discovered an itch on his face and scratched the side of his nose. He lowered his head. 'You wouldn't expect me to confirm or deny that.'

He had confirmed it.

We stood a tissue paper apart. For a moment, I thought he would step back, or embrace me, but he did neither. I held my ground and waited.

'I'll tell you this much, Kate, Conroy is distraught over Armstrong's death. Utterly distraught.'

'I can hear the thirty pieces of silver clinking as he flings them into the gutter.'

'He was acting from the best of motives, to save Ethan from himself, and from exploitation by men who do not have the good of our country at heart.'

He caught my hand as I turned to go. 'I'm booked into the Red Lion, but if you'd like me to come to you tonight ...'

'Best not come to me, Marcus. But thanks for telling me where to find you.' I should have left it at that but I had to say it. 'Miss Trimble was poisoned because of something she knew. Bob Conroy was in the village that afternoon, supposedly posting letters to comrades. He was in the churchyard when I came from the vicarage. He'd spoken to Miss Trimble on Sunday and was going to make a donation to the church.'

'There were no suspicious circumstances surrounding Miss Trimble's death.'

'Country doctors never want suspicious circumstances. How many unexplained deaths are passed off that way because it's easier for all concerned?'

'What possible reason would Conroy have for killing her? Only one that I can think of and that's because she claims to have seen a person answering Mrs Armstrong's description by the quarry. That wouldn't help your case at all.'

Marcus insisted on walking me back to my car. 'Thank you for coming, Kate. I know this must have been difficult for you.'

He expected me to ask if I could stay until after Mary Jane's interview and was already thinking of some polite way of refusing me. But I would not ask. I wanted to catch Sykes before he left for Great Applewick with his supply of stockings for mill girls.

As I left the police station, a suave gentleman in a grey mohair suit and a bowler hat walked into the courtyard, a minion trotting a few steps behind, carrying a briefcase.

We looked at each other and I guessed who he was. A solicitor employed by the Ledgers would not wear a worn tweed country suit. A solicitor employed by the Ledgers would buy his silk shirts from the top drawer and his suits from Savile Row.

I drew myself up to my full height, and was glad to be wearing a touch of silk of my own, the coffee and cream suit had been a good choice after all. Which one of us would speak first?

I did, because I had nothing to lose and he had nothing to gain. His fee would come from Ledger and to him this was simply another bit of business.

'Excuse me.'

'Yes?'

'I believe you're Mr Nelson, appointed by Colonel Ledger. I'm Mrs Shackleton, a friend of Mrs Armstrong.'

He feigned surprise though I guessed he knew well enough who I was. The colonel would have briefed him thoroughly.

'If there's anything I can do to help, Mr Nelson . . .'

He raised his hat. 'Bad business,' he said as if commenting on a rainy day spoiling play. 'But worry not, my dear lady. I shall have Mrs Armstrong out of here in no time.'

Stupidly, I felt myself light up at this unexpected show of support. 'I'm glad to hear that because she wants to be home with her children.'

He lowered his voice, not that anyone could hear, except the minion with the briefcase. 'Of course you know the police, especially where Scotland Yard is involved. I shall probably have to bargain a little. Have her released into the care of a responsible person.'

'Well, if I can . . .'

'And of course people don't come more responsible than Colonel Ledger. He has expressed a willingness for her to be in his care until we can clear up this . . . misunderstanding. I believe the children are being well cared for in the meantime.'

He raised his hat. 'My card, madam. Please don't hesitate and all that.'

He was gone.

The minion produced a card and thrust it at me.

Colonel and Mrs Ledger were taking no chances. Mary Jane would be incarcerated with them, until they could be sure she would be silent.

Two

Sykes waited by the mill gates, notebook at the ready. In his attaché case were thirty-seven pairs of stockings, individually wrapped in tissue paper. He had a list of names and a pocketful of pennies to give correct change. He felt in two minds about this caper. It was a useful cover, and a nice way to earn a little extra cash but, as he braced himself for the surge of females, indignity prickled. He felt a serious longing to be in uniform and on point duty.

The mill doors opened and the workforce poured out. Sykes wondered where they would all fit. Great Applewick was no more than a mile across and a mile wide. Some of them must be dashing to catch a tram.

'There he is!' It was the red-haired beauty who had asked him to the pictures.

'Changed your mind have you?' she asked. 'Tekin me out tonight?'

'Sorry, love. I'm spoken for.'

'Shame.'

He laughed. 'Catch the bouquet at tomorrow's wedding, let some chap glimpse your stockings and he'll ask you out for the rest of your days.'

'I might just do that.'

So tomorrow's wedding was still on. Mrs Shackleton was right. The bridegroom at least had not been kept in custody. She had asked him to find out what he could about Bob Conroy, but he couldn't see how he would do that. You could only go to a farmhouse once to sell stockings.

Pockets heavy with coins, he headed for the Fleece to think over strategy while supping a pint of bitter. The only occupants of the pub were a couple of old men in the tap room, their boneyard of dominoes spread out on the table.

One wore a Rip Van Winkle beard that must have saved him a lot of time over the years. He had nothing to say for himself but nodded a lot, a nervous palsy. The other sported a wispy moustache, eye patch, and a growth of pirate stubble.

Sykes hated dominoes, an old man's game. There'd be time enough for that if and when he reached his dotage. But when Pirate Stubble asked him to join the game for a halfpenny, he did, as a way to pass an hour and ingratiate himself.

They were all related to each other round here. Pirate Stubble, who picked up double six to start, was father to Turnbull, quarry foreman, grandfather to young Raymond, the pair who had dug out Ethan's body. This had earned Pirate Stubble an extra pint or two and he was still playing on the glory. Sykes treated Rip Van Winkle and Pirate Stubble and when they asked what line he was in, Sykes owned up to buying and selling. He'd be a figure of ridicule here if he mentioned ladies' stockings.

Sykes turned talk to the quarry.

'Do you reckon it was accidental?' Sykes asked. 'A landslip, a rock fall?'

Pirate Stubble chuckled mirthlessly with the glee of the man left standing. 'Can 'appen. Who's to say?'

'Not foul play then, as some are saying?' Sykes prompted.

'For foul play thah'd need a foul player, and ahm pointing no fingers.' The old domino player suddenly swallowed the pickled egg he had been saving, popping it into his mouth. Sykes watched his throat to see if it would bulge like a cobra's.

Sykes followed his opponent's five-two with a two-three. This could be a long night. When he looked through the hatch into the tap room and spotted the man Mrs Shackleton had described, Sykes planned his escape. That's Bob Conroy, Sykes said to himself as he looked at the gaunt, weatherbeaten man with high cheekbones and deep-set eyes. Mrs Shackleton had described him well. Conroy was already drunk.

Sykes bided his time a little longer. He did not flee the old men's company until the side of a mountain filled the doorway of the snug. The man wore a red neckerchief knotted at his throat, corduroy breeches, and a jacket that had once been tweed, all deeply ingrained with quarry dust. 'Nah then, son,' said the old man.

Sykes made room for the man he guessed to be Josiah Turnbull, quarry foreman, and escaped in the direction of the tap room.

He walked slowly enough to hear the old man's opening gambit to his son. 'Where's young un on his last night as a free man?'

'Drinking hisself silly with his pals. They're tekin him to every pub in Guiseley.'

Ethan might have been with him had he lived, Sykes thought. He would have treated his former apprentice to a drink on his last night as a bachelor.

As Sykes walked into the tap room, there was a lull in the talk. *Bloody hell, they think I'm a plain-clothes copper. I'll get no joy here.*

But Conroy was oblivious. He ordered a pint and a chaser. The landlord said, 'Sit down, Bob. I'll send it across.' He nodded to the old waiter.

'No, I'll stand where I allus stand.' Conroy fumbled for his brass and spilled coins onto the counter. The landlord counted the coins and shrugged, in no mood to tell the unsteady Conroy that he had underpaid.

Forgetting that he intended to stand where he always stood, Conroy turned and blindly made for the corner by the fire where people shoved along to make space. Men on either side spoke to him, but he said nothing, as though not hearing or seeing anyone or anything bar the flames chasing up the chimney back.

Sykes watched through the mirror that covered the wall behind the bar.

Space was made on the table for the waiter to place Conroy's pint and chaser. Conroy picked up the pint and gulped, smacking his lips.

Through the mirror, Sykes watched Conroy down his chaser.

Flush with the price of thirty-nine pairs of stockings, Sykes bought two whiskeys, one for himself and one he pushed to Conroy when he next approached the bar. 'You look as if you need it.'

Conroy stared at him, with something like recognition. *He thinks I'm plain-clothes, too. He thinks I'm keeping an eye on him, but he's not taking that ill. Mrs Shackleton was right. He's the man that shopped Ethan to his bosses. Reported on Ethan to Special Branch. He's a patriot. But now he wonders did he do the right thing.*

The landlord said, 'Are you all right for getting home, Bob?'

'I'm . . . I'm all right.' Conroy downed his whiskey.

Sykes drank with Conroy till the landlord called time. He was feeling none too steady himself, and remembered he had not eaten. And this dratted attaché case, making him stick out like a sore thumb.

By chucking-out time, Bob and Sykes had struck up a bit of camaraderie. Sykes was good at banter. In the cool night air, they fell into step. Bob Conroy zig-zagged through the village street. He passed the Methodist chapel and turned into Over Lane. You're going the wrong way, Sykes thought. You're taking a long road home. Only when Bob turned into Nether End did Sykes realise that he was going to Mary Jane's cottage.

The cottage was in darkness. Conroy went to the door. He spread his arms akimbo and brought his head forward so that his forehead knock-knocked against the door. Over and over, he banged his head against the door.

Sykes went to him, raised him up. 'Come on, Bob. Come on, lad. She's not here. Let's get you home, eh?'

'What have I done?' Conroy wailed. 'What have I done?'

That's exactly what I'd like to know, Sykes thought, but if I put it that directly I'll never find out.

'Come on, lad. Your missis'll be looking out for you. Let's have you, eh?'

With encouraging words, putting an arm around the man, Sykes drew him away from the door, but he realised he was not sure how to get to the farm without going back into the village and starting again. There was a back way, he knew that. Mrs Shackleton described going to the quarry with the little lass. Conroy was stumbling in that direction, criss-crossing the back garden and along some path.

Sykes took the risk of hiding his attaché case under a bush in the Armstrongs' back garden. He had brought his torch, in his inside pocket, but for now the moon shed enough light to give the hawthorn hedge its shape.

'We might see him,' Conroy said. 'What if Ethan's ghost comes walking along, as he always did?'

Sykes said. 'One foot then the next, that's the way.'

'I don't know your name.'

'Jim.'

'If we keep going, Jim, we'll go to Hawksworth Moor, that's the place on a night like this. We'd walk on Hawksworth Moor and set the world to rights.'

'Another time, eh? We've both taken a drop too much.'

Nearby, an owl screeched. A tree sighed.

Conroy said, 'You stride out, like he did. Purposeful like, a man with an appointment to keep, a job to do. The best. Ethan put a steeple on the church. That's why Mary Jane had to have insurance. A mason, he might fall.'

'Did someone help him fall?' Sykes asked.

But Conroy had stopped talking. He slid from Sykes's arm. On his knees on the rough path, he lowered his head and was sick into the grass, the moonlight catching the whiteness of his ear as his cap fell off.

He turned and looked at Sykes. 'I know who you are. I know who sent you.'

He thinks I'm Special Branch. Well, there'll be no sense got from this man tonight, only drunk's talk, moon talk and madness.

Sykes left Bob at the farm gate. He watched as the man zig-zagged across the farmyard.

Three

The thumping on the door woke Harriet from a dream. She shot up, thinking, it's Dad. He's home. And then she remembered. She shifted her foot to touch Austin with her toe. They lay top to tail and he slept, but was hot, giving off waves of heat. She kept her foot by him to make sure of being awake, to make sure this was no dream. Then she remembered, she was at the Conroys' and didn't want to be here. She wanted to be at home with Mam and Dad.

She'd liked Auntie Kate, but now she didn't like her because she had brought them here and dumped them.

The banging got louder.

She went to the window. There was Uncle Bob, braying on his own door. 'Georgie, Georgina! I'm locked out.'

He stepped back and looked up, moving unsteadily. Drunk. Uncle Bob never got drunk.

A window was flung open. 'Aye, you're locked out. I can't abide drunkenness. You can stop out there till you sober up.'

'Let me in.'

'Go and sleep in the cowshed!'

Harriet felt sorry for him. He looked as if he might fall

294

down. Auntie Georgie should let him in. He's drunk because Dad is dead, she thought. He's drunk because his heart is broken. Should I be drunk? Should I be outside in the middle of the night, ready to fall down? Instead, here I am, as though nothing has changed.

Uncle Bob let out a cry like a dog howling at the moon. He wouldn't stop howling.

Auntie Georgie shut the window. Harriet heard her treading softly down the stairs. She would let him in. The bolt on the door slid back.

Uncle Bob moaned, saying her mam and dad's names, Ethan, Mary Jane, Mary Jane, Ethan, as Auntie Georgie opened the door.

Auntie Georgie's voice came out hard and mean. 'If you can't stomach ale you shouldn't sup.'

'Have a heart, woman.' He slipped and let out a curse and lay for too long on the ground before struggling to his feet.

'What time do you call this? Where've you been?'

'I wanted to see Mary Jane. They've taken her. I tried to explain . . .'

What did he mean? Who had taken her? No one should take her. Without Mam, she'd be a full orphan for sure. Bad things happened to orphans.

Harriet watched. Instead of letting Uncle Bob in, Auntie Goergina pushed him away. He staggered back. She was angry. 'Shut up your mouth. I've the man's bairns sleeping up there. Show some respect.'

'Mary Jane . . . and Ethan, poor Ethan.'

'What about your wife? What about me? Mary Jane was planning to leave Ethan. He told me. She was going to leave the lot of them.'

'No, never, never in this wide world.'

Uncle Bob staggered. Auntie Georgie got behind him, to bring him in, Harriet thought, but no. 'You're sleeping in the cowshed, my man, till you know how to respect a respectable wife and two fatherless children.'

He made a kind of sobbing sound, as if about to cry.

Uncle Bob is crying, Harriet thought. Men don't cry.

They had moved away into the shadows. Harriet could hear their voices but not the words. This would be like her mam sending dad into the coal shed. Something that would never happen. It wasn't right. And it wasn't true what Auntie Georgina said. She would tell her. She would say, Mam isn't going to leave us. It's not true.

Harriet waited at the window until Mrs Conroy came back inside, until she heard her climb the stairs and go back into the room next door. Austin still slept. But you never knew with him. Sometimes he pretended. The room was too dark to tell if he was pretending or not. Harriet listened to his breath, too even and quiet for him to be awake.

Harriet lay down. What if Dad is not dead? This is all some mistake or some dream. A story. She would not have to go to school and be stared at. She would not be half an orphan. If she went to sleep, she might wake in the middle of last week when everything was normal and ordinary.

How long she slept, she did not know, or whether she slept at all. Something woke her. She moved her feet left and right. All she felt was the crumpled sheet beneath her heel and the top sheet on her big toe. She sat up. The bed was flat at the bottom and on either side. It wasn't like him to get up for a pee. He'd prefer to wet the bed.

She felt suddenly scared. What if he had not been asleep earlier, when Uncle Bob made his racket? He might have gone downstairs, let himself out, and tried to find Uncle Bob in the cowshed. No. He would have wakened her. He was too afraid to be brave.

The light at the window was not like morning, and not like the moon. Harriet went to look.

Flames licked from the wall of the barn. Red sparks flung themselves into the darkness. She flung open the window, and smelled smoke.

Four

Trust the moon to slide behind a cloud when you needed her. Jupiter shone brightly, but not brightly enough. Sykes took out his torch. He felt like bloody Goldilocks because where else could he go but the three bears' cottage – the Armstrong cottage where he would risk a few hours' sleep and be careful not to eat porridge or break baby bear's chair.

The wind was behind him now and it brought a tang, a dryness, something like smoke. He turned to look at the sky. It was lit red over the farm. Sparks flew into the sky. For a moment, Sykes stood like a statue, as if some master of ceremonies had put on a display and demanded his appreciation. And then he started to run, back towards the farm, along the track, past the ominous quarry with its forbidding shadows, up the dirt road, along the farm track. And by the time he reached the farm track, he was not alone.

Someone else had seen the fire. A man came running out of the farm cottage, pulling a cap onto his head. 'Bloody hell fire,' said the man. 'It's the cowshed. My beasts! My poor beasts.'

'How many are there?' Sykes asked, catching the sound of his own panting, wishing he had not spoken.

'Four.'

Sykes could hear the braying of distressed cattle and the barking of a dog.

It was like a circle of hell come to life. Wind blew the smoke and sparks towards them. Sykes thought he saw the girl he had given chocolate to, saw her flit by and disappear behind a great lumbering shape that in this light looked more wild elephant than milking cow.

'The beasts is free,' the man said and ran past the burning cowshed towards four wild-eyed creatures that mooed and bumped into each other as though at any moment they would dash back into the flames.

If the wind changes, the house will catch fire, Sykes thought. He saw a bucket by the horse trough. Sykes lowered the bucket into the water, filled it, and threw it on the flames. Useless.

The man paid no attention to the fire. Sykes was vaguely aware that he was talking to the cows, smacking their flanks.

Sykes heard her before he saw her. The shriek came from behind. He turned to see the woman who had bought stockings. Mrs Conroy. 'Bob, my poor Bob.'

A banshee wail came from the house and a small nightgowned figure charged in their direction.

That must be the little girl, Sykes thought. I saw a shadow before.

But it was a different girl, and she called a name over and over. 'Austin, Austin.'

'Back, Harriet, back!' Mrs Conroy ordered. 'Stay clear.' She grabbed the child's arm.

'Where's Austin!'

'Austin?' The woman stared at the flames, at Sykes and back at Harriet. 'Oh my God.'

Harriet pulled free and ran towards the burning cowshed. Sykes caught her and held her fast. 'You don't know he's in there, and if he is there's no helping him.'

She struggled and kicked. 'Let me go!'

One kick hit Sykes where it hurt and as he involuntarily relaxed his grip, she wriggled free. She ran towards the cowshed. The girl – he remembered her name, Millie – appeared from nowhere, like a wisp of smoke. She blocked Harriet's path, tripping her, catching hold of her as she fell. For a moment, the two girls struggled on the ground, Harriet screeching to be let go.

A rafter fell into the burning cowshed, sending out sparks and new flames shooting to the sky. Choking black smoke billowed into the farmyard. Sykes began to cough. He stuffed his hanky over his mouth.

When he picked up Harriet again, all the fight was gone out of her. He carried her into the house, kicking the door shut behind him to keep the smoke from entering.

'Austin,' she said. 'Find Austin.'

'I will. I'll find him.'

Or his charred bones, his ashes.

They were on the stairs. Sykes was carrying her to a bedroom, but which one he didn't know.

She pointed.

'You go back to sleep, and keep the windows shut.'

'Austin,' she whimpered. 'Find Austin. He's with Uncle Bob. Millie told me.'

Mrs Conroy called up the stairs. 'Is he there? Is the little one there?'

Slowly, Sykes came down the stairs. Mrs Conroy stood at the bottom, staring at him. He shook his head.

'You're the stockings man.'

He felt accused, unmasked. 'I was walking back from the pub. I saw the flames.'

She closed her eyes. 'The little lad sleepwalks. He must have walked outside when I opened the door. I'd made Bob stop outside because he was reeling drunk, and the little lad . . .'

'Are you saying he went in the cowshed?'

'I left the door, but only for a moment. I was in the yard with Bob. A moment's all it takes.'

Harriet was on the stairs. 'Look for him. Somebody look for him.'

Sykes pulled out his torch. 'I'll go. You search the house, Mrs Conroy. I'll search outside.' He added quietly, 'Your poor husband must have dropped a cigarette.'

She indicated a row of pipes on the mantelpiece. 'He doesn't take them out. He only ever smokes the odd roll-up if someone hands him one.'

Mrs Conroy called after Sykes, 'Don't try and save that damn barn. Just find the child.'

In the yard, the farm worker stood, watching the flames.

'There's nowt we can do, gov. Bob must've let the beasts loose when he could have saved his life. But that's Bob. He loved them beasts.'

'If the wind changes, get Mrs Conroy and . . . Get Mrs Conroy and Harriet out of the house.'

'Aye. I've thought of that. And I've teken the beasts downwind.'

'Did you see the little lad?'

'No.'

'What about Millie?'

'She'll be with the beasts, talking to them.'

'Show me.'

Sykes's torch shook as he shone his and the man's way across the yard to the barn. Four pairs of cows' eyes looked at them expectantly. But there was no sign of Millie, or of Austin.

SATURDAY

On a cloud I saw a child,
And he laughing said to me:
'Pipe a song about a Lamb!'

William Blake

One

At dawn, Sykes stood with Sergeant Sharp in the farm-yard. A sullen red glow lit the grey ash and charred wood, which was all that remained of the cow shed. Do I tell him now, Sykes asked himself, or keep quiet?

Sergeant Sharp poked with a stick at the hot ash, as though searching out a lost roast chestnut. 'Poor Conroy. What a shocking end.' He shook his head. 'Mrs Conroy thinks Austin Armstrong sleepwalked, matches in his pocket. She says she caught him trying to set fire to the hen hutch last week.'

'That makes no sense to me.' Sykes drew the toe of his boot away from the hot ash. 'No kid would come out in the middle of the night and start a fire. Cigarette more likely, or combustion.'

'Bob wasn't a cigarette smoker. A kid would do it, if it's in him to do it. Fire raising takes a hold of some kids, like a disease. But you did right to take him and Harriet home, away from the scene.'

'It was only Harriet I took back to their cottage. Austin was already there.'

'Run off, guilty like. I'll have a word with that lad. You see it's in him. It's in him to do summat bad and run off.'

Sharp was determined to think badly of the children, even after his experience of misjudging Harriet. Sykes decided what he would do.

From beyond the farm gate came the distant sound of a motor engine.

'That'll be the fire engine. They'll search this lot and find poor Bob.' Sharp sucked a finger and held it in the air. 'We're fortunate the wind didn't carry the fire to the house.' He held out his hand. 'Thank you for what you did. Lucky you was nearby.'

'It would have been luckier for everyone concerned if I'd seen Bob Conroy through his own door and not just to the farmyard gate.'

'Leave it to me now,' Sharp said. 'You get off home. Where do I get in touch with you if needs be?'

Sykes pulled out his notebook, scribbled his name and address, and handed it to the sergeant. 'Shall I call in to the station when it suits you?'

'Aye. You do that.'

Sykes turned up his collar and pulled down his hat as he turned his back on the burned-out building. The fire brigade engine had reached the gate. Sykes lifted the latch, swung the gate open and waited until the vehicle chugged through.

Behind it was one of the North Riding Alvis motors, Chief Inspector Charles sitting in the back seat. Bad timing. The chief inspector had spotted him. Sykes clutched his ridiculous attaché case, having retrieved it when he took Harriet back to the cottage. He'd be mortified if asked to open it and reveal the solitary pair of artificial silk stockings. He stopped a grin. Be a bit rich if the chief inspector bought a pair for Mrs Shackleton.

Chief Inspector Marcus Charles looked straight at

Sykes, and then through him. He remembers me all right, Sykes thought, but he's choosing not to let on. Damned if I'll acknowledge you then. I'm no toadeater. The man's probably busy loathing me because I spend more time with Mrs Shackleton than he does. But at the thought of Mrs Shackleton, Sykes knew that he would have to speak to the man, even at the risk of having been discovered somewhere he shouldn't be. No difficulty about that. If asked, Sykes would simply say he had arranged to meet an old chum in the Fleece last night, and got chatting to Conroy. And if the chief inspector believed that, he'd believe anything.

Two

My mother is the most relaxed of women. Dad and I once speculated about this. Dad maintained she was simply born that way. I came to the conclusion that her permanent state of equilibrium is due to her privileged girlhood in her family's country pile where Care, Want and Anxiety not only never appeared, they did not exist. She is now aware that there are worries in the world and that life does not run along smooth lines for everyone, but it is as if the difficult side of existence is somehow slightly unreal and does not touch her in a deep part of her being. This makes her very comfortable to be with. It is rare for her to fall into a tizz. So when she telephoned to me in an agitated way, asking me to meet her in Marshall & Snelgrove's café in Leeds at ten o'clock, I knew something was up. I especially knew something was up when I arrived at a minute to ten and she was already sitting at a table, sipping coffee.

Of course she never comes straight to the point and so we chatted about her journey from Wakefield and I told her about visiting Mary Jane in Otley Courthouse.

'Goodness me, was it very horrid?' she asked.

Well, it's a gaol as well as a police station, Mother, and she is near enough to being charged with mariticide. But I said,

'It's a not an unpleasant part of Otley. And Mary Jane could have been in a worse frame of mind. But you didn't ask me here to talk about that.'

'No, you're right. Only my information seems so trivial by comparison.' She brought out a letter from deep within her reticule; someone as grand as my mother would never carry a simple handbag. She sighed. 'This came by the first post this morning, from the well provided woman. I opened it, as you instructed.'

I took the letter from her and read.

Dear Mr Wright

I thank you for your communication and your suggestion that we meet with which I heartily concur and look forward to that event.

It is good of you to think of seeing me in so salubrious a place as the Griffin Hotel. However, I prefer to meet privately if that is agreeable to you. You were kind enough to give your address. I know my way well to Wakefield and instead of meeting at the Griffin, I shall call to see you in your home on Sunday afternoon at four o'clock. If this proves an embarrassment to you in respect of your landlady, I shall be glad to be introduced as a distant relation on this one occasion!

Although this may appear a bold venture on my part, be assured that I am a respectable and childless widow of a generally retiring nature, left well provided by my late husband and sometimes longing for a little male companionship.

I trust this will be agreeable to you and that you will excuse my boldness. Be assured that from my point of view our meeting will hold you to no further obligation unless you are so inclined.

I remain, sir, yours sincerely
Gertrude Alexander (Mrs)

I looked at Mother and she looked at me. 'What do you make of it?' I asked.

'She wastes no time and wants to see the bird in his own bush. But you see my difficulty, Kate?'

'Yes. She's left no opportunity to reply. It's one thing to ask Mr Duffield to make a trip to the Griffin, and quite another to have the poor man come to your house in Wakefield under the guise of Mr Wright, to receive a lady visitor.'

'Sunday,' she stressed. 'Four o'clock? Does that ring a bell?'

My hand flew to my forehead. 'Oh no! Sunday dinner. You've invited Marcus.' I looked at the letter again. 'Mrs Alexander doesn't give an address for reply. That's a bit much of her. What a cheek.'

'Well, exactly. The dreadful woman is going to turn up on our doorstep at four o'clock, and your father will be there, and Mr Charles. I don't know how I shall explain this.' She lay the letter down next to the sugar basin. 'Either we answer the door and tell her there has been some mistake, or your Mr Duffield must be there to meet her.'

I looked at my watch. 'This is a pretty pickle. I'm not sure what hours Mr Duffield works on Saturdays. Either way, he'll have to know.'

Mother held up her hand to calm me down. 'Let me think.' She closed her eyes, sighed, and thought, a small frown creasing her forehead. When she opened her eyes, she gave her isn't-this-easy smile. 'What's he like, this Mr Duffield?'

'He's about fifty years old, a very cautious sort of man – I was surprised he agreed to my scheme; a little eccentric perhaps, clever . . .'

'In appearance, and manner?'

'In appearance a typical bachelor, a little shabbily turned out, but a most amiable man, quite charming.'

'Is he a good conversationalist?'

'I have always found him interesting. He's a librarian and not short of a story or two.'

'Then we shall give him lunch on Sunday . . .'

'But you don't like odd numbers. We can hardly get in touch with . . .' I checked the woman's name, 'Gertrude Alexander . . .'

'Mr Duffield will come to lunch, and afterwards he will be on the spot to receive his visitor.'

'But . . .'

Mother held up a hand. I was about to receive a lesson in etiquette. 'I know that Sunday has the purpose of your Mr Marcus Charles becoming acquainted with your father . . . No wait, Kate, let me finish. By having two more guests we shall make the occasion less weighty. Also, I am going to quite a lot of trouble over this lunch and I know well enough that your chief inspector could cry off at the last moment, and so could your father. That would leave us feeling rather flat. Since you are asking this great sacrifice of poor Mr Wright . . .'

'That's not his real name, Mother. His real name is Duffield.'

'Of course. Since you are asking this great sacrifice of poor Mr Duffield, wanting him to meet this obvious gold digger, this desperado of a woman who is vulgar enough to advertise for a husband, and set her own terms as to where she will meet him, then the least we can do is give Mr Wright, I mean Mr Duffield, lunch. Tell me, does Mr Duffield play bridge?'

'I have no idea.'

311

'Really, Kate! Call yourself a detective and you can't tell me whether a man plays bridge.'

'Mother . . . what are you planning?'

'Why, nothing at all, dear. Only obviously I must make up the numbers for Sunday and it would help to have the gentleman's measure. I shall invite Martha Graham.'

'You're matchmaking, and you haven't even met the man.'

'Kate, your Mr Duffield would never have agreed to this scheme if he were not on the look out for romance.'

When the waitress brought our pot of coffee she was followed by the restaurant manager, bringing me a message.

Telephone communication from Mrs Sugden. Mr Sykes has sent telegram: do not be in least alarmed but please go to the cottage in Great A as soon as possible.

I thanked the manager and passed the note to Mother.

'Good heavens, Kate. Poor Mr Sykes must have his hands full. To say you have only recently met these members of the Whitaker family, they certainly know how to make demands. Let us hope for your sake the other ten Whitaker siblings do not find themselves in the same kind of quandary as Mary Jane.' Mother poured coffee. 'You will travel better for having a cup of coffee and a small sweet bite. There's nothing that cannot wait for a moment's refreshment, and I am partial to their curd tart. As to Mr . . . Duffield, please leave him to me. I shall call at the newspaper offices myself. It's proper that I should extend the invitation personally, and I should like to take a little look at him.' She chose a dainty chocolate-covered bun. 'It may be that the gentleman is a confirmed bachelor, and you hadn't noticed.'

Three

It was not out of my way to call home and pick up a few items, including a change of clothing, in case I needed to stay the night at the cottage. As I drove to Great Applewick, I wondered about the reason for Sykes's telegram; a development in the investigation, perhaps. I fervently hoped that Marcus had come to some break-through and released Mary Jane. Or there could be something the matter with the children. I remembered Austin's reluctance to go to the farm. The Conroys may have had enough of them, but that seemed unlikely for two such good-hearted neighbours.

As I drove, I began to regret following up the personal advertisement and involving Mr Duffield. Dad would not take kindly to his drawing room being used as a matrimo-nial agency by Mr Duffield and the mysterious Mrs Alexander.

Too late now.

When I arrived at the cottage, I heard voices from the garden and walked round to the back. Sykes was drawing water from the well, supervised by Harriet and Austin. The children were laughing at something and I felt full of admiration, and a little envy, that they were so at ease with him and that he had somehow managed to amuse them at what must be the darkest time of their young lives.

Sykes greeted me, pretending pleased surprise. So the children did not know he had contrived to send me a telegram.

Harriet and Austin looked at me, and then past me, to see if I had brought their mother.

'Your mam will come as soon as she can,' I said. 'She has a few things to attend to. And I'm to be sure and take you to your granny tomorrow.'

Austin said, 'I was in a fire. Dad fetched me home.'

He stared at me, daring me to contradict that his father had reappeared and rescued him.

'There really was a fire,' Sykes said quietly. 'The cowshed caught light.'

Before I had time to ask whether anyone was hurt, Harriet said, 'Austin, what did Dad smell of when he fetched you home? Did his hair smell of stone?'

'He smelled of Bonfire night.'

'Dad never liked Bonfire night so he wouldn't smell of that.'

'He did smell of it, he smelled of fire.'

'It must have been Uncle Bob who brought you home.'

A small explosion went on inside Austin as he burst to say something and could not find the words.

Sykes gathered the two together and whispered something to them. They went inside. When they had gone, Sykes told me about the fire at the farm, the horrible fear that Bob Conroy had been burned alive, and the failure to find his remains in the ashes.

We sat on opposite sides of the well. I pressed my hand against the cool stone.

'Do you mean that Conroy was so badly burned that nothing remains?'

'That's what the police and the firemen are allowing people to think. He escaped. I'm sure of it. It could have been a terrible accident or a ploy by him to make it look that way. At present, the firemen are saying only that they are examining the scene.'

'Then how do you know he escaped?'

'Millie told Harriet. She saw Conroy running from the cowshed, carrying Austin with him. I think Conroy's gone to ground.'

'But he voluntarily went into the police station yesterday. Mary Jane thought he must be there to protest her innocence.'

Sykes fiddled with the well handle. It creaked. 'I spoke briefly to Chief Inspector Charles this morning. Of course he gave nothing away to me, but I believe he connects Bob Conroy with the death.'

I could hardly bring myself to ask. 'And Mary Jane?'

'She's not out of the woods. I don't know whether your sister is involved or not, Mrs Shackleton. But it's looking bad for Bob Conroy. People know he and Mary Jane were very close. Perhaps that's why Ethan went to talk to Mrs Conroy. They shared a sense of betrayal in common. A double betrayal for Ethan, if he'd found out that Bob was reporting on him to Special Branch.'

'Is that why you've asked me to come here, to be with the children? Mrs Conroy's not going to be up to it.'

An image flashed behind my eyes: myself miscast in the role of dutiful aunt thrust into caring, having to look every day at children whose mother died swinging on the end of a rope.

Sykes said, 'I want to look for Bob Conroy.'

315

'Aren't the police searching?'

'Yes, but something he said last night, and something Harriet said, gave me a hunch as to where he may be. And there's another thing . . .'

'What for God's sake?'

'That little girl who works for Mrs Conroy, Millie. She's missing too. She wasn't caught in the fire. Perhaps she's run away, expecting to be in trouble, expecting to be blamed.'

'What on earth is going on?'

'I wish I knew. Will you take the children to their grandma's today?'

'No. They've been shifted about enough. Let them have a day and a night in their own home.'

Sykes began to wind up the bucket from the bottom of the well. 'I sent them inside to unpack the hamper, and surprise you by setting it all out on the table. Lady Bountiful sent it.'

'Lady Bountiful?'

'Mrs Ledger. Didn't you say she's the nearest Great Applewick has to lady of the manor?'

'Yes. And that solicitor of theirs intends to have Mary Jane released into the Ledgers' care, God help her.'

I closed my eyes for a moment, to gather the strength to go in and be normal with the children, whatever normal is. 'I'd stake my life on Mary Jane's innocence.'

Sykes' said, 'Of course you would. How could you bear to believe otherwise?' He picked up the bucket of water.

'Is anyone looking for the little girl?'

'Arthur and the other chap from the farm. Mrs Conroy was casting round for who to blame for the fire. Apparently Millie has run away before.'

We began to walk up the path, the overfull bucket swinging and spilling as we went.

I tried to picture the little girl, talking to the lamb by the fire, talking to the sheepdog. 'Where do you think that little girl comes from? She's not local.'

'Millie?' Sykes smiled. 'She's surely not. We had a chap in the force talked not unlike her. If he was pointing out a fair-haired female, it'd be, "Hur thur with the fur hur." I'd put her down as being from Lancashire and if I had to pinpoint it a bit sharper, I'd say Blackburn.'

The contents of Mrs Ledger's hamper were spread on the table: ham on the bone, bread, butter, soup, pie and cake; eggs and milk; tea and dandelion wine.

'I want Mam to come home and have some,' Harriet said.

'We'll save some for her. Tell me, Harriet, do you have an atlas of the British Isles?'

She went to the pile of books above the chest of drawers and found the atlas. I made space on the table. 'See if you can you find the page with Lancashire. I'd like to know how close are Blackburn and Clitheroe.'

It occurred to me that the reason for Miss Trimble's untimely death may be nothing at all to do with having seen a female in a plaid cape by the quarry at four o'clock. Miss Trimble had spent the previous week in Clitheroe.

Harriet measured the distance between her thumb and finger and looked at the scale on the map. 'It's about nine miles from Clitheroe to Blackburn.'

There was something that I was missing, but what?

Bitter, Miss Trimble had said. Dandy, Miss Trimble had said. We had thought of all the dictionary definitions of that word, dandy, and of dandy fever. But what if it was only part of a word. Bitter. Dare I taste the dandelion wine sent by Mrs Ledger?

Four

Sykes clambered into the Jowett. He now regarded himself as a confident driver. He was less confident about his ability to find the missing Bob Conroy, and he knew he was still missing because Sergeant Sharp had called at the cottage twice under the pretext of checking whether the children were all right. Even Harriet had said, 'The sergeant's looking for Uncle Bob.'

While waiting for Mrs Shackleton to arrive, and while keeping the children occupied, Sykes had recalled the previous evening in the pub, the smell of bitter ale, slops, full ashtrays and unwashed bodies. I was the one playing clever, Sykes thought, escorting Bob home, leaving him at his gate. What if he played me, played me for a fool? You see it on the music hall, rubber-legged comics, sober as a judge, acting the intoxicated buffoon. Sykes dismissed the thought. Conroy had been throw-up-and-fall-over drunk, stinking of ale and whiskey. If he'd been in that cowshed a moment longer, he'd have lit up like a Roman candle. Getting out of that blaze alive should have sobered him up quickly. Where would the man have gone, and why? Did he really think he could fake his own death in a fire?

Sykes drove to the edge of the moor. This was the place

Bob had spoken of in his cups, where he used to come with Ethan. He and Ethan had hiked this way every Sunday as lads, and had continued when the opportunity arose. The wind helped Sykes on his way, a light rain whipping the back of his neck. He hitched up the scarf Rosie had knitted for him and wound it tightly.

This was the place Harriet said her father and Uncle Bob sometimes brought them on a Sunday, the walk that Bob Conroy had described, as he cried into his beer last night.

By driving, Sykes had chopped off what he imagined may have been the early section of Conroy's hike, but he was left wondering whether he had struck out from the right spot.

The path led through rough moorland. Sheep nibbled coarse grass. Trees grew sparsely. This part of the moor offered no protection from the elements. When the land dipped unexpectedly, it turned boggy. The stout boots, that had formed part of Sykes's payment when he worked in security for the boot and shoe company, were soon caked in mud.

It was what a bookmaker would call long odds, but Harriet had supplied clues: walk upstream, cross a rickety bridge, pass the standing stones shaped like upturned mushrooms. Look for a copse and an abandoned bothy.

It had sounded simple, and no doubt would be if Harriet were doing the walking. Country children could read a landscape in a way that a townie never would. With no street signs, pubs or shops to guide him, Sykes felt like a landlubber crossing a choppy sea on a sledge.

After a good hour's walking, he began to guess he had struck out in the wrong direction for the woods that Harriet had described as an enchanted forest. Where to now? Bob Conroy had boasted of the splendid views from high rocks.

In the dampness of the afternoon, and with the light mist, his field glasses were not much help. Not a solitary human could he see. There must be a hundred secret places, caverns, disused mines, where a man familiar with the landscape could hide.

In the distance, Sykes saw a clump of trees and, to his left, farm buildings.

Somewhere far off, a dog barked.

He veered off, to try the farm buildings that he could see on the horizon. A man out on such a night as last night would need shelter. Bob Conroy would know the farmers, but Sykes knew that the police would have set up their own search, drawing on reserves of manpower and local knowledge.

When he finally reached the farm, he half expected to have to supply difficult explanations. He searched a barn, full of farm machinery that looked like medieval torture instruments, and stacked with sacks of something that stunk; an empty cowshed; a stable where a horse cheered up at his approach and let him stroke its flanks. Defeated, he knocked on the door, asked for a glass of water, and whether his friend Bob Conroy had passed this way. The water was supplied with hospitable speed, but the question about Bob drew a blank.

Instinct kept him moving. Hadn't Mrs Shackleton once said to him that if he were an animal, he would be a bloodhound? But a bloodhound would have tracked its prey by now.

He reached the edge of the wood, where bracken crunched underfoot. Part of him had given up even a shred of hope of finding Bob Conroy. Leave it to the proper police, the voice in his head mocked. You'll be hard pressed to find your way back to the motor. The movement he saw from the corner of his eye could have been a squirrel, or a crow, but then he glimpsed the figure, sitting on the low branch of a nearby tree, legs dangling, looking like an illustration from a children's story: the green man, or an agile King Lear, all rags and dirt.

Bob's face was smeared, his clothing torn. He looked down from the branch with a wild look that told Sykes the man did not remember him, did not recognise him. Bob dropped from the tree and, like a startled animal, ran.

'Bob!' Sykes called after him. 'It's me, your drinking pal! Wait!'

Bob Conroy ran. He had lost a shoe so surely couldn't keep up much of a pace, but he twisted and turned through the trees so that now Sykes saw him, now he was gone. A twig cracked. A startled pheasant flapped its wings and came so close to Sykes's face that Sykes held his hands in front of his eyes. When he opened them, there was no sign of Bob.

'Bob!' he called again. 'Bob Conroy!'

And then he had a thought, and stopped still under a tree, his back to it, looking up at the branches.

Sykes pursed his lips. He repeated the whistle that Kate told him Harriet used when she reached the quarry last Saturday and wanted to let her father know that she was there.

He let out a single long trill, followed by a short one. Paused. Repeated the signal.

After several moments, he heard a sound close behind him. Sykes stood his ground, his back to the tree, and waited.

A hand appeared round the side of the tree and touched his arm. Only with great effort did Sykes stand still.

'Is that you?' the voice said.

Sykes did not answer. Slowly, Bob came round from the other side of the tree. His jacket bore scorch marks from the fire. He smelled of smoke and of bracken. 'You feel real. Not a ghost.'

'I'm no ghost.'

'You take different forms, is that it? It's you. You came to me in the fire. You warned me.'

'Who did?'

'You. Ethan. You've taken a different . . . I think . . . Have I lost my wits?'

He fell to the ground. On all fours, he scrabbled among the tree roots, pulling at a wild mushroom, digging his knuckles into the dirt. He shoved a mushroom in his mouth.

'Don't do that, man!' Sykes said, helping him up from the ground, feeling the tremble of cold or fear that rushed through Conroy's being.

'I'm with you now. You'll come to that farm. It's not so far.'

'No!'

'You'll be safe. It's time to . . . find your shoe. Come with me.'

'Are you . . . do you take different shapes now that you're dead?'

'Your mind is tired. I'll take care of you now.'

'Take me with you. Take me to . . . where is it we go? Across the river . . . what's it called? Didn't we say that once?'

'Yes.' Sykes took his arm. Either the man had run mad or was feigning madness, and if he feigned, then he should tread the boards. If he feigned, it may be because he had murdered a man and wanted to be regarded as mad, not bad.

Side by side they walked back through the wood. And what made Sykes believe Bob did not pretend was that he never winced whether his bare foot touched a stone, or a bramble. He walked like a lamb beside its mother.

'Where are we going?' Bob asked.

Trusting Bob's madness did not extend to a loss of his sense of direction, Sykes asked, 'How far are we off Otley?'

'Otley?' Bob repeated, as though the place were the far side of Tasmania.

'Yes. That's where we'll find Mary Jane. She's asking for you.'

The long Saturday afternoon stretched into evening. Harriet and Austin stayed outdoors, to play on the swing, Harriet said. But when I looked out, they were perched on the dry-stone wall by the Jowett, watching, waiting for their mother.

Eventually, I went across to them. 'Why don't you come inside? We can have a game. Do you have snakes and ladders, or a pack of cards?'

Reluctantly, they gave up their vigil, when I explained that their mother would not be back today, and that tomorrow they'd see their grandma.

Harriet dug out a set of draughts and set up the board on the table. 'Austin can be on your side, Auntie Kate.'

Again, I had that feeling that she was the adult, obliging me, taking her responsibilities seriously. I had not told them that Mary Jane was at Applewick Hall. It was too close. They might ask to go there and fetch her home.

The room grew more gloomy as dusk gathered. Austin and I won a game. He liked kings, because they could move in any direction.

Harriet took a taper from the mantelpiece and lit the lamp.

Another hour passed before Sykes returned. He joined the game on Harriet's side and in quick succession the pair of them took two of our kings for huffing.

Sykes supped a glass of dandelion wine and ate a slice of pork pie as we played one more game. He looked through the window. 'Drawing in dark. I'm sorry to say I've put a bit of a scratch on your motor, Mrs Shackleton. You'd better come and take a look while we can still see.'

We went outside and carefully examined an old scratch. 'I found Bob Conroy. I've taken him to Otley Courthouse. The chief inspector's having a doctor to look at him and he could be sent to hospital. He's in a state of shock and confusion, with burns to his hands and arms.'

A chill wind made me shiver. The setting sun gave the sky an orange glow.

'What does Conroy have to say for himself?'

'Nothing, that makes sense, not to me at any rate. The chief inspector may get something out of him.'

'How is he?'

'Raving. Incoherent. He said that he realises now there never was a lost lamb. That Ethan was right. His brother was murdered. I tried to calm him down.'

'Is there any news of Millie?'

A pair of wood pigeons came to rest on a nearby tree.

'No. Let's hope someone has taken her in and that she'll be found soon.'

He was holding something back. 'Spit it out, Mr Sykes. What else did Bob Conroy say?'

Sykes stared at his muddy boots. He rubbed the side of his sole against a tuft of grass. 'Nothing of consequence. What persuaded him to come along quietly, come to

Otley station with me, was when I said he would see Mary Jane.'

I knew what he was not saying: that Bob Conroy and Mary Jane conspired over Ethan's death. Sykes was no longer looking at me, but staring at the scratch on the car.

I turned back and looked at the cottage window. The scratch on the car story had not fooled Harriet and Austin. They peered out, reading our moves. We would have to go back inside. Before we did, I said, 'I don't know whether Conroy is guilty of murder or not. What I hate is that he makes it appear that Mary Jane wanted rid of Ethan and she didn't. If treacherous Conroy ever does cough up for a decorative window for the church, it should feature a full-length Judas. Mary Jane's fond of Bob Conroy, that's all.'

Was it all? I didn't know. If anyone else were doing as I did now, trying to be convincing, I should think they had a weak case.

'What do you want me to do, Mrs Shackleton? Shall I go on looking for the little girl?'

'I'll go inside and ask the children. Perhaps they may know Millie's hiding places.'

Harriet and Austin were back at the table, pretending interest in another game of draughts.

'Mr Sykes says that your uncle Bob is being looked after by a doctor. He's going to be all right. But do you know where Millie may have gone? We're worried about her.'

'Run away,' Austin said. He leaned on the draughts board, knocking a couple of pieces to the floor.

'Where might she have gone?'

Neither answered.

'Did she say where she came from?'

Harriet picked up the draughts pieces. 'From that place

you said, that I measured.' She set the pieces back on the board.

'From Blackburn?'

'No, the other place. Clitheroe.'

'You make a start on the game. I'll be back in a minute.'

Outside, I told Sykes what the children had said.

'I'll pass it on to the chief inspector shall I, Mrs Shackleton? He can have a call put through. But I don't see the child will have found her way back there. And surely Mrs Conroy will have already told them all they need to know.'

A streak of red in the sky promised a fine day in the morning.

'How about you go over there tomorrow, Mr Sykes? I know it seems unlikely, but perhaps Miss Trimble didn't die because she claimed to have seen Mary Jane by the quarry. Perhaps she died because of some connection with Clitheroe.'

Sykes waited, his long-suffering what's-she-up-to-now look asking for more information.

'Miss Trimble's cousin Clara is married to the verger at Clitheroe Parish Church. Mrs Percival Watmough.'

'Why would I contact her?' Sykes sighed. 'That'll be a great assignment. Sorry to burst in on your trouble, but my boss thinks your cousin Aurora Trimble was poisoned, and it could have been because of something you said. And there's a girl with some sort of Lancashire accent who's gone missing.'

'I'm sure you'll handle it beautifully. If you look in the folder on my dining room table, you'll find photographs. There's one of Millie.'

'All right. I'll see what I can do, but it will be Millie I'm searching for. I can't go around claiming a woman was

326

poisoned when we've no evidence, and the police aren't investigating that.'

'We don't know what they're investigating. Marcus tells me what he thinks it's helpful for me to know.'

Sykes nodded, but with no great enthusiasm. 'All right. I'll go tomorrow.'

'How will you get there?'

'I've a pal with a motorbike.'

'Don't tell me, he owes you a favour.'

Sykes laughed. 'How did you guess?'

When he had gone, and I went back inside, Harriet said, 'We usually have a bath on Friday and last night we didn't.'

'Well then, you must have a bath tonight. Tell me what to do.'

Ten o'clock Saturday night. Harriet and Austin had gone to bed. I sat in the rocker by the fire, in Mary Jane's cottage, feeling useless.

'When will Mammy come back?' Austin had asked, as he waited his turn for the bath, and again when I tucked him in bed.

'I can't say for sure, but it will be soon.'

'Tomorrow?'

'We'll see.'

He snuggled down into the bed.

'How do you know our mam?' Harriet was sitting up, retying the thread that fastened the end of her single plait.

I considered telling her that I was more than a courtesy aunt, that I was the real thing. But piling on such information seemed an unnecessary burden. 'Our families have known each other for a long time. Your mam and I will tell you all about it one day.'

She left it at that. I trod carefully down the stairs,

327

holding the candlestick, disinclined to climb into Mary Jane and Ethan's bed. Lantern in one hand, coal scuttle in the other, I went outside.

Setting the lantern down, I shovelled coal. It was madness to think Mary Jane would have hidden Ethan's tools here. If she had been guilty, she could have left them in the quarry, or tossed them into the river. Whoever put the tools there did it for the purpose of casting suspicion on Mary Jane.

I still had not let the quarry foreman off my list of suspects, in spite of the fact that Marcus no longer appeared to show any interest in him, or in his son who had married today in the local church and would no doubt be taking over this house in the not too distant future. He would be the one coming out here to shovel coal.

In the darkness and quiet, the scraping of the shovel along the coal shed floor sounded like Satan's orchestra, tuning up for a night of evil symphonies. I filled the bucket, breathing in the coal-dust smell. In the lantern light, black cobs shone like dark diamonds.

When I stopped shovelling, another sound caught my ear, a rustling, a brushing, as though a small animal dashed for cover. Perhaps I had disturbed some night creature.

I shook off the feeling. The countryside is full of such sounds, and though only a quarter of a mile from the centre of the village, this was countryside.

Back in the cottage, I picked up the tongs and mended the fire. Unaccountably, I thought of my mother who has never in her life made a fire, and of my original mother, Mrs Whitaker, who no doubt had times in her life when simply having fuel for a fire would be a luxury.

Well, this would be a good fire, just for me. I would sit in the chair, and pass the night. I went to the basin to wash my hands. The blind was raised, thanks to Austin's certainty that his Mammy would look through the window when she came back, to see if they were here.

As I reached to draw down the blind, a movement caught my eye. Someone was in the Jowett, and had ducked out of sight. Probably a curious village lad. Well, I wouldn't risk the local daredevil making off with my motor for a bet. I opened the front door, trod silently down the path, reached the car, and jerked the door open.

A small shriek of alarm came from a gnome who tried to dart past me. I made a grab, and caught a wriggling child.

'What are you doing?'

I set her down, expecting her to run. She seemed beaten, with as little energy as I had myself. 'I'm cold.'

It was the Millie from Conroys' farm. 'Where have you been? You've had half Yorkshire scouring the countryside for you.'

'I'm cold.'

She was, too. Shivering.

'Come inside. Be warm.'

'Don't send me back.'

Afraid she would dash away, I took her hand. 'Come on. It's all right; everything's going to be all right.'

If ever I had children, I would say to them, Never believe a person who tells you that everything will be all right.

Once inside, she shrank back towards the door. The light from the fire and the lamp filled the room with shadows.

'Sit by the fire and warm yourself.'

She walked to the hearth and held out her hands to the flames that burned through the newly placed coals.

'Not too close or you'll get chilblains.' I poured her a glass of milk.

She took it from me, and drank.

'Drink slowly.'

I could get the hang of ordering children about. Perhaps I had missed my way and should have been a school mistress. Although there was the slight drawback that she seemed not to be listening.

She looked all about her, as though expecting some trap. 'Where is the kind man?'

That would have to be Sykes. 'You mean the man with the stockings?'

'And chocolate.'

'Tonight he's with his own children.'

'Are you his mother?'

I think she meant wife, but I didn't argue. 'No. I'm here to look after Harriet and Austin.'

The child looked half starved, inside and out. I lifted a shawl from a hook behind the door and wrapped it around her shoulders. There was a small buffet, just the right size for a changeling creature. I set it by the fire. 'Sit there. I expect you'd like something to eat.'

She stared into the fire.

I had begun to slice bread. My hand slipped. I barely missed chopping off my index finger. Was she the one who had set fire to the cowshed? I had let in a little fire raiser. That's why she ran away.

I could see it now. Mary Jane released from police custody without a stain on her character, standing before the charred ruins of this cottage. Sergeant Sharp saying, 'Sorry, Mrs Armstrong. It would appear that Mrs Shackleton inadvertently let in a small arsonist. She and your children were quickly incinerated. We righteous villagers were asleep in our beds at the time.'

'Here.' I handed the child a plate with buttered bread and a slice of ham.

She wolfed it down. 'I'm warm. I'll go now.'

In her haste to be off, she knocked over the buffet.

'It's too dark and cold. Stay here for tonight.'

She thought this over.

'Where?'

'Where you please. There on the rug. I'll find a blanket for you, or there's a bed upstairs.'

'Here.' She sat down in the centre of the peg rug.

I slid into the rocker, passed her a cushion and Mary Jane's shawl. For a while, she gazed into the fire. Perhaps there would be a variation on a theme and instead of matches, she would easily manage the tongs and place lighted coals in strategic places about the house.

She lay down, her head on the cushion, and let her eyes close.

When she was soundly asleep, I lifted her in my arms and carried her upstairs; her stick-like arms and legs hanging in a way that reminded me of Ethan Armstrong on the stretcher, his fingers pointing to the ground.

Pushing open the door of Mary Jane and Ethan's room, I carried her in, awkwardly turning back the covers, and lay her on the bed. Several fleas had jumped from her to me during the three or four minutes this journey took.

Sorry, Mary Jane. You'll have to boil all your sheets, if you ever get back.

I stood by the bed. She had woken, but pretended to be sleeping. There was something like an electric current of caution running through her. I would have to watch out that she didn't come downstairs, steal a taper and set about her work.

I gave up on the thought of slipping to the outsales department of the Fleece and buying a bottle of gin. It was too late anyway.

She opened her eyes.

'Whose child are you?' I asked.

'I'm nobody's child.'

'What's your full name?'

'Millie Featherstone.'

'How do you come to be in Yorkshire, when you're a Lancashire lass?'

But her eyes had closed. I left her sleeping.

Next I looked in on Harriet and Austin. Harriet was wide awake.

'Who's come in?'

'Only a little girl who was lost. The girl from the farm.'

'I'm glad she's come. She pulled Austin from the fire.'

'What?'

But Harriet closed her eyes and would say no more, except, 'Don't tell on her. She didn't mean it.'

The rap on the door came so gently that at first I thought it must be the wind, blowing a bough of the apple tree.

I opened the door to find Marcus, standing a little way back. 'You should call out to ask who it is,' he said. 'You never know who might be wandering about on a night like this.'

My first thought was for Mary Jane, that something had happened to her, or that she had confessed.

'Come in.' He stepped inside, and for a moment we stood in the light of the lamp.

'Sit down, Marcus.' I returned to my chair.

He remained standing. 'I can't stay long.'

'Are you on your own?'

'I have a sergeant driving me. He's in the motor. I stopped a little way down the lane so as not to disturb the children with the noise of the engine.'

Marcus reached for a bentwood chair from the table. He sat astride it, his arms folded across the chair back. 'Bob Conroy . . .'

I interrupted him by pointing to the ceiling, and reminding him that the children may hear.

He lowered his voice to little more than a whisper. 'Bob Conroy has confessed to killing Ethan Armstrong. He says Mr Armstrong worked out who must be informing on his political activities, and when he challenged him about it, Conroy admitted everything.'

'But he's sold the farm. He's going away. Why would it matter so much that Ethan knew?'

'He couldn't bear the shame of what he'd done. He felt sure Ethan would denounce him to everyone, including his own wife, and Mary Jane, so he killed him.'

'Do you believe this confession?'

He looked at the fire, and then at me. 'No. I think he's trying to protect Mary Jane.'

In spite of his low tone of voice, I felt a sudden horror that Harriet would be out of bed, her ear to the floorboards.

'He could be telling the truth, Marcus.'

'It's possible. I'm keeping an open mind. Ethan Armstrong had married the woman Conroy loved. There's been talk in political circles that Mr Armstrong planned to stand for parliament.'

'That's why Special Branch took an interest in him?'

'Yes. He was charismatic, a born leader. Conroy and he were school chums and comrades, and perhaps Conroy couldn't bear the thought that he would forever be held in contempt by a man who – apart from his mad politics – was better in every way than Conroy himself.'

'Marcus, your men searched this cottage and the

outbuildings. Have you ordered a similar search at the farm?'

He hesitated. 'Not yet.'

'And those papers of Ethan's I handed over, has anyone gone through them?'

'Yes. Most of it was familiar, a few surprising names.'

I felt sick at the thought that I had handed over the names and addresses of working men who only wanted better conditions and pay. But I put the thought aside and clutched at another straw. 'That advertisement by a well provided woman seeking a well provided man, Dad thought it might be some sort of code, but I asked a friend to write a letter. It's a real person, Marcus.'

He listened while I told him about Mr Duffield's letter, written as Mr Wright, and the reply, and the meeting scheduled for tomorrow afternoon.

'Please don't get your hopes up, Kate. There was probably some perfectly simple explanation as to why Mr Armstrong had that cutting in his possession. He was interested in all sorts of social issues and women's rights – at least in theory.' A tone of slight rebuke entered his voice. 'You'd no need to go to the lengths of having a reply written to the advertisement. I would have had the box number checked. Saved your friend Mr Duffield and this enterprising lady a little embarrassment.' He was about to say something flippant, but thought better of it.

'Have you told Mrs Conroy that you have her husband in custody?'

'Sergeant Sharp paid her a visit. He told her that Conroy is being treated in hospital for burns and shock, and that he's under sedation.'

'I expect she was mightily relieved.' She would also be relieved to know that Millie was safe and sound.

'What is it, Kate?'

'The little girl, Millie, she turned up here not long ago, frozen and half starved. She's terrified of getting into trouble. I've fed her and put her to bed. Do you think . . . I mean, having another child here would help Harriet and Austin . . .'

That was not entirely true. Harriet and Austin had each other and tomorrow would be with their grandma. It was Millie who worried me. If she really had set fire to the cowshed, she needed help, not punishment.

Marcus did not seem concerned about Millie. He nodded. 'I'll have someone call on Mrs Conroy and tell her we've found the child and she's being taken care of. Is she hurt?'

'No. Just dirty, exhausted and flea-bitten.'

He smiled. 'Well, it's very noble of you. We both have our work cut out.'

'I expect this means we won't see you for Sunday dinner at my parents' tomorrow?'

He bent and kissed my cheek. 'Don't you believe that, Kate. I wouldn't miss it for the world. A man has to eat, and . . .' He left out the fact that as far as he was concerned, this case was all but concluded. He drew me up from the chair and into his arms. 'Try not to worry too much.' He kissed me again. 'Get some sleep, Kate. And bolt the door after me.'

I watched from the window as his figure disappeared into the darkness. The motor started, and the car drove off into the night.

SUNDAY

Will the day's journey take the whole long day?
From morn to night, my friend.

Christina Rosetti

One

The three children sat at the table, each with a basin of porridge. Harriet pressed the lumps in the porridge with the back of her spoon. Austin sported a lump of porridge on his chin, like a joke beard. Millie ate quickly, not taking her eyes off the food. When she finished, she licked the dish clean.

'Millie. Tell me what happened on the night of the fire.'

She looked at her dish as if to read an answer.

'It want me!' Austin cried.

'And it want me neither,' Millie echoed.

'I'm not blaming anyone. I just want to find out. Millie, where were you when the fire started?'

'In my bed.'

'She sleeps downstairs,' Harriet said, 'in a bed that pulls down from the wall in the kitchen.'

'Tell me what you saw, Millie.'

Millie recognised a bargaining situation. 'I want a sup of tea.'

Harriet poured some of her own tea into Millie's porridge dish. Millie picked up the dish and began to drink. When she had finished, I asked her again.

She stared at the empty dish. 'Mr Conroy brayed on the door. That waked me up. Mrs Conroy come down. She wouldn't let him inside because he had drink on him. She went after him.'

'What do you mean?'

'Making sure he went off from the door and didn't mither her. I shut my eyes again. And I heard more noise and I didn't want to look.' She stared at Austin.

'It want me,' Austin wailed.

'No it want him,' Millie confirmed. 'Austin'd woked up and was crying outside. Some flames was taking hold.'

Austin began to cry, as if he must illustrate this story with his actions. 'I wa' cold, right cold, and Harriet want there.'

Harriet shushed him. She turned to me. 'Sometimes Austin sleepwalks.'

That did not explain how he came to be outside, unless the door had been left open, or Millie had taken him out there to lay the blame for the fire on him.

'What happened next, Millie?'

'I knew summat was up. I went and saw the flames. I let the cows loose.' She turned red and looked away. I guessed that she had shown more care for the cows than for Austin.

I smiled at her. 'That was very good, to set the cows free. You saved their lives. What then?'

'Mr Conroy, rolling hisself on the ground. His clothes was on fire, and he rolled and rolled and he picked Austin up in his arms and run.'

'Where was Mrs Conroy?'

'She'd gone back to bed after shutting Mr Conroy out.'

A loud knock on the door sent all four of us into an attitude of statues. I watched as the string that held the key began to move. And then I leaped across and grabbed it, and held the key.

'Anyone home?' It was Mrs Conroy.

I nodded to Millie to go upstairs, which she did, silently.

I opened the door, but only a fraction. 'Mrs Conroy. I'm sorry but I can't ask you in. The children are exhausted.'

'Mrs Armstrong gave me care of them. I can't let her down.'

I stepped outside, closing the door behind me.

'You have troubles of your own, and the children are expected at their grandma's today.' I reached out a hand and grazed her arm. 'I've heard about the fire. It's beyond me to know what to say. My heart goes out to you. I shall tell Mary Jane how kind and thoughtful you were to come looking.'

My heart was beating fast. If she chose to force her way in, this could be a nasty scene.

'My girl went missing too. The police have her in custody though of course they don't say it in so many words.'

'How dreadful. Go see Sergeant Sharp. I'm sure he'll put your mind at rest. I would come with you, but the children's grandmother will be here shortly.'

That did it. Perhaps I was not sufficient of a deterrent, but with the addition of an arriving grandmother, Mrs Conroy retreated.

I wished her goodbye, went inside, and shut the door. When I locked it and turned my back against it, I was trembling. What I was up to amounted to abduction, but Millie looked too frail to bear the brunt of blame for the fire.

Harriet went to the window and closed the curtains.

'I don't like it dark,' Austin complained.

'You have to have the curtains shut when someone died,' Harriet said gently.

'Who died?'

'Dad died.'

'But that was before. That wasn't today.'

Harriet ignored him. 'Is Grandma really coming here?'

It didn't do to tell lies in front of children. 'I think it will save a great deal of trouble if we go there. And it will take Millie's mind off things if she comes with us.'

On the way, I would call home, freshen up and collect my outfit for the all-important family Sunday dinner.

Once again I found myself in White Swan Yard, the Wakefield courtyard where I was born. Mrs Whitaker's old dog lay on the flags. It thumped its tail, without bothering to lumber up until Harriet and Austin reached the door and rushed inside.

Millie hung back shyly. I felt sorry for the child, having yet more strangers to contend with. 'Can't I come with you?'

I considered. Shortly I would be at my parents' house in Sandal. Something told me it would be complicated enough, with Marcus meeting Dad for the first time; valiant Mr Duffield arriving for his teatime appointment with the well provided woman; and Mother's friend along to make up the numbers at dinner, and give Mr Duffield the once over.

I was saved an answer. Mrs Whitaker came to the door and held a hand out to Millie. 'Come on, lass. Don't be left out in the cold. It's Millie isn't it?'

Millie brightened up straightaway and went inside, accompanied by Benjie the dog.

Mrs Whitaker turned to Harriet and Austin, told them to look after the little guest.

She stepped into the yard. 'Hello, love.'

'Hello.'

She wore a bright silky Sunday pinafore, printed with spring flowers. 'Any news?'

I couldn't call her mother. I couldn't call her Mrs Whitaker; that would be too formal. 'Mary Jane has been released by the police, for now. She's staying with the Ledgers. Their solicitor is acting for her.'

She frowned at that. Perhaps Mary Jane had told her the secret about the Ledger children, or Ethan had confided his opinion of these particular members of "good" society. 'What does your father ... what does Superintendent Hood say about it all?'

That your former son-in-law was an agitator, under surveillance, and that your daughter may be a murderess.

'I'm going there now. Just as soon as there's a development, I'll let you know.'

She thrust her hands into the pocket of her pinny. 'I feel that helpless. Would it do any good if I went to speak up for her? She wouldn't ...' Mrs Whitaker could not bring herself to finish the sentence.

'I'm sure we'll get to the bottom of this and she'll be back home.'

'She won't have a home though will she, without Ethan. The house goes with the job.'

'Let's take it a step at a time, Mrs Whitaker.' It slipped out, the Mrs Whitaker, and that made me add something more optimistic than I felt at that moment. 'I'm sure it will turn out all right.'

No I'm not. I have no idea how this will turn out.

'I hope so, Catherine. I pray so.'

'Goodbye then. I'll call back for the children.'

It seemed unkind to leave her so hastily, but I needed to get to my parents' house. My stomach churned. I wanted Marcus to be too busy to come. I wanted him to arrive early and announce that he had charged Bob Conroy with murder, and Mary Jane was free to go.

I dreaded the solemn look, the gentleness in his voice if he said the words I feared. Banish the thought. Thanks to me, dear Mr Duffield would be foregoing his usual Sunday routine, straightening his tie and steeling himself to meet strangers, and the mysterious Mrs Alexander, placer of a small advertisement. She may well turn out to be a secret code. An anarchist, black bomb under her arm stumbling into the house on the stroke of four and blowing us all to kingdom come.

Whenever Dad knows I am visiting, he arranges with his motor-mad neighbour to check over the Jowett as he does not trust me to keep the tyres in good condition.

The next-door neighbour, a young man with wild hair and tidy beard, lives with his mother. He was waiting, watching out for me, like a fussy old lady. He called out, 'Keep her running!'

He was beside me in an instant, listening to the sound of the engine, like a conductor who has detected a wrong note. 'Have you checked the boiler lately, Mrs Shackleton?'

I confessed I had not.

'Leave her to me.'

I smiled, thanked him, and picked up my bag. He is a man my mother once thought of in connection with her widowed friend Martha, but reluctantly concluded that Martha Graham did not have sufficient cranking parts to be of interest to an amateur motor mechanic. My Jowett disappeared into his garage and, if cars can look pleased, it did.

Mother ushered me upstairs. While I washed away motoring dust and brushed my hair, she laid my dress on the bed.

'This is lovely, Kate.'

It is a new wrap-around style in turquoise silk crepe, with narrow panels gaily embroidered in darker silk and metallic threads. I don't like the metallic, but Mother disagreed.

'What you need is my turquoise pendant with the matching bracelet.'

She only just had time to fasten the pendant for me when the doorbell rang.

'Our first guest.' She listened as Pamela the maid let him in. 'It's your newspaper librarian.'

'Mr Duffield. Good. I should like to have a chat with him before the others arrive.'

'The sherry is in the drawing room. Pamela will take him in there. I'll let you greet him and give you five minutes.'

Mr Duffield shone with brushing and scrubbing. His face was pink from close shaving. The usually unruly eyebrows lay plastered in straight lines. His hair might have been parted with a sword. I wished he had chosen a more sober suit and a regimental tie of some sort but it was too late for that. Mr Duffield had dressed for the occasion, in his inimitable fashion. He wore a maroon bow tie and a long jacket that gave him the air of having stepped from a Wild West saloon. I could not place the era from which his footwear dated. A pixie could have admired its reflection in the sheen of his pointed toe caps. He smiled at me with a look of pure relief as though I was the cavalry and had just ridden across the hill in the nick of time.

'Thank you so much for coming, Mr Duffield. Will you have a glass of sherry?'

He accepted a dry sherry and immediately confided, 'I arrived a little early because I feel most uneasy about this enterprise. The more I think about it, that poor lady coming to meet me under entirely false pretences ... If you could go over what is required of me ...'

'Of course.' Now was not the time to admit that I felt equally uneasy. 'First there'll be lunch, Mr Duffield, with my parents, Mr Dennis Hood, and my mother Virginia, Dad calls her Ginny.' Mr Duffield visibly shuddered at the thought that I might suggest such familiarity. I did not add that Mother is also entitled to her Lady Virginia moniker.

'I had the pleasure of meeting Mrs Hood yesterday when she called at the newspaper offices.'

'Ah yes, of course.'

'A charming lady.'

'And there'll be a friend of my mother's, Mrs Martha Graham, a widow, and Mr Marcus Charles.'

'And Mr Charles is ...?'

'A friend of mine.' I took a breath. 'He's a chief inspector at Scotland Yard.'

Mr Duffield's hand trembled. The sherry made waves. I watched, wondering would he crush the stem or spill the contents onto the rug. He did neither but carefully placed the glass on the mantelpiece, as though too distraught to see the occasional table next to him. He bit his lip. 'Superintendent Hood, and Chief Inspector Charles, and I am here to partake of Sunday lunch, and then perpetrate a deception upon an unwitting lady. Surely ...'

'My father and Mr Charles are aware of this. It is part

346

of an investigation. You will have the gratitude of the West Riding Constabulary, and Scotland Yard.'

I may not, but you will.

He waited for me to say more. This is the trouble with men who have been in the army. They either want to give orders, or take them. In his empire at the newspaper offices, Mr Duffield gave orders. But this, in his eyes, was my domain. I rose to the occasion.

'We will finish lunch in time for you to be ready to meet your teatime guest, Mrs Alexander. You will bring her into this room, so please make yourself familiar with it. Sherry glasses there, sherry dry, and sherry sweet. As soon as she arrives, Pamela the maid will admit her and take her coat. She will be shown in here where you will walk to meet her, offer your hand, and welcome her. We get the sun through this window in the afternoon, so make sure you sit with your back to the window, so that you can observe her well. Once she is seated, even if she accepts sherry, pull the bell cord by the fireplace. Pamela will return, and you'll order tea.'

He held up his hand, schoolboy fashion. 'What if Mrs Alexander doesn't want tea?'

'There will be cake, to have with the sherry. Give a truthful account of yourself, but keep it very simple, sticking to what you said in the letter.'

With a look of panic, he said, 'I can't remember what I said.'

I reminded him about his widowhood, his income, his properties, and his reasons for living here.

'What if her advertisement was a secret code, as you half suspected, and she asks me questions I can't answer?'

'Well then, she will realise you are an innocent party, unaware of the code. If she asks you everyday sorts of

347

questions that you find awkward, say that you would so much like to hear about her, and how delighted you are to entertain such a fragrant lady in your humble home.'

He looked around the drawing room with something like dismay. 'It's not humble.'

'Be your charming self. Give her admiring glances, whether she merits them or not. Listen to her.'

'What if I find myself engaged to be married, under false pretences?'

'It will be all right, believe me.'

Before he had time to worry further, Mother glided in. She wore a peach dress with tiered skirt, and her second-best pearls. 'Why Mr Duffield, how delightful to see you. My husband is so looking forward to hearing all about your work at the newspaper library. I told him how very well informed you are on every topic under the sun.'

Mr Duffield stood to attention. Under her flattery, his worries dropped away. I left him in her capable hands when the doorbell rang. It was Marcus.

He kissed me. 'Kate, you look ravishing, as always.'

The always was a lie, but turquoise does suit me.

We stood for a few moments in the hall, and I wished we were going to be alone, but of course there was a purpose to the visit. Dad emerged from his study, and I introduced them, then we all went into the drawing room for sherry.

Martha Graham arrived last. She is a slender live wire of a woman who only truly lights up when she plays bridge. Mother introduced her to Marcus, and then drew her into conversation with Mr Duffield. This helped take his mind off the task ahead, and perhaps gave him a little time to practise being suave.

Dad cornered me at the far end of the room. While

making it appear that we were chatting about his visit to the dentist, he said, 'What on earth are you thinking of, Katie, setting up some lonely hearts meeting here?'

'It wasn't meant to be here. They were to meet at an hotel.'

'It'll look grand, won't it, if your man over there fluffs it and we end up with some insulted female suing for breach of promise and I'm to stand up in court and explain how this came about under my roof.'

'Dad . . .'

'Don't Dad me. This was meant to be an opportunity to meet your friend Mr Charles.'

'Well, you are meeting him!'

It was a relief to me when dinner was served and we all sat down to tuck into Yorkshire pudding.

'We always eat the Yorkshire pudding first,' Mother explained to Marcus.

Dad said, 'When Katie was little, she would never eat her Yorkshire pudding until I cut windows and doors into it and made a little house.'

Marcus caught my eye and we smiled.

Mr Duffield turned out to be the perfect guest. He speculated as to who would replace Bonar Law; would it be Mr Baldwin or Lord Curzon? He thought Mr Baldwin because the Conservatives were trying not to appear so aristocratic and patrician. He and Dad agreed that they could see no end to the lawlessness in Afghanistan. Mother successfully steered the conversation away from politics, to give Mrs Graham the opportunity to talk about her garden.

Only when the little French clock chimed the quarter hour, did some shifting about on the chairs take place, and Mr Duffield glanced in my direction, awaiting orders.

Mrs Graham had clearly been primed as to her time of

departure, looked at her watch, uttered a goodness me and was off as fast as Cinderella from the ball, but not before saying a warm goodbye to MrDuffield.

Mr Duffield took up his position in the drawing room.

Not until ten minutes past four did the doorbell ring.

I almost jumped out of my skin.

We dining room inhabitants sat in unnatural silence while Pamela opened the front door. I listened, ear to the crack in the door.

Pamela asked the visitor in, and offered to take her coat.

'Thank you. It's rather chilly out.'

The voice was cultured, with rounded vowels and carefully enunciated word endings; too careful, perhaps. It was the voice of someone who has just filed her nails.

'Mrs Alexander?' Mr Duffield asked, with a smile in his tone.

'Yes. You must be Mr Wright.'

The door closed.

I heard no more.

Marcus caught my eye, silently asking who or what I had expected, or suspected. When I did not respond, he flashed me a smile that was both kind and annoyingly indulgent.

Mother whispered something to Dad whose face took on a thunderous look.

Pamela stepped smartly along the hall and tapped on the drawing room door, delivering a tray. She was supposed to come in and give a description of the woman, but did not.

Twenty minutes stretched to half an hour, stretched to forty-five minutes. What was Duffield doing in there? It was supposed to be a brief tête-à-tête, not the development of a ten-year plan.

I could bear the tension no longer and rang the bell for Pamela, not daring to step into the hall and break Mr Duffield's cover.

Moments later, the door opened. Pamela mouthed exaggeratedly, 'Sorry. I forgot.'

Forgot? How could she forget?

She tiptoed to the table.

'What does she look like?'

She thought for a moment. 'You know that picture of Pola Negri, with the beauty spot?'

'No.'

'Well, she's like her, but without the beauty spot and her eyebrows don't come quite as far down her temples as Pola Negri's do.'

'So she has dark hair?' I asked.

'Yes.' Pamela looked at my mother.

Mother said, 'Pola Negri has a sort of round face, a little sultry looking.'

'She wears gold-rimmed spectacles,' Pamela added. 'The lady, not Pola Negri.' She thought for a moment. 'Solemn looking.'

'Her figure?'

'Buxom.'

'Well?' Dad asked.

At the same time, Pamela whispered, 'How is my ginger tom, Mrs Shackleton?'

Ginger tom? I hesitated to ask.

Mother said, 'Oh, you know, Kate, the ginger tom in Sookie's litter that you promised for Pamela.'

'Ah.'

Sookie had not had a ginger kitten. 'He's very well, Pamela. I've told him all about you. Only he's not entirely ginger.'

Dad looked ready to explode.

Pamela smiled and turned to leave. I caught up with her at the door, still desperate to have the smallest hope that I had been right. 'What does she wear, this Mrs Alexander?'

'A dark skirt and blue blouse, quite nice stockings in artificial silk, and a pair of court shoes with a heel. Her coat is reversible.'

'Oh?'

'Yes. It's a cape. Bottle green on one side, plaid on the other.'

'Bring it in, quickly.'

She brought the cape and handed it to me. I held it up, as though it were exhibit A in the most notorious Old Bailey trial – first the green side, and then the plaid. It was exactly the plaid of Mary Jane's cape. 'It's her. It's the woman who was seen near the quarry'

I handed the garment back to Pamela.

She left the room and hung up the coat just in time because seconds later, the drawing room door opened. 'Pamela,' Mr Duffield called cheerily. 'I shall escort Mrs Alexander to the railway station.'

'No need, Mr Wright,' the lady protested.

'Please,' said Mr Duffield, giving the orders this time. 'I insist.'

No one at the dining table had responded to my claim, 'It's her.' I said again, the moment that the door closed. 'A woman in plaid was seen by the quarry. Ethan had that advertisement in his pocket. We must do something!' I looked from Marcus to Dad and back again.

There was a pause, during which looks passed around the table. What were we to do? Dash into the street and confront her?

'If you won't go after them, I will.'

'We have to follow it through,' Marcus said, biting his lip. 'I should have asked a constable to be on hand, only . . .'

He kindly refrained from saying he didn't believe me.

Dad stood up. He held out his hand to Mother. 'Come on, Ginny. We're going on a jaunt. Kate, fetch your mother's coat.'

Mother stood up, about to say that she needed to change her shoes but I did not give her the time. The moment the door closed behind Mr Duffield and Mrs Alexander, I rushed into the hall and grabbed Mother's coat from the hall stand.

'It's probably a wild goose chase,' Dad said, 'but we can't come this far and not follow it through.'

Marcus said, 'Wait, sir. My driver's in the kitchen. He'll take you to the tram stop and you can follow the tram, see if she really is going to the railway station.'

Dad nodded. 'Good point.'

He looked grim and there would doubtless be a lecture later.

When they had gone, Marcus said, 'Your parents are sports.'

This was not how the afternoon was supposed to go. They were humouring me because of Mary Jane. Later they would be able to say, we kept an open mind. We tried to clear her name.

Two

From the early days of her married life, when she shocked her aristocratic family by marrying a police officer and moving to Wakefield, Lady Virginia, or Ginny Hood as she became, had never felt easy about taking a supporting role. Once, when asked to step in as temporary matron to a woman in custody, she had brought two ounces of Lapsang Souchong and a sponge cake to the Wakefield cells. After that incident, Dennis, then Inspector Hood, never again asked for his wife's assistance.

Now here she was again, once more trying to do her best as she and Dennis, now Superintendent Hood, settled themselves in the motor ready to tail Mr Duffield and his mysterious companion, and follow the tramcar. She must try, for Kate's sake, to manage this surveillance with the utmost diligence and discretion.

Dennis and Ginny climbed from the motor at Westgate Station. She watched as that nice Mr Duffield waved goodbye to the lady, who entered the station without looking back. Ginny avoided the temptation to meet Mr Duffield's eye, but she certainly looked forward to meeting Martha Graham tomorrow and finding out if she was correct in thinking there had been a little spark of interest between them. Mr Duffield had passed Mrs Graham the gravy boat with immense courtesy.

At W H Smith, Ginny picked up the *Sunday Pictorial* and a bar of Five Boys chocolate. On the platform, she and Dennis chatted calmly about she knew not what. He listened politely, nodding agreement, and checked his watch against the station clock. Now and then, Ginny cast a surreptitious glance in Mrs Alexander's direction as she stood calmly, a couple of feet back from the platform edge, showing no sign of pleasure or excitement at having just met a potential suitor.

When the train steamed in, Mrs Alexander was first into the carriage. Ginny was ready to shoot in after her, but Dennis held her arm and allowed a young family to go ahead.

Ginny gazed out of the window. Don't let me be drawn into conversation, she said to herself. I would feel so bad to have struck up a liking for a female criminal. It would be the Lapsang Souchong all over again.

Dennis read the *Pictorial*.

At Leeds station, Ginny allowed a few moments before she followed Mrs Alexander into the Ladies' Waiting Room. Ginny powdered her nose and tidied her hair for what seemed an interminably long time. If it had not been for the description of the reversible cape, she would have paid no attention to the woman who emerged from the lavatory, blonde bob, no spectacles, and much slimmer than the plaid-caped lady from the train.

Ginny gave her hair a last pat, dropped tuppence in the attendant's saucer, and followed the woman out.

Dennis was waiting for her, a little way off from other travellers. Even so, she whispered, 'That blonde woman with the bob, it's the same woman who just parted from

Mr Duffield. She went into the lavatory and came out having shed a disguise. She was wearing a dark wig, Dennis, and has reversed her cape.'

Dennis nodded to a railway guard.

Ginny swelled with pride. She'd done it; been a help to Dennis, and to Kate. Lapsang Souchong and sponge cake were consigned to ancient history.

Three

Marcus and I had said little to each other while we waited, side by side on the sofa. The moment the doorbell rang, I leaped to my feet and went into the hall to meet a gloomy Mr Duffield, returned from the station. He took off his hat, refusing to step into the drawing room, intending to catch the next tram. 'I feel such a cad regarding that lady. Just for a moment, Mrs Shackleton, she touched my heart. It briefly came to me that we would marry, that she would delight my life and that of an evening we should sit either side of the fire, me reading Trollope and she with the Good Book, or a pair of knitting needles.'

'I could be wrong, Mr Duffield. Perhaps Mrs Alexander is who she says she is. I am only going by a feeling, and by her reversible cape.'

'No,' he said sadly. 'She would not give me her address but will contact me. Something about a sister who disapproves, and something else ...'

'What else, Mr Duffield?'

'I watched her walk into the station. She waved. I waved, and turned, but then looked back. Her gait had changed. Don't ask me how, but something altered in her step, and the way she held her head. I know we are all a different person when alone, but this was something else, and I can't say what, but I knew. These things are perhaps instinctive, as you hinted, Mrs Shackleton.' He sighed. 'Instinct, you know, whether a life spreads out just as it did before, or with some subtle change. My life spreads out as it always has.'

He smiled bravely, hiding disappointment.

Marcus had stepped into the hall and was listening. 'Thank you very much for your assistance, Mr Duffield. It's most public spirited of you to help us in this way.'

I smiled at Marcus, glad that he now at least pretended to treat my wild scheme with such sober appreciation. The change in Mrs Alexander's gait might be accounted for by her knowledge that she had made a conquest, or her relief at being able to escape from an eccentric.

Mr Duffield replaced his hat. 'Well, good day to you both.'

I watched him slowly walk away, head bowed.

'Don't feel too bad about all this, Kate.' Marcus placed a hand on my shoulder. 'Who knows but that you may have given the old chap an idea or two? Perhaps he'll be placing his own personal advertisement for a wife before too long.'

'Or brushing up on his bridge to please Mrs Graham.'

Back in the drawing room we sat beside each other on the sofa, a little way apart this time. 'Kate, when this business is settled, I have something to ask you, and I hope you'll say yes.'

I knew what the question would be, or at least thought I did. A Scotland Yard chief inspector does not have Sunday dinner with a West Riding Constabulary superintendent and his wife while planning to ask their daughter to live in sin or continue a clandestine affair.

Marcus is a dear man, but we were treading warily around each other. He wasn't saying so, but he believed my scheme to have Mr Duffield answer the letter had come to nothing and that because of a reversible cape, I had sent my mother and father on a wild goose chase. Like a finely adjusted set of scales, something hung in the balance between us.

'Pamela!' I ran into the kitchen. The woman wore artificial silk stockings. So did a thousand other women.

Pamela turned from stacking dishes. 'Pamela, did the lady wear jewellery?'

She thought for a moment. 'Earrings, a ring on each hand.'

'A ring on each hand, one a wedding ring?'

'Yes.'

'And the other, a buckle ring?'

'I think so.'

'What kind of earrings?'

'Pierced. I don't come across many ladies with pierced ears, and I expect they was gold.'

'Pear-shaped hoops, smallish?'

'Yes. If they'd been any bigger you'd call them vulgar, gypsy like.'

'Thank you, Pamela.'

'That kitten, what colour is it if it's not entirely ginger?'

I pictured the peculiar little creature. 'It's ginger, tabby and white.'

'Oh.' She could not hide her disappointment. 'Mrs Hood said it was a ginger tom.'

'I've no idea what sex it is.'

Marcus was listening in the hall. We went back into the drawing room before he spoke. 'So who is the mysterious Mrs Alexander?'

'Georgina Conroy.'

He sighed. 'You have a limited choice of suspects.'

'That's not the reason. It's her jewellery.'

'Pamela is suggestible. You gave her the information.'

'Georgina married Bob Conroy in January, 1922. I remember seeing the date in the church register and thinking that he took his time to find a wife. Bob and his brother Simon jointly owned the farm. Four months later, Simon was dead – an accident, tumbling into the quarry while trying to rescue a lamb.'

'Yes, an accident.'

'With Simon out of the way, the farm is owned by Bob, and when he dies, in another accident, it will come to her. She'll move on. I asked her about the advertisement that was in Ethan's pocket. She claimed to know nothing about it.'

'Did you ask Bob about it?'

'Yes, but by then she'd told him to say nothing, probably claiming she would be embarrassed to own up to her method of finding a man. He was holding something back. I should have pressed him.'

'I'll interview him. But he was drunk when the fire started, Kate. She didn't arrange that.'

'She's clever, takes advantage of whatever opportunity comes her way.'

Marcus reached for my hand and said softly, 'And she lets Mary Jane off the hook because she has a reversible cape? I don't think so.'

There was no point arguing. If I did, it would only fix him more firmly on Mary Jane. So I simply tried to offer him another idea. 'Ethan went to see Georgina, supposedly to confide in her about his marital troubles with Mary Jane. What if he went to see her because he knew she had schemed to have Bob sell the farm? Ethan had found the latest advertisement, the exact same wording as her previous one, and he knew she was behind it.'

'There's an awful lot of supposition there, Kate.'

I had said too much. A hint should have been enough. If Marcus would not investigate Georgina Conroy, then Sykes and I would. But his doubts dented my confidence.

The telephone rang.

Pamela got to it first.

A moment later, she opened the drawing room door. 'Mr Charles, it's the station master at Leeds, wishing to speak to you.'

'Thank you.'

Marcus went into the hall. I did not follow him, to watch him pick up the speaking device, to listen to half a conversation. I waited.

Either this was nothing to do with the well provided woman, Mrs Alexander, or I was right and she and her advertisement amounted to something. Only it could not be Georgina Conroy. Even the voice was wrong.

Pamela stepped into the room and closed the door on Marcus's conversation.

She looked sheepish. Had she come to tell me that the kitten would not be suitable?

'What is it, Pamela?'

'That lady visitor, when I said about her hands.'

'Yes?'

'She has a wart on her right middle finger. Was I right to notice it? No one can help warts can they?'

'No, I suppose not. Thank you, Pamela.'

'Do you think . . .'

'What?'

'I could take the tram to where you live, and I could look at the kittens.'

Wakefield must be teeming with unwanted cats, but Sookie's strange hybrid intrigued. 'What a good idea,' I said, trying to make myself sound convincing.

She looked pleased with herself. 'I'll talk to your mother about it.'

When Marcus came back, his face was unreadable. He looked at me as though I had hailed from another planet, and then he said, 'It looks as if you may have been right.'

'Oh?'

'Mrs Alexander took off her wig and spectacles in the ladies' room at Leeds railway station. She emerged blonde and rather well less well endowed than the person who called here, and with her cape reversed to bottle green. She may not be connected to the murder, Kate, but she's up to something. Your father had the ticket collector report on her destination. Great Applewick.'

'Georgina Conroy.'

'It's possible. I'm not jumping to conclusions. Sergeant Sharp will meet the train.'

I felt a sense of panic. Sergeant Sharp would frighten her off. She'd bolt.

He read the look on my face. 'I want him only to confirm that she gets off the train, and make a note of the time, in case we need that information for evidence. I'd like some answers from that lady.'

'About Ethan's murder?'

'Not yet. Personation is a misdemeanour but only if it's for the purpose of fraud or to obtain property.'

'Personation! Marcus, she killed Ethan.'

'I'll speed up the search warrant for the farm.'

'Marcus, I have an idea.'

'Go on.'

'That farmhouse and the outbuildings will be devilish to

362

search. There's one person who'll know every nook and cranny of the place.'

'Bob Conroy? He's in no fit state and he's still under suspicion.'

'The little girl, Millie. She's browbeaten and scared of Mrs Conroy; but little girls look into everything. Let me go there with her, and see what we find.'

Marcus frowned. 'And have Mrs Conroy deny all knowledge of whatever you find, say that Mary Jane's sister went to the house to incriminate her? No. We'll do this in the usual way, Kate, no unorthodox methods.'

'All right. But I have one small suggestion.'

Austin stayed with his grandma, in the second house on the right in White Swan Yard. Safety in numbers, that seemed to be Millie's feeling. She would only come with me to the farm if Harriet came too. The two girls sat side by side in the motor, sharing Gerald's motoring coat, and with a blanket around them. The goggles were too big, but they did not seem to mind.

I stopped the motor on the lane that led to Conroys' farm, outside the farm cottage. Arthur opened the door, but it was Mrs Sharp, the police sergeant's wife, who stepped forward to meet the children. Billy, the sheepdog, pushed past her and leaped at Millie, licking her face, wagging his tail.

Harriet shot me a glance. 'When can I see Mam?'

'Soon.'

I hoped it would be soon.

When they had disappeared into the tiny cottage, I drove on, finally leaving the Jowett by the farm gate.

Carrying my satchel and brown paper carrier bag, I stepped into the yard.

Mrs Conroy took a long time to come to the door. While I waited, it struck me that a pie and a fruit cake might be overdoing the commiserations, and one would have been enough.

She smiled with something like relief on seeing me. 'Come in. I feared it would be bad news about Bob.'

'Haven't you seen him yet?' I followed her into the spotless kitchen.

'They keep promising. You know hospitals, never tell you a thing.'

I handed her the carrier bag. 'I thought you might not be up to preparing food.'

She took the bag from me, and lifted the cake and pie onto the table. 'Thank you, but I've no appetite.'

I noticed the tea chest at the side of the table. She had been packing. When she saw me looking, she said, 'No point in shillyshallying. Now the farm's sold we shall move on just as soon as Bob's well enough. The livestock is sold.'

'Mrs Conroy, I want to ask you something.'

'Sit down then.' She sighed. 'I'm sorry I haven't put on the kettle since this morning. But you'll have a drink of something?'

'Yes, if you'll join me in a slice of cake.'

'You've talked me into it.'

She disappeared, returning with glasses, a bottle, plates and a sharp knife. 'Ask away,' she said as she cut into the fruit cake.

For a few seconds, I couldn't avert my eyes from her hands. A ring on each hand, one of them a buckle ring. From somewhere the words popped into my head. By our deeds will you know us. By our hands will you know us. 'She has a wart on her middle finger,' Pamela had said.

She poured a glass of homemade wine.

On the middle finger of her right hand, Georgina Conroy had a wart.

'Mrs Conroy, when Ethan came to see you, what was that about?'

She handed me a slice of cake. 'I don't suppose there's any harm in telling you now, though I would hate to hurt Mary Jane.'

I sipped the wine, a little sweet for my taste. 'I can't imagine what would make things worse for her than they are already.'

'He came to me because he was unhappy, and he asked for my advice.'

Poppycock. Why had Ethan really come? Because, voracious reader of newspapers, he had spotted her personal advertisement and linked it with a previous one that Bob Conroy had replied to.

She poured a glass for herself and raised it to me. 'Here's to better times. All things will pass.'

'Cheers.' I raised my glass. 'Why would Ethan have come to you, and not to Bob? After all, those two were old friends.'

'I was a shoulder to cry on. Ethan and Bob had a fall out over something or other, like little boys. Ethan was dead set against Bob selling the farm, and there was something else too, but I'm not sure what.'

I did not tell her that it was because Ethan had discovered Bob informed on him and his political activities. Perhaps she did not know that, though I guessed not much would pass this woman by. Keep her talking. Hope that she will give herself away.

'Mrs Conroy, I'm trying to understand what was going on. This is a little awkward, but Mary Jane and your husband, were they ... well, closer than they ought to be?'

She bit her lip. 'Do you know ... Now that you say it,

366

I wonder if Ethan did suspect something going on between Bob and Mary Jane. They always got on so well. There was something there when you saw them together, an understanding.'

I took a chance. 'Perhaps that's why Ethan encouraged Bob to marry. Bob told me it was Ethan who urged him to answer your advertisement I think.'

She looked at me quickly. Her lips parted but she said nothing.

'Sorry. He did wish he hadn't told me.' I continued. 'Of course Mary Jane didn't know how you and Bob met. You'll have to excuse that he told me. I caught him at a weak moment, in the churchyard, at his brother's grave'

She wouldn't be able to catch me out in a lie, not with Bob in hospital and in no position to make a denial. No doubt she had sworn Bob to keep quiet about how they met. She was not speaking. I was meant to make her talk, and all the words were coming from me. She would be a hard nut to crack. 'Bob said he'd seen you leave the vicarage. That you must have been having a word with Miss Trimble.'

The denial came quickly, too quickly. Her lips formed a grim line. 'What are you getting at? I did not leave the farm on Monday.'

I had not mentioned Monday. Now it was my turn to wait.

She steered the conversation. 'I didn't visit Miss Trimble. Bob went to see her. He was thinking of having a commemorative window designed in honour of his parents and his brother.'

'Ah yes. His brother met with an accident shortly after you and Bob married.' I kept my voice light, sympathetic, without a hint of accusation. 'Miss Trimble

367

thought she saw Mary Jane by the quarry. But that was you, wasn't it?'

She reached for the wine and poured herself a drop more, offering the same to me. I declined.

Her hand was steady as she returned the bottle to the table and raised the glass. 'It's been such a bad business. It puts us all on edge. But you're wrong.'

'What puzzled me was Bob's brother's death, when he was searching for the lost lamb in the quarry. But then, there was no lost lamb was there? You told him a child had come reporting the lost lamb. No one ever found out who that child was. But of course there was no such child. You made that up. You went with him. You pushed him. That's why no lamb was ever found.'

She laughed. 'Are you mad? Why would I do that?'

'So that when you killed Bob, there would be no one else who could lay claim to a share of the farm. Only Ethan was very inconvenient. He'd noticed that you got a little ahead of yourself and advertised in the paper again. When I showed the advertisement to Bob, it gave him quite a shock.'

'Have you told anyone about your wild ideas, Mrs Shackleton?'

I turned the bottle around so that the label faced me. 'Dandelion wine. It should be sweet, unless it's laced with something. You should have stayed with Miss Trimble until she died.'

For the first time, Georgina Conroy looked rattled. She rubbed the ball of her thumb against the wart on her finger. 'She was dead.' Immediately, she realised her mistake and tried to swallow her words. 'The doctor pronounced her dead.'

'She talked to me. She tried to tell me. You gave her a

bitter drink, and told her it was dandelion wine. You thought there'd be plenty of time for her to die before her brother returned, and her housekeeper. She'd already begun to lose feeling in her feet, her legs, her lower body. But somehow she tumbled off the sofa, dragged herself across the room. And then there was me, being nosey.'

Mrs Conroy grabbed at the sharp kitchen knife. As she lunged at me, I jumped from the chair, grasped the chair back and whipped it round, using it as a shield. She came at me. With all the force I could muster, I brought the chair down on her arm. The knife clattered to the floor. We faced each other.

'Miss Trimble's words meant nothing, until today, until you kindly brought out your homemade wine. Is that what you took with you when you visited her? Do you have a special dandelion wine recipe, for murder?'

She stared at me, her face a mask. 'What do you want?'

'I want to have Mary Jane freed, and she will be set free, because Bob has confessed. Mary Jane will need money. I expect as a well provided woman you already have a little nest egg. Is that why Ethan cut out your first advertisement, because he thought Bob would find a wife who could help him financially, bring the farm through difficult times?'

'Oh yes, Ethan thought that all right, that I would pour good money into this place. A fool and money are soon parted, but I'm no fool. As a going concern, this farm isn't worth a pint of sour milk. But I'm admitting nothing. Your accusations are preposterous.'

'I don't care what you've done. I want to help Mary Jane. Bob's confessed to killing Ethan. Mary Jane will be freed, but she'll need money.'

'I like Mary Jane. If she needs money, I'll help her. But

369

what is it you want? Why are you saying these things to me?' She was walking a tightrope of denial, and yet testing me out. Could I be bought?

'For myself? Nothing, except to know why you killed Ethan.'

We stood at some distance from each other. I still held onto the bentwood chair like a shield.

'Why would I kill Ethan? Bob has confessed. You didn't know Ethan. He had a sneaking admiration for me, someone who cocks a snook to all that's holy. So what if I advertised for a husband?'

At last, an admission. Would that be the only one? If Ethan had fallen out with Bob, he could still have wanted to spare his friend's feelings, and his pocket, by giving Georgina a warning that she must leave without taking Bob's money, the proceeds of the farm sale.

My silence worked. She spoke again. 'You can't connect me to what happened to Ethan.'

'We'll see.'

She gave a lopsided smile that curdled my blood. 'So . . . I'm a murderess am I? Well then, you think because we both drank from the same bottle of dandelion wine you are safe. But what you did not see was what I sprinkled at the bottom of your glass. If you're helpful, I could fetch the antidote.'

She was bluffing, or was she?

'Then fetch the antidote for yourself, because I switched the glasses while you were cutting the cake.'

She laughed. 'Clever. You and Ethan would have liked each other.'

'Yes, I think we might.'

'Whereas Bob is a drippy sort, trailing on Ethan's coat tails, slavering after Ethan's wife.'

She took a step towards me, and perhaps there was nothing threatening in it, but I didn't take the chance. I brought the full of force of the bentwood chair down against her knees. 'Is that how you felled Ethan before you hammered him to death?'

She gave a cry of pain, and then, 'You can't prove a thing.'

I am not usually a violent person, but there was one thing Georgina Conroy was right about. I would have liked my brother-in-law. And it made me angry to think of Harriet and Austin growing up without a father. All the same, I resisted the urge to execute her and claim self-defence.

'I won't have to prove anything, Mrs Conroy. But I have a feeling you'll have an awful lot of questions to answer.'

Through the window, I saw Marcus striding up the yard towards the house, his sergeant beside him, with the confident glow of a man with a search warrant in his pocket. Sergeant Sharp brought up the rear.

I went outside.

Marcus hurried towards me, motioning the other two on towards the farmhouse. 'Kate! You were to wait in the farm cottage with the children.'

'Oh? Sorry. I thought it might be helpful to make sure Mrs Conroy was home. Now, unfortunately, she's had an argument with a chair.'

'What was going on in there?'

'Hold your horses, Marcus. I think you might be interested in what Mrs Conroy had to say.'

I told him of our exchange, and about the mystery of Miss Trimble's last words: bitter, dandy. 'You'll find the dandelion wine on the table, and more in the pantry I should think.'

Marcus gave me a shrewd look. 'Unless we find a poison it would be difficult to make your suspicion stick. We could not test for every single poison, and they don't all stay in the body.'

'Test for hemlock, if that's possible.'

His sigh was a little exasperated, as if he had enough to do without being given tasks by me. But he waited to hear the reason behind my suggestion.

I described seeing Miss Trimble through the window, going into the house and finding my way to the parlour. 'My first thought when I went in the room was that she had seen a mouse and tripped, and when I thought about the colour of her dress the word "moleskin" came to mind, though it was only an ordinary grey.'

'A mouse? Moleskin? How does that take you to hemlock?'

'I must have caught a whiff of something mousey. The only poison I remember from my *Materia Medica* that is described as having a mousey smell is hemlock. And it would explain why she could still speak. It's a poison that spreads upwards, paralysing the body slowly.'

He stared at me, and then nodded slowly. 'I'll talk to you later, Kate.'

As he reached the farmhouse door, I called after him, and caught up. 'Will you need the children again tonight?'

'No. Mrs Sharp helped me to get Millie talking. No mean feat. Millie said Mrs Conroy started the fire in the barn. From what the child tells me, her own father died under suspicious circumstances.'

'In Clitheroe?'

'Yes.'

'That was where Miss Trimble spent last week. Georgina Conroy must have feared she would make some connection.'

The farmhouse door opened. Sergeant Sharp brought Georgina Conroy into the yard. Her look of hatred turned me cold.

'Take her to the car,' Marcus said.

We watched her go.

'Marcus, am I to take it that Mary Jane is free to leave the Ledgers'?'

'There'll be paperwork to complete.'

Bugger Marcus's paperwork. Mary Jane had suffered enough. I would gather up Harriet and Millie, and fetch Mary Jane from the Ledgers'.

Five

Sykes rode up just before midnight, disturbing the silence of our quiet road with the roar of his borrowed motor-bike. I pulled on my dressing gown and went downstairs to let him in.

He brought a breath of fresh air into the hall as he pulled off his helmet. 'Sorry. I saw you were in darkness but with a light in your room, and I thought you'd want a report.'

'You look half frozen.'

'I've come from Otley. I took the information to Chief Inspector Charles. He was still at his desk.'

I led him into the sitting room where Sookie was sitting by the embers of the fire, her kittens in the trug brought from upstairs.

Sykes rubbed his hands over the dying fire. 'My teeth are chattering ten to the dozen. Have you got a drop of something warming?'

It took an hour for his long story to come out, over glasses of brandy. The verger's wife, Miss Trimble's cousin, had chapter and verse on the woman we knew as Georgina Conroy, née Waterhouse. In Clitheroe she had been married to a retired solicitor's clerk. He died of heart failure, only six months after his only son met an accident in their garden, falling from a ladder while tying up the branch of an apple tree. After Georgina left the area, police from Manchester came looking for her in connection with the death of a previous husband.

'I wonder why she took Millie with her?'

Sykes grunted. 'A useful little slave. It was the way she treated Millie that made me think less highly of her than you did. She's personable, and a good actress. It was a small thing. Mrs Conroy didn't buy socks for Millie. The child seemed so forlorn, with her couch grass fire, clogs and no socks. I thought, something's not right here.'

'I hope Marcus will be able to pin her down for this.'

'Oh he thinks he will. He's having every inch of the sundial fragments tested for her fingerprints. A single print will put her at the scene. And he found some useful stuff when searching the farmhouse.'

It surprised me that Marcus had confided in Sykes, but then, we had done most of the work. 'What sort of things did he find in the farmhouse?'

'He's having some substances tested by a chemist. And there were different identity papers, bank books, the deeds of houses inherited from previous husbands. I wonder when she would have stopped.'

'Perhaps she didn't know how to stop.' We sat in silence for a while, looking into the fire. A coal cracked and blue and orange flames sparked.

Sykes said, 'It's Bob Conroy I feel sorry for. They're letting him out of hospital, so I thought I'd visit him, see if he needs a hand. Him and me struck up a bit of camaraderie that night in the Fleece, and then when I found him wandering on the moor. I wonder what will become of him, without his farm?'

'I feel no sympathy for the idiot. He betrayed Ethan. He should have found his own wife without resorting to newspaper advertisements, then Ethan would still have been alive.'

'All the same, he's suffered for what he did.'

'Good.' I gazed at the fire, as though it were a crystal ball. 'He'll take up with Mary Jane, after a decent interval. He's a well provided man, after all, and she'll be a well provided woman.'

'I'm going to ask him about Millie, whether he intends to look after her.'

'She and Harriet seem to hit it off. Perhaps Mary Jane will take her in.'

I put a log on the fire. A little extravagant at such an unearthly hour, but all thoughts of sleep had fled.

Sykes leaned back in his chair, staring at the sparks the log made as it settled onto the embers. 'I'm still not sure why Mrs Conroy killed Ethan.'

'She made the mistake of using identical wording when she placed the advertisement that netted her Bob Conroy, and the latest one that Ethan cut out of the paper. She couldn't risk being found out as a bigamist, and a murderess – though poor Ethan wasn't to know that. When she claimed that Ethan came to talk to her about his problems, that was poppycock. My guess is that he told her to sling her hook. His mistake was in not telling Bob, but by then he and Bob were estranged. From what I've learned of Ethan, I believe he would still have wanted to spare Bob's feelings. We'll never know for sure.'

'And she smashed the sundial because she could. And because it would help cast suspicion in other directions, on fellow workmen, or even Ethan himself – suggesting he'd got into a rage and abandoned his family and his work.'

'But she planted the tools on Mary Jane, just in case.'

We talked in circles for another half hour or so, watching flames take hold of the log. Finally, Sykes stood up and pulled on his coat.

'What will you do tomorrow, Mrs Shackleton? Take a well earned rest?'

'I have a private matter to attend to that will take me up to the North Riding.'

'Do you want a driver?'

'No. This is something I need to do alone.'

MONDAY

The saddest birds
A season find to sing

Robert Southwell

Epilogue

The weather did its worst – a fierce mixture of wind and rain. Sheets of rain obscured my view. Rain leaked into the car from under the canvas. Dad's neighbour, when he checked the motor, had pronounced it sound but extolled the virtues of newer models. On higher ground, the wind threatened to blow me and the Jowett into the ditch. Well, if I were to die of pneumonia, I had arrived at the right place. Catterick Hospital.

It was made up of so many buildings that I had no idea which way to go. Eventually, I spotted a chap trying to right his inside-out umbrella and asked for directions.

I parked outside what I hoped was the right building. The short dash for the door felt like walking through a waterfall. If I knew anything about matrons, I would be in trouble before I began – for dripping onto the tiled floors.

A porter took me to the matron's office, where I introduced myself.

'Ah yes, I have your letter,' she said. 'As I said in my reply, I doubt very much we can be of help. Let me give you a towel, and you can dry yourself a little. Here, let me take your coat. I'm sure I can find you a pair of slippers while your shoes dry.'

It was an unexpected kindness. I sat by the fire, drying my hair. She insisted on providing tea, a boiled egg and bread and butter soldiers, as though I were a child come crying home from school and in need of special care.

As I ate, she told me about the only two men who remained unidentified. One had total memory loss, and was lodged with a farmer and his wife a mile or so away. His description as short and stocky did not fit Gerald. The other man was brain damaged, and unable to speak.

'I'll take you to him when you are ready,' she said. She had cleverly timed her words about the brain-damaged man so that I had finished the egg, bread and tea. Otherwise, my appetite would have flown up the chimney.

We walked in silence along an endless corridor, and turned into another shorter corridor. 'He has been out of bed today, undertaking some exercises with the physiotherapist. If he's asleep, we won't disturb him.'

She opened the door to a private room. The man lay still. His head was shaved on one side, his eyes closed. Glad of the soft-soled slippers, I trod silently to the bed and looked down at him. I could see why she had brought me to him. His hair and eyebrows were dark. His face had been handsome once. But it was not Gerald. I shook my head.

We left the room. But it might have been, I told myself. I'm right to go on looking. 'Why is his head shaved?'

'He had an operation to relieve pressure on his brain. It's not beyond hope that there'll be some recovery.'

'Has he been here . . . all this time?'

She nodded. 'Look, there's one other chap you might talk to. He's not the man you're looking for, but he was in the same areas, and the same regiment. He's in because

of an infection that's taken hold in his leg. It was ampu-
tated at the knee. And he's blind. It's too far for his family
to visit, and I'm sure he'd be glad of a new voice. He's
even brought a book, that he's always pressing the nurses
to read to him.'

'What book?'

'John Masefield, *The Old Front Line*. You'd think they
would have had enough of it, wouldn't you?'

She thinks he knows something about Gerald, I told
myself. But she doesn't want to get my hopes up. 'What's
his name?'

'Walter Barker. Nice chap.'

His bed was at the top end of a ward, under a high
arched window. I was glad not to have to run the gamut
of beds. Matron brought me a chair and introduced me.

'Mrs Shackleton came hoping for news of her husband,
but I've persuaded her to chat to you for half an hour. Not
that you deserve it, of course.'

He grinned. 'I'm your star patient, you mean. You
want to show me off.'

The banter was meant to hide that they had already
talked about me. Walter Barker raised his hand in my
direction. I took his hand, trying not to shake with nerves
at the thought he might have some news for me. It was
ridiculous after all this time. Five years since the end of
the war.

'Leave you to it then,' Matron said.

He released my hand and I sat down. *The Old Front Line*
was on the top of his locker, the page marked with a post-
card.

'My name's Kate,' I said, not wishing to spend an hour
reading aloud and putting off that awful moment of
finding out something, or nothing. 'My husband Gerald

was in your regiment. He was the Regimental Surgeon. I got the usual telegram, but I've never been able to find anyone who could tell me about his last moments. And I believe that's why Matron has brought me to you.'

'Yes. She told me. Captain Shackleton, our MO. I think I saw him, twice.'

'You think?'

'Well, yes. I saw him. He . . . took photographs.'

'Yes.'

'That's why I remember him, the doctor with the camera. I saw him twice.'

If he was going to repeat himself, this could take a long time. I wanted to tell him to get to the point. Did he see him at the end? Did he see him die? But I could not ask those questions. I waited.

'Yes, I saw him twice. Once in Albert, where the Virgin dives from the church tower.'

He paused. Perhaps his mind was affected, and I would be compelled to sit and listen to his ramblings.

'Don't think me mad,' he said, as though he had picked up on my thoughts. 'The church was built by the local priest to attract pilgrims. She's a gilded statue, the Virgin and Child. An iron stalk attaches her to the summit of the tower. But a shell bent the stalk and she's suspended, quite horizontal, precarious, looking as though she'll come flying down at any moment. Men marched beneath her, up to the line, hoping she wouldn't come toppling down on them. That's when I saw him first.'

His voice had fallen to a whisper. Was he going to tell me that Gerald was killed by some falling statue of the Virgin Mary? It almost made me want to laugh. Gerald was not a believer, and especially not a believer in the

Scarlet Woman, as he called the Catholic Church.

'He was setting up a tripod, on a day in May – but not like this day in May. It was fine, sunny. It was spring. I couldn't see how it would make a good snapshot. She was too high. I was marching men in an easterly direction to Fricourt. Very straight line we formed, except where the marchers bowed out, to avoid trampling the man with the tripod. That's it, I'm afraid. But that was the first time. I marched past your husband.'

'That was Gerald,' I said softly. 'I remember now. He wrote to me about taking that photograph. He said it had come out better than he hoped. Trust him to go on developing and printing in the middle of a war.'

Walter laughed. 'He had medical supplies to transport. That's how he'll have done it. What's a couple more bottles of chemicals, or a dish or two when you are setting up a field station or a first aid post?'

Rain battered the window pane. 'Is it cold out there?' Walter asked.

'It is. And I got soaked on the way here.'

A man on crutches made his slow way up the ward.

'You said you saw Gerald a second time.'

'Yes. He was setting up a first aid station. There was a quarry nearby, and that's where he stored his supplies. But he'd come up to the front line, with a medic and a couple of privates. There was a chap further along he'd attended to.' He paused again, and I guessed he was remembering that chap who needed attention, or some other, or seeing the day again in his mind's eye.

'We'd been hearing a bird with an unusual song. You always get countrymen or bird watchers who know every song there is, and can whistle them too. But no one knew what bird this was.

'It was early morning, and I saw the Medical Officer – Captain Shackleton – going out into No Man's Land with his camera, and a ladder. Someone had told him about this unusual bird. His sergeant was carrying the tripod would you believe? Madness. We were in full view of the Germans. They could have shot the pair of them at any time. But it was dull. Dull, dull, dull. The tedium ground you down. Nothing ever happened for hours, or sometimes days. The Germans may have been intrigued, watching to see what the mad Englishmen would do.

'The pair of them followed the bird song. I watched him set up the tripod and the camera. *It'll fly away,* I thought. No bird would sit there, waiting for them to point a camera at it. And some German will take a pot shot.

'We all watched. No one spoke.

'The sergeant climbed on the ladder, moved a branch to one side, and the MO clicked his camera.

'Then they walked back. If any of the top brass had seen, they'd have been on a charge, but no top brass came that close. He looked very pleased with himself, Captain Shackleton. I asked him what kind of bird was it. And he smiled. He said that it was a golden oriole.'

For a long time neither of us spoke. Being blind, he could not see my tears. His hand moved across the counterpane, reaching for mine.

On the bookshelves in the drawing room was Gerald's childhood set of encyclopaedias. Or was it in some natural history annual? Somewhere in the house nested a picture of a golden oriole. I wanted to know what it looked like.

I was looking through the pages when I heard footsteps in the street outside and recognised Marcus's tread. He was coming to take me out to supper. Tomorrow, he would be returning to London, and so I felt sure his Big Question would come this evening, in the restaurant, or perhaps afterwards when he brought me home.

The wife of a policeman. Mother, years ago, taking Lapsang Souchong and cake to a female prisoner in Wakefield. Mrs Sharp sitting with Mary Jane, or with the children in the farm cottage. Of course, the wife of a chief inspector would not even be called upon to do that. She would wait at home, and certainly not do any investigating on her own account.

The doorbell rang.

'He's here!' Mrs Sugden called.

But I had found the picture I was looking for. A golden oriole, sharp eye, serious beak, glossy. "The male has a bright yellow body with black wings; the female a paler yellow. This bird is difficult to see and stays high in the tree canopy. A secretive bird."

I wonder did Gerald hear the golden oriole sing.

ACKNOWLEDGEMENTS

For help with research into quarrying, thanks to Kevin Mone, Mick Holstead, Jason Lee, Alistair Mitchell, Craig Morrell, Ian Pickersgill and John Middleton Walker.

Charlie Holmes kindly shared his experiences of farming in the Yorkshire Dales.

Dr Barry Strickland-Hodge, Senior Pharmacy Lecturer and Head of Medicines Management at Leeds University, gave me the benefit of his expertise.

John Goodchild guided me through his Aladdin's cave: a superb archive of Wakefield history. Steven Dowd and staff at Leeds and Wakefield Libraries were most helpful.

Thanks to Emma Beswetherick, Lucy Icke and all at Piatkus, and to my agent, Judith Murdoch.

Thanks also to Anna Clifford, Sylvia Gill, Christine Law-Green, Ralph Lindley, Pat McNeil, Vanessa Rosenthal and Peter Walker.

The village of Great Applewick is fictional; but you knew that, of course.